Mr Hammond and
the Poetic Apprentice

Mr Hammond and the Poetic Apprentice

Mellany Ambrose

Matador
Unit E2 Airfield Business Park,
Harrison Road, Market Harborough,
Leicestershire. LE16 7UL
Tel: 0116 2792299
Email: books@troubador.co.uk
Web: www.troubador.co.uk/matador
Twitter: @matadorbooks

ISBN 978 1803136 769

British Library Cataloguing in Publication Data.
A catalogue record for this book is available from the British Library.

Printed and bound in the UK by TJ Books Limited, Padstow, Cornwall
Typeset in 11pt Adobe Garamond Pro by Troubador Publishing Ltd, Leicester, UK

Matador is an imprint of Troubador Publishing Ltd

For Danny and all the other hardworking GPs in the NHS,
the Thomas Hammonds of today.

So answered I, continuing, 'If it please,
Majestic shadow, tell me: sure not all
Those melodies sung into the world's ear
Are useless: sure a poet is a sage,
A humanist, physician to all men.

John Keats, *The Fall of Hyperion*

PROLOGUE

February 1817

A pale pink glow, the first light of day, suffuses the room. Thomas watches Susannah as she sleeps curled in a chair at his bedside. Her hair is still glorious despite the grey, her face still beautiful despite the lines, each line a record of their years together, their four children. He doesn't want to wake her, but he needs to tell her something.

He reaches out and strokes her cheek. Her eyelashes flicker and her eyes open. Pain grips him and although he tries to hide it, she must see it in his face and picks up the laudanum bottle. He swallows the dose she offers, choking on its bitterness which even cinnamon fails to disguise. Laudanum, tincture of opium, beloved of the apothecary surgeon. Harvested from *Papaveretum somniferum*, the sleep-inducing poppy. In summer in his garden large papery petals crinkled in the wind, a flimsy flower holding a powerful hidden heart, the bluish-grey seed pod topped by its crown of thorns. An antidote to suffering.

The laudanum dulls his pain and his mind. There's something he needs to remember, before he fades into oblivion. He struggles to form the words, his tongue thick and unwieldy.

Send for John.

Chapter One

July 1814

It had been a good morning. Mr Tuke's leg ulcer was healing at last, baby Smith's fever had settled and Mrs Brown's cough had eased. Mr Reed had brought six freshly laid eggs and Mrs Wood a jar of honey. Thomas Hammond sent the last patient on his way and entered the dispensary with his son, Edward. Sunlight shone on the blue and white apothecary jars decorated with angels, peacocks, shells and flowers, highlighting the face of Apollo. The pleasing scents of aniseed and cinnamon made him imagine the exotic lands his medicines had come from. The steady pound of pestle on mortar echoed around the walls. Hardly changed since his father's time, the room reminded him he was part of a grand medical tradition.

John stood at the scratched, wooden bench crushing herbs. His hair was a mass of reddish-gold curls, eyes blue, forehead high, mouth wide and the upper lip projected over the lower. His nose was sunburnt. The boy was forever running off to the orchard or the fields. An open book lay on the counter in front of the mortar. Thomas lifted the cover and read the title. Silence fell as John stopped mixing.

'I don't think you'll find the recipe to cure Mrs Taylor's gallstones in Virgil's *Aeneid*,' Thomas said.

'I know it by heart,' John replied. 'I could mix it in my sleep.' He bowed his head, clenched the pestle so the sinews in his wrist and hand stood taut, and scraped it so hard against the iron mortar it screeched.

'No need to murder the herbs,' Thomas said, trying to lighten the dark mood that hung between them.

Edward sat on a high stool, drew his horn snuffbox from his pocket and clicked it open and shut. Where John was fair Edward was dark, with large brown eyes and black hair curling over his collar. His mobile face with its ready smile could charm anyone when he chose. Sitting, he was as tall as John standing and his shoulders were broader. Hard to believe the boys were both eighteen.

'I think that must be my hundredth tooth extraction,' Edward said.

'And a tricky one,' Thomas replied. 'You've surpassed the blacksmith, without fracturing any jaws.' His son was talented, a quick learner with deft fingers.

'It came away perfectly. The woman was extremely grateful.'

'Edward,' Thomas said, 'I want you to make the pills today. I'm taking John on my visits.'

John stopped grinding the pestle against the bowl and looked up. 'Me?'

'But I always go on the visits. John's only training to be an apothecary.' Edward's aggrieved tone might have swayed his mother, but not Thomas.

'The Apothecaries Act changes all that,' Thomas said.

'I don't see why.'

'Because he must attend Guy's. It will be the law. Six months for an apothecary and twelve for a surgeon.'

For Thomas the question was not why John should attend Guy's Hospital but who he might meet there. He was bound to be taught by Astley Cooper. Even after the terrible mistake

4

which had ended his career at Guy's, Thomas still had some pride. He might not have shown the eye of an eagle, the hands of a lady and the heart of a lion Cooper said every surgeon needed, but he wanted to prove that he trained his apprentices well. Edward would be no problem. He'd been preparing him to attend Guy's Hospital to be a surgeon for years. But John was another matter.

How was he going to teach this boy everything Edward knew? It would be an enormous challenge. To bleed with leeches and lancets, to pull teeth, set limbs, assist childbirth and diagnose fevers. And in one short year. He'd put John in the dispensary because his Latin was excellent, which helped with mixing, and it was more important for Edward to see patients.

Damn the Apothecaries Act. There had been talk of it for years but until now he'd never believed it would come to anything.

John held out the pestle to Edward, who snatched it from him and spun it in the air. Thomas's heart lurched at the thought it might crash and be damaged, but his son caught it. John fetched Thomas's medical bag and stood by the door.

'Who are we visiting?' John asked.

'Mrs Foster first.' Thomas needed to see if the veronica and hyssop expectorant was working. Mrs Foster wasn't improving as he'd hoped.

The village of Edmonton, with its dusty roads, few fine houses, rows of thatched cottages, two inns, church, workhouse, provincial shops and a charity school, was only ten miles from Guy's in London but it could have been a hundred. It was separated from the metropolis by meadows and clumps of elms. To the east coaches travelled up and down the main London road, stopping at the Cross Keys Inn.

Church Street was hard and dry under Thomas's boots, the sun beating down on the back of his neck. The medical bag hung from John's hand, almost dragging in the dirt. John's pale coat was shabby. Perhaps there was an old one of Edward's at home which could be passed on.

John dropped behind and when Thomas turned around to find him, he was standing by a small pond.

'Look!' John pointed. Several dragonflies clung to the rushes, hovered or darted above the surface of the pond. 'The colours. Azure and emerald. That iridescence! Such beauty.'

Thomas glanced at the insects. Years ago, when he was a boy, they would have excited him. He remembered playing in Salmon's Brook catching minnows, the water cold on his feet; digging for earthworms in the herb garden, examining their segments; catching tadpoles and keeping them in a jar, watching them metamorphose into frogs which he held, feeling their moist skin expand against his hands. But he had grown up and had no time for those things anymore.

'I wish I was a dragonfly,' John said. 'To possess that radiance and fly wherever I wished.'

'You would have a very short life, and a useless one. All they do is procreate and die.'

'But those few days would be filled with such delight, more than fifty common years could ever contain.'

'I'd prefer fifty common years myself.' Thomas started walking again. John caught up with him, but his eyes kept straying to the hedgerows. Thomas quickened his step. Apart from his anxieties about Mrs Foster there were several cases at the workhouse to see as well.

At the Fosters' house the maid let them in. A boy poked his head from behind her skirts and cut through the air with a wooden sword.

'Away with the infidels!' he cried.

'Master Fred, let Mr Hammond enter.' The maid grabbed for the sword but missed.

John dodged sideways and raised an imaginary sword. 'We will fight to the death to enter your castle,' he said.

'Stop!' Thomas said, and the boys froze. 'We've come to see your mother.'

John ruffled Fred's hair. 'Put down your sword for now. Even knights need a rest from rescuing damsels in distress.'

Mrs Foster lay on a chaise longue in the parlour, wearing a summer dress. She wore no cap and her reddish-gold hair was gathered at the back of her neck, but much had escaped and hung around her face in a wild fashion as if she'd been blown in a strong wind. Her cheeks were flushed. Thomas had attended her four confinements, treated Mr Foster's lumbago and asthma, and the children's illnesses. Last year three-year-old Isabella had died of croup despite his treatments and the taint of unspoken blame hung in the air like a miasma.

A pendant, depicting a blue urn and a willow tree, hung at Mrs Foster's throat. The willow tree was made of Isabella's blonde hair. A flash of Isabella, gasping for breath, came to him. He had ordered a warm bath before the fire, steamed the child and applied leeches to her throat. Her skin had turned dusky blue and her gaze had gone blank. He'd watched in disbelief, dreading Mrs Foster's reaction, her grief. Now he reminded himself he'd done all he could.

'Where's Edward? He always cheers me up.' Mrs Foster clutched a fresh white handkerchief in one hand.

'This is my second apprentice, John Keats.'

'Mrs Jennings's grandson? A lovely woman, your grandmother.' She lay back on several pillows.

'How are you?' Thomas asked. 'Is the new expectorant helping?'

'I'm feeling better, thank you, only spitting a little blood.'

Thomas touched the back of her warm hand and felt her fast pulse.

'I'll bleed you today.'

'Are you comfortable?' John asked. 'Let me help you rest higher on the pillows.' He put a hand behind her and lifted her up with surprising strength.

'Stop fussing. Let's get started,' Thomas said.

John removed the engraved, silver lancet case and bleeding bowl from the bag.

Mrs Foster closed her eyes. She'd aged in the past few months, her full face growing thinner and exposing her bone structure, despite all Thomas's medicines.

'Hold the bowl, John.' Thomas applied the tourniquet to her arm and patted her thin veins. They took time to swell. He grasped the mother-of-pearl handle of the lancet and cut. Blood dripped into the pewter bowl. 'We'll only take a cup today.'

The bowl wobbled in John's hands and Thomas told him to be careful or else he would spill blood all over the Turkey rug. When the bowl was nearly full Thomas tied a bandage tightly around the cut.

'You're taking the medicines as directed?' Thomas picked up the bottles by her side and studied their levels.

'Yes.'

'And sticking to the strengthening diet?'

'I try, but my appetite is poor.'

She began coughing. Small, delicate coughs at first, as if clearing her throat, which gained in volume. Spasms wracked her body, her narrow shoulders. John helped her sit up and patted her back. She coughed and coughed into her handkerchief until she looked too exhausted to cough anymore. It stopped and she settled back on her pillows. Then she sat up abruptly, took a great inhalation and emitted a loud, whooping cough. A blot of red appeared in the handkerchief she held to her mouth, spreading outwards until it was soaked, flowing onto her hands and dripping onto her muslin dress.

Ruby-red blood. Arterial blood. A chill seized Thomas. His eyes were deceiving him.

'Stop it, make it stop!' she cried. Her eyes stared into his in sheer panic.

John took out his own handkerchief and wiped her hands, but it also became saturated.

'John, go and tell the maid to bring some towels,' Thomas said. 'But don't let the boy in.' It would upset Fred to see his mother like this.

John left and Thomas was alone with Mrs Foster. 'Try to keep calm,' he said. 'Panic will only make it worse.'

Mrs Foster held her bloody hands above her dress and hung her head, her hair falling around her face. He didn't know what to say.

An arterial haemorrhage. Sometimes the treatments worked, but other times they only sent the illness into remission, until it roared forth with renewed might. The shadow would hang over the rest of the family; it was hereditary, so likely Fred and the other children would succumb. What was the cure for this dreadful disease, the great imitator, the thief of life? He had given her dozens of remedies already.

He couldn't save her. Just as he'd been unable to save Isabella. He felt seized by a palsy, as if he'd eaten the shiny black berries of nightshade, *Atropa Belladonna*. Impotent. The worst thing for a man of action, a man who helped by bleeding, prescribing medicines, setting broken bones, assisting childbirth, even amputating limbs. With immense effort he pushed the feeling back down and shut it away.

John and the maid entered with water and towels. The maid washed Mrs Foster's hands and John dabbed at her lips with a moist towel.

'I will be well again, for my children, won't I, Mr Hammond?'

'Of course. There is much room for improvement. You must continue the treatments.'

He couldn't tell her she might not survive the winter. It would only upset her more and her condition would deteriorate further.

He poured a dose of laudanum onto a medicine spoon and she swallowed it. He would study his books again tonight for mixtures to prevent further haemorrhages.

'John will mix you some more cough syrup and deliver it later,' Thomas said.

'Thank you.' Her eyes closed and Thomas knew she'd soon be asleep.

Thomas and John left the room quietly. In the hall Fred waited in a corner.

'Can I see Mama?' he asked.

He looked directly at Thomas. It disconcerted him.

'Not now,' Thomas said.

John knelt to his level. 'She needs to sleep, Fred. But you can see her later today, I think.'

Fred bit his lip and looked as if he might cry. 'You must go and fight some dragons with your sword,' John said. 'I see several in the garden.'

'Do you?' Fred picked up his sword and ran outside.

How quickly children forgot their troubles. John was good with the child, who on previous visits Thomas had found to be indulged and obviously needing more discipline.

Thomas and John walked in silence, back towards the workhouse. John's light coat was stained by blood on the sleeves and front. Thomas always wore a black coat and black breeches, so blood wouldn't show. His wife said he looked as though he was forever going to a funeral, and he'd once replied with gallows humour that often he was. She had winced and he'd regretted the remark.

A cart piled high with furniture passed them, the driver whipping the horse. John stopped at the pond and looked at the dragonflies again.

'Sometimes patients cough up small amounts of venous blood, rust-coloured or like autumn leaves,' Thomas said. 'But that was arterial blood, bright red and full-flowing. Remember it.'

'Her face, when she saw the blood…' John said. 'You must be able to do more for her.'

'I've tried most of the remedies I know for consumption. Sometimes they don't help.' As John should know from his own mother's case. The boy had insisted on administering her medicines himself and nursed her in his holidays from boarding school. He'd scurried about the room, overwrought and agitated, getting under Thomas's feet.

John turned and looked at Thomas, his face contorted as if he'd suffered a physical agony. 'Why be an apothecary if you can't cure disease?'

'I can ease their pain, make them more comfortable.' Thomas forced himself to look John in the eye. His legs felt weak, probably from the heat. He didn't want to admit it to John, but often even that was impossible and caused him grief. However hard he tried, however much good he did, there was always some pain he couldn't relieve, some suffering that was too formidable for him to help.

'It's distressing to watch such suffering,' John said.

'One must be strong to help others, and not be affected by it.'

'So you're heartless?'

'Not heartless. Becoming agitated by emotion won't help the patient and interferes with the work.'

When Thomas was an apprentice, he'd been shocked by the things he'd seen. The first time he'd witnessed a compound fracture, the splintered bone sticking out of the skin, the man screaming, he'd wanted to run away. But his father had remained calm, dispassionate, practical and dealt with it. Thomas had learnt to imitate his father. He'd erected a wall to protect himself. And that had worked, until the tragedy of the boy at Guy's had demolished the wall and he'd never been able to rebuild it.

'How do you cope with the pain it causes you?' John asked. Dragonflies flew around his head, shimmering and reflecting the light. John reached out as if to catch one, but it was too quick for him.

Why was this boy squandering precious time asking him this? They needed to go to the workhouse. Thomas's patience snapped.

'You work harder,' Thomas said.

Chapter Two

After dinner Thomas settled back on the compacted stuffing of his father's old armchair in the drawing room. He worked loose his boots and rested his feet on a small stool. Susannah sat in the yellow velvet chair. She'd brought this – along with the matching chaise longue, needlepoint cockatoo fire screen and Wedgwood vases on the mantelpiece – with her from her former home in Ludgate Street. She'd sat in that chair almost every day of their marriage and Thomas felt she was reproaching him for not being able to buy such nice things for her.

Susannah picked up a piece of confectionery from an occasional table and popped it in her mouth. The sweets made him think of her first husband. He'd never met the man but knew he was older and imagined him as corpulent. Even now, after nearly twenty-five years of marriage, he didn't like to think of his plump fingers touching her soft skin.

Evening light spilled in through large windows. Susannah began mending a dress, her dark hair escaping from the edge of her cap. Thomas picked up *The Times*. Foreign news was quiet with Napoleon imprisoned on Elba, but domestic news of unrest over rising corn prices was prominent. He saw the effects every day, his patients unable to afford bread, numbers at the workhouse increasing, cases of malnutrition and even starvation.

Edward bounded into the room and sat on the chaise longue. He picked up his fiddle, tuned it and played a cheerful folk melody. Edward's fingers moved quickly; the manual dexterity involved would help him become a skilled surgeon. Thomas tapped his foot. The music gained speed, the notes tumbling over each other. Thomas felt a lightness of heart, a joy in his being, here with his son and his wife and the music. If only there could be more moments like this, lifted by the music away from misery and pain.

Edward put down his fiddle, pinched one of Susannah's marzipan fruits and ate it. And another and another, popping them into his mouth. Like eating money. The cost would feed a family in the village for a week. He reached for another.

'Edward, stop gorging on your mother's sweetmeats,' Thomas said.

Edward's hand hovered over the plate, his expression petulant.

'Let him eat them,' Susannah said. 'It won't do him any harm.'

Edward chose a pink macaron, shoved it into his mouth whole and chewed, his lips smacking.

'Mary tells me since the wedding Anne and Joseph Henry Green are always visiting them,' Susannah said. 'They hear all about Guy's and Henry Cline.'

'I'm sure they do.' His brother William had done well, marrying his daughter to the nephew of a famous surgeon.

'Mary suggested Edward should go to William's to learn new things and benefit from William's connections.'

'Oh, yes, please, Father,' Edward said.

'You can learn everything you need here.'

'I would see different patients, different illnesses.'

'Illness is the same everywhere. I need you here.'

'You have John, especially if you're now taking him on visits.' Edward sat on the edge of the chaise longue, leaning forwards.

'At least consider it, Thomas.' Susannah looked up from her sewing. 'I can do the bills while Edward is away, and John can work harder. I caught him reading a book in the orchard the other day. He said he'd finished the chores, but I didn't believe him and sent him back to the dispensary.'

'Please, Father,' Edward said. The pleading look in his eyes almost convinced Thomas, but he mustn't spoil the boy.

'No, definitely not.'

'Fine, then, have it your own way as usual!' Edward stormed out of the room, the back of his coat swinging.

'Edward! Don't talk to me like that.' The air in the room felt turbulent from Edward's outburst. He longed for the days when Edward was younger, asking to help dig the herb garden, to learn the meaning of the symbols on his apothecary weights and to look at his surgical instruments. Running and laughing in the orchard, splashing and swimming in the brook. Playing leapfrog with his little sisters and giving them piggybacks. Climbing trees, although he'd once ignored Susannah's pleas and Thomas's commands to come down, saying he liked to be higher than anyone else and see further, and had fallen and broken his arm, which Thomas had set.

'Are you plotting again?' Thomas asked Susannah.

'Of course not. Why shouldn't our son learn from your brother?'

'I worry William's more interested in money than his patients.'

'I know Edward can't be a lawyer as I wished, but I want him to be successful. Joseph Green could introduce Edward to Henry Cline. Surely one of the surgeons at Guy's and St Thomas' would be useful to know?'

'Edward can be a surgeon on his merit.'

'Thomas, let him go, to humour me. You've told me how lack of a patron hindered your own surgical career.'

Except that wasn't the main hindrance. The real obstacle had been something deeper, something he'd never told her, even though he'd wanted to many times especially early in their marriage.

'There must be someone from your time at Guy's? Someone who's done well whom you could ask to help Edward.'

Thomas shook his head. He hadn't seen his one influential connection for over twenty-five years and didn't wish to renew the acquaintance. Memories he'd rather forget crept into his mind. The first day in the dead house. The last day in the operating theatre.

'Thomas? Are you listening?'

Susannah's voice dragged him back to the present. To his annoyance, Susannah was right. William's connections would help Edward's career. It was a golden opportunity. Thomas could offer him nothing like that.

'I'll ask William, if that will please you,' he said.

'It would.' She reached across and touched his hand gently, then picked up her sewing again. 'How was today?'

'Mrs Foster's not well. The consumption is worse.'

'Poor woman,' she said. 'It must be terrible not to see your children grow up.'

Her words made the hairs on the back of Thomas's neck stand erect as if she was predicting his future.

'I'd hate not to see Edward become a great surgeon, Eliza married and our two little girls well settled,' she continued. 'Or see my grandchildren. Didn't Mrs Foster lose a child last year?'

'Yes, from croup.'

'And Fred is such a lively lad, running round at church. He'll miss his mother terribly.'

Thomas felt his eyes moisten. Sometimes Susannah went straight to the heart of the matter and expressed things he was frightened to even think about.

She looked at him with her large brown eyes. She was still a beautiful woman. He remembered that he'd thought this at their first meeting, a party organised by his older brother, William. Thomas had stood in a corner holding a glass of wine, observing the guests, wondering if he could leave, until he noticed her. She was dressed in dark grey and unadorned by jewellery so must be just out of deep mourning, but she looked young, in her early twenties like him. She was striking despite her plain attire, her face oval, jet-black hair piled high on her head, curls cascading down. She had a fine figure. She looked into the eyes of the man she was talking to, threw back her head and laughed at something he'd said. Thomas felt intensely jealous of the man and turned away.

His brother had come up behind him and introduced her as Mrs Styles. His body trembled at her closeness. She asked him about his work. Usually people changed the subject when they discovered he was a surgeon, but she seemed genuinely interested and said it was a more noble career than her deceased husband's, which was confectionery. Her eyes met his and he knew he wanted to get to know her better, to take care of her, to possess her, to marry her. He pursued her, and to his joy she agreed to marry him, even though with the money she'd inherited from her husband she could have done much better.

Could he talk to Susannah now, tell her how helpless he felt at being unable to save Mrs Foster? Would she understand? He didn't even understand it himself. The clock on the mantlepiece ticked and the voices of the girls playing outside floated in on the warm air. He was on the verge of speaking, but his tongue stuck to the roof of his mouth.

'I hear a new family has moved into Pymmes House,' Susannah said. 'You should call on them.'

'Why? Do I know them?'

'To improve your clientele, Thomas. And I think you should buy a new coat that isn't black. Burgundy or forest green would suit you.' She reached for another macaron.

Thomas shook his head. Susannah wouldn't understand. She was a wife and mother, not an apothecary surgeon. She had no real idea what his work was like.

The wheels of the carriage bounced over ruts in the track. Thomas had lowered the calash, as he often did in summer when it wasn't raining. Cinnamon knew the way home and Thomas only had to rest the worn reins loosely in his hands, but he felt every jolt in his weary bones. Today was Wednesday, John's half day, and Edward had disappeared somewhere, so Thomas had been too busy to ask William about him. Although it was late in the evening, the summer light lingered.

He was returning from visiting a young woman with smallpox, her face covered in pustules, not one piece of skin spared. He hoped her eyes would not be affected. A disfigured woman, however badly scarred, might still find a husband, but a blind one would be a burden to her family. He tried to vaccinate all his patients by scratching cowpox into their skin, but many were suspicious of the procedure, fearing it would cause the illness. He'd ensured his family were all protected, and his apprentices.

A figure appeared in the distance, travelling in the same direction, walking along the verge and stopping every so often for no apparent reason. As he gained on him, Thomas recognised John's pale coat and gold hair. Coming alongside, he halted Cinnamon. John was staring intently at the field of wheat.

'You're out late in the middle of nowhere,' Thomas said. 'What are you looking at?'

John turned around to face him. 'The poppies, in the wheat, don't you think they look like the scarlet coats of soldiers?'

To Thomas they looked like splashes of red flowers in a field of green wheat. He squinted but still couldn't imagine them as soldiers.

'Do you think the poppy fumes could send us to sleep?' John asked.

'Of course not, the latex from the seed pods needs to be dissolved in alcohol. And those aren't opium poppies.'

'But wouldn't it be wonderful if they could?'

What was he talking about? Falling asleep in a field of wheat wouldn't be very comfortable.

'Let me give you a ride back.'

'I'm happy to walk.'

'You'll need to wake early tomorrow to mix the medicines.'

John yawned. 'Thank you.' He climbed up next to him and they set off, Cinnamon walking at a gentle pace. John held a book in his hands.

'Is this what you do on your free afternoon?' Thomas asked. 'Wander the hedgerows?'

'I go to Clarke's school.'

'But why?' Now his brother Tom lived with John in his lodgings in Edmonton, John had no reason to visit the school.

'To see Charles Cowden Clarke.'

'The headmaster's son?' Thomas had met Clarke on his visits to the school to treat the boys. He must be several years older than John.

'The Clarkes invite me to their table and the talk is lively and interesting. Then Charles and I sit in the arbour listening to the nightingales and discuss all sorts of things.'

'Such as?'

'Everything! Literature, books on history and travels and geography. He borrows plays and poems for me from the school library.'

'What did you discuss this evening?' Thomas had never heard John talk so much or seen him so animated.

'We looked at Tasso's epic poem *Gerusalemme Liberata*. We were still talking about it when he walked me as far as the bridge over Salmon's Brook.'

The road forked and they took the path towards Wilston. The sun had set and a large moon floated above the horizon.

'Isn't the moon beautiful?' John said. 'I see why the ancient Greeks have a story of the shepherd Endymion falling in love with it.'

'They do? How strange.'

John held tight to his book, wrapping both arms around it.

'What book do you have there?'

'*The Faerie Queene*, by Spenser. I want to read it again.'

'Spenser?'

'One of our greatest poets, from the age of Queen Elizabeth.'

'I'm curious, not being a literary man myself, what attracts you to poetry?'

'With Spenser, I admire his *spring-headed Hydras and sea-shouldering whales.*'

'Sea-shouldering whales?' Did whales even have shoulders? Thomas had never seen one. Why not just say the whale broke the surface?

'It's such an eloquent, powerful image.'

'We'll agree to differ,' Thomas said. 'But what do you gain from reading all this poetry?'

'A world of beauty.' In the moonlight John's face was soft, his eyes dreamy.

'There's no space for beauty in an apothecary's world. We're rooted in pain and disease, human suffering.'

'Poetry harnesses the imagination and opens a door to another realm; it celebrates a world of nature and ancient virtues. Like our universe but transformed.'

'So it's an escape? A distraction?'

'It can help one transcend the troubles and circumstances of the world. It reveals truth and can change the world.'

'I don't see how that's possible.'

'One must read to discover it. Shakespeare and Milton. They tell of noble action and sound the depths of human nature.'

'A nice thought, but I don't have time.'

'Have you never read a poem that transported you away from the world and lifted your spirits?'

'I can't say I have. Have you?'

'Yes, many a time.'

John rested his chin on his hands and gazed out at the fields and hedges passing by. The horse's flanks shone luminous in the moonlight. The wheat in the fields extended to the horizon, soft and glistening. For a moment Thomas thought

21

he would like to hear such a poem, but he could not imagine he ever would. The image of the woman with smallpox came back to him: no poem could banish that.

'I hope you're not neglecting your medical books,' Thomas said.

'I can read both. I feel I'm two people, my apprentice self and once a week my literary self.'

'Make sure it stays that way. You'll never help anyone with poetry.'

When Thomas arrived at William's fine house in Southgate, early in the evening a few days later, his sister-in-law Mary sent him to the treatment room to find his brother. It was connected to the rest of the house but had its own entrance and resembled a parlour with a large fireplace, walnut furniture and thick velvet curtains. Thomas couldn't imagine his patients there. He was so used to seeing them in his bare, cramped room in the small building separate from Wilston.

In the dispensary across the hall William, in a fancy waistcoat embroidered with gold thread, was barking instructions at his son James, to retrieve a jar from a high shelf. With his shock of greying hair, long sideburns and aquiline nose, it was uncanny how closely William resembled their father. He was now fifty-four, only three years younger than their father when he died.

James, standing on a ladder to reach the jar, was dressed in trousers and a smart coat with brass buttons as if he were going out to a party. His hair needed a good brush. Next to him and William, Thomas felt unusually conscious of his own worn coat, faded waistcoat and breeches. Perhaps Susannah was right and he should ask the tailor to make him some new clothes.

James removed a jar from the shelf and climbed down. The jars were all creamware decorated with gilt. The scales and pill machine looked new, and the polished wooden bench shone.

'Thomas.' William came over and shook his hand. Veins snaked across the back of William's hand and it was freckled with age spots, but his grip was still firm. The same firm grip which had beaten Thomas at arm-wrestling and held him down mercilessly when they were young.

'Hello, Uncle Thomas,' James said. He weighed a quantity of dried flowers from the jar and crushed them with a Wedgwood pestle and mortar. Thomas's father had always insisted on iron.

Thomas had never understood why James, who had been dresser to Astley Cooper at Guy's four years ago and passed the membership of the Royal College of Surgeons, hadn't tried to become a hospital surgeon. Working for William was a waste of his talent.

'What are you mixing?' Thomas asked.

'Camomile flowers with cloves and vervain,' James said. 'To help a lady's nerves.'

The sharp smell of cloves rose into the air.

'I would add some laudanum too,' said William. 'That will calm her down.' William took the bottle of laudanum from the shelf and poured in a generous glug as if it were cordial. The lady would sleep for a week if she took that, unless she was accustomed to it, of course.

Thomas questioned his own judgment in sending Edward to William. He must speak quickly before he changed his mind.

'Would you take Edward for a few weeks?' Thomas asked. 'He's keen to learn from you.'

'You'll never manage without him,' William said.

'John Keats can help me.'

'He won't be much use.'

'He'll have to go to Guy's for six months because of the Apothecaries Act so I'm training him up.'

'The cockney son of an innkeeper going to Guy's, whoever heard of such a thing?' William laughed and his jowls wobbled.

'Why shouldn't he go? I don't see why only the sons of medical men should be allowed in, or those with connections. Surely nepotism is wrong?' Except here he was trying to use William to help his own son's career.

'Oh, Thomas. I'm only joking. Why do you take everything so seriously?'

'Because it's a serious matter.'

'Edward told us all about Keats,' James said. 'How he nearly killed him over some leeches.'

'That's not the whole story. Both boys were to blame.' To his surprise Thomas felt strangely protective towards John, who had no father to defend him since Thomas Keats had fallen from his horse and died from his injuries ten years ago. John wasn't a bad boy, just rather unusual.

'This whole Apothecaries Act is ridiculous,' William said. 'It won't get through Parliament.'

'I'm convinced it will,' Thomas replied. 'It's needed to stop quacks, horse doctors and charlatans.'

'Do say yes, Father,' James said. 'Edward is good company.'

William tucked his thumbs in his waistcoat pockets. The buttons strained across his stomach, in danger of popping off.

'He'll certainly see a different class of patient,' William said. 'I don't know why you persist in treating those wretches at the workhouse. I leave all the poor to the new chap in town and concentrate on the ones who appreciate my attention and pay their bills.'

'I've just visited two spinster ladies who suffer fits of the vapours,' James said. 'They're our most rewarding customers.'

How could they be rewarding? Except in monetary terms. The vapours were an illness of underoccupied, wealthy women. Thomas really was starting to question if he should send Edward to William. But William was a well-respected apothecary surgeon, trained by their father and Guy's Hospital.

'Will you take him?' Perhaps William didn't want Edward, or didn't think him good enough? If William didn't say yes soon Thomas would just walk out.

The trouble with having a brother six years older was that Thomas could never win, never be better than him. He'd discovered this at an early age. William was always stronger, cleverer, more accomplished, more sociable. When Thomas started helping in the dispensary age eight, William was already skilled at mixing and being taken on visits. When William went to Guy's, and Thomas at age fifteen officially became his father's apprentice, the shadow of William hung over him. His father was always saying how well William had done this or that. William would come home to visit from Guy's, feted, dresser to Billy Lucas. He passed the Diploma of the Company of Surgeons and everyone fussed over him. By the time Thomas was nineteen and off to Guy's himself, William had set up practice in Southgate, married, and become a success. But in the end he'd refused their dying father's last wish. Thomas could never forgive him for that.

William opened his mouth to speak and Thomas held his breath.

'Of course, no question. We'd love to have him. He can stay as long as he likes.'

'I can give you something for his board and keep.'

'No need, we're family, aren't we?'

'Thank you.'

James labelled the bottle and left to deliver it to the lady with the vapours. Thomas was sure he would be charming, and William would charge a fat fee she would happily pay. Their father had taught them his guiding principles of integrity and charity. When had his brother abandoned real medicine, treating the poor and needy?

'Why don't you come over to Abernethy's at Field Manor in Enfield one evening?' William said. 'It's full of medical men from far and wide. Abernethy discusses cases and Hunter's Vitalism and theory of life. Joseph comes with me, and often brings Cline. Lawrence comes too, the debates are tremendous. It's very lively with good food and drink.'

'Maybe I will.' How Thomas would love to listen, even join in these discussions. He ordered books and medical journals from London, at vast expense, Susannah complained, to keep up to date, but discussing these things in person would be stimulating and rewarding.

'Astley Cooper even comes occasionally,' William said.

The name dropped into the air like a chemical into a clear solution, clouding everything.

'Wouldn't you like to see Cooper again?' William gave him a shrewd look. Thomas had no idea how much he really knew.

Thomas's palms were sweating and he wiped them on his breeches. 'It's kind of you to invite me, but I couldn't possibly. I'm far too busy.'

'If you say so,' William said.

'I'll just say hello to Mother while I'm here.'

William led Thomas to their mother's sitting room and left them. She sat upright in a chair, her face wrinkled, her body frail, wisps of thin grey hair emerging from her cap. He sat next to her. Mementoes of her life at Wilston surrounded her: the gateleg table on which stood her tea caddy and chipped china tea set, a pair of earthenware candlesticks above the fireplace, a small portrait of her husband on the wall.

'Shall I call for hot water for tea?' she asked.

'No need, I must set off soon.'

'I never see you enough, Thomas. Or the children.' She reached for his hand and held it. It felt fragile as a small bird in his.

'Edward is coming to stay for a few weeks.'

'Wonderful. He's so amusing and can play his fiddle. I almost want to rise out of my chair and dance at the thought.'

'Well, why don't you?'

'Because I'm an old woman. I'm surprised Susannah's letting him come.'

'Oh, she sees all the advantages of William's connections and wealthy patients.'

'Don't be jealous, Thomas. It's not becoming.' She removed her hand from his.

'Of what? His wealth? Or his ladies with fits of the vapours.'

'Your father would be proud you still treat the workhouse patients.' She looked at the portrait on the wall. His father stared out sternly into the room.

'Susannah wishes the workhouse paid more,' he said.

'So she can spend it on crimson flock wallpaper? There was nothing wrong with the old wallpaper at Wilston.'

'I know, Mother, but she wanted to change it.'

'After I'd lived in that house all my life, and your father had just died. It was prohibitively expensive. Imagine mistaking Wilston for Carlton House.'

'Please be kind about her, Mother.'

Susannah had kept telling him how distinguished the new paper would look, how it would attract a better class of folk to use his services, despite his pleas to humour his newly widowed mother. In the end he sided with Susannah, of course. How could he bring himself to be harsh to this beautiful creature who'd chosen him? Soon afterwards his mother had moved to Southgate to live with William.

'It's because of her background, the daughter of a shopkeeper. Your father and I never understood why you chose her.'

'I love her. She's my wife.' Only his mother's age and his respect for her stopped him walking out.

'She's given you lovely children.'

At least they could agree on that. He sat a little longer then took his leave.

Thomas patted Cinnamon's neck, feeling his soft coat under his fingers. The horse whinnied in response. The sun was sinking but the air was still warm. William had said his colleagues debated the theory of life at Abernethy's. Thomas had discussed that endlessly with Astley Cooper during his time at Guy's.

They'd met in the dissecting room, the dead house. On entering the smell hit first, a wall of stench. A dozen bodies in various stages of decay, rot and putrefaction lay on tables, each surrounded by six or more students. Vapours rose from the bodies like a foul mist, towards a square lantern hung from the ceiling.

Specimens in glass cases rose up the walls. Bones were boiled in a copper cauldron. Rats ran around the edges of the room and sparrows hopped in through the tall, open windows.

Cooper had been only seventeen, surgical apprentice to Henry Cline and already a brilliant dissector. He stopped by Thomas's table and warned him not to cut himself, on a spicule of bone or a knife. That could mean death.

The smell of rot and the smell of the alcohol some of the bodies were pickled in bathed Thomas and permeated his skin. He woke at night to it. He found scraps of fat or tissue on his boots when getting undressed. As an apprentice to his father he'd seen patients dying, an amputation, great suffering, but nothing had prepared him for this: the shock and horror and desecration.

Astley helped him calm his terror. His matter-of-factness was reassuring, his enthusiasm to learn everything about anatomy and the human body inspiring, his fearlessness admirable. Astley loved dissecting and would dissect anything. He had bodies delivered to his house and experimented on live cats. Under his guidance Thomas rolled up his shirtsleeves and plunged his arms in up to his elbows to learn the anatomy of the human body. Afterwards the stains would never wash out.

The bodies became things, not people. The students joked about their bad teeth and sagging breasts, their shrunken members. Sometimes in the face of death all one can do is laugh, especially when one is young. Thomas rummaged amongst organs and threw the sparrows titbits.

They also attended surgical lectures given by Henry Cline, Astley's mentor. They sat on the tiered benches in the lecture theatre, underneath the oval skylight, scribbling notes, taking in every word. The enthusiasm Thomas had then; he wanted to know everything. He didn't share Astley's interest in radical politics but was fascinated by natural philosophy and vitalism. They sat up late and discussed John Hunter's theories by candlelight. What made up the stuff of life? How were rocks different from animals? Hunter's belief in the living principle, the necessity of a soul. Astley made Thomas believe they were at the cliff edge of a revolution in medicine, that human lives could be improved and suffering could be tackled. Their future seemed limitless.

Now Astley Cooper was a world-renowned surgeon, writing books and treatises, lecturing, teaching medical students. And who was Thomas Hammond? An apothecary surgeon in a village a few miles outside London who pulled teeth and dressed leg ulcers.

But that would change when Edward attended Guy's and became a surgeon. His own hopes might be gone, but Thomas would achieve something of worth through his son. That would be his legacy.

Chapter Three

The queue of patients wound around the surgery: men dressed in farm labourer's clothes, children in rags clinging to their mothers' skirts, the elderly leaning on sticks, a patient with a cloth tied under her chin, another with blood oozing through a dressing on his leg. It would be a long morning and Thomas regretted allowing Edward to go to William's.

Inside the dispensary John, who should have been performing his chores, leant over the bench reading something which wasn't the *Pharmacopoeia Londinensis*. When he saw Thomas, John flipped over the thin pages and jumped up to dust.

Thomas walked to the bench and picked up the magazine.

'Where did you get this?' Thomas had never taken *The Examiner* in his house.

'Charles Cowden Clarke lent it to me.'

'*A Sunday paper on politics, the domestic economy and theatricals,*' Thomas read the subtitle aloud. He flicked through its pages. 'Radical nonsense and gossip.'

'Leigh Hunt calls for parliamentary reform and less extravagance,' John said. 'That's only fair.'

'I didn't know you were interested in politics.'

'Hunt believes the political and the literary are two edges of the same sword.'

'Poetry can no more change the world than I can bring a dead man back to life.'

'Hunt and I disagree.' John's eyes shone with a zeal Thomas

had seen before in the eyes of men when he was young. The eyes of Astley Cooper when he'd discussed the situation in France.

'Radical ideas mutate into terrible actions. Do you want a revolution like the French, your head chopped off by Madame Guillotine while the crowds bay for blood?'

'That wouldn't happen here.'

'I suspect the French thought so too.'

'How else can we change things?'

'Help patients, John. It will do more good than these pretentious ideas.'

'We need to change the system which is at fault.'

'You may as well try to change human nature. Men are driven by money, power and their own interests.'

'Leigh Hunt isn't. He's a friend to liberty.'

'He went too far vilifying the Prince Regent.'

'He's one of the greats like King Alfred and Milton, the patriots.'

'I hear he lives the life of luxury in prison. He'll abandon his principles when it suits him.' Astley Cooper had returned from France, where he'd seen atrocities and helped operate on the casualties, and renounced his beliefs to secure the surgeon's job at Guy's.

John's face went red. 'Don't speak like that about Libertas.' He clenched his fist and raised it. 'He's a true hero.'

Thomas almost spluttered with laughter at how ridiculous John looked, but part of him felt anxious at his naivety. John was a slight eighteen-year-old raising his fist in idealism. Edward would never even contemplate such ideas.

'You're young, John, but you'll learn,' he said. 'Unclench your fist. I don't want a fight with you. Let's start work.'

Mary Curtis and her daughter Rachel walked into the

surgery. The little girl handed Thomas a bunch of cornflowers and he smiled. When Mary was in labour the midwife had called him to use the destructive instruments to remove the baby and save Mary's life, but he'd detected a faint movement and insisted on using forceps. The baby hadn't breathed and he thought he'd failed, but then she cried. After that Mary had haemorrhaged and almost died, but he'd controlled the blood with cool cloths and pressure. The relief had been enormous and every time he saw them, he thought of them as his miracle.

Rachel had eczema and he recommended a salve. Next the butcher, Mr Trew, whom years ago he'd treated for syphilis, wanted something for his manhood. Thomas gave him a special mixture, promising it would work. As long as Mr Trew believed in it, Thomas knew the sugar and water solution would help him. Mrs Wilson had headaches again; he couldn't see them ever improving but prescribed chamomile in hope. Sam Trisker's dyspepsia was no better because he refused to alter his diet. Thomas sighed. He'd told Sam so many times, but the man never listened. There were several cases of fever, none too serious thankfully. Near the end of the morning a patient walked in with a deep cut from a scythe and he sutured it.

'I'm going to visit Mrs Foster,' Thomas said after the patients had gone. John rushed to collect Thomas's medical bag. Thomas had laid the cornflowers from Rachel on the bench and John picked them up.

'You're not taking those, are you?' Thomas asked.

'Why not?'

'We're calling as her apothecary surgeons, not her lovers.'

'But they're medicinal. Cornflowers cured the centaur Chiron when he was wounded by an arrow tipped with the blood of Hydra.'

'She's not been shot by an arrow and even if she had you'd need to put them into a medicine to have any effect.'

'They're so beautiful I'm sure they'll make her feel better. They're like pieces of the sky fallen to earth.'

'You'll never get anywhere at Guy's with these ideas. They don't give the patients flowers.' What would Astley Cooper think if John behaved like this?

'But I don't see—'

'John, I'm the master and you're my apprentice. I know best.'

'About diagnoses and making medicines, but not about how patients feel.'

'Now you're being impertinent. Put them down and hurry up.'

John held the flowers tightly in front of him and Thomas wondered if he would continue arguing. Thomas saw how deep blue the cornflowers were, unnaturally so. John placed the flowers back on the bench, but only after he'd picked the head of one and put it in his buttonhole.

Mrs Foster breathed with fast, shallow breaths, her chest stained yellow from mustard plasters. Despite several visits in the past two weeks, more bleeding and new medicines, she'd deteriorated. John helped raise her higher on a bolster. She was shivering, wrapped in a blanket which she threw off.

'I'm so hot,' she said, 'but then it feels like the middle of winter.'

'Mama's no fun anymore,' Fred said. 'Make her better!'

Thomas believed in a quiet, orderly sickroom. It was no place for a child, but the boy had followed them in.

'Well, you must help.' John squatted so his face was near

the boy's. 'You can plump her pillows, bring her food, give her medicines and read to her.'

'Fred is only eight years old, John,' Thomas said.

'And I don't read very well,' Fred said. He looked forlorn.

'Perhaps I can read to her.' John looked up at Thomas.

Mrs Foster had recovered her poise and her breathing was a little easier. 'I would love to hear a novel.' She smiled then looked at Thomas. 'What am I saying? That would take John away from you, Mr Hammond.'

'May I, Sir?' John asked.

'I need you at the surgery, you know that.' John's attachment to Mrs Foster was becoming unhealthy.

'It might help take her mind off her illness. I used to read to my mother.'

'We're too busy, John.' Thomas reached for his bag and took out the silver leech case and bowl. He hoped John wouldn't make a scene. 'Let us bleed you, Mrs Foster.'

The maid took Fred from the room. John bowed his head and removed the leeches from their cramped case with shaking fingers. Thomas positioned them on Mrs Foster's arm. She averted her head, saying she couldn't bear to look. Thomas saw it now, her resemblance to Frances Keats: the reddish-gold hair, the wide mouth, the pale freckled arms. It was intensified by the concave temples, sunken eyes and prominent cheekbones caused by her disease. At some point all victims of the illness looked similar.

Four and a half years ago Thomas had opened the door to the sickroom at 3 Church Street, two doors down from Wilston, to find John sat by his mother's bed reading aloud. He'd insisted on finishing the chapter, keeping Thomas waiting. Frances Keats lay propped up on pillows, her eyes shut, her breathing rapid and there was a faint rattle from her lungs. Thomas had waited in a bad temper. A bedraggled goldfinch sat in a cage in the corner of the room. After Thomas had bled Mrs Keats, John lifted her on her pillows then ran around adding coal to the fire and puffing the bellows. He refused to let his grandmother and little sister enter the room. He fed his mother, telling Thomas he'd cooked the food himself in line with Thomas's strict regime. Mrs Keats coughed, and John sat her up and put his arm around her shoulders. He held her and talked gently to her, and the fit passed. She called him her angel.

Thomas thought John's devotion unnatural, way beyond the call of duty, especially as his mother had abandoned her children three years earlier. Edward would never have cared for Susannah in that way, even though he loved her dearly.

Over four years later, in another sickroom, the leeches writhed and sucked until they were so swollen it seemed they must burst, but they relaxed their jaws and John caught them in the bowl. Afterwards John was attentive to Mrs Foster, plumping her pillows and pouring her a drink from a jug. Thomas reviewed her medicines and advised continuing his regime.

They said their goodbyes and once the front door shut behind them John asked, 'Is it wise to take so much blood?'

'Shh. She might hear you.' Thomas waited until they'd both passed through the garden gate into the road. 'It's to balance her humours.'

'But she's so weak already.'

'You know better than Boerhaave, do you?'

'The medicines aren't working.'

'They take time.'

'She doesn't have much time, even I can see that. There must be a new treatment.'

'If there was, I would have heard or read about it.'

'Can't you ask at Guy's? Someone must be working on a new cure.'

Thomas had once thought like that. When he'd started at Guy's there was such excitement. New theories of fibres and nerves were set to augment the centuries-old therapeutics of balancing the four humours. But in the end, as far as he could see, nothing revolutionary had come of them.

'Alas, I don't think another opinion would add anything.'

'Isn't it worth a try? You can't just give up on her like this.' John's voice was shrill, but sobs hid just beneath the surface. Thomas was reminded of the time when John started as his apprentice. John had been unstable with grief, even after five months, crying at the smallest upset or sad thing. Thomas had decided it was best to ignore these episodes and they'd become less frequent then stopped. He hoped they weren't coming back.

'I don't have time to go to Guy's.'

'Someone local then?'

The sun was overhead now. Out of the shade of the house it shone mercilessly on Thomas's dark clothes.

'My brother in Southgate has connections with Henry Cline at Guy's and John Abernethy at Bart's,' Thomas said. 'I'll discuss the case with him next time I see him.'

Why had he said that? Something pleading in the boy's tone, the hope that he might find the answer and save this woman. He knew he wouldn't, but he was a man who kept his word. He would ask William.

The herb garden was bursting with growth. Thomas pressed his foot hard upon his garden fork and twisted the tines in the dry earth. He loosened weeds and pulled them up with his bare hands, cut back sprawling bushes and deadheaded flowers. He needed to make room for the less strong plants, so they weren't crowded out. The trouble was fitting it around his patients. Thomas missed Edward, his practical help and enthusiasm, but to his delight after they'd seen Mrs Foster the day had been quiet and he'd finished early.

He wiped sweat from his brow. Plants didn't answer back or complain. When he tended to them they grew, returned his care. Occasionally one would wilt or die, but not often. They took the sun, soil and water, and made stems, leaves, flowers and seeds which grew again. He'd planted the arnica plant from a seed and now it was two feet tall, covered in yellow flowers. His hands were dirty, but he enjoyed the feel of soil on his skin and didn't wear gloves. It was strange how the soil didn't stick to the long white scar on his right hand. He shuddered at the memory of how he'd acquired it.

'Father, catch us!' Mary Ann and Harriet ran up to him from the orchard, their cheeks pink, their hair glowing in the sun. He brushed the soil from his hands and chased them round the trees, through the long grass, letting them escape when he came near. At last he caught Harriet and swung her high in the air. Her dress flared out around her as she screamed with delight.

The three of them sat on a blanket, breathless, next to Susannah and Eliza. The remains of their picnic were spread out and Thomas ate one of Martha's pork pies, savouring the salty meat and flaky pastry. Harriet cradled the cat whose leg he'd fixed at the girls' request. He'd told them that he'd never set an animal's broken leg before, that he wasn't a horse doctor, but Mary Ann begged him with her serious face and said it couldn't be that different from a person. She'd wanted to know how bones knitted together and how long it would take, but Harriet had only wanted the kitten to be well again.

Eliza helped Harriet make a daisy chain while Mary Ann studied a butterfly. Eliza wore a white muslin dress and her long dark hair was loose. Thomas lay on the rug, next to Susannah who knelt surrounded by her skirts. He rested his head against her and she stroked his hair. He closed his eyes, feeling the soft touch of her fingers, smelling the scents of herbs, listening to the chatter of the girls and the buzz of bees.

'Eliza, we really must start thinking about suitors for you.' Susannah stopped stroking his hair.

'Do we have to, Mama?'

'Unless you want to be a spinster.'

'Perhaps I do.'

'Of course you don't.'

'What do you think, Father?' Eliza asked.

'There's nothing wrong with marriage. Your mother and I have had over twenty happy years.'

'Exactly,' Susannah said. 'We must have a new dress made for parties. And I'll do your hair. We want to attract the best class of men.'

'I suppose you mean the richest,' Eliza said.

'You don't want to be a pauper,' Susannah replied.

Eliza grabbed Thomas's hand and pulled him to his feet. 'Teach me a new herb,' she said, and they walked to the herb garden. The scents of peppermint, dill, sage and lavender mingled in the warm air, their sweetness overpowering. Eliza plucked a leaf of lemon balm and rolled it in her fingers releasing lemon scent.

'*Melissa officinalis*, lemon balm or bee balm,' Thomas said. 'Used for headaches, to dress wounds, soothe tension, a cure for toothache and mad dog bites. When you're married and have a family you'll need to know these things. I'll give you my mother's old recipe book for remedies and buy you a medicine chest.'

'I won't need a medicine chest, I'll have you,' she said.

'You may not be near me.'

'I'll refuse to marry any man who lives more than a mile from Wilston. Teach me another one.'

'*Viola arvensis*, wild pansy, heartsease.' He picked a small flower, its five petals a mixture of white, yellow and purple, and handed it to her.

'What's its use?'

'It's said to be good for a broken heart, but I find it more useful for lung complaints.'

'I'm worried who Mama will select for me. What if he's too hairy or has foul breath?'

'Then say no! I'll support you.'

'Thank you.' She embraced him, her warm arms encircling him. The thought of her leaving him caused a pain like angina over his heart.

Out of the corner of his eye he saw hyssop with its small leaves and dark blue flowers. He was reminded of Charlotte Foster.

'Eliza,' he said. 'Perhaps you would read to a patient for me?'

She smiled and the ache in his chest eased.

'Of course I will, Father. Who is it?'

'Mrs Foster. You've probably seen her at church. Her son Fred runs wild.'

'Yes, I know her a little.'

She still held the small wild pansy in her hand and twirled it between her fingers. Would it be too much for her?

'I think I should warn you she's quite unwell, with consumption. You may find it distressing.'

'I want to do it. Maybe I can help ease her suffering a little.'

'Very well, but remember, if it becomes too difficult you can always stop.'

The waiting room was full and the patients restless. The summer heat persisted and the small treatment room was close and stuffy, the noise of babies crying and an old woman groaning carrying through the thin wall. Thomas wiped his brow with the back of his hand.

'Mr Hammond?' John asked. 'What do I do with this?'

What now? Couldn't the boy do anything himself?

'Wait a minute.' Thomas finished examining a baby with a fever and a rash and told the mother he would send some medicine later.

John showed him a large abscess on Mr Cannon's leg. A yellow mound was surrounded by spreading redness.

'Lance it with a heated silver pin,' Thomas said.

'Won't that hurt? Even touching near it is very tender.'

'Relieve the pressure and the pain will go.'

'I'm not sure I want it done if it will hurt,' Mr Cannon said.

'Best to do it quickly,' Thomas replied. 'Light a candle.'

John obeyed and Thomas showed him how to hold the pin in the flame with small forceps. What more did he have to do? John cut too lightly and didn't bleed patients enough. He was too tentative, frightened almost. He'd never be ready for Guy's at this rate. He'd probably faint by the bedside. And he was always worrying about hurting the patients. It was harder work fixing John's problems and having to help him than working alone.

The door swung open and someone walked into the room behind Thomas. Some patients thought they were in more pain, or more deserving, or just more important and tried to jump the queue by barging in. 'We're busy, wait outside,' he said.

'Father!'

Thomas turned around to see his son.

'Can I help?' Edward said. 'Your waiting room's full to bursting. John, that boil needs lancing. Let me do it. It won't take a minute.' He grabbed the forceps from John and plunged the red-hot pin into the tense yellow mountain on Mr Cannon's leg. The old man cried out. Pus burst from the lump and flowed down the sides.

'Should I squeeze a little, to get more out?' Edward asked, and started to do so before Thomas could reply. Mr Cannon roared in pain.

'Gently, Edward,' Thomas said.

'But look how much more I've encouraged to escape.'

'I was going to lance that,' John said. He shook his head like a bad-tempered horse.

'It's done now,' Edward said. 'Dress it and I'll call the next one. I smell cloves so there must be a tooth to pull.'

'Can I do that?' John asked Thomas.

'I've much more experience. You can do it next time.' Edward picked up the tooth key and went to call the patient.

'What right does he have to barge in here and steal it from me?' John's face was red and his voice strident.

'Just today, John, because we're so busy,' Thomas said. He didn't approve of Edward's attitude towards John, but Edward was so helpful. 'You can pull a tooth tomorrow. I promise.'

John clenched his jaw but picked up a bandage and wound it round the now-deflated abscess.

Edward pulled the tooth easily. He bled Mr Trew, the butcher with enormous muscles and a glowering expression, for his sore throat. He diagnosed the rash of scarlet fever in a small child by its rough feel. He recommended cinchona for a relapsing fever. It was crowded with the three of them in the treatment room. Their elbows knocked and they tripped over each other. Patients were squeezed in. John took three times as long as Edward to question a patient, then dithered about the necessary treatment. Thomas sent him to the dispensary to make pills, overriding his protests. The morning passed quickly and Thomas enjoyed it. He was proud of his son.

When they'd finished Thomas and Edward went to the dispensary. John was staring into space, but when they entered he placed a sausage of pill mass on the pill machine, banged the grooved brass plate on top and rolled vigorously.

'Have you come back for good?' Thomas asked Edward.

'No. Mama wrote and said she longed to see me and I must visit for the day. William agreed.'

Thomas tried to ignore the sinking feeling of disappointment in his gut. Seeing Edward made him realise how much he'd missed him.

'What have you learnt?'

'We've visited so many great houses. William treated a Lord the other day.'

'A Lord?' Thomas had never treated a Lord.

'I must tell Mama. The house was furnished with gilt mirrors and chairs and a sparkling chandelier.'

Thomas thought of the hovels, cottages, farmhouses and modest brick buildings he visited day in and day out. Not a grand house among them. The money a Lord would pay for one visit was probably more than he earned in a week.

'His patients like their pills covered in silver or gold leaf, not talc,' Edward said. 'He can charge much more for that.'

'They work the same whatever the coating,' Thomas said. 'Have you learnt any new skills?'

'How to mix some different medicines.'

'Speaking of which, can you mix this for me now?'

Edward agreed and Thomas opened the large, leather-covered *Pharmacopoeia* which lay on the bench to find the recipe.

'What does *Taraxaci* mean?' Edward said. 'Why can't they use English? Then anyone could understand and make medicines.'

'Dandelion,' Thomas said. 'It cleanses the liver and boosts the blood.'

'Latin is boring.' Edward leant forwards on one elbow, his dark hair falling over one eye.

'The *Aeneid* in Latin isn't boring.' John stood straight, his stiff body the same height as Edward leaning.

'I'm sure it's just as great a work in translation.' Edward took down two jars from the shelves.

'A good translation can only capture some of its power,' John said.

Edward stirred the mixture briskly with the fat end of a silver spatula. Drops splashed up and stained his hands brown. 'Pass me the *Tincture Rhei*, John. It doesn't matter what it means.'

John surveyed the rows of jars and ran his finger along them, his lips mouthing their labels. He handed one to Edward, who measured it and added it to the mixture.

'Next, *Sodae carbonatis*!' Edward pulled down one of the jars and told John to hold the scales. Edward put a weight on the pan and measured the powder to balance it.

'Edward, the recipe calls for a scruple but you've put a dram,' John said. 'That's three times too much.'

Thomas read the *Pharmacopoeia* and observed the weights. 'John is correct,' he said.

'I know that, Father. I just wanted to see if you and John noticed.'

'Edward, if that were digitalis you would have poisoned the patient and killed them. Paracelsus tells us the only difference between a medicine and a poison is in the dose.'

Edward swapped the weight and tipped the excess powder on the bench. 'Tell us more about poisons. What is the best way to kill a man without being detected? With wolf's-bane or yew berries?'

'An apothecary respects life.' Thomas swept the unwanted powder into his hand and replaced it in the jar.

'But you could slip something into the drink of someone you despised.'

'Never, not even my worst enemy. I will only use my learning for good, and you must do the same.'

'I'm only jesting.' Edward continued making the mixture.

'You shouldn't jest about such serious matters.'

Edward had so much talent – look at how he'd helped with the patients. Thomas dearly wished to believe Edward about the mistake with the weighing, but part of him doubted whether it had really been a test to see if he and John noticed. Such errors were not that unusual among apprentices, but it was best to admit them and learn from them, to show integrity. He hoped William wasn't filling his head with inflated ideas.

'Now write the label,' Thomas said. 'One third part to be taken three times a day in dropsical and visceral affections.'

'You know John's writing is much neater than mine,' Edward said.

His son stared at him. Edward had often said this sort of thing before and Thomas had accepted it, seeing it as reasonable to ask John, but now it perturbed him, and he saw it as defiance. Thomas perceived his son's height, his muscle bulk, his width and felt his power. He felt flustered. Now was not the right time to confront Edward, especially as John was watching.

'John. Would you mind writing the label for me, please?' Thomas was annoyed with himself that he was having to plead with John to do a task he'd asked Edward to do. He was as bad as Susannah, indulging Edward.

John met his eyes and Thomas saw him weighing up his choices. Obey his master but appear weak and submissive to Edward, or refuse and challenge Thomas's authority. John breathed deeply for a few moments, his shoulders rising and falling, then abandoned pill making and wrote the label with quill and ink in a neat hand. Perhaps he remembered the leech incident and thought better of arguing.

Early in John's apprenticeship, when the boys were both fourteen, Thomas had sent them to Pymmes Brook with his father's leech jar to collect more bloodsuckers. He'd returned home from his visits and found them fighting like bare-knuckle boxers. Edward was losing, despite being considerably bigger. John was barefoot and blood ran down his bare lower legs. Thomas stepped forwards and yanked John by his collar at the back of the neck, separating them. John told him Edward had tricked him into wading into the water first, so the leeches attached to his legs. He seemed unaware this was how they were caught. Edward had laughed at him and refused to enter the water himself. Thomas told them they were acting like infants and John ran away along Church Street.

Thomas tended to Edward, applying comfrey paste to his bloodied nose, while Susannah fussed around her son. Later Thomas crushed dark green, hairy comfrey leaves in the mortar to make more paste. Juice bled out of them. The door to the dispensary opened and John crept in. His grandmother had begged him to return. Thomas lectured him on controlling his temper and trying to get on with Edward. He told him an apothecary needed to be calm, like a pond on a windless day with no ripples. There was enough commotion and choppiness caused by illness and disease.

John's right hand was scarlet and puffy over his knuckles. Thomas offered to dress it. John hesitated, then held out his injured hand. Thomas had placed the comfrey paste on a square of muslin, settled it over John's swollen knuckles and tied the ends to make a bandage.

'Father?' Edward asked, and Thomas was back in the dispensary four years later. 'Why didn't you become a surgeon?'

Blood rushed to Thomas's ears and he heard the thump of his heart in them. He felt as if he was swaying on his feet.

'Why do you ask?'

'James says when he was dresser to Astley Cooper, Cooper often spoke of you and said you were very talented. That you could have been a great surgeon.'

'I…' His throat was so constricted he couldn't speak. What else had Cooper told James about him?

'Are you feeling unwell?'

'My throat's a little dry, that's all. I did want to become a surgeon, but my father became ill and I came home to take over his practice. William was already established in Southgate and didn't want to move. I'd just married your mother and needed an income.'

'But you've never mentioned knowing Astley Cooper,' Edward said. 'He's the most famous surgeon in the country.'

'We were students together, that's all. I didn't think it was important.'

'Do you regret not becoming a surgeon?'

'No, of course not.' He wondered if Edward and John could tell he was lying. 'Now you better go and see your mother or else she'll accuse me of monopolising you.'

All through the next few hot weeks of summer Eliza read to Mrs Foster. Thomas and John sometimes saw her leaving the house as they were entering. Work was busy with difficult labours, diarrhoeal illness, several cases of scarlet fever, broken bones and heatstroke. He took John on most of his visits and let him attend morning surgery. Thomas missed Edward's help. At times he didn't remove his boots for thirty-six hours. He kept thinking he must visit William to fulfil his promise to John, but there was always another case to see, another complication, another emergency.

One evening, leading Cinnamon to the stables, he saw Eliza and Edward talking in the orchard, sitting on a bench. He rubbed his eyes; his lack of sleep must be causing hallucinations. Edward was at William's. But it was John, in Edward's old coat which was too big for him. Their heads were bent close together, almost touching. Eliza wasn't even wearing her bonnet.

As far as he knew Eliza hadn't talked to John for years. When John had lived above the surgery and taken his meals in the house, he'd been quiet and rarely joined in the dinner conversation. Since he'd moved into lodgings in Edmonton with his brother Tom in January she couldn't have seen him much at all because the worlds of the surgery and the house were so separate.

Thomas shouted across the orchard to John. He had to call several times before John looked up and came over.

'Please stable Cinnamon for me.' Thomas handed John the reins.

There was the usual tension, the delay, before John took them from him and led the horse away. John seemed to think stabling the horse beneath him, although his father had been an ostler.

Eliza stood up and crossed her arms. She wore a fine muslin dress, almost transparent in the evening sun. Far too revealing.

'What were you talking to John about?' Thomas asked.

'Books for Mrs Foster. He can lend me some or borrow from Clarke's school.'

'Doesn't Mrs Foster have sufficient books?'

'She wants to hear new ones.'

'What about the ones in our house?' His study was full of medical books and journals, but he'd also inherited some Shakespeare, religious tracts and Swift from his father. And Susannah read sensational novels like *The Mysteries of Udolpho*. Were John's books so superior?

Thomas remembered when John started as his apprentice he'd brought his books from his grandmother's and unpacked them in the room above the surgery where he was to sleep. There were several large books about heathen gods. Thomas told him the classics were useful for learning Latin to read the *Pharmacopoeia*, not for their ridiculous romantic stories of gods and goddesses. A *Dictionary of Merchandise* looked interesting, as many of the entries were ingredients used in medicines. There was a book on the Incas of Peru. Thomas told

49

him the Incas used Peruvian bark for fever, from the cinchona tree. There was also some Shakespeare and *Robinson Crusoe*. Thomas said he would bring William Cullen's *First Lines of the Practice of Physic* over for John to read in the evenings.

He brought his attention back to Eliza, who was talking.

'She likes poetry and John is very knowledgeable. He recommended a poem by a lady, Mary Tighe. Did you know women can write poetry? It's called *Psyche* and I think it's helping her recover.'

'Not my medicines?'

'I didn't mean that, Father. Only it takes her away from herself for a time and she seems calmer and more hopeful after I've read to her.'

'Do you talk to John a lot about poetry?'

A pink flush appeared on her cheeks and she looked down at the ground. A grasshopper jumped from the grass, startling her.

'I don't think your mother would approve.'

She grabbed his arm and held it tight. 'Please don't tell her. We only discuss books. If Mama knows she'll stop us.'

The feel of her small fingers digging into his arm was unpleasant. Her face was white, her neck muscles tense.

'I won't tell her, but you must promise me to behave properly.'

'Thank you, Father.' She threw her arms around him.

A few days later, Thomas entered the dispensary and found John engrossed in something, his head bent low. John wrote on a sheet of paper, resting on the open pages of the bulky *Pharmacopoeia*. His intense absorption stimulated Thomas's curiosity and he crept up behind him and peered over his shoulder. He could read the first line. *Fill for me a brimming bowl.* He leant closer.

And in it let me drown my soul. John's quill travelled across the paper. *But put therein some drug, designed.* Thomas stretched his neck to see the next line, but John must have sensed the movement and slammed his hand on the paper to cover it.

'What are you doing?' Thomas asked. He felt alarm at the overblown tone, the desire to drown.

'I've mixed all the medicines, Sir.'

'Scribing a poem about bloodletting, are you?'

John blushed and bit his lower lip. He removed his hand from the paper and folded it, but not before Thomas read the next line. *To banish Woman from my mind.* For a moment Thomas worried the poem was about Eliza, that John was obsessed with her, but the last line reassured him. It was an excellent sentiment; his apprentice had no time for romance.

'Let us mix this medicine I need for Mr Brown,' Thomas said. 'It's an unusual one and needs great care.'

Mrs Foster's condition fluctuated. Some days she rallied, sitting up and smiling, and Thomas hoped she would do better, but then the next day she relapsed and lay on the chaise longue struggling to breathe, unable to find enough air to greet them. He detected the sweetish smell of decay rising from her rotting lungs. He found himself praying for a miracle. He rarely prayed except in church, otherwise he would be constantly praying for his patients rather than working for them.

At the end of a busy day Thomas and John went to the dispensary. There was enough light not to need the lamp. Thomas placed his bag on the bench and began to restock it from some of the blue and white apothecary jars on the shelves. Many of the jars were chipped around the pedestals and spouts from years of use, their glaze worn, but Thomas would never swap them for the white creamware and gilt jars William used; these were his father's jars.

The tin-glazed jars were white decorated in shades of blue. The fat-bellied ones were for dry ingredients, the ones with spouts for wet. Vellum or parchment lids sealed their contents. Each had a label inscribed in capitals in Latin. Cartouches surrounded the labels, either plain dark lines or swirling and rolling like waves. Around the cartouches were symmetrical pictures of leaves, flowers, birds and shells. On many a cherub or angel's face peeped over the label, his wings spreading either side. One had the head and shoulders of Apollo, a halo blazing behind his head, his gaze directed downwards. Another had a two-legged winged dragon, a wyvern.

As a child he'd stood at this same bench watching his father and William mix medicines. Books had lain open showing the recipes, handwritten notes in the border. He'd learnt Latin from the names of plants.

'What does that inscription mean?' John pointed at one of the jars Thomas had taken down. 'I don't know the word FLAN.'

Thomas inspected the jar. 'O:LAUR:FLAN: Oleum Laurinum Flan. Oil of yellow bay berries. I think the Flan is a misspelling of FLAV for flavour.'

'What does the dragon symbolise?'

'Pestilence. It's a wyvern not a dragon.'

John studied the picture. 'He's always flying, wings extended, arrow-tip tongue protruding, tail curled. He's trapped forever on the jar.'

'So we can never defeat him, but we have to try. And Apollo, on that jar, with the halo around his head, helps us. The god of medicine. That's one of your Greek gods and goddesses I do know.'

'Apollo is also the god of poetry.'

'Now that surprises me. I don't see how the two can be linked.'

'I think the poetry is helping Mrs Foster.'

'I doubt it's the poetry.'

'I noticed her bottle of veronica and hyssop is low so I'll mix some more.' John measured the ingredients and pounded the herbs with vigour in the iron pestle and mortar. 'And then I'll make some more liquorice and Peruvian balsam pills.'

'You'll wear yourself out. Shouldn't you go home to rest?'

'No. I want to do it now.'

John's sleeves were rolled up. There was a ferocity in his mixing, a determination Thomas hadn't seen before.

'John, I think you should prepare yourself for the worst.'

'What do you mean, the worst? She was so cheerful today when we arrived and said she felt better.'

'That's the *spes phthisica*, John. The feeling of euphoria near the end.'

John stopped mixing. Flecks of herbs which had flown out of the bowl lay spattered on the bench and along his freckled forearms. John, his eyes wide, stared at Thomas. He looked younger than eighteen and Thomas saw again the boy who'd nursed his mother.

'John, you mustn't become too attached to the patients. Learn to harden yourself or you'll never be an apothecary. You'll drive yourself mad and end up in Bedlam.'

'I don't believe you. She's definitely getting better.'

'I think it would be best if you didn't come on the visits to Mrs Foster anymore.'

'No! I will come. You can't stop me.' John breathed heavily, his face pale.

What should he do? Assert his authority? That would make John even more enraged. Thomas remembered as a boy refusing to do a chore, stamping his foot and his father hitting him, but he couldn't beat John. He wasn't that sort of master. He abhorred violence in all its forms.

'You're overwrought, John,' Thomas said. 'Calm down.'

John's face crumpled and tears flowed. 'Please, Sir,' he said.

Thomas looked away, at the wyvern and Apollo. The boy was too delicate; he had an excess of feeling, which wasn't healthy especially for an apothecary. Thomas listened to John's sniffs until he could bear it no longer.

'Here.' Thomas handed him his handkerchief. 'Don't cry.'

John wiped his face and blew his nose. 'Have you asked your brother about new treatments yet?'

'I've been too busy, but I will. If it means so much to you, you can still visit Mrs Foster, but I want you to promise me, no more scenes. You must control yourself.'

'Thank you,' John said. 'I promise.'

'Now, I insist you leave the mixing and go home. She has enough for tonight. You can do those first thing tomorrow.'

To Thomas's surprise John obeyed. Thomas showed him out and shut the door to the surgery. He watched John walk down the street, his shoulders hunched, his pace slow. Thomas felt a deep discomfort, a foreboding, in his belly. The boy had a lot to learn.

Chapter Four

The sounds of Martha singing a folksong about blackbirds drifted from the kitchen. Thomas enjoyed listening to her repertoire of country songs and hymns. She looked up from rolling pastry, a short, plump woman with a cheerful face, her nose dusted with flour.

'Mistress said to tell you she wants to see you, Sir,' Martha said. 'She's upstairs doing the accounts.'

'I think I better fortify myself first,' Thomas said.

Martha looked down and concentrated on rolling her pastry thinner, but he saw her smile. Martha had been thirteen, the youngest maid, when Thomas and Susannah moved back to Wilston. Over the years the other staff had taken umbrage against Susannah and left. She hadn't replaced them, citing reasons of household economy. Martha cooked and did the work of two maids but seemed happy in her position. Thomas sometimes wondered why she'd never married but hadn't thought it his place to ask her. She'd been eternally grateful after he'd treated her mother who had nearly died of pneumonia many years ago.

'There's some ham in the larder,' she said.

He took ham and butter from the cool larder and a piece of bread from the side. He buttered the bread evenly, tore it into chunks and ate it quickly, then started on the ham. When summoned, no one should face Susannah on an empty stomach.

Susannah sat at the desk in her sitting room, the evening sun slanting through the window onto her figure bent over the ledgers. Her quill flowed across the paper, leaving behind a beautiful curled path of ink on the left-hand side. On the right-hand side she jotted figures in neat rows. He trusted her addition more than his own. Her father had been a shopkeeper and sent her to a dame school to learn reading, writing and arithmetic. Then she had kept her father's accounts and become an astute bookkeeper.

She finished the entry and placed her quill in the glass and silver inkpot before she spoke.

'What's this I hear about Eliza? Is it true?'

'Eliza?' Had she seen Eliza and John in the orchard from her window? 'It's nothing to be concerned about, I've spoken to her.'

'So she won't be visiting your patients anymore?'

'What? Yes, she will. I asked her to read to Mrs Foster.'

Susannah stood in front of the window. Her blue dress made a pretty picture in front of the gauzy curtains. Was it new? He didn't recognise the fabric, but he knew if he asked she'd deny it and call him an unobservant man.

'My daughter reading to a consumptive woman. Why did I have to hear it from Mrs Draper in the village? It's not seemly.'

'Other women do it.'

'Married women, not young girls, and a brief visit suffices. What if she catches something?'

'It's not contagious.'

Susannah came round and took his hands in hers. His hands dwarfed her small ones. His were brown, hers pale as milk. His warm, hers cool. She tipped her face up to his.

'We should be looking for suitors for Eliza.'

'She's too young to be married.'

'She's nineteen. I was married at that age.'

'That was different. She doesn't need to marry.'

She dropped his hands and turned her back to him. He saw the outline of her stays through her dress, holding in her figure. When she released them at night the ravages of four childbirths and her fondness for confectionery were evident, but he still desired her.

'I wish you'd socialise more, Thomas. How can she meet appropriate men if you don't?'

'You know I'm too busy.' He crossed his arms.

'It's a question of priorities. Doesn't your daughter come before patients?'

'Of course she does, but can't you just leave her be for now?'

'You want her to be an old maid?'

'No, but let's wait a little.'

'I'll throw some card parties for the ladies of Edmonton and ask Eliza to attend so they can meet her.'

'If you must.'

Susannah sat down at her desk again. She picked up her quill and pressed it into the paper of the ledger.

'And you'll stop her visiting Mrs Foster?'

'Susannah, I don't think you need worry about Eliza reading to Mrs Foster for much longer. The poor woman hasn't long left on this earth.'

'I'm sorry to hear that.' She did genuinely look sorry, her face compassionate.

'It would be cruel to stop now.'

Susannah played with the lace ribbons on her cap. 'And you won't send her to any of your other patients? Those rabbles of children riddled with lice? Those old men in rags?'

57

'You have a low opinion of my patients.'

'I'm just trying to protect her and her reputation.'

'After Mrs Foster, no more.'

She ran her hand across the ledger, her gold rings catching the light.

'I saw Mrs Bunton in the haberdasher's buying lace. That woman owes you a guinea. If it wasn't for the money I brought to the marriage I don't know how we'd survive.'

'But we do survive, quite well, in fact.'

'Why bother to send bills when you know half of them won't pay?'

'Then they would think it charity and feel offended.'

'So they're less offended but live in fear of the bill? They think you are soft, Thomas.'

'I'm not just a tradesman like a confectioner or a carpenter. It's a vocation. I want to live up to my father's ideals.'

'The yellow velvet in the drawing room needs reupholstering.'

'There are more important things in life than yellow velvet. It will just have to wait.'

'I better send out more bills. Perhaps some of them will pay.' Susannah bowed her head, picked up her quill and went back to her columns and figures.

Thomas watched her for a few moments, wondering how they'd become so far apart in their ideas of the purpose of his work. Then he headed to his dispensary.

Thomas rubbed his eyes in the hot and smoky room. The village women supporting the mother clustered around her top half. The baby's legs, bottom and torso hung from the mother's perineum. Thomas sat on a stool with his hands held together in his lap, waiting for the head to descend. John stood next to him holding a lamp. Why did so many babies enter the world in the early hours?

'Shouldn't you try and birth the head now?' John asked.

'Patience, John.'

'It looks so unnatural.'

'I've delivered hundreds of breeches. I learnt at Guy's Hospital.'

The whispers of the women comforting the mother circled the room. He thought he heard snatches of doubt about his method, the name of Ellen Lock, whose breech baby had been born dead last year. He would tell John off later, for questioning his authority.

The mother's cries drowned the whispers when a contraction came.

'Now.' Thomas grasped the baby's feet and with gentle traction swept them upwards in an arc over the mother's abdomen. The baby's head emerged slowly. He cleared the mouth and lay the baby on the mother. The midwife rubbed it and it started to cry. The women laughed with relief and John whooped with joy. Thomas smiled and washed his hands in a bowl of water. Bringing new life into the world was one of the best parts of his work. Perhaps now he and John could get some sleep. The labour had been long, but he'd wanted John to experience a breech delivery.

There was a knock at the door and a boy told them Mrs Foster was very ill and asked them to come. A look of alarm crossed John's face and he quickly packed Thomas's bag. Thomas pulled his shoulders back and straightened his coat. The joy at the safe birth of the baby disappeared, and a sick feeling settled like a stone in the pit of his stomach.

Thomas and John walked along the village street in silence. John hurried so fast Thomas struggled to keep up. The air had a cool bite after the hot room. It felt as though they were the only people in the whole world awake in the dead of night. The houses themselves seemed asleep, but at the Fosters' there was light in the windows and noise from people awake inside.

'Remember, control your emotion,' Thomas said to John. 'Whatever happens, it's God's will.' His heart beat fast in his chest after the brisk walk.

The room was lit by several lamps. Mrs Foster sat up in bed struggling to breathe. Her thin chest pulled in and out like a bellows and the noise of her breathing was loud. She clawed at the air with her hands, grasping invisible birds. Her hair was loose and tangled. Distress and sheer panic showed in her eyes, but she did not, could not speak. She flung back the cover and tried to leave the bed. Her husband tried to stop her. His face was ashen.

'Do something, Hammond,' Charles Foster said. 'She's been like this for an hour.'

Thomas picked up the silver medicine spoon from the side of the bed and poured a dose of laudanum.

'Mrs Foster,' he said. 'I need you to take your medicine. It will calm you down.' She was still for a few seconds and he held the spoon towards her dry, cracked lips. 'That's good, just swallow this.'

Her hand flew up and knocked the spoon from his hand. The liquid sprayed in the air. 'No!' she shouted. Her eyes fixed on his and he swore there was a clarity there that had been absent a minute before.

'Charlotte, dear,' her husband said. 'Mr Hammond is only trying to help.'

She plucked at the covers and tried to get out of bed again.

'I can't bear this any longer,' Foster said. 'I'll be in my study.'

'You must stay in bed, Mrs Foster,' Thomas said. 'You'll feel better if you rest.'

She sat with her thin legs hanging over the side of the bed, leaning forwards to breathe more easily.

'That's good, now some medicine will help you.' He poured another spoonful of laudanum and advanced it towards her lips. His hand was shaking a little. He wasn't normally clumsy. The spoon touched her lower lip. 'Open wide now.'

She jerked her head away and the liquid spilled on his coat. She laughed and lay back again but started muttering, all the while gasping for breath in a desperate effort to draw air into her lungs.

'John. I need you to hold her down,' Thomas said. 'Sit on the bed and hold her head so I can give the medicine.'

'No,' John said. 'Mrs Foster, let Mr Hammond give you the medicine, please. I know it will help you.'

She swatted at him with her hand.

'John, hold her down,' Thomas said.

'Let me try something else.' John seized a book from her bedside table.

'Mrs Foster, is this the book Eliza, Miss Hammond, has been reading to you? She told me you liked to hear poetry.'

Mrs Foster stared at John and lowered her arms. She looked puzzled.

'Let me read you a poem by William Cowper.' John flicked through the pages.

Thomas wiped some drops of laudanum from his face. What a ridiculous idea.

'This is called *Light Shining Out of Darkness*,' John said. '*God moves in a mysterious way, His wonders to perform; He plants his footsteps in the sea, and rides upon the storm.*'

John continued reading the verses, but Thomas didn't hear them. God did indeed work in mysterious ways. To make a young wife and mother suffer so. To afflict her with a protracted, distressing, wasting illness. What was the purpose of her suffering? She was a good woman; she didn't deserve it.

Mrs Foster turned away from John and started clawing at the air again.

'It's not working,' Thomas said. The laudanum would calm her, ease her breathing and her distress. 'We need to restrain her.'

'I can't.'

'I'll hold her down, and you must pour the laudanum down her throat, straight from the bottle. That's an order.' Thomas pushed Mrs Foster against the pillows, holding her face either side and opening her jaw. It was brutal but necessary. He tried to avoid her sharp fingers and kicking legs. Her strength was unworldly for one so ill. 'Be quick,' he said.

John picked up the laudanum bottle and poured the liquid into her mouth. She spluttered and choked. 'More,' Thomas said. John hesitated. 'More,' Thomas shouted, and John obeyed.

Thomas held her head until he was sure she'd swallowed and couldn't spit it out, then let go. She wiped her lips which were covered in the laudanum. She looked at him and he saw she recognised him. It was a look of hatred.

'You… killed… Isabella,' she said, gasping between her words. 'Murderer.'

The vehemence of her words stunned him like a physical blow. Her eyes locked with his. He swallowed. She didn't mean it. She was delirious. She didn't know what she was saying. He must push aside his feelings and be strong to help her.

'Let's lie you down so you can rest,' he said.

John rushed to rearrange her pillows, but she wouldn't lie against them. She struck out and kicked and muttered. Whenever she tried to climb out of bed Thomas would gently push her back, trying to avoid her scratches and slaps. John stood, pale and horrified. Her sharp nails scratched Thomas's cheek and he jumped back, touching the area and feeling blood. It wasn't her fault. She didn't know what she was doing.

Slowly the laudanum started to work. Her movements weakened and she collapsed, exhausted, on the pillows.

Thomas went to the study to find Mr Foster, who sat at his desk in front of a closed Bible.

'She's settled,' Thomas said, 'but I don't think she has long left. Do you want to sit with her?'

Mr Foster shook his head. Thomas crept back to the sickroom, dimmed the lamps and sat with his patient and John. Every so often she would cough, look startled and try to lift her head and arms but could not. Her pupils shrank to pinpoints. Her breathing slowed. John sponged her brow with cool water. His face was pained. The sound of secretions in her throat and air passages gurgled like a monster and Thomas gave her drops of henbane, which she accepted without resisting.

'You must do something,' John cried. 'Save her.'

'I can't.' Thomas raised his head. She lay like a breathing corpse, her face skeletal, her skin falling from prominent cheekbones in loose folds, her collarbones protruding. She had once been a beautiful woman, full of life. He couldn't save her. He had no more medicines, mixtures, tonics, draughts or potions, no more leeches, no more lancets to offer. He was powerless. Stranded in a sea of despair.

Each breath moved her chest less until the movement stopped, the death rattle died and she was gone. Thomas folded her pale, thin hands on top of each other and bowed his head.

'Her suffering is over,' he said to himself as much as to John.

John sat still as a cut silhouette. Thomas's eyes felt moist; it must be from the smoke at the earlier delivery. They sat in silence; he had no idea how long for.

Thomas went back to Charles Foster in his study. His legs felt heavy.

'She's at peace,' Thomas said.

'How will I cope without her?' Foster asked. 'How can I tell the children?'

'I'm sure you'll find the courage.'

'I don't think I can.' He sobbed into his hands.

The sight of a grown man crying made Thomas want to run away. He felt stiff, out of place. He couldn't bring himself to speak the platitudes he knew others would. That she was in a better place, with the angels, chosen by God, reunited with their daughter Isabella.

'Shall I send for the vicar?' he asked.

Foster reached towards the Bible then withdrew his hand. He looked up and shook his head.

'I'll mix you a draught for your nerves and bring it round later.'

'Thank you.' Foster made an effort to stop his tears. 'I'll sit here for a while then go and see her.'

'I did all I could for her,' Thomas said.

'I know.'

Thomas took his leave and went back to the bedroom, where John sat by Mrs Foster's bedside. His head was bowed and his hands clasped together, but not in prayer.

'Come, John,' Thomas said. 'We should leave. There will be work to do in a few hours and we can do no more for her now.'

John turned his face to him and it was blank, as if he had never seen Thomas before in his life.

Outside the Fosters' house a sliver of pink over the horizon signalled dawn. Thomas was relieved to escape the confined atmosphere of illness and death. John walked slowly beside him, the bag dragging down his arm and Thomas took it from him. John hadn't spoken since Mrs Foster passed away. Thomas recognised the shock of death, the disbelief.

'It's very sad, John, but we must go on living,' Thomas said. 'Remember the baby we brought into the world? He'll now be suckling at his mother's breast, snuggling against her for warmth. Life and death. Two sides of the same coin, my father always said. A medical man must be able to deal with both, there's no escaping that fact.'

John still didn't speak.

'Why don't you sleep in your old bed above the surgery for a few hours rather than go back to your lodgings?' Thomas said. 'It's not long 'til the patients arrive. They don't know we've been up most of the night.'

He detected a slight nod from John.

Thomas pulled back the covers and climbed into bed beside Susannah. As soon as his body brushed against hers he felt great desire arise in him. He kissed her face, her lips, lifted her nightdress and kissed her breasts. She woke and he made love to her with an urgency, a need to possess her. Lying spent, his head on her chest below her shoulder, he felt the warmth of living skin and heard her heartbeat. It told him he was alive.

He awoke to bright light and was annoyed to find he'd overslept. A few patients waited outside the surgery. He asked them to wait a little longer, entered and shut the door behind him. The surgery was deserted. Dust motes floated in the air, settling on the surfaces.

'John?' He climbed the stairs. 'John?' He pushed open the door.

John sat by the window, his back to him. He didn't turn around. He still wore his coat from the night before.

'Have you slept?' Thomas asked.

'I couldn't.' John's voice was thick and muffled.

'Never mind. You'll sleep well tonight.'

John turned to face Thomas and his eyes were red as if he'd rubbed them. He then turned back to the window. He showed no sign of rising to see the patients. Thomas sank onto the bed. He remembered the first time John came to this room, four years ago.

When they had signed the indentures, John swore to be bound to Thomas for five years and refrain from consorting with women, haunting inns or gambling. In return Thomas had promised to train him in his profession, provide meat, drink and lodging, and in case of sickness proper physic and other necessaries. John had seemed surprised he was to sleep in the room above the surgery and not in the house. Thomas led him up to the hot attic room and opened a window which overlooked the orchard where Eliza walked in a white dress among the trees. John lay his bag on one of the beds, the shapes of books distorting the fabric from inside.

After he'd unpacked his books, Thomas told him he would

start his duties the next day and they would be to dust the bottles, sweep the floor, deliver medicines and care for his horses. John asked when he would see patients and learn to treat disease. Thomas told him the chores must be done first, he must be trained like a soldier, do drills and work his way up the ranks. As his apprentice he must obey his orders and do his bidding without questioning his authority. In return, Thomas would teach him anatomy, physiology and materia medica, how to bleed patients and mix medicines. Most important of all he'd learn by observation. John nodded his head slowly, but his expression was sullen.

The noises outside brought Thomas back to the present. 'It's time to clean the surgery,' he said. 'The patients are already waiting.' He went downstairs and after a short pause John followed, his tread heavy on the wooden stairs, as if he were laden with a sack of grain on his back.

'I'm too exhausted to clean today.' John's body shivered. 'Can't Edward come back and do it?'

'John, I'm the master. I'll decide who does what.'

'You decided I would be your footman and mind your horse outside my old school where the boys came to gawk at me. What would my father think? He always said he would never again sink so low as to mind another man's horse.'

'It's part of an apprentice's duties.' What had the boy expected?

'I fear I'm your servant, while Edward is treated like a prince. He sleeps on a feather bed and feasts on kippers.'

'Don't sound so bitter, John. It doesn't suit you.'

'You decided I would make thousands of pills while Edward accompanied you and bled patients and learnt medicine. Until the past few weeks all I've done is chores.'

'I've taught you anatomy, physiology and materia medica, and how to mix medicines.' How ungrateful could the boy be? Other apothecary surgeons didn't teach their apprentices at all. Edward needed more instruction and experience as he was destined to be a surgeon.

'But I need to learn how to diagnose fevers and diseases and operate. When will I learn to fight the war against disease?'

'Come, John. Calm yourself. That's what I'm trying to teach you now. Why this outburst? Mrs Foster was an interesting case.'

John rested his outstretched hands on the bench and hung his head. It was cool in the surgery. He raised his head and looked into Thomas's eyes.

'Did you ever ask your brother about her treatment?'

A stab of guilt pierced Thomas. 'I intended to, but I didn't have time before her condition worsened.'

'You didn't care enough to find the time.' John's voice was as sharp as shards of glass.

'That's not true. Do you expect me to devote all my energies to one patient?' How dare John talk to him like this.

'She was weak from your treatments and so much bleeding.'

'I was balancing her humours.' So now John thought he knew better than him. 'John, you're tired. Go home to bed this once and I'll manage by myself.' It would be busy, but John wouldn't be much use like this. He showed no stamina.

John stood in the surgery, in front of the apothecary jars with their Latin inscriptions, their pictures of Apollo, the wyvern, cherubs and flowers. The light fell on his reddish-gold hair, which reminded Thomas of Mrs Foster.

'How did my mother die?' John asked. 'Did she suffer like Mrs Foster? Struggling to breathe, out of her mind, held down while laudanum was forced down her throat?'

Thomas opened his mouth, but no words came out.

'I was at school when they told me. I hid under the desk, unable to believe it. They said you'd comforted her, that she'd fallen asleep peacefully.'

'John, calm down. You're overwrought. It's been a long night.'

'My mother died taking your medicines.' John turned his back to Thomas and ran his hand along the apothecary jars, and for a moment Thomas feared he might knock them off and break them. 'I insisted on giving them myself, following your instructions precisely. So many medicines, pills, draughts, balms, tonics, stimulants, brandy and finally laudanum.'

'Those are the standard treatments for the symptoms of consumption.' Didn't the boy understand anything? What more did he want from him?

'I trusted you. She trusted you. But your treatments made her worse.'

'Your mother was weakened by her past living.' No one could have saved her.

Frances Keats had returned to her mother and four children in great distress. Thomas didn't like to listen to gossip in the village, but his wife delighted in telling him she'd been living with a man in Enfield who wasn't her second husband.

He was first called to see her because she suffered from rheumatism, her joints red and swollen, and struggled to rise from bed. She looked much older than her thirty-four years and he'd smelt the alcohol on her breath. She developed sweats, chills and a persistent cough. Over the spring and summer her condition had improved but deteriorated with autumn and winter. She had died the next spring.

'We can't save everyone,' Thomas said. 'Even Astley Cooper

with his operations, however fine a surgeon he is. It's God's will.'

'God's will?' John turned to face him. 'That's just an excuse for your failings.'

'I tried my best.' Had he failed Mrs Foster? And Isabella? And Frances Keats and the boy at Guy's? He'd read the books, the journals, followed their instructions. He'd tried so hard, but he hadn't been able to save his patients.

'You let them down.'

Thomas saw Mrs Foster, his hands holding her face, while she scratched and fought; Frances Keats coughing, unable to breathe, panic in her eyes; the terror in Isabella's face when he attached the leeches to her neck; the boy at Guy's screaming and bleeding to death. He should have saved them. All the useless medicines, the leeches, the lancets. He'd failed them all and many more. Before it had prickled at his skin, pricked his consciousness, but he saw it clearly now. The pain of this knowledge was acute, the sharp jagged blade of a surgical saw cutting deep into his core and not stopping. Even if he'd not saved them, he should have eased their suffering.

'Your mother died more peacefully than Mrs Foster, John. A little distressed, but she fell asleep.' She'd gladly taken the brandy and laudanum he'd offered, swallowing it greedily.

'Liar!' John's face was red, on fire. 'How many lives have you saved? None which I've seen. All you do is dispense useless mixtures and send bills for them.'

'I've saved many lives and when I couldn't I've tried to ease symptoms.' He didn't understand why he felt he had to defend himself to this little upstart. He should just ignore him, but John's comments were eating into him like maggots.

'I've seen nothing that shows me you're a healer.'

'I trained at Guy's Hospital,' Thomas shouted. 'I'm a member of the Corporation of Surgeons. I'm one of the Hammonds of Edmonton.'

'How can you live with yourself? You're a fraud. A quack!'

Billy Lucas Junior had called him a fraud. After the boy at Guy's had died. When he'd come into the operating theatre and seen the boy's body. Deaf, stooped, ungainly Billy Lucas Junior with his thin lips and pale eyes. The worst thing was in that case Thomas knew it was true.

Anger rose within him like a fever, climbing higher, heating his body to combustion point. He couldn't bear that this boy was calling him a failure and a fraud.

'You, my boy, are insolent and ungrateful, unworthy of my teachings,' he said. 'I've tried my best, but you've been difficult, resentful and churlish. Why shouldn't I promote Edward? He has a cheerful face. I refuse to teach you anymore. If you think so little of me, then you won't mind. Leave. Get out of my sight. The apprenticeship is over!'

Chapter Five

'Mr Hammond?' Martha stood over Thomas in the drawing room holding a plate of food and a glass of beer. He took them from her and drank half the beer straight down. Susannah cleared her throat. She preferred him to eat in the dining room, but it was late and he was tired. The ox tongue was tough and he swallowed it in great chunks.

'They don't eat tongue at Uncle William's.' Edward lounged with his legs hanging over the side of an armchair. Thomas had summoned Edward back home to help. It was three days since his argument with John, but his anger was like an inflammation of heat, redness and pain, exquisitely tender when touched by memories of John's words.

Susannah sat on the yellow chaise longue with the two younger girls, showing Mary Ann how to fasten the thread on her embroidery. When he'd told her he'd dismissed John she'd looked astonished and asked him why, but he said he didn't want to discuss it further.

'Have you mixed all the medicines I needed, Edward?' Thomas asked. 'The antimony and rhubarb and opium?' Why couldn't Edward sit up straight, not slumped in a chair that would damage his spine?

'I've mixed as many as I can.'

'I expected you to still be preparing them.'

'The wine needs to sit in the antimony cup for longer before I can use it.'

'Thomas, he's been working all day. I can vouch for that,' Susannah said. Harriet leant against her side.

'Can I go back to Uncle William's soon?' Edward picked up his fiddle and plucked the strings. 'They're having a dance.'

'Last year you sprained your ankle jumping about and couldn't walk for a week.' Eliza looked up from her book.

'But it's such fun with the music and the pretty dresses. You should come too, Eliza.' Edward flicked his hair away from his face.

'Haven't you noticed how busy we are, Edward?' Thomas started on his potatoes.

'I mix all day without a break! I never even go on a visit with you or bleed patients anymore,' he said. 'Since John left I'm working twice as hard.'

'And I thrice as hard!' A tinge of indigestion started in Thomas's stomach, but he ignored it and finished his beer. It was as good as a tonic.

'When I'm at Guy's training to be a surgeon I won't need to mix medicines,' Edward said.

'You're mistaken.' At Guy's Thomas had mixed endless pastes and ointments and plasters.

Susannah looked up from unpicking Mary Ann's embroidery. 'Edward should have the chance to go to the party.'

'While patients are dying?' Thomas said. Susannah mouthed his name and nodded towards Mary Ann and Harriet.

'Maybe John would come back?' Eliza said. 'I'm sure I saw him going into Mrs Jennings's the other day.'

Thomas had ridden past Mrs Jennings's house several times but spurred his horse on to avoid the possibility of meeting John. He half expected the old lady to step in front of him and ask why he'd dismissed her grandson.

'That's not possible, Eliza,' Thomas said. 'His behaviour was unforgivable.'

'But what did he do?' she asked. 'Kill a patient?'

'He questioned my authority and competence.' Thomas saw John's face and heard his voice accusing him of killing his mother. His muscles tensed at the memory.

Edward picked up his bow and drew it lightly across the strings. The sounds hung in the air. Eliza went back to her book. When he'd told her Mrs Foster had passed away her face had turned pale. He'd seen she was trying to be brave and wanted to ease her pain, but he couldn't dose her with laudanum and brandy. There was nothing he could do to help her and that upset him. He should never have asked her to read to Mrs Foster in the first place.

'Why don't you take on another apprentice, Thomas?' Susannah asked.

'I'm too busy to look for one.' There was no question of taking John back, so why did he hesitate to replace him? 'And it would take time to train a new apprentice to John's level.'

'Henry Cline will be at the party,' Edward said.

'Eliza should go too, to meet people,' Susannah said. Her plans to find a suitable suitor for Eliza among the relations of the ladies of Edmonton hadn't materialised.

'I don't wish to, Mama.' Eliza didn't glance up from her book.

Edward played a melody on his fiddle, a country tune. Although it was cheerful the notes made Thomas feel melancholy.

'Stop that, Edward. I can't think,' he said.

'What about the party for me?' Edward asked. He still bowed his fiddle, but softly.

'When the work is quieter you can go to your cousins.' The

boy had no sense of duty. Thomas would never have questioned his father so. He knew his obligations.

They stared at each other. Thomas saw defiance cross Edward's face, but his son suppressed it. Perhaps he could hear his irritation.

'Thomas,' Susannah said, rising to put Harriet to bed. He waited for her to intervene to forward Edward's case. He was determined not to give in to her. She spoiled Edward. But to his surprise she didn't continue to support Edward's request to go to William's. 'This came earlier.' She handed him a letter, which he opened.

Mr Abbey, the guardian appointed by John's grandmother, wanted him to come to his office. Well, Mr Abbey, like Edward, would have to wait until his patients improved. He couldn't abandon them now.

'What's it about?' Susannah asked.

'Abbey wants to discuss my treatment of John Keats,' Thomas said. 'You realise this is all your fault, don't you?'

However much Susannah might deny it, Thomas blamed her meddling for his predicament. Four years ago his apprentice had left prematurely and Susannah had arranged with Mrs Jennings for her grandson, John, to replace him. Behind his back. The first he knew of it was when Mrs Jennings thanked him for allaying her worries over John's future.

John had come to the surgery to look round. In daylight, away from his mother's sickroom, he looked pale, as though he would faint at the sight of blood. Thomas hadn't seen him since his mother's funeral five months earlier. John had asked about the Latin inscriptions on the apothecary jars, saying he knew Latin but not Greek.

Thomas had tried to dissuade John, telling him an apothecary saw illness, suffering and death. Courage was needed. John told him he'd wanted to join the military like his uncle who fought at the battle of Camperdown, but he was too short. Instead he'd fight the war against disease. A shaft of light struck the wyvern on the jar on the shelf. Its wings seemed about to beat, to lift off in flight. John looked at Thomas and spoke. 'I want you to teach me how to relieve suffering, Mr Hammond.'

A strange request, from a fourteen-year-old boy, but a boy who'd already lost his father and mother, a mother who'd suffered from a cruel illness. The boy must still be grieving. The desire in John's eyes was mesmerising. Thomas saw his passion to learn from him and knew its rarity. He felt a conversion, an almost religious experience, with the light striking the wyvern. He would take him on and teach him all he knew.

Now, rising out of his chair to review a case of childbed fever, he reflected he hadn't done a very good job of teaching John how to relieve suffering. He didn't even know himself.

A light rain fell as Thomas rode the ten miles towards London. He rehearsed the arguments he would present to Abbey. John Keats had acted unreasonably. John Keats was unsuited to be an apothecary. It was perfectly right that Thomas had ended the apprenticeship. His stomach contracted with apprehension. Abbey had sent a second letter demanding his attendance, the tone intimidating, and since his most ill patients had improved he'd not dared refuse.

He stabled Cinnamon at an inn at Moorgate outside London Wall and walked into the City of London. The streets were crowded with people from all walks of life hurrying to get out of the rain.

As he turned into the Poultry an unholy stench emanated from the barred windows of the Comptor. He pitied the debtors and vagrants locked up there. The smell reminded him of the dissecting room at Guy's, and he breathed through his mouth not his nose. By comparison Edmonton smelt sweet as new-cut hay. In the doorway, a dog ate from a bowl, watched over by a warden. He suspected the dog was better fed than the inmates. Nearby the grand bricks and square tower of St Mildred's Church rose above the slick cobbles. Loaded carts and carriages full of passengers trundled past him and he kept close to the buildings. He turned into narrow Pancras Lane and arrived at number four unscathed.

A clerk showed him to an office and announced his arrival. His eyes took a few seconds to adjust to the dark, wood-panelled room. Richard Abbey rose from behind a large desk and came round to greet him. He wore a well-dressed wig, white stockings and knee breeches. Abbey shook his hand firmly and invited him to take a seat. The walls were hung with framed maps and botanical drawings of tea plants.

'Mr Hammond, would you care for some tea?' Abbey asked. 'I have several new blends just arrived.'

'No, thank you.' Thomas hadn't come here to drink fancy tea.

'I regret the circumstances which have forced me to summon you here today,' Abbey said with a hint of Yorkshire accent. A large globe sat by his right hand and a pile of ledgers by his left.

'As do I, Mr Abbey.'

'Mrs Jennings asked to be present at this meeting.' Alice Jennings, dressed in black, sat to Thomas's left almost in the corner of the room. He hadn't seen her on entering because she merged with the shadows.

'I fear there is no amicable solution, Sir,' Thomas said. 'I can't have my apprentice call me a quack.'

'The boy is apt to talk without thinking.' Abbey set the globe spinning. 'He is tainted by the weaknesses of his parents. Your firm guidance is necessary to correct that.'

Mrs Jennings moved on her chair, her black silk rustling. Her hands in black gloves were clenched around the top of her ivory-headed cane. 'Mr Abbey,' she said, 'that is my daughter you are talking about.'

'I've been a patient man,' Thomas said, 'but I've run out of that commodity.'

Abbey adjusted his wig. 'I know you're a charitable man, apothecary to the workhouse and on the vestry committee. You will want to help an orphan boy and be forgiving as the Lord is.'

'The boy keeps questioning my authority. And he daydreams so much.'

'He's only eighteen. Give him another chance.'

'He's suffered with his mother dying,' Mrs Jennings said.

'I'm sympathetic to that, but it can't be used as an excuse forever more. He must mature and take responsibility.'

'Mr Hammond,' Mrs Jennings said, 'you offered to take him. I trusted you, but you've let me down.'

Thomas bowed his head. Mrs Jennings sat like a boulder on his conscience.

'I'm informed that you haven't taught or treated him well,' Abbey said. 'John has been used by you to saddle your horse, mix pills, write bills and deliver medicines.'

'Those are the duties of an apprentice, ask any apothecary or surgeon.' Thomas looked Abbey in the face. Abbey's eyes were bulbous and grey.

'You've neglected his instruction while favouring your own son.'

'My son is destined to become a surgeon so needs more experience.'

'John is tired and in poor spirits from his hard work,' Mrs Jennings said.

'He's tired because he treks across to Enfield to see Cowden Clarke, and then reads literature.'

'That school is a subversive and dangerous place. I wouldn't send a child of mine within fifty miles.' Abbey's complexion suffused red.

Alice Jennings coughed into her handkerchief.

Abbey picked up a quill, twirled it round and pressed the tip into his forefinger.

'Mr Hammond, you signed the indentures, a legal document. You accepted the premium of two hundred pounds. This is a contract you must abide by.'

'I cannot. The boy has forfeited his apprenticeship.'

Mr Abbey looked down his nose at Thomas. He placed his hands on his desk and stood up, leaning forwards.

'You will return the premium then.'

'I've apprenticed him for four years. At considerable cost and effort to myself.'

'So you will refund part of the premium?' Abbey said.

'I will not.'

Abbey paced behind his desk. 'If you don't take him back, I will have to implement legal proceedings against you.'

'Then you must, Sir, for I cannot have that boy back in my surgery.'

'Hammond, don't be so stubborn. The boy needs a profession to provide for himself and his family. Have you seen anything which suggests he wouldn't make a good apothecary?'

'It's his character I object to, not his abilities.'

'He was upset and said things he shouldn't, but that isn't his character forever,' Mrs Jennings said.

'He will apologise to me and retract his allegations?'

She bowed her head.

'I thought not.'

'You must take him back, Hammond.'

Thomas's breath came quick at Abbey's audacity. 'And if I refuse?' Thomas stood up, his legs shaking.

Abbey put his hands together as if in prayer, touched them to his lips and took them away. 'Then I may have to take legal action. I'm sure you wouldn't relish the stain on your reputation, that you abused a poor orphan boy from a good family and broke your word. A dishonest apothecary wouldn't be trusted. Even the vestry committee wouldn't employ him for the workhouse. And the cost of defending yourself could be considerable.'

'You're threatening me, Abbey.'

'I'm following legal process.'

Thomas stood up, turning one way then the other. The maps on the walls showed possibilities, places he would never travel. Abbey was a powerful and stubborn man. Gall rose in his throat.

'I need to think,' he said. 'I will let you know in a few days.'

He walked back through the darkening streets where hunched figures cast long shadows. If only he'd never signed the indentures.

The bust of Hippocrates surveyed Thomas from a shelf above the fireplace. The eyes had no pupils carved in them but were smooth almonds, staring blankly. When he'd arrived home from seeing Abbey at his offices he'd gone straight to his study where bookshelves rose from floor to ceiling, crammed full of medical books. He often ordered new ones to keep up to date. All that knowledge in black and white, more than he could ever hold in his head. The opinions and advice of experts, across the centuries, but what use was it if he couldn't apply it correctly? He collapsed into his cracked leather armchair. The mahogany and brass clock ticked on the mantlepiece, time running away from him with each soft sound.

He was so deep in his thoughts he didn't know Susannah had entered the room until he saw her standing before him.

'What did Abbey say?' She touched his sleeve. He hadn't removed his outer coat and the wool was heavy with rain.

'He's threatened legal action and to blacken my reputation if I don't take John back.'

'Surely he can't do that?' She pulled up a chair and sat opposite him. Her knees touched his through her dress and his damp breeches.

'He's a powerful man. I don't wish for any trouble from him.'

'Will you reconsider?'

'I won't surrender and take the boy back.'

'It's not a war, Thomas. You're not fighting Napoleon.'

'It feels like one.'

'And look where war has taken us. Men! Why can't you and John both admit you said some things in the heat of the moment, then make a fresh start? Like a new dawn or a birth.'

'Wouldn't it be easier without him?'

'Not if it threatens your livelihood, and your happiness, and Edward's. John's a nobody. All you must do is take him back and train him a little. How difficult can that be?'

Thomas sighed and looked to Hippocrates, who he was sure would have understood his dilemma if they could have conversed across the centuries.

'It's impossible,' Thomas said. 'I can't train someone who doesn't respect me. I'm the master.'

'Forget his words. He's a headstrong eighteen-year-old.'

'Every time I think of him, I see his face and hear his words and feel angry.' But it was more than anger; it was despair too. And pain.

'But why? He's a young apprentice and you're an experienced surgeon.'

Thomas hung his head and held its heavy weight in his hands. He saw the coffin of Charlotte Foster being lowered into the ground, next to Isabella's small headstone. He heard the voice of the vicar ringing out like iron striking the anvil.

'Why couldn't I save Mrs Foster and Frances Keats?' he asked, his warm breath puffing into his hands. The warmth told him he was alive.

Susannah leant nearer to him and took his hands from his face. She kept hold of his hands, connecting him to her. 'Because their disease was stronger than your medicines, more powerful than your lancets and more formidable than your leeches, Thomas.'

'Why do so many of my patients die?'

'It's God's will.'

A sob escaped from somewhere deep inside him. 'I want to rant at God, forgive me for saying that, but I do. The deaths seem so undeserved, so random, so cruel. He must be laughing at me from above.'

'We cannot know God.'

'Perhaps John was right and I am a quack. If I'd tried

harder I may have saved Mrs Foster, and John's mother and many other patients.'

Susannah stroked his face. 'Thomas, this isn't like you. I know you did your best for them.'

'Did I? Mrs Foster suffered, especially towards the end. The worse thing is she trusted me and I let her down.'

After Mrs Foster had the large haemorrhage, the day they saw the dragonflies and he remembered the frogs, John had asked how he coped with the pain his patients' suffering caused him and he'd been irritated because he felt the question was irrelevant. He could have told him the way he'd always dealt with it, the way his father had taught him, by denying it hurt him. And after he'd witnessed the extreme suffering of the boy at Guy's and knew it was his fault, by burying it six feet deep.

That had held it at bay, but since the night of Mrs Foster's death he'd had nightmares where he saw Mrs Foster's frightened eyes, John's mother struggling for breath, and heard Isabella screaming. When he woke he felt his distress at their suffering seeping to the surface. It was a weakness. What would his father say?

Susannah put her arms around him and held him tight, but his feeling of despair did not abate. Rain beat against the windows, breath entered and left his body. He thought of the twenty-four years they'd been married, bound together. He wanted to tell Susannah about what was happening to him, but he didn't know where to start.

He'd failed his patients. He'd done a terrible thing to the boy at Guy's. How could he tell Susannah he wasn't who he pretended to be? That he wasn't a brave, noble, invulnerable surgeon. That he wasn't who she thought he was?

After some time, she removed her arms and sat up straight.

'What are you frightened of, Thomas?' she said. 'Take John back. Make him respect you.'

Chapter Six

September 1814

Thomas woke with the dawn and felt the warmth of Susannah's body next to him. Light slipping through the bed curtains showed that her night cap had fallen off. Her dark hair streamed across the pillow, her eyelids flickered and she breathed gently. Perhaps she was dreaming of life as a surgeon's wife, in London, the life she'd quite rightly expected when she promised to marry him. He remembered the nights long gone, before the children were born, when she'd risen with him, wrapped a shawl around her shoulders, lit the lamp and waited for his return from a visit.

No need to dress. He still wore stockings, breeches, shirt and waistcoat from his night visit, a little rumpled but the creases would soon fall out. Martha had left hot water outside the door and he took it to the dresser, soaped his face and scraped the razor across his skin.

After his talk with Susannah, Thomas had written to Abbey. She was right about teaching John respect, and today he was returning. The razor jerked and nicked Thomas under his chin, stinging him. Damn. He pressed his handkerchief against his face. Blood oozed from the cut, through the weave, reminding him of the blood Mrs Foster had coughed.

His eyes stared back at him from the mirror, fathomless. Croup season was approaching. Children would die. He would block the feelings, the pain he felt about patients and their anguish, which kept catching him unawares. John had found a way under his skin and unsettled him. He needed to vaccinate himself against John, show him who was the master.

He must ensure that John impressed Astley Cooper at Guy's, though how anyone could turn that dreamer into a competent apothecary was a mystery. Susannah had suggested letting Edward go back to William's for a short time and Thomas had agreed. At least he wouldn't have to referee the two boys' disagreements. He parted the curtains, leaned over and kissed his wife.

Crossing from the house, Thomas shivered in the first crisp morning of autumn. Smoke rose from the surgery chimney, a good start. John must have arrived already and lit the fire. He nodded at the waiting patients but tried not to meet their eyes. If he let them in before the allotted time, they would come earlier every day. Inside the dispensary the lamps were lit and John knelt by the fire with his back to Thomas.

'Good morning, John.'

John's back rippled as he jabbed the logs with the poker. Sparks flew into the air.

'We'll be busy today,' Thomas said. 'Edward is at his cousins.'

John turned around. His eyes glittered and his cheeks glowed. 'I only came back because my grandmother begged me.' Behind him the fire crackled and spat.

If any other boy talked to Thomas like that, even Edward, he would briskly admonish him, but something stopped him, although he'd resolved to make John respect him. John was the embodiment of the avenging angel the vicar had warned of in last week's sermon. The anger which had led to the fight over the leeches was still there but harnessed to a new purpose.

'Your grandmother is a wise woman,' Thomas said. 'Now let's fight the war against disease.'

John stood and Thomas noticed for the first time that although still short he'd grown in stature since he'd started as his apprentice.

When Thomas opened the door, patients poured into the waiting room. Peter Trew, the plethoric butcher, was at the front of the queue. Thomas had seen his burly arms swiftly wield his knives and saw, and he'd thought he might make an excellent surgeon, even amputate a leg faster than Astley Cooper. Trew told him he had a severe sore throat and Thomas asked John to look while he held the lamp close.

'What is your prescription, Mr Keats?' Thomas asked.

John stared at him blankly. 'The throat is red and ulcerated, Mr Hammond.'

'From your reading you must have some idea how to relieve Mr Trew's suffering.'

John looked from Thomas to the scowling butcher.

'I hope you're not letting this stripling practice on me, Mr Hammond.'

'Do you think I would do that, Mr Trew? With your trade I know you would be after me with your meat cleaver. Mr Keats has been my apprentice for four years and is very skilled.'

John swallowed then spoke. 'I recommend bleeding then a mixture.'

'Of…'

'Parsley?'

'Perhaps sage may be more effective in this case. Bleed him while I see the next patient. Then you can mix the medicine.'

Thomas stepped into the corridor. John followed and grabbed his sleeve.

'Leeches or lancets?' John asked.

'Your choice,' Thomas said. 'But if it's lancets, cut deep.'

'I can't bleed and hold the bowl.'

'Mr Trew is used to blood and makes an excellent black pudding. He can hold his own bowl. Or ask one of the other patients, but make him sit down, just in case he faints.'

'Asking me to decide on treatment in front of him wasn't fair.'

'I thought you wanted to learn how to be a proper apothecary surgeon? I can't hold your hand forever. Bleeding is the most basic of procedures.'

Thomas brought in the next patient, a child with a rash. Behind him Mr Trew let out a loud roar and a string of curses when John cut him. Thomas kept talking to the child's mother. He went to the dispensary to collect a salve. On his return the bowl of blood was dangerously near to overflowing. Mr Trew looked pale.

'How do I remove the bowl and stop the flow?' John asked quietly.

'I'm sure you can work it out.' Thomas instructed the mother how to apply the salve and sent her on her way. John removed the bowl and blood dripped over the floor, forming a red puddle.

'Press hard on the cut,' Thomas advised. John took a piece of cloth and pressed. Every time he stopped more blood flowed.

'Hammond!' said Mr Trew. 'Your apprentice is killing me.'

'It will do you a lot of good,' Thomas said. 'Tie a tight bandage, John.'

After Mr Trew had left, looking far less plethoric, Thomas told John he might have cut a little deep but not to worry. He could practise on the next patient. John wiped the blood from the floor, but it left a patch which Thomas walked in all morning, the soles of his boots sticking to the flagstones. He saw three patients to every one of John's, but they worked through the mass. John bled several more, dispensed medicines and ointments – which Thomas checked or suggested alternatives to so no one was harmed – mixed others, and dressed wounds. Thomas had never seen such untidy bandages but didn't have time to redo them. He ran later than usual without Edward to help and his stomach grumbled.

'Now you can finish dusting the surgery,' Thomas said. 'Then prepare the horses for our visits.'

'But—'

'I don't think you can tell Mr Abbey I haven't taught you any medicine. In return you must do chores.'

John glared at Thomas but then picked up a duster. Thomas felt pleased he'd shown John who was the master.

Cut. Bleed. Bandage. Attach leeches, catch them gorged on blood. Over the next days John became much better at judging the right depth to cut, doing it swiftly and learning how long to press to arrest bleeding. There were no more puddles of blood on the floor and surgery sped up a little. In the early morning and the evenings Thomas and John made medicines. The afternoons were taken up with visits.

Thomas liked to ride when he could, rather than take the carriage. He enjoyed the exercise, moving up and down in the saddle in rhythm with the horse, and the fresh air. Edward had taken his bay gelding to William's, but Thomas had borrowed an old grey nag for John. The nag was lazy but John's early years living at his family's coaching inn showed and he had a knack with her.

Thomas and John rode their horses past stubble fields and trees whose leaves were changing hue. John spent more time looking around him than at the road ahead and didn't talk much, but Thomas was happy with that.

They visited one of the Bailey children. The child was four but the size of a two-year-old, a shrivelled creature. He was tired all the time and listless. Mrs Bailey held a young baby, also underweight, and the other children were all twig-thin. There was no work now the harvest was in. Thomas said he would send a tonic.

When Thomas had first taken over his father's practice he had been shocked at the poverty he saw. At Guy's it had been different. He treated the patients and sent them back to their world. Here he lived among them. He'd tried to give some of the poorer patients money. Most had refused it. A few accepted and seemed to expect more, but he'd quickly seen this was unsustainable. He would become poor himself. Instead he undercharged and didn't demand payment of his bills. He was apothecary to the workhouse, as his father had been, although it paid a pittance, and he strove to improve conditions at the interminable vestry meetings.

'Those children need food not medicine,' Thomas said to John as they rode away.

'Maybe now the wars in Europe and America are ending the government will spend less money on fighting and more on feeding people,' John said.

'I very much doubt it. The Baileys' only option is the workhouse.'

'The workhouse?'

'The father doesn't want to go. Even if there was room for them all. The vestry committee tell me the landowners can't afford to contribute any more to parish funds, but I see them riding around in new carriages.'

'We must get rid of the king,' John said with feeling. Thomas was reminded of how he had waved his imaginary sword at Fred Foster.

'Been reading *The Examiner* again, have you? I warned you, look at the French Revolution.'

'And give all men the vote.'

'Now that's a fairy tale. It'll never happen in my lifetime.'

'Perhaps men like Leigh Hunt will see it does.'

'He needs to be released from prison first. We could be waiting forever.'

'I still have hope.'

'The only way to help is on an individual level.' Thomas squeezed his heels and Cinnamon trotted, leaving behind the starving Baileys. He would send them milk and eggs. Often patients would accept food, especially if he said it was medicine.

He soon arrived at Ellen March's cottage, John catching up with him. Vines climbed around the thatch eaves.

Thomas had known Mrs March for many years. She'd worked as a dressmaker and sewn outfits for Susannah, but the past few years she'd been losing her reason. When they arrived she was crying with pain and reluctant to let them near her. Thomas couldn't get sense out of her. She held her face and the skin over her jaw was red. He asked her to open her mouth. She refused.

'Now, Mrs March, I think you may have an infected tooth. If I extract it you'll feel better,' he said. John passed him the tooth key from his bag. 'Open wide.'

She shook her head vehemently.

'I can't help if you don't cooperate,' Thomas said. 'I'll be quick. You'll hardly feel it.'

'Go on, Mother,' her daughter said, but Mrs March stubbornly clenched her jaw. Thomas reached towards it, but

91

she jerked her head away. He sighed, not relishing the thought of asking her daughter to restrain her and John to force her jaw open, but he saw no other option.

'Mrs March, would you like to hear a poem?' John asked. Mrs March didn't look up.

'Not that again, John,' Thomas said. 'It didn't work last time.'

'Would you?' John asked again. Mrs March didn't say no and John seemed to take that as a signal. '*Now Morning from her orient chamber came, And her first footsteps touched a verdant hill.*'

Mrs March's eyebrows drew together in a frown. Of irritation or concentration, Thomas wasn't sure. Maybe just puzzlement.

'John, she's an illiterate old woman. Your fancy poems won't mean anything to her.'

'*Crowning its lawny crest with amber flame, Silv'ring the untainted gushes of its rill.*'

Mrs March's head tilted upward, her eyes fixed on John. His voice rose and fell, rhythmically casting a spell over her. '*There the kingfisher saw his plumage bright, Vying with fish of brilliant dye below.*'

'Can you open your mouth?' John said. 'For Mr Hammond?'

To Thomas's surprise Mrs March obeyed. '*Whose silken fins, and golden scales light Cast upward, through the waves, a ruby glow.*' Thomas touched the woman's face gently and she didn't flinch. '*There saw the swan his neck of arched snow.*' He spied the rotten tooth, surrounded by red, swollen tissue. '*And oared himself along with majesty.*' He inserted the tooth key, hooked it under the tooth and twisted it. The tooth popped out. Mrs March's mouth remained open.

'Ahhh,' Mrs March said. 'I do feel better now. Thank you.'
Thomas wasn't sure if her remarks were directed at him or John.

'That was wonderful,' Mrs March's daughter said to John. 'Thank you.'

Outside the cottage Thomas attached his bag to his saddle, while John untied the nag from the fence.

'You were lucky,' Thomas said, his fingers struggling with the stiff buckles. 'She was so surprised she forgot to object.'

'I think she liked it.' John patted the nag's mane.

'I never saw much use for poetry before,' Thomas said. 'Perhaps you can recite it at all my tooth extractions, and operations and childbirths. It will save the cost of laudanum.'

They both laughed.

Although Thomas was teasing John, he was struck by the sounds the words had rung in his head, the pictures they'd conjured, the colours. Amber flame, a kingfisher with plumage bright, fish with golden scales and the swan his neck of arched snow. He knew a swan's neck couldn't be made of snow, but he couldn't rid the image from his mind. The neck would feel cool and glisten in the sun.

'Who wrote that poem?' Thomas asked.

John looked down at his boots and Thomas thought he wouldn't answer. Maybe he'd forgotten the author. Then he mumbled a few words and Thomas asked him to repeat them.

'I wrote it.' John lifted his head and his face burned red.

'You?'

'Is there something wrong with that?'

'No, it's just, I thought it was rather good.'

'It was my first effort. I've a long way to go to write good poetry.'

'What's it called?'

'*Imitation of Spenser.*'

'The sea-shouldering whale man?'

'You remembered.'

'Why do you imitate Spenser? Don't you have ideas of your own?'

'It's the same as my apprenticeship with you. I watch and imitate to learn the art of the master.'

It wasn't openly disrespectful, not by any means, but Thomas knew that John was mocking him. He wanted to shake him but restrained himself. He was the master and must behave as such. The images and words John had conjured in his mind dissolved.

The spot where Edward's fiddle had leaned against the wall in the corner of the drawing room was empty. Although Thomas appreciated peace and quiet, Edward's absence had begun to feel a gaping, yawning space. There were no sudden bursts of singing, no embraces for Susannah making her smile, no laughter from the younger girls at their brother's antics. His son had been gone for four weeks now, since John had returned, but Thomas missed Edward more than he'd expected and he worried whether William was teaching him bad habits.

'We should send for Edward,' Thomas said.

'He's hardly been away,' Susannah said. 'Let him stay longer at William's to build up connections.'

'It would be a help to me. And the girls miss him.'

Susannah picked up one of his shirts from her mending basket. She'd made them herself all through their marriage and mended them over and over. He liked the feel of the worn linen held together by her neat stitches next to his skin.

'But you have John,' Susannah said. 'How's he progressing?'

'Your guess is as good as mine. He's taken to bleeding with gusto, but then he was quoting a poem he wrote at Mrs March.'

'Mrs March the dressmaker?'

'The strangest thing was she listened, as if bewitched, and let me remove her rotten tooth.'

'Well, I never.' Susannah smiled. 'Perhaps I was right to suggest you take him on.'

'Suggest? You offered the position to Mrs Jennings without even consulting me.'

'Mrs Jennings was terrified her grandchildren would end up in the workhouse when she passed away. The poor woman was desperate to find John a career.'

'So you were being charitable?' This was a trait Susannah did not instinctively possess, which puzzled him when he considered her impoverished upbringing.

'Yes.'

She looked down at her mending, engrossed in a seam. A faint flush spread across her face. She rarely flushed. It must have been some other reason. What would be the advantage of offering John to be his apprentice?

'You were hoping I'd let Edward be a lawyer if John was my apprentice.'

She paused in her sewing. Although he'd never realised this at the time four years ago, it was clear to him now.

'He could have risen far in the law with his quick mind and personable ways, his energy and ideas. I thought it would suit him better. He has a refined nature.'

'You think my profession isn't good enough for you and Edward?'

She looked up at him with her large dark eyes. 'You know I respect the work you do.'

'Do you?'

'Yes,' she replied, and for a moment he saw the woman he'd courted all those years ago, but that didn't mean he was going to forgive her for meddling.

'And I suppose the premium of two hundred guineas for the apprenticeship didn't hurt.'

'Money doesn't appear out of nowhere. I work hard to economise. I make and mend your shirts.'

'You had it all calculated. You knew I wouldn't want to disappoint Mrs Jennings.'

Her remembered the distress of thinking he'd have to tell Mrs Jennings no. How difficult it had been when John came to the surgery and asked him to teach him to relieve suffering. He'd nearly abandoned his dream of Edward becoming a surgeon, but in the end he'd solved the problem by declaring he would have two apprentices.

'I've accepted Edward being your apprentice,' she said, 'but I want him to have the best chance of being a great surgeon.'

His annoyance festered. She had tried to manipulate him, but he'd been naïve and taken it at face value, wanted to believe in her good nature. No more. He was the man in this house.

'I'm sending for Edward to come home, now,' he said.

She pulled her cotton so tight it snapped. 'If he comes home he must keep up his connections with William. Mary told me when he goes to Guy's he should become dresser to Astley Cooper, like James was. The most eminent surgeon in the country.'

'Becoming a dresser is difficult. Only a few students are picked.'

'If William introduced you to Cooper you could ask him to consider Edward.'

Thomas tried to calm his rapid breathing and pounding heart. Ask Astley to take Edward? Impossible. He lacked the courage to do it. Images of the boy at Guy's came to him, one of his last times with Astley.

'Are you sure you didn't meet him when you were a student? You must have overlapped.'

'There were many students and it's so long ago I really don't remember.'

She frowned, concentrating. 'Who were you dresser to again?'

'William Lucas.'

'Why couldn't he help you get a job after you passed your surgeon's exam?'

'Nepotism.' That was the easy but not the full answer. 'He wanted his son to succeed him. And my father needed me here, remember?'

'Is his son still a surgeon at Guy's?'

'Yes. But Billy Lucas Junior isn't well thought of. Edward should definitely avoid coming within a hundred miles of him.'

Thomas felt the scar on his hand itch. He tried not to scratch it, but it became so irritating he couldn't prevent himself. Angry welts formed around it.

Chapter Seven

Thomas whistled one of Edward's fiddle tunes as he walked across to the surgery. Neither the long queue of patients outside nor the slight headache, probably from one too many glasses of claret last night, dulled his good mood. Edward had arrived home yesterday evening and they'd eaten a meal. His family was back together again, complete. The two younger girls had clamoured for Edward's attention. Edward told anecdotes of his time at Southgate, his cousins and his adventures. How he'd passed on the road minutes after a highwayman held up a coach. One of the occupants had been shot and Edward had taken him to William. Luckily it was only a flesh wound. He'd visited many grand local houses with eccentric inhabitants and particularly vicious dogs he'd had to avoid. Even Eliza, usually unimpressed by his tales, had smiled, although she looked pale and had retired early. Today would be easier with his son's help. He'd wanted to wake Edward, but Susannah had said let him sleep in a little and he'd agreed. Just for today.

In the dispensary John stood holding a duster, staring at the apothecary jars. The fire was lit and smoke snaked across the room. Thomas cleared his throat to alert John to his presence.

'What do you think the cherubs stand for?' John asked. 'So many of the jars have them.'

'It's just decoration,' Thomas said.

'I wonder if it's to do with Cupid?' John started dusting the jars. 'He wounded himself with his own arrow, which made him fall in love with Psyche, but I don't see how love is an illness.'

'On the other hand, I do have the occasional patient ask for a love potion,' Thomas said. 'Which I refuse to give, of course.'

Thomas went to open the door. By the time Edward arrived an hour later tying his cravat, Thomas and John had seen several patients each.

'What can I do, Father? Are there patients to bleed?' Edward asked. Thomas stood in the waiting room deciding who to call next. A baby wailed but a small boy sitting quietly was wheezing. He would see the boy first. It wasn't always those who made the most fuss who were most ill.

'You can hold the bowl for John next door,' Thomas said. 'He's applying leeches to Mr Potts.'

'Hold the bowl for him?'

'He's become proficient at bleeding while you were away.'

'I've become proficient at much more at my uncle's. He should hold it for me.'

'Let's not argue when there's work to be done.'

Several faces watched them with interest. The man nearest had a red swollen cheek from a bad tooth.

'Let me pull this man's tooth. I can see he's in pain,' Edward said. He was nearly as tall as Thomas now and his shoulders had broadened. A fleeting vision of his mortality, the certainty his son would replace him, flashed before him. He hesitated, sensing the challenge to his authority but reluctant to argue in front of the patients. What if he insisted Edward help John but he refused?

'You may do that,' he said. Edward smiled and led the man to the treatment room while Thomas brought the quiet child,

Davy Field. John was attaching leeches to Mr Potts's arm. The room was crowded with all three of them, and the patients and Davy's mother.

As Thomas assessed Davy, lifting the boy's shirt, he watched Edward from the corner of his eye. Davy was breathing fast, the muscles of his chest indrawing. Edward chatted to the man with toothache briefly then removed the tooth easily, with a flourish. He could have been performing a show for an audience. Thomas dosed Davy with ipecacuanha, the vomiting it induced was a cure for asthma, and sat him and his mother back in the waiting room. As he handed them a bowl Martha appeared at the door, which was unusual, and Thomas spoke to her in the corridor.

'The mistress sent me, Sir. Miss Eliza is unwell with a fever and she wants you to come and see her.'

Thomas surveyed the waiting room. The asthmatic boy, three leg ulcers to dress, a few elderly people, a smiling baby. Apart from Davy, none were seriously ill. He instructed Edward and John to continue and told them he would return soon.

Back at the house he ran up the stairs to Eliza's room. Susannah sat by her bed and rose to meet him.

'I'm worried,' she said. 'She's so hot.'

Eliza lay in bed, shivering, her teeth chattering, the quilt pulled up to her chin. Her forehead was beaded with sweat and her face flushed. Thomas touched her cheek with the back of his hand. It burned like a fire. Susannah leant across and wiped Eliza's face with a cloth.

'My throat,' Eliza whispered. 'It's sore. And my head hurts.'

Thomas felt her neck where glands had arisen like small mountains. Her pulse was full and frequent. She shivered again. His mind raced. She had a high fever, which could be any cause, but the sore throat pointed towards tonsillitis. He examined her throat and saw it was red, which supported the diagnosis. But the headache might be due to something more serious such as meningitis. He tried to banish his mounting anxiety. It was probably tonsillitis which a fit, strong girl would easily recover from.

'I must bleed her,' Thomas told Susannah.

'Promise me you'll use the lancet not the leeches. I can't stand the thought of their wriggling bodies and rubbery skins on my child.'

'I promise.'

He rushed back to the surgery. In the waiting room Davy had vomited but his breathing was still wheezy. Thomas stopped to assess him and gave another dose of ipecacuanha. In the treatment room he found an old man with his leg outstretched, a long bandage unwound, his leg ulcer exposed. Voices from the dispensary led him to John and Edward standing in front of the apothecary jars.

'Uncle William uses *Unguentum Aegyptiacum*,' Edward said.

'*Unguentum Eleni* is better because it's an old ulcer,' John replied. 'He's been coming for weeks.'

'Well, it's obviously not working. Time to try something new.' Edward reached towards the *Aegyptiacum* jar with its birds and shell.

'But your father—'

'Boys,' Thomas said. 'I need one of you to hold the bowl while I bleed Eliza.'

Neither boy volunteered. Edward held the *Aegyptiacum* jar, verdigris boiled with honey, close to his chest.

'One of you, come on.'

'John can do it,' Edward said. 'I'll stay here and finish seeing the patients.'

'Why should I hold the bowl?' John said. 'I want to stay here and see the patients.'

'But I'm so much more experienced than you.'

'I've learnt a lot in the past month.'

'At my uncle's I've been seeing important patients, not these waifs and strays no one cares about.'

'I've delivered a baby.'

'That's women's work. No self-respecting surgeon undertakes obstetrics, my uncle says.'

'I've set an ankle fracture.'

'I've been taught by Joseph Green and I've met Henry Cline, who advised me on treating bladder stones.'

'Boys!' Thomas shouted. 'I can't believe you're arguing when Eliza is ill. Your own sister, Edward.'

The two glared sullenly at each other. John's eyes protruded slightly; his nose ran in a straight line from his sloping brow, giving an impression of strength that was weakened by his receding chin. Edward's expression was haughty, his head tipped back, his full lips protruding below his aquiline nose and fine nostrils.

John's shoulders drooped and he turned to Thomas. 'I'll help you,' he said, and began collecting the bowl and case of lancets.

'Thank you. Edward, continue here and keep an eye on Davy in the waiting room. Call me if he's worse. And use the *Unguentum Eleni* on that ulcer.'

On the way out Davy's wheezes followed by his retching made Thomas pause to listen. He told himself he wouldn't be long.

Susannah sat by Eliza's bed, leaning over and wiping her

daughter's brow, stilling her restless hands. Eliza was mumbling gibberish.

He freed Eliza's arm from under the quilt and pushed up the sleeve of her nightdress. He pulled the small mother-of-pearl-handled lancet from its silver case and held it above her skin, ready to strike, but he hesitated. He couldn't cut the perfect pale skin of his own daughter's arm, the white unblemished flesh. Perhaps he could ask John. No, he must. He braced himself and cut quick and deep. She cried out and arched her back. He found it painful to watch. A pool of ruby-red blood welled up and John caught it in the pewter bowl, which filled to the brim. Thomas concentrated on the blood flowing into the bowl. This procedure would help her recover. He bled her ten ounces that day.

Back at the surgery Edward had dressed the ulcer and seen the smiling baby, but Davy's wheezing was no better. Thomas told Edward he must go to the house and ask Martha to make very strong coffee for the child.

'But—'

'Just go! Stop objecting. I don't know what William taught you, but you seem to have forgotten your place.'

'My place? I thought my place was as your son, your senior apprentice, a future surgeon. Not some lackey running round. I've only been gone a few weeks and you're favouring John.'

'Edward, that's not true.'

'Yes, it is! I'll go and get your coffee now, like the drudge you expect me to be.' He stormed out.

Thomas turned to see John watching him, open-mouthed.

'Stop gawping and mix some medicines,' he said. He went to sit with Davy and his mother. What a day, and it wasn't even over yet. His whistling seemed a lifetime, not hours ago.

The next day Eliza struggled to swallow and Susannah dripped water into her mouth. She still had a high fever and Thomas bled her ten ounces again, with John's help. Susannah asked if they should send for William, but Thomas said that wasn't necessary. The closest he'd come to this situation before was attending Susannah in childbirth, terrified she might die and leave him, but she'd given birth without too much fuss, crying out but coping with a determination he admired. His children luckily had strong constitutions and had remained healthy apart from minor illnesses. This was a new experience for him and Thomas found it hard to stay in the room because of the distress he felt at Eliza's suffering and illness. As her doctor he should be immune, but as her father he couldn't be.

He was relieved to have the excuse of a busy morning surgery to escape to. Davy was improving, his wheeze much less, his mother grateful. She told him she'd stayed awake all night listening to her son's laboured breathing, and he wondered how she'd borne it. Seeing patients distracted him, but every so often his stomach would contract with fear.

During the afternoon he took Edward on his visits, leaving John at the surgery. There was a stiff silence between them after yesterday's outburst, but Thomas was too worried about Eliza to care. He hurried through the visits and back to the sickroom. She was still feverish and confused. He mixed sorrel tea and gave it to her on a spoon, then tried to sit with her but became restless. Her beautiful face, flushed and covered in sweat, her tangled hair, her mumbling nonsense, the cuts on her arm where he'd bled her, all caused a pain in his chest as if a heavy stone was crushing him. A pain as real as any physical illness. He longed for something to do, but he'd seen all the patients and it was too soon to mix another medicine for Eliza.

Outside the window grey clouds scudded across the sky and trees bent in the wind. He couldn't stand to be confined in the bedroom any longer.

The herb garden was dying back, the flowers gone, seed pods rustling in the wind, bone-dry leaves clinging to stems. It needed clearing. He pushed the fork with his foot, turning over the dark soil, spearing balls of roots with the tines, picking up matted clumps and separating them with his fingers. His arms and legs ached from the effort, but that felt good. The wind rose and blew cold on the back of his neck, stirred his hair. He shivered.

He crouched down to pull brown leaves from a vervain plant. Underneath sat a frog, one of the frogs he saw regularly, which lived in the garden near the pond. Every year they laid frogspawn and new ones metamorphosed from tadpoles. It felt right that he and the frogs shared the garden. The frog had large black eyes and olive-green skin splashed with blotches the yellow brown of ground cumin seeds. He was struck by the colours, their beauty. Usually a frog would leap away when disturbed, but this one stayed still. He touched its damp back with his finger. Nothing. His finger sank into the moist skin and it still didn't move. He stepped back, nearly falling over the plants. The beautiful frog was dead. His breath came fast, rasping in his lungs, and he felt dizzy. He told himself he didn't believe in omens.

The third day of Eliza's illness her cheeks were flushed, her mouth developed a white ring around it and her tongue resembled a strawberry. Red spots started at her neck and spread over her body, darker in her flexures, turning her skin the colour of a boiled lobster. The rash had a roughness to the touch and Thomas knew it was scarlet fever. Her throat was red and ulcerated, a poor prognostic sign, and fear gripped him. Susannah begged him to save Eliza and he promised he would do his utmost. He bled her again and blistered her. He mixed powder of hartshorn with cochineal for her. Susannah helped him wrap her legs in flannel wrung out with hot water and soaked in camphor liniment.

He rushed between the house and the surgery, supervising Edward and John but in reality struggling to concentrate. In the afternoon the boys offered to do the visits by themselves and he accepted gratefully. He went back to the house and up to Eliza's room. A broad back in a maroon coat stood over the bed. Susannah stood nearby wringing her hands. William turned round to face him, and at the sight of his older brother, Thomas stepped forward and embraced him.

Eliza was still confused and feverish, her eyes sunken, lips cracked and tongue dry. William assessed her, holding her small hand and feeling her fast pulse, examining her throat. William was experienced, trained by their father and Guy's Hospital, and he knew Henry Cline and Abernethy. William would know what to do.

'You've tried milk vetch?' William asked.

'Yes, but it hasn't helped.'

'Blessed thistle?'

'And sorrel and hartshorn. Bleeding, of course, and blistering and wrapping her legs.'

William stroked his long sideburns. Thomas found his resemblance to their father reassuring. 'There's only one thing to do. Give her mercury.'

'Mercury?'

'It will help, I assure you. I've used it often for severe scarlet fever.'

'What about side effects? Ast…' He closed his mouth. He didn't want to speak Astley Cooper's name, but Astley advised against using mercury apart from venereal disease. It was too dangerous.

'You've run out of options, Thomas.'

'Please, Thomas, listen to William,' Susannah said. Her eyes implored him to follow William's advice. Thomas looked from William to Susannah to Eliza lying in the bed restless and whimpering.

'I can't expose my beautiful daughter to mercury. The risk of side effects is too high.'

'It's that or likely death,' William said.

Susannah let out a little scream and collapsed onto a chair. Thomas rushed to her side. She buried her head in her hands.

'I'll take my leave,' William said. 'You're making a big mistake, Thomas.'

William's footsteps on the stairs echoed between them. Susannah took her hands away from her face and looked at him.

'You promised me you'd do your utmost,' she said.

'Yes, but I can't do that.'

'If she dies, I'll never forgive you.'

'You have to have faith in me, Susannah.' Thomas tried to take her hand, but she pushed him away. For the first time he wondered why William had arrived. It couldn't be coincidence; Susannah must have sent for him. It hurt him that she didn't trust him to treat their daughter.

'If I give her mercury,' he said, 'I'll never forgive myself.'

Thomas ran his fingers over the spines of his medical books. Cullen's *First Lines of the Practice of Physic*, John Hunter's *A*

Treatise on the Blood, Inflammation and Gunshot Wounds,
Cooper's *A Treatise on Dislocations and Fractures of the Joints.*
There must be something here to save Eliza. He took down
Cullen's and Hunter's. Nothing new. He pulled out several
magazines but found none were relevant. He was an apothecary
surgeon, highly trained and experienced, but he couldn't save
his own child.

On the middle shelf, at the end, sat the Bible. He laid the
heavy book on his desk and opened the cover. Inside were
written the names and dates of birth of his mother's family, his
mother, himself, Susannah and all his children. His mother's
father and his own father also had the dates of their death.
He imagined having to write the date of Eliza's death in a neat
italic hand. Spots swam before his eyes and he thought he
might faint. He mustn't think like that. He turned the pages of
the book and read passages, but the language felt old and dead.
Full of punishment and damnation.

He returned the Bible to its place and knelt on the floor in
front of his bookshelves. On the bottom shelf, at the far end,
were a few volumes of Shakespeare, inherited from his father.
Why had his father owned Shakespeare? He wasn't a literary
man and Thomas had only ever seen him read medical books.
He took out a volume. Perhaps his father had intended to
read them to educate himself, or were they bought to impress
others?

Thomas flicked through the pristine pages of *The Tempest.*
Shakespeare was a poet, the greatest poet in the English
language. He remembered John's words when they'd talked in
the carriage that moonlit night. How poetry could take one
away to another world and transcend troubles. A few lines
caught his eye.

Full fathom five thy father lies; Of his bones are coral made. The lines blurred before his eyes. He focussed on the words and read them aloud. His voice sounded cracked and hesitant.

Why all those "f"s in the first line? Bones of coral would be strange. The skeletons of sea creatures. He'd once treated a wealthy woman, a visitor to Edmonton, who'd worn a necklace of smooth, round coral beads the colour of ox blood as a talisman against disease.

Those are pearls that were his eyes: Nothing of him that doth fade. Pearls for eyes would be blind. If he were fathoms down he must be drowned. *But doth suffer a sea-change Into something rich and strange.* A vision of a corpse wearing a red coral necklace, its eye sockets replaced by pearls, rose in his mind. The only sea-change he saw possible was a transformation into rotting flesh.

This was not helping. It was meaningless. He slammed the book shut so hard it hurt his hands. He must return to Eliza. He would kneel by her bed and pray. God would decide her fate.

Thomas woke the next morning, after fitful dreams of running girls wearing red coral necklaces, and crept into Eliza's room. He stroked strands of matted hair away from her hot forehead. She slept but her breathing was fast and she mumbled meaningless phrases. He pressed the inside of her wrist; her pulse raced but was weakening. Outside the wind moaned.

Susannah slept in a chair by the bed. Last night Thomas had knelt at the bedside and prayed, but it hadn't comforted him. The sight of Eliza so ill and Susannah's frosty, disapproving manner had driven him from the room to his bed, telling her to wake him if Eliza deteriorated.

Perhaps he should use the mercury as William suggested. Or call someone else. But who? He could hardly ask Astley Cooper for advice. He'd done everything he could for her, but it hadn't worked. He felt helpless. It was like the suffering he'd felt with Mrs Foster, and the boy at Guy's, but a thousand times worse. He couldn't block out the fear and pain. His heart felt squeezed in a press every time he thought of losing her. Why love someone if the thought of losing them was this painful?

Susannah stirred and woke, blinking. Her cheek was crumpled where she'd rested against the chair and she looked older, with dark shadows under her eyes.

'Is she better?' she asked.

'No.' The word caught in his throat, nearly choking him. 'But I'll fetch John and bleed her.'

Eliza was restless and John had to move the bowl to catch the blood. He looked serious but didn't speak until the end.

'Shall I see the patients, Sir? With Edward.'

'Thank you, John. Call me if you need me.'

'I will. I hope she recovers.'

Thomas administered more sorrel tea and milk vetch. He sat with his head in his hands.

'What about the mercury?' Susannah asked.

He hung his head. 'Don't ask me that. I can't.'

'I still don't see why. But promise me one thing.'

'What?'

'You won't leave her.'

He wanted to run away. This was too difficult. He'd rather be in the surgery seeing patients and mixing medicines. He raised his eyes and saw she was crying. He had to do this, for her. 'I promise,' he said.

They sat for hours, Eliza feverish and delirious. Martha

brought cool drinks which Susannah tried to give her. The world contracted to the room, the three of them, the bed.

Sometime in the afternoon Martha knocked on the door and entered. She also looked older and worn. She came over to Thomas and whispered.

'The midwife wants you, Sir.'

'She does?' Were there still women in labour and babies being born outside this room?

'There's a woman in obstructed labour.'

Susannah must have overheard. 'Can't you send one of the boys?' she said.

'It will be too difficult for them,' Thomas replied. 'They're not ready.'

'What about calling another surgeon?'

'It would probably take too long for them to come.'

'Doesn't she know there's illness in this house?'

'She does, Ma'am,' Martha said, twisting her apron in her fingers. 'But she says it can't wait.'

'Sarah Dunn's a good midwife. She'd only call if she really needs me,' Thomas said. 'I have to go.'

'But you promised me you wouldn't leave.'

'I'll come back as soon as I can.'

'It's always the same with you, isn't it? Patients over family. Well, I've put up with it for myself, but I won't let you neglect our daughter.'

'Susannah, I'm not neglecting her. I can't do any more for her.'

'Except give mercury, which you refuse.'

'I can deliver the baby with forceps, do something. I can be useful. I might save its life, and the mother's.'

'You don't understand, do you? I need you here.'

111

The wind howled at the window and tree branches tapped against it with ghostly fingers. Martha twisted her apron tighter.

'What shall I tell the boy?' Martha asked.

'Tell him I'm on my way,' Thomas said.

Susannah cried out, but Thomas didn't stop to look at her. He ran down the stairs and to the surgery to collect his bag.

Chapter Eight

The room was lit by candles and a fire in the grate, the air hot as a high fever. The smell of ale and allspice rose from a pot hanging over the fire. However much Thomas had tried to convince the midwife that ventilation was good for women in labour and caudle not beneficial, she persisted with the traditional ways. But Sarah Dunn was otherwise sensible, competent with normal births and sent for him when she needed help. Unlike the old crone who'd been the village midwife when he took over the practice, who had waited until the mother and babe were nearly dead to call him, then crowed when they didn't survive.

The young woman, Jane, sat on the horseshoe-shaped birthing stool, leaning forwards. Her face was pale and puffy, her lips cracked and her hair stuck to her forehead. Her shift and petticoat were stained with blood.

'How long has she been in labour?' Thomas asked.

'Two days,' Sarah said. 'She's too tired to push. Can you use the forceps?'

Thomas placed his hands on her swollen belly, on top of her shift. He felt a faint ripple beneath his fingertips. The baby was still alive.

Between them they lifted Jane onto the table. Thomas unwrapped the forceps, which clinked together, and Jane twitched at the noise. He slipped his hand under her petticoat to check the position of the foetal head. They must wait a little for the head to descend more. With each contraction Sarah encouraged Jane to push. Thoughts of Eliza kept intruding, but Thomas tried to banish them. He must concentrate on the task in hand. Jane was exhausted. He saw he had to act soon and slid one curved blade of the forceps around the baby's head, followed by the other, locked them together and waited.

'Push, Jane,' he said when the next contraction arrived. 'You must push.' She tried her best and he pulled on the forceps. The first long tug was always the most difficult. Nothing shifted.

He applied more traction. The head moved a tiny jolt. The room was so hot his shirt was drenched. He continued pulling, his hands clenched around the forceps handles, his muscles feeling as if they were tearing with the effort, until the head descended the birth canal and crowned. The head was now out in the world, but the body must wait for the next contraction. He must be patient.

He remembered when Eliza was born, his first child. She hadn't breathed for a minute and he'd held his breath, tapping her gently, then blowing on her, wound tight as a clockwork spring. When she'd given a cry he'd felt such relief, such happiness. He'd gazed with love at her tiny wrinkled face, her dark hair, her long eyelashes, her miniature clenched fists.

The contraction came at last; he delivered the baby and placed it on Jane's abdomen.

The cord pulsated, but the baby, blue and lifeless, didn't take a breath. Thomas held it upside down by its feet and slapped its bottom. It didn't respond and he slapped it again. And again. Still no breath. Thomas reached for a cloth, grabbed the slippery infant and rubbed it vigorously. No response. He rubbed it harder.

The baby hung loosely from his hands, flaccid, like the

puppy he'd once drowned because it was deformed. Soon he was going to lose Eliza. He couldn't bear the pain.

'Come on, breathe.' He lifted the baby up. 'Breathe!'

He wanted to shake the baby, shake it into life.

'Mr Hammond!' Sarah cried. 'What are you doing?'

He stood stock-still, the weight of the baby in his hands, its lifeless body dragging him down.

'Give it to me.' Sarah reached out her arms for the baby and he handed it to her. She placed it back on Jane's abdomen, while he turned away and wiped blood from the forceps.

What had he been thinking of? To nearly shake a dead baby because he so desperately wanted it to live. He'd seen many stillbirths. He knew they couldn't all survive, and at least the mother would live, but somehow this one had seemed so important. He'd been desperate to prove something to himself.

He wrapped the forceps in cloth and put them in his bag, then bent over and rinsed his blood-stained hands in a bowl of water. As he stood up, bracing himself to tell Jane the bad news, he heard a weak cry. The noises strengthened. Unbelievable. The baby had come to life.

He checked the scrawny but perfectly formed infant, and Sarah cut the cord. 'Well done, Jane,' he said. 'You have a girl.' Sarah swaddled the baby in a blanket and placed her in a box for a crib. She handed him a cup of caudle, from the pot over the fire, and he sat drinking the alcoholic, sugary, spicy liquid while she waited for the afterbirth. The baby lay in her makeshift crib, her small face squashed but undeniably human, the bones of her skull overriding each other after struggling to come through the birth canal, the soft spot at the centre pulsating. She opened her eyes and looked at him.

He finished the caudle. He couldn't delay any longer. He

walked back to Wilston, holding on to his hat in the strong wind. His footsteps slowed the nearer he came. He pushed open the squeaking gate, walked up the flagstone path with weeds growing in the cracks, opened the heavy oak door with its brass lion knocker, dropped his bag on the black and white checkerboard tiles, climbed the stairs one at a time, gripping the worn mahogany banister.

He stopped outside the door to Eliza's room. It was quiet within. Was she lying the other side of the door, pale and lifeless, waxen? His stomach hardened to stone, dragging his innards downwards. He couldn't lift his hand. He wanted to run away.

Was this the point where his life would change forever? He wouldn't only have lost Eliza but Susannah too. He couldn't stand not knowing any longer. He turned the handle and pushed the door. It was dim in the room, a few candle flames fluttered. He crept up to the bed. Eliza lay still, her face pale, her eyes shut. He reached out his hand and touched her forehead. It was cool. His heart juddered. The coolness of recent death. He knelt by her bed and grasped her hand, which was damp from perspiration. He'd never felt a pain like this before, never thought it possible. His body rent asunder.

'Thomas,' Susannah said from behind him. She rested a hand on his shoulder as if trying to anchor him to earth, but he felt completely untethered.

His beautiful daughter. He couldn't bear the pain of having her torn from him as if from his own flesh. He squeezed her hand harder.

And then it happened. Her eyelashes flickered and she opened her eyes.

'Father?'

'Eliza?' He stared at her as if she were a ghost, risen from the dead. 'Eliza?'

'She's better, Thomas,' Susannah said, smiling a wide smile. 'She perspired terribly and was so hot, but then the fever broke. I think she's going to be fine.'

'Yes! Yes!' Of course. Thomas wanted to dance around the room, but his legs felt too weak. He kissed Eliza on the forehead and held both her hands. He smiled from ear to ear. Then he stood up and embraced Susannah.

She hit her fists against his chest, crying and shouting, 'I'll never forgive you, Thomas Hammond. I never will.' He held her tight until she tired and collapsed against him.

Eliza's recovery was slow and Thomas mixed her draughts and tonics. When he visited her, lying in bed in her nightgown, he examined her joints for puffiness and listened to the rhythm of her breathing, watching for the heart and joint complications of scarlet fever. He insisted she rest. Her palms and fingertips were still red and the skin peeling off, a common sequel to the illness.

'Can I get up, Father?' she asked.

'You may get dressed and sit in the drawing room, but no more.'

'I'm so bored of resting.'

'Why don't you read to amuse yourself?'

'Mama did bring me a book, but my eyes are so tired the words blur and it makes my head ache.'

'I could ask Edward to read to you.'

'Edward? He'll jump around the room and act out the parts and become overexcited and throw my pillows.' She sat up. 'I want John to read to me.'

'John?'

'He has a pleasant voice. Do you know, I had the strangest dream he was here when I was ill?'

'Who will perform his apprenticeship duties?'

'Edward can do them. Please, Father.'

She clasped one of his hands tightly between hers. The dry, peeling skin of her palms scratched against his, callused from endless mixing with pestle and mortar and holding Cinnamon's reins. The memory of how white and soft her hands had been before her illness upset him. He told her he'd send Martha to help her dress. He couldn't refuse her request. She was so precious and he'd almost lost her.

He found John rolling pills. The small, perfectly formed spheres dropped into the catching area of the pill machine. The accounts books rested on the bench ready for him to write the bills afterwards.

'John, how would you like to read to Eliza? I feel it would benefit her, help time pass more quickly.'

John stopped rolling and looked at him. The light from the window struck one side of his face. 'I would like that, Sir.'

'You can choose a book from my library.'

At the door John paused, looking back at the paste he still had to roll into pills.

'I'll make sure Edward finishes here,' Thomas said. John ran out the door and Thomas went to find his other apprentice.

He discovered him in the kitchen pilfering things to eat and instructed him to finish the pills. Edward grumbled but did amble over to the surgery. Thomas imagined the deformed pills he would roll and the messy bills he would write and sighed.

'Was that John coming indoors?' Susannah entered the kitchen, which was warm and cosy from the fire.

'Yes. He's going to read to Eliza.'

'Is that appropriate? You might have consulted me.'

'What harm can come of it?'

'What about her reputation, being alone with him?'

'She'll be in the drawing room. I'll go now and check all is well. I'll insist the door be propped open.' Thomas left the kitchen before she could argue further.

John's voice travelled along the corridor, clear and expressive. '*Fair is foul, and foul is fair: Hover through the fog and filthy air.*' Thomas peered around the door, keeping out of sight. Eliza lay on a pillow on the chaise longue, her long dark hair spread on the white linen. A blanket covered her body, her eyes were closed and her chest rose softly. She might be asleep. Thomas cleared his throat and stepped into the room. John stopped reading. He sat in Susannah's yellow velvet chair and held the book open in both hands.

'Why have you stopped? I'm still listening,' Eliza said.

'Your father is here to see you,' John said.

Eliza opened her eyes.

'I just wanted to see…' Thomas said. 'Your mother is concerned…'

Both she and John looked at him. 'Tell Mama there is no need to make a fuss,' Eliza said.

'I will. What are you reading, John?'

John closed the book and showed Thomas the spine. *Macbeth*. Thomas had never read it but knew it was about murder and magic.

'I don't think *Macbeth* is suitable in your condition, Eliza. It may give you bad dreams and make you melancholy.'

'But Father—'

'John, put the book away and choose something more cheerful.'

Eliza's recovery marked the end of Edward and John's brief period of cooperation. The day after Thomas asked John to read to Eliza all three plus their patients were squashed into the treatment room. A woman was complaining of her cough to Edward, while John looked at an inflamed foot and Thomas examined a baby with a rash.

'Mr Keats will mix some ipecacuanha syrup for your cough,' Edward said.

'I'm examining this foot, Edward.'

'You're taking your time. It's obvious what it is.'

'Rheumatism?'

'Ha! No, it's gout.' Edward touched the patient's scarlet foot and the man yelped.

'Mr Hammond, what do you think?' John asked.

Thomas peered at the foot. 'I think it is gout. From his age and the site over the big toe. How will you treat it, John?'

'Colchicum!' Edward said.

'Perhaps a cool flannel might reduce the inflammation and help the pain?' John said.

'Perhaps, but you better go and mix the colchicum, too.'

'And my cough syrup,' Edward said.

'Edward, you can mix that.' Thomas turned back to the baby with the rash.

Thomas caught up with them in the dispensary a few minutes later. John took down the jar containing *Colchicum Autumnale* and weighed a pinch of the stamens on the small balance.

'I can't believe you thought that swollen foot was rheumatism, John,' Edward said. 'It was obviously gout. It's good I spotted your mistake.'

'It wasn't a mistake,' John said. 'That was a differential diagnosis.'

'Uncle William has lots of patients with gout.'

'I'm sure he does,' Thomas said. 'Mine can't afford to eat so much rich food and drink so much wine and port.'

John lowered his head and crushed the crocus stamens in the pestle and mortar, rather more forcefully than necessary.

'You'll need to do better to get into Guy's and do well there,' Edward said. 'Joseph Green told me all about it. He now demonstrates anatomy.'

John thumped away with the pestle some more. His face was red and his hair flying with his exertions. Specks of the crocus flew over the side.

'Steady on, John,' Thomas said. 'We don't need it all over us.'

'You should be studying, not reading novels to my sister,' Edward said.

John stopped mixing and looked directly at Edward. 'I can read novels and learn medicine. They're not exclusive to each other.'

'Ha! Do you hear that, Father? John thinks he can learn medicine from poems and literature.'

'I didn't say that. But I think reading might help medical men understand patients better.'

'Stop talking, both of you,' Thomas said. 'You're like a pair of old women. Mix the ipecac syrup for your patient, Edward! And John, make sure you put the right dose on that or it's toxic.'

'No need to get agitated, Father. I'm just waiting for John to finish so I don't get in his way.'

'Well, hurry up. After that John can read to Eliza and we'll visit at the workhouse.'

'Do we have to? Isn't there anywhere more exciting?'

'We have to because patients are sick there. I don't want to hear any more nonsense from you, Edward. This is my practice and we do things my way.'

Edward opened his mouth to speak, but Thomas held up his hand to stop him. Somewhat to his surprise, his son shut his mouth.

The Edmonton parish workhouse building had not changed much in the twenty-four years since Thomas was appointed the surgeon and apothecary there after his father's death. It lay immediately to the west of All Saints Church, but Christian charity did not travel very far. The local landowners who contributed funds thought the poor lazy and undeserving, despite the vicar's readings from the Bible. Obtaining money from the vestry committee for repairs was near impossible. How he would love a hospital wing! A fever ward! The Chase Farm workhouse had a pest house and a schoolhouse.

The fifty pounds a year the parish paid him sounded generous, but for the work involved, caring for fifty inmates, many elderly or infirm or women giving birth, it was not. Susannah sometimes asked if it was worth it, but Thomas felt it his duty to continue, as his father had. Like him, he also wanted to be known as a man of strict integrity and friend to the poor.

Edward and Thomas stood on the doorstep, Edward holding the bag, which he'd moaned about carrying from Wilston. There was a nip in the air heralding the onset of winter and more illness.

'Why can't John do this?' Edward asked.

'You know he's reading to Eliza.'

'Uncle William doesn't visit the workhouse in Southgate. He says its unprofitable.'

'When our father died we were both apothecaries to the workhouse here. It was his wish.'

'Why would he wish that?'

The master answered the door, wringing his hands. Mr Pike was portly for such a relatively young man. He had taken over when the elderly Mr Danvers passed away from apoplexy last year. Mr Pike had come from London with a good reference which bore no relation to the man before Thomas. His red nose and cheeks told him he drank too much and probably suffered from gout.

'Mr Hammond, thank goodness you've come. The young woman is getting worse.' They followed him down a long, dark corridor and upstairs to a large room packed with beds with hardly room to pass between them. Thomas knew from night-time visits the women slept two to three to a bed. Today the more infirm inmates lay on them, the elderly who struggled to walk, a woman with a small baby. The curtains were drawn. In the corner a thin figure curled up on her side under a blanket.

'Sit up, Rebecca,' Mr Pike said. 'The apothecary has come to see you.'

The woman struggled to sit but fell back. 'Let her remain lying,' Thomas said. He touched her hand. Her skin was burning, as hot as the forge where the blacksmith shod his horse. She cried out in pain and clutched her abdomen.

He felt her pulse, which was high, and examined her tongue, which was furred. 'She may have peritonitis,' he whispered to Edward. He opened his case and fed her a little laudanum.

'Can we open the curtains?' Edward asked. He walked over and drew them. Bright light shone into the room and startled Rebecca, who blinked. Edward peered into her face. 'Do you not think her eyes are a little yellow?' Edward said. 'William

123

told me always to look at the whites of the eyes.'

Thomas looked more closely. It was true her eyes did have a yellow tinge.

'What colour is your urine?' Edward asked.

'Dark,' she said, looking down in embarrassment.

'And your stool?'

'Pale,' she whispered.

'Ah ha! She has hepatitis,' Edward said. 'Doesn't she, Father? We must bleed her.'

Thomas stood, confounded. His son was correct. And he'd nearly missed it.

'Is it dangerous?' Rebecca asked.

Edward ignored her as he extracted the lancets and leeches from the case.

'It may sometimes be serious, but we will do the best we can,' Thomas said.

Edward and Thomas tried to sit her up, but she cried out. Edward persisted, seemingly unaware of her pain, and Thomas told him to be more gentle. Then Edward grabbed her arm and cut without warning and told her to be quiet when she screamed. He lifted her nightgown and attached leeches over her liver, ignoring her protests about the creatures.

'They will do you good,' Thomas said. 'Try and bear it. I'll mix some milk thistle for you too, which will help.'

'You must keep the windows shut, Master,' Edward said. 'To stop the miasma causing more cases.'

'She would benefit from a warm bath,' Thomas said. 'Can your wife arrange that?'

The master called his wife. She stood back from the bed and covered her nose with a handkerchief. Her cap, trimmed with lace and ribbons, looked more suitable for a party.

'I'm not a nurse, Mr Hammond,' she replied. 'And we don't have hot water.'

'If she is able to eat you must give her nourishing broth, then a strengthening diet,' Thomas said.

'Mr Hammond, do you know the price of bread? I struggle to feed them at all with what the vestry gives me.' Mr Pike jammed his hands against his sides.

Thomas bit his tongue. He knew exactly how much the vestry committee paid him to feed the paupers. He doubted Mr Pike was even giving them four ounces of bread and an ounce of butter each, as specified, let alone any meat or cheese. But he had no proof and accusing the Pikes of fraud would only antagonise them and probably make life harder for the inmates.

'I'll send some broth,' Thomas said. 'Who else is there to see? I think we still need to bleed Mrs Collins. Edward, I'll leave you to do that.'

Thomas walked quickly back past the church, trying to suppress his anger at Mr Pike. He wondered if he could do more for the paupers. He had influence in Edmonton but not enough among the rich landowners. He could perhaps try and get the Pikes dismissed, but their replacements might be worse. All he could do was his little bit, treat the inmates' illnesses and press for changes. Sometimes it helped, but sometimes it felt as inconsequential as a drop of rain splashing into Pymmes Brook.

On the bright side, Edward was making great strides. His diagnoses were excellent, the gout this morning and the hepatitis just now. He was efficient and competent. He would impress his teachers at Guy's and have a chance of becoming a dresser. He remembered how good William had been when they were younger, his accurate knowledge, his clinical skills. Their father had delighted in pointing this out to Thomas. Something nagged at his mind, though. When Thomas compared Edward's interaction with Rebecca to the way John had carefully lifted Mrs Foster on her pillows, he was troubled by his son's lack of compassion. But compassion wouldn't cure disease, and in the hard life of a surgeon it might actually be a hindrance.

John continued to read to Eliza each day. He seemed happier and hummed as he carried out his chores. Edward was sullen and rarely spoke except to complain that John wasn't working hard enough or to comment about how much better William did something. Thomas counselled himself to ignore him, but he found it difficult. He hoped if he remained calm his son might follow his example and learn from him.

Eliza's cheeks recovered some of their freshness and her hair its gloss. Thomas would often pause outside the drawing room, listening, then enter to say hello. He used the excuse of checking her pulse or joints. John was reading *A Midsummer Night's Dream*. Thomas didn't like to ask what it was about and didn't understand most of what he heard. Eliza listened, enthralled, hanging on every word. Sometimes she laughed. Seeing her so happy made Thomas happy. He didn't like to remember how close he'd come to losing her. John was dramatic, a showman, standing up and pacing the room, waving one hand while the other held the book. Slowly a fear came on Thomas, that Eliza adored John, and he decided to speak to Susannah.

'Do you think it's right to let John read to Eliza?' Thomas asked.

'You're the one who arranged it.'

'But is she becoming too fond of him? In a romantic way?'

126

'No, she has more sense. He's hardly any taller than her. And has no prospects.'

'Are you sure?'

'Of course. No woman in her right mind would fall for him. He's too conceited and strange.'

'She likes discussing books with him.'

'Stop worrying. In a few more weeks I'll invite Mrs Godolphin Cobb to one of my card parties. She's well connected and has a lot of sons. I'll arrange for Eliza to meet one of them.'

George Smith clutched the arms of his chair. He was wheezing, gasping for air, drowning in his own fluids. His bare feet and lower legs, too swollen for shoes or stockings, resembled the legs of an elephant Thomas had seen as a boy near Queen Charlotte's House with his father. George coughed into a handkerchief and his phlegm was frothy white tinged with pink. His eyes communicated his terror of death.

Thomas had known George since he took over his father's practice. He'd fixed his broken leg, which had not healed straight so he limped, seen his wife with female complaints, and his nine children with coughs and fevers, two of whom had not survived.

George's daughter stood nearby. 'He hasn't been able to lie down for three nights, Mr Hammond. He sleeps in the chair.'

Thomas greeted him and felt his pulse, instructing John to do likewise.

'Well?' Thomas said.

'It's very fast and weak,' John replied.

'And irregular.' Thomas pushed his finger into George's grossly swollen leg to demonstrate pitting oedema. 'Your diagnosis, Mr Keats?'

'Dropsy?'

'Correct.' Thomas turned to George. 'I'll give you some laudanum for now, to ease your breathing, and send John with some medicine later. In a few days you'll feel a new man.'

Thomas measured a dose of laudanum which George could hardly swallow. His daughter thanked him.

Outside the small cottage John untied the grey mare from the fence. 'How can you lie to him?' he said. 'A new man! In a few days, maybe even tonight, he'll be dead.'

'The laudanum will ease his breathing until the other medicines start to work.'

'Laudanum does nothing but induce numbness and send the patient to sleep. To Lethe! It won't make him better.'

'So you know more than your master now?'

John struggled with the knot he'd tied earlier, finally succeeding in loosening it. He patted the horse's neck to calm her.

'Mr Smith would be better drinking the whole bottle of laudanum.' His hands on the reins were white from squeezing so hard.

'John, while it is acceptable to use laudanum to ease suffering it should never be used to end life.'

'That's what happened with my mother and Mrs Foster.' He must have pulled on the bit because his horse flattened her ears and swished her tail.

'I think we should agree not to discuss your mother or Mrs Foster. I need your help in the dispensary. Let's go back there now.'

John turned his back on him.

'We need to make the medicine for Mr Smith,' Thomas said. 'We must put patients first, before personal feeling. It's important.'

John mounted the horse, setting off at a fast trot. Thomas followed the trail of dust he left.

In the dispensary Thomas instructed John to crush scilla with its small blue star-shaped flowers in the pestle and mortar. 'It will produce a diuresis,' he said. 'Then we'll add digitalis. It's very important to mix the correct strength as an overdose is lethal.'

John kept his head bent over his work.

'The common name for *Digitalis purpurea* is foxglove,' Thomas said. 'People talk nonsense about the flowers being fairies' gloves, witches' thimbles or witches' hats.'

John looked up. 'Flora slipped one on her thumb and touched Juno's stomach to help her conceive the god Mars,' he said.

'The god of war? Maybe it would have been better for the world if she hadn't.' Thomas weighed the digitalis, explaining to John that he must take account of Mr Smith's size, his age and whether the digitalis was root or leaf.

They boiled the mixture on the fire to make a decoction. Once it cooled Thomas instructed John how to bottle and label. 'Mr Smith is to take one dose tonight and another tomorrow morning, then we will reassess him. When you deliver it, make sure you stress not to take more.'

John set off on his horse and Thomas sat by the bench. Digitalis should help ease George's symptoms, but finding the correct dose was difficult. It was a delicate matter to achieve the right balance and it wasn't always successful. Wittering had published his observations of its effects just about the time Thomas went to Guy's and the materia medica teacher had lectured enthusiastically about it.

The next afternoon they set out to visit George Smith

again. As soon as they walked in Thomas saw he breathed more easily and his leg swelling was reduced considerably.

'That medicine was magic, Mr Hammond,' George said.

'Not magic, but science. Now we must decrease the dose to a quarter of the amount a day.'

He caught John's eye. He saw something glowing, deep in his large, dark pupil. A flicker of respect.

On the way to the next visit he lectured John on some of the other miracles science could perform: to cure scurvy with limes, to vaccinate against smallpox and treat rickets with cod liver oil. He thought he better not tell him the effect of the digitalis would eventually wear off and George would need laudanum to keep him comfortable before he died.

Despite Susannah's reassurances about Eliza and John, Thomas felt suspicious. One day he went inside to fetch a fresh pocket handkerchief and heard John's voice coming from the drawing room. Something drew him to the open door to listen to his words.

'*Yet mark'd I where the bolt of Cupid fell: It fell upon a little western flower, Before, milk-white, now purple with love's wound, And maidens call it love-in-idleness. Fetch me that flower; the herb I shew'd thee once.*'

'Father has love-in-idleness in his herb garden!' Eliza said.

'*The juice of it on sleeping eyelids laid Will make or man or woman madly dote Upon the next live creature that it sees.*'

'It would be fun to pick some and smear it on our eyelids and see if the play is true.' Eliza laughed after she said this. In the hall mirror Thomas saw her sat up on the chaise longue, her hair brushed but loose. Her shawl had fallen away from her shoulders and she wore only a thin dress underneath. Susannah was wrong. The look on her face told him all he needed to know.

'John,' Thomas walked into the room and John dropped the book at the suddenness of Thomas's entrance, 'I need you in the dispensary.'

'Father, can't he stay a little longer?' Eliza asked.

'No, Eliza. He can't. He's my apprentice not your personal reader.'

'But when will I hear the end of the play?'

'You can read it yourself. Your eyes must be recovered by now.'

Eliza stared at him in disbelief. An atmosphere like that before a summer thunderstorm hung in the air.

'I should go. Goodbye, Eliza,' John said.

John had always called her Eliza, but surely it was time for him to call her Miss Hammond now they were both older? John picked up the book, put it on the table next to her and backed out of the room. Eliza pulled her shawl tight around her shoulders.

'You're ruining my enjoyment, Father. After I've been so ill, don't I deserve some fun?'

'He's not a suitable companion for you, Eliza.'

'He'll be an apothecary like yourself.'

'There's no comparison. I'm also a surgeon and inherited my father's practice. He has very little.'

'Is that all you care for? Monetary wealth?'

'It's important to live a good life.'

'What about love?'

'You need to find both. As I and your mother have.'

'Except you always argue about money. Was it really a love match as you always say?'

Thomas was lost for words. She'd never said anything like this before.

'I'm in love with him, Father.' Her voice was clear and pure, her face angelic.

'You're too young to understand love.' Thomas remembered the first time he saw Susannah, the longing. Perhaps he was now too old to understand love.

'It's not a childish infatuation. I'm in love with his voice and Shakespeare and the way we talk about the play.'

'Is that really love?'

'It's being in love with something bigger than oneself, learning a new language, seeing the world differently.'

The book rested on the table, bound in calf skin with gold-tooled lettering. The cover was now slightly dented and a little scratched, no longer pristine.

'I don't wish John to read to you anymore.'

Eliza picked up the volume and held it to her chest. 'Much as I love you, Father, I see you'll never understand. It's not in your nature.'

Her withering look cut him as painfully as a knife. He saw he'd forever lost the young girl who'd played in the orchard, chasing butterflies and asking to learn about herbs.

At the end of a busy morning, just when Thomas thought they'd finished, Ned Barlow walked in, clutching his left arm with his right, his face grimacing in pain. 'I tripped,' he said through gritted teeth.

In the treatment room Thomas cut open the front of Ned's shirt with scissors. Ned protested a new shirt would cost a whole month's wages. Thomas pointed out he could stitch it back together and there wouldn't be any more wages unless they fixed his arm. Once the shirt was removed it was obvious his shoulder was visibly deformed.

'What do you think of this, Mr Keats?' Thomas asked.

'The shoulder is very square and he can't move his arm, but I don't think it's broken.'

'It's dislocated. Lie down, Ned, and Mr Keats will reduce it.'

'I don't want Mr Keats to do it. He's no bigger than a miniature pony. Can't you do it, Mr Hammond?'

'What about laudanum for pain?' John said.

'Quiet! Both of you. We need to do this as quickly as possible. Mr Keats does it or it doesn't get done. Pain relief afterwards. Lie down.'

Ned lay on the bench. Thomas tied a towel tightly around his upper arm on the affected side, ignoring his cries.

'Take your boot off,' Thomas told John. John's stockings were in a poor state, threadbare in places. 'Put your heel in his armpit.'

John obeyed, balancing awkwardly on one leg. Thomas instructed him to pull on the towel while pressing into the axilla with his heel.

'Pull harder, keep up the traction,' Thomas said. John puffed and tugged. Ned cried out. John, his face white and drawn, turned to look at Thomas.

'Push your foot in deeper and pull out slightly,' Thomas said.

Ned's cries increased. John was flagging.

'Let me help.' Thomas held the towel and pulled. Ned begged him to stop. The arm wasn't shifting. Thomas told John to push his foot deeper into the axilla. Ned screamed in agony. Thomas's clenched hands burnt with pain. He sweated. This had been one of Astley's favourite manoeuvres. He thought it showed off his legs, clad in white silk stockings, which he was proud of. He would have managed it.

If he failed at this, what would John think? Perhaps John was right and he was a failure as a surgeon, a fraud. Astley could do it. Why couldn't he? The shoulder would not shift. His hands slackened around the towel. He was useless, powerless. He looked up. John was tugging, his face red. He recalled his glittering eyes and glowing cheeks the day he'd returned to Wilston. He had to show this boy he could do this; he was the master.

He must keep going, block his ears to Ned's shrieks, ignore their lacerating edges. Show John he was a skilled surgeon, he could save people. Thomas pulled with all his strength. One last heroic effort. The humerus popped back into place, sending Thomas and John flying backwards and landing on their buttocks.

Ned sighed with relief. Thomas burst out laughing and John stared at him.

'Don't move, Ned,' Thomas said. 'We need to tie your arm to your side and you must keep it like that for three weeks.' He sent John for bandages then helped him tie them. He gave Ned laudanum, although he hardly needed it now, and sent him on his way.

'Do you still say I haven't healed anyone?' he asked John. 'I'd like to see a quack do that.'

John collapsed onto the bench. 'I didn't think I could pull any longer.'

'You need to develop your strength, John. Maybe get back to that fighting you used to do?'

'I'm not sure I can do this.' His voice was small and

defeated. He no longer looked like an avenging angel but a bewildered, disheartened boy.

Thomas's triumph seeped away. Perhaps he shouldn't have pushed John so hard. He was acting like his father, taking pleasure in showing his superiority, something he'd vowed never to do.

'You said you only came back because your grandmother begged you?' Thomas asked.

John's mouth sagged at the corners. 'I do still want to be an apothecary.'

'To relieve suffering?'

'Yes.'

'Good. Failure is part of learning. We need it to push us to do better. Don't lose faith. Next time it will work. And if not then the time after.'

'You believe so?'

'I know it.' Except some failures, like the boy at Guy's, couldn't be made better; there wasn't another chance for him. However hard Thomas worked and strived, nothing atoned for it, but it wouldn't help John to be told that. They must get on with the day's work; there was lots to do still.

Chapter Nine

December 1814

Girls must grow up and become women and married, but Thomas missed Eliza's company and confidences. Susannah enjoyed discussing finding a suitor for her. If Thomas was present during these conversations Eliza would look at him as if to say, see what you have forced onto me? But she didn't speak it aloud. As far as he saw she had no contact with John.

Thomas wasn't sure what John made of the matter. He'd become quiet and withdrawn, but there was another reason for that.

The pile of coals glowing in the grate couldn't take the chill from the room at 3 Church Street where Alice Jennings rested on several pillows to ease her laboured breathing. Wisps of white hair escaped from under her yellowing mob cap. Candles burnt to light the room on this day in the depths of winter. Their flames flickered across a miniature of her late husband, John Jennings, which lay by her bed.

Thomas had applied the cups and recommended a strengthening regime, but she was very weak and frail. John sat by her bed and held her hand. His young, straight fingers contrasted with her gnarled bones. Footsteps sounded on the stairs along with the mumble of voices. George and Tom Keats entered, and the small room felt crowded, but Thomas couldn't escape without pushing through so waited quietly in the corner.

George greeted his grandmother and stood by the bed. He was smartly dressed, taller than John and might have been taken for the eldest. He had darker, thinner hair but the same high forehead and wide mouth.

Mrs Jennings opened her eyes and took time to focus.

'George,' she said. 'I didn't expect to see you so soon.'

'Tom told me you haven't been well, and Mr Abbey gave me permission to come and visit.'

'There was no need for that. I'm sure he needs you at the counting house.'

'You'll soon be better, Grandmother,' John said. 'Mr Hammond had me mix up a new medicine for you.'

Mrs Jennings looked at John. 'Child,' she said. She took a few breaths, the effort exhausting her. 'No, you're a man now, John. You must look after the family when I'm gone.'

'Don't talk like that. You'll recover,' John said. 'It's just a chill you caught.'

'I'm an old woman of seventy-eight.'

'I can help look after the family,' George said. 'Mr Abbey is pleased with my work.'

'I'm sure Mr Abbey will do what's best for you three boys and Fanny as your trustee and guardian. But promise me, John, you will complete your studies with Mr Hammond.'

'I will,' John said.

'Now let me rest.' Alice Jennings sank back and closed her eyes. Thomas gestured to the three boys to leave her and they went downstairs.

George turned to him. 'How much time does she have?'

'Mr Hammond will make her better so she lives many

years,' John said. 'Why, only last week he brought Mrs Hart, who is ninety, back from near dead.'

'Your grandmother has been very ill indeed,' Thomas said to George, looking him in the eye.

'She'll regain her strength like Mrs Hart, with the medicine,' John said.

'She's lived a long life, John. You can see how weary she is. There's no cure for old age. Her body and mind are worn out.'

'She can't die,' John said.

'Should I write to our sister Fanny?' George asked.

'Yes, she may want to visit soon.'

'I'll sleep at the house until she is recovered. I can read to her,' John said. 'You'll let me do fewer duties for a while, Mr Hammond?'

Thomas felt he couldn't say no. He knew it wouldn't be for long.

George wrote to Fanny, but she didn't arrive in time. Mrs Jennings's maid knocked on the door of Wilston one morning and told Thomas that Mrs Jennings had passed away in her sleep. He entered the house, its rooms dim and silent as a tomb. Upstairs John knelt by the bed, his upper body lying across his grandmother, his arms spread out.

'He won't leave her,' the maid said.

Thomas put his hand on John's shoulder. 'John, let me see her.'

John turned his face, his eyes swollen from crying. 'She can't be gone. She can't leave me,' he said, his voice hoarse from tears.

Thomas rested his hand on John's thin, bony shoulder, which felt as fragile as the old woman's.

'She's gone to join your grandfather, mother and uncle, but

she's still with you in spirit, John. See how at peace she looks.'
Alice Jennings's face did indeed look at peace.

John lay across her body again as if protecting her from
the world. Thomas left him for a time with her, then called
Susannah to help her maid lay her out.

It was a bitterly cold day, just before Christmas. The Thames
had half frozen and the horses' hooves clanged on the icy roads
into town. Thomas looked up at the tower of St Stephen's
Coleman Street where a gilded vane in the form of a cockerel
captured the sunlight and glinted: the rooster of Peter and
the message of God's pardon to sinners who repent. But Alice
Jennings could not have had many sins; she had lived a good
life. Thomas walked past a gateway with a skull and crossbones
and an image of doom above it.

The interior was a single space with large round-headed
windows. At the front of the church with their backs to him,
stood John, George and Tom, their hats bound with long
black ribbons. Mr Abbey was in the pew behind them. Some
people Thomas didn't know, they looked in trade, perhaps old
acquaintances from Mrs Jennings's days at the Swan and Hoop
at Moorgate, and some villagers from Edmonton sat near the
back. Thomas sat in front of them but behind Abbey.

Mrs Jennings had told him she was from Lancashire, but
Thomas had first met her through her husband. Those visits to
Mr Jennings nearly two miles away in Ponders End had become
a burden. A Londoner who moved to the country to retire, his
health slowly deteriorated until he called for Thomas every day.
He was always jovial and boasted about his inn, the Swan and
Hoop at Moorgate, how it was 117 feet long, had two coach
houses and stabling for fifty horses, but he was irritable and

impatient with his wife. Even then, before all her troubles, she was nervous and easily startled.

After her husband's death nine years ago she'd moved to Edmonton, two doors away from Thomas. Her parlour was cramped with furniture: tables and chairs, a small writing desk, and a glass-fronted bookcase stuffed with books. On his visits she always offered him raisin and cherry cake, along with a small glass of plum wine. When her son-in-law died and daughter disappeared she looked after her granddaughter Fanny and her grandsons John, George and Tom in their school holidays. Thomas remembered her face when her daughter, John's mother, had died, the grief etched into it, but she had borne her burden and been there for her grandchildren, more like a mother to them than a grandmother.

The coffin, covered in an embroidered cloth, was brought in on the shoulders of the pall bearers. Alice Jennings would lie in the family vault of this church near where she had spent her working life. She would lie beside her husband, her son, her daughter, John's mother, and her son-in-law, John's father.

Thomas listened to the service. He hoped the vault would be sealed tight and cringed with shame at the memory of the time he went bodysnatching. One night Astley Cooper had asked him to accompany him on an adventure with some other students. Astley said there would be money in it for them and although money would have been helpful that wasn't why Thomas went. He was flattered to be included. It was a dark, windy night and they wore dark clothes. They skulked along the narrow, winding streets of the Borough to the graveyard next to Guy's. Astley drew a shovel from underneath his cloak and began digging up the earth of a fresh grave.

'Stop! You can't do that,' Thomas said.

'We need bodies and this is the only way to get them.' Astley shovelled dirt over his shoulder. The other students laughed around him, but Thomas detected fear in their shrillness.

Astley held out the shovel to Thomas. 'Your turn. Be quick.' Thomas felt revulsion, but he didn't want Astley to think him a coward. He grasped the wooden handle, slick with sweat and covered in grimy dirt. Shadows among the graves spooked him and the wind sounded like ghostly footsteps behind him. When they had enough space Astley wrenched the coffin lid open with an iron bar and they slid the body of a young woman from her shroud. She was heavier than Thomas expected, her limbs stiff and unyielding. Her pure white body glowed in the moonlight and he felt overcome by nausea. Astley had brought sacks to cover her and they carried her body down dark streets to a house and deposited it on a table in the back room. Thomas wondered if Astley was selling it or would come back later to dissect it. Astley shared coins amongst them, and Thomas took his, but it felt as if the money was burning into his palm and blackening it to charred flesh. He never went bodysnatching again.

The words of the vicar reading the thirty-ninth psalm brought him back to the present. '*Lord, make me to know mine end, and the measure of my days, what it is; that I may know how frail I am.*' He wondered if he would live to three score years and ten, or only fifty-three like his father. That would mean he had only five years left. A cold sweat passed over him at the thought.

He focussed his attention on the people in the church. In the front pew the Keats boys' straight backs, clad in mourning black, looked too fragile to bear their burden, left on their own in the world with John at their head aged only nineteen.

Mr Abbey was officially their guardian, but Thomas vowed he would do all he could to help them.

Christmas was busy that year. At Wilston Thomas rested his damp, cold boots in front of the Yule log burning in the fireplace. His body ached from riding Cinnamon all over the parish, visiting cases of ague. He couldn't feel his toes. He hoped he hadn't developed frostbite in his feet. Last year a man found half frozen in a ditch had suffered gangrene and needed his toes amputating. When Thomas rode out in the winter, the country roads being impassable for the carriage, he protected himself with leather gloves and a muffler wrapped tight around his nose, cheeks, chin and ears, but his leather boots were cracked.

Martha brought him a plate of leftover goose and rewarmed potatoes as he'd missed dinner. She also brought a glass of mulled wine. Boughs of evergreen hung on the walls of the drawing room, releasing their pine scent in the heat from the fire. He ate the goose, his cold fingers just able to hold the cutlery.

'I'm fed up of goose,' Edward said.

'I've just visited a house where they're burning the furniture to keep warm and living on gruel.'

'What have they done with the food in the boxes we gave out only a few days ago?' Susannah asked.

'Can I go to Uncle William's for Twelfth Night?' Edward picked up his fiddle and plucked the strings. 'They play bob apple and snap dragon.'

'Last year you burnt your mouth on the raisins.' Eliza looked up from her book.

'But it's such fun with the blue flames dancing on the brandy and everyone looking like demons.' Only Edward could think picking raisins from a burning bowl of brandy amusing. Edward flicked his hair away from his face. At nineteen he had the look of a grown man but many of his mannerisms were those of a child.

'I need you here 'til John comes back,' Thomas said. He'd allowed John a few days off to spend with his brothers and sister. Tom was planning to move in with George so John would be on his own at his lodgings in Edmonton.

'Can I go to Uncle William's when John's back?' Edward asked.

'Let's wait and see.' He wasn't promising anything. He wanted his family around him, where he could keep them safe. Thomas started on his plum pudding, eating fast in case he was called out again. A tinge of indigestion started in his stomach, but he ignored it and drank the mulled wine.

The upstairs window was small, its frame covered in flaking paint, the glass dirty and the curtains drawn. Snowdrops poked through the hard ground outside the cottage. Thomas knocked at the door and Polly Bates answered.

'I've come to see my apprentice,' Thomas said.

'Good luck to you. He won't get out of bed. I'm at my wits' end. I wish I'd never taken him in.'

Thomas climbed the dark, narrow staircase to the room where a figure lay huddled on the bed under wool blankets. The room was cold and Thomas rubbed his hands, put a few pieces of coal on the fire and stirred it with the poker, but the coal was damp and smoked. He drew the curtains but that hardly admitted more light. The room was bare apart from a shelf with books and a small chest of drawers.

'John, I expected you back at work yesterday,' he said. The

shape under the blankets didn't move. 'It's very busy with ague and Edward and I are fully stretched.'

John's head emerged from the blankets and he rolled over onto his back. 'I can't.' His voice was weak.

'Do you have a fever? Ague?' Thomas stepped to the bed and touched John's forehead, but it was cool. His hair was uncombed and the collar of his nightshirt grimy. A bowl of broth lay untouched by the bed. Thomas dipped his finger in it and found it lukewarm.

'Let's sit you up.' Thomas helped raise him on the pillows. For one so small, it was like lifting a sack of flour. 'What's wrong?'

John shrugged. The corners of his mouth drooped and his face lacked its usual expressiveness.

'Are you ill?'

John shook his head slowly. He lay back against the pillows and closed his eyes. The coal in the grate spat a little and collapsed on itself.

'Try and eat this.' Thomas held the spoon of broth against John's lips, but John sealed them tight. His eyes opened but were unfocussed as if he'd taken belladonna. 'Come on, you need nourishment.' Thomas pushed the spoon between John's lips as if he were feeding a baby and John's lips opened. Thomas fed him the broth slowly, wiping drips from his chin with his handkerchief.

'That's better. You're grieving for your grandmother. Everyone finds it difficult.' Thomas remembered the heaviness when his father died, the pain of his loss. He'd only been twenty-four. He hadn't expected it to be so all-consuming.

John was silent for a time then spoke. 'She was always there for me. After my father died, after my mother left us.'

'You must miss her very much.'

'I do, but I can't cry for her loss.'

'That's not uncommon. Grief isn't always screaming and shouting and wailing.' What to say that would console but not upset or belittle?

'I've suffered grief before. With my father and my mother, I felt wretched, inconsolable, abandoned, but this is different. I feel as cold as a marble statue.'

Thomas felt the sadness oozing out of John. It frightened him, the intensity of it. It might suffocate a person.

'There seems no point to anything,' John said. 'The future is dark, empty. I know I must get up and help my family, but I remain anchored in the bed.'

'You must try and make the effort.'

'It's difficult when my thoughts are so gloomy. I think of Chatterton.'

'Chatterton?'

'He poisoned himself with arsenic.'

The hairs on the back of Thomas's neck rose. 'John, I forbid you to do anything so extreme and sensationalist. It's a sin in the eyes of God. Think of the effect on your brothers and sisters. You're head of the family now; you must set an example.'

'I have no will. I'm paralysed.'

'I think you're suffering from melancholy,' Thomas said.

'Melancholy?'

'Yes.'

John grabbed Thomas's sleeve and held tight. 'Please don't send me to Bedlam. When I was a child I saw the mad going into Bedlam opposite our house. Some were ranting and wild and had to be restrained, but others were like walking corpses, hollowed out.'

'I promise I won't send you to Bedlam. I'll mix you some medicine to take. There are many recipes in Burton's.'

'I don't believe they'll work.'

'But you must at least try them. You must hold on to hope.'

'What hope is there?'

'Burton says he writes of melancholy to avoid melancholy. Hard work and keeping busy can help. I found that after my father's death. Doing something difficult but meaningful, helping patients.'

'You felt the same?'

'A little.' He'd drowned his sorrows in work, in twenty-four-hour shifts addressing suffering. The gloom had lifted after a while and he was thankful. 'You can recover, John, I know.'

Thomas sat in his study resting Burton's massive *The Anatomy of Melancholy* on his lap. The book was informative and Thomas often consulted it for cures. It was also satirical and amusing in places, but he generally skimmed over the quotations, many in Latin, the numerous references to literature and the Latin poetry. He was searching for advice to help John.

He'd visited John's lodgings every day and dispensed the medicines to make sure he took them, but John hadn't improved. Thomas knew it might take time, but he felt worried because the case was very severe. Some cases didn't recover. What then? His *Times* told him the Apothecaries Act was due its first reading in Parliament soon. There would be a second reading a few months later and it would then be voted into law. John had to attend Guy's to become an apothecary. If he didn't recover, his years of training would be wasted. He'd made good progress but still had much to learn. Thomas felt ashamed he'd been concerned about the impression John would make on Astley Cooper. This was John's life, his means to earn an income and support his family. It was life and death.

All this thinking was making Thomas melancholy. He turned the pages of the heavy tome, heavy as the weight of grief crushing John.

'Father?' Eliza opened the door. 'Can I borrow a book?'

'Of course.' He was surprised. Since he'd ended the readings with John, Eliza had avoided Thomas and hardly spoke to him.

Eliza knelt by the lowest shelf and pulled out a book. She flipped through the pages then returned it and pulled out another.

'What are you going to read?' Thomas asked.

'Another Shakespeare, I think.' She opened the cover of the book. 'It seems a long time since John read *A Midsummer Night's Dream* to me. How is he?'

'Melancholy. He feels the loss of his grandmother greatly. I wish I could help him.'

'You could prescribe something.'

'I have, but it's not working as I hoped.'

Eliza stood up and hugged the book to her chest. Her hair was loose and she reminded him of the girl in the herb garden, not the sophisticated young lady who now went to parties.

'When I had scarlet fever I found John reading to me helped. It gave me something else to think about, to be interested in.'

Thomas felt discomfort from the weight of Burton's across his legs and looked down. Lines of Latin poetry spread across the page. Of course. John needed something to interest him, to draw him out of the illness.

'Eliza, thank you. You've given me an idea.' Thomas shut the book, leapt up and hurried with it, carrying it awkwardly due to its size and shape, attracting stares from a few villagers, to John's lodgings.

He helped John balance *The Anatomy of Melancholy* on his knees to read while he lay in bed. John read a few lines and Thomas saw a spark of interest.

Each day after that there was a small improvement until John recuperated enough to come to work, but he was very slow and unsure of himself so Thomas had to supervise him closely.

Thomas was thankful Edward mostly ignored John and treated patients. Edward worked hard and showed skill, and Thomas was reassured.

Susannah was sympathetic to John's plight and suggested they invite him to dinner.

'Now Tom has gone to work for Abbey and lives with George it must be very lonely for him,' she said.

And so they did, but John hardly said a word and picked at his food. He didn't even smile or blush when Eliza tried to cheer him up. After a few meals he apologised to Susannah but said he would eat alone at his lodgings.

One day in early February Thomas saw John leaving the surgery looking flushed and excited, holding a letter in his hand.

'May I go, Mr Hammond?' he asked. 'The chores are all done.'

'Yes,' Thomas replied, 'but what's the rush?'

'Leigh Hunt has been released from prison. I must go to Charles Cowden Clarke and find out if he's seen him yet! Libertas is free! I will write a sonnet for the occasion.'

Thomas felt hope that as Leigh Hunt had been released from prison so maybe John was finally being released from his internal prison of melancholy.

Chapter Ten

Recently Thomas found his body ached after riding in a way it hadn't used to, and he'd been relieved that the roads were clear enough of mud to use the carriage. John sat next to him and Edward rode alongside. He'd taken both boys to see an interesting case, a patient with a popliteal aneurysm. The bulging, pulsating mass behind the man's knee might rupture, thrombose or spin off emboli causing ischaemia or gangrene so needed treatment. Tying off the artery above the bulge encouraged new vessels to grow, forming a collateral circulation, but it was a dangerous operation.

He would need to refer the man to a hospital. The obvious one was Guy's, where Astley Cooper was an expert at ligating the popliteal artery, having learnt from John Hunter himself and practised on live dogs. As a Guy's man, Thomas had referred patients to Guy's over the years, so why did he hesitate and think of sending him to Barts instead?

In the distance a rider galloped towards them, dust flying from his horse's hooves. He drew up sharply and the horse rose on its hind legs.

'Mr Hammond, thank goodness I've found you.' Matthew Trot, who worked on a nearby farm, struggled to calm the horse. 'A tree has fallen on Robbie Brown.'

'Robbie?' Robbie was a young man with a wife and baby. Thomas had seen him in surgery only last week. How could a tree have fallen on him?

'His arm's pinned beneath it.'

A seed of fear germinated in Thomas, spreading shoots through his body, but he forced his mind to remain calm. It was probably nothing, an overreaction. Matthew was panicking.

'Show us,' Thomas said. 'Let's go.'

They followed Matthew at speed, the carriage rattling and jumping over ruts in the track. At Shaw's farm Matthew told them they must proceed on foot. In the field behind the farm a tree lay on its side, its branches pointing to the sky like broken, gnarled fingers under bunched grey clouds. Small figures gathered around it. Thomas ran towards them, his heart straining in his chest, his breathing fast and sharp.

Axes lay around the bare stump. At first Thomas couldn't see the body for the branches springing from the severed trunk. Then he saw a figure curled on its side, facing the tree. He touched his back.

'Robbie? It's Mr Hammond.' Thomas knelt in the dirt, on the thin grass.

Robbie's face was screwed up tight, his eyes closed. Sweat beaded on his brow. His left arm was trapped beneath the tree trunk, only the shoulder and part of the upper arm were visible. Thomas's intestines twisted like a knotted rope being pulled tighter and tighter, producing severe cramps, as they had the time he nearly died of typhoid.

'We'll get you out of this,' Thomas said, removing his coat and placing it over Robbie. He saw boots standing next to him and looked up to see Edward, wide-eyed.

'What will you do, Father?' Edward asked.

'My bag, I need my bag.' Thomas turned around to see John hurrying towards them carrying it. Thomas undid the buckles, his fingers clumsy as he pushed the stiff leather straps. He grabbed a bottle and gave Robbie a large dose of laudanum.

Robbie shivered, white and spectrelike. The arm under the tree must be mangled. The only question was whether he should amputate it in the field or try to get him inside the farmhouse. It would be difficult here in the field; he wasn't sure he could wield the saw, and the soil was dirty. The saw. He needed his saw. But first they must try and free Robbie.

'Matthew!' Thomas shouted. 'You must try and roll the tree off him.'

'We've tried already,' Matthew said.

'With me and the two boys as well maybe we can.'

The men climbed over branches and lined up along the trunk. They pushed as hard as they could, but to no effect. 'All together now, one more effort,' Matthew shouted. Thomas pushed with all his strength, his shoulders straining, pushing even more when he felt exhausted. The other men gave a great roar, like wild beasts. The tree shifted and rolled away.

The arm was crushed beyond recognition. Fetid acid rose in Thomas's mouth and his stomach threatened to expel its contents. He had to look away from the mass of bloody pulp. He wasn't sure he could do this.

Around him the men stood, silenced by the horror, their faces ashen. They were all looking at Thomas, as were Edward and John. He had to act; he couldn't run away.

Thomas took deep breaths of cold air. He applied a tourniquet above the injury and sent Matthew to the farm to bring a blanket for a stretcher.

'One of you must fetch my saw,' he told John and Edward. 'The other can stay and comfort Robbie.'

Edward was motionless, his eyes shocked. John was harder to read. He bit his lower lip, emphasising the overhanging upper one.

'I'll go, Father. I know where it's kept and I'm a fast rider.' Edward ran back towards his horse.

John and Thomas helped the men carry Robbie inside. The laudanum was starting to take effect, so he was drowsy, but he cried out in a sort of delirium. They lay him on the kitchen table in the farmhouse and Thomas asked for a pillow for his head. Time passed interminably. The men wanted to leave but Thomas asked for Matthew and two others to stay. Matthew offered them brandy, but Thomas refused. He asked him to find a small length of wood which he wrapped in a cloth. John stood at the head of the table and wiped Robbie's brow.

Thomas hadn't performed an amputation for some time. The last one, when a boy's leg was trapped under a cart, was before John and Edward had started as his apprentices. He'd had to perform the surgery in the street as they couldn't move the cart. The poor lad had developed an infection afterwards and died. Thomas laid out the equipment he would need from his bag: forceps, sutures, a needle, gauze and bandages, then sat quietly to prepare himself. William Lucas senior, the surgeon at Guy's he was dresser to, always said a calm mind was as important to success as a steady hand.

Edward arrived with the saw and Thomas instructed Matthew and one of the other men to stand by Robbie's legs. 'When I start you will need to put the full force of your weight upon them,' he said. He told the third man to hold the uninjured arm. 'John, you will put the biting stick between his teeth and Edward will hold the injured arm above the crush.'

'Father,' Edward said. 'My legs feel weak from the ride and I fear I may not be strong enough.' He did indeed look shaky and sat on one of the chairs.

'Very well then, you can help with the biting stick of wood. John, come here.'

Thomas instructed John to hold the arm tight above the point where he would amputate.

'You will need to be stronger than you can imagine,' he said. 'Stand firm, like your uncle on the deck at Camperdown.'

Edward stood by Robbie's head and inserted the cloth wrapped stick between his teeth. John squeezed the upper arm. Matthew and the other man pressed on Robbie's legs. Thomas picked up the saw, held it above the mutilated arm and laid the jagged blade on the unspoiled flesh above the crush. The teeth dug into the skin. He must cut quickly and efficiently. The most merciful thing a surgeon could do was be quick. Astley Cooper was renowned for being swift.

Start sawing now. Now. Thomas's arm refused to move. Perhaps he should transport Robbie to a hospital, even though any delay could be fatal. Let Astley Cooper do it, someone competent. How could he even think of doing this? After what had happened that night at Guy's with the boy? Around him the men breathed deeply and noisily.

'Mr Hammond?' John said.

Thomas looked up and saw John's eyes fixed on him. At the head of the table Edward was also staring at him. He had to show John and Edward what it meant to be a surgeon. To relieve suffering, even if that involved inflicting great pain.

Thomas pulled the saw deep against Robbie's skin. Robbie cried out through teeth clamped on the wood. Thomas pushed the saw through muscle and sinew. Robbie's body bucked and the men pressed hard on his legs. Thomas forced the blade back and forth. Noise filled his head. Metal grating against bone. Robbie screaming. 'Hold firmer, John,' he said. John's fingers were white. The bone splintered, the last remnant of flesh was cut and the arm fell to the stone flags.

The small thud was followed by a larger one. Out of the corner of his eye Thomas saw Edward's body slumped on the floor. 'Shall I go to him, Mr Hammond?' Matthew asked.

'No, hold on to Robbie.' Blood leaked out of the cut vessels despite the tourniquet and Thomas tied them to stem the bleeding, then sutured the stump. His fingers were sluggish and his stitches weren't neat, but beauty wasn't important. John helped him dress the stump, winding the bandage. Relief flooded Thomas. It was over.

Edward groaned and sat up slowly. 'My head hurts,' he said. 'I see stars.'

'Sit in the chair and put your head down, Edward,' Thomas said. Matthew offered Edward some brandy, which he accepted. Thomas asked for some too and downed it in one.

The stick fell from Robbie's mouth. He was now crying.

'There, there, it's all finished,' Thomas said. He felt as numb as the missing arm, amputated from himself.

'How will I live without my arm?' Robbie asked. 'I'd rather you'd killed me.'

Thomas gave him more laudanum. John looked from Robbie's face to the stump. He placed his arm on Robbie's shoulder.

'Well done, John,' Thomas said. 'You're stronger than you look. In mind as well as body.'

'Thank you, Sir,' John said.

Edward rose from the chair and walked towards the door. 'Are you hurt, Edward? Did you bang your head?' Thomas asked. But Edward was out of the door before Thomas's words were finished.

Edward's horse was gone. John and Thomas had spent some time with Robbie, checking the bleeding had stopped and that he was fit to be taken home lying in the back of a cart, before they left him. Thomas reasoned if Edward could ride his horse he couldn't have hit his head too badly. In the carriage John didn't speak or show emotion and Thomas thought he was probably still in that state that sets in during an emergency and protects the mind from the reality of what's happening. It's only later that the body shakes and the mind flashes with terrible images of the trauma.

He pushed thoughts of Edward away. It was difficult, to assist at the first major surgery. The body reacted in a physical way the mind couldn't always control. So why did he feel ashamed that his son had refused to hold the arm and fainted? While this slip of a boy next to him, the son of an innkeeper, had shown enormous strength and mental resolve.

'Will Robbie survive?' John asked.

'If the wound doesn't fester he has a good chance.'

'But how will he earn a living with one arm?'

'Some patients adapt well, others less so,' said Thomas.

'I can't imagine…' John said.

'My advice is don't even try. You handled yourself well, John,' Thomas said. 'You could train to be a surgeon when you go to Guy's. I think you should seriously consider it.'

'Be a surgeon?'

'Edward plans to, and you're as competent as he.'

John shook his head and looked ahead at the road. 'Being an apothecary will be enough for me.'

Thomas decided he would leave this discussion for another day.

At Wilston Susannah was waiting in the hall. 'How could

you choose John over Edward to help with the amputation?' she asked. 'Edward is very upset.'

'He told me he felt too weak, that's why I asked John. It was just as well because Edward fainted.'

'Did he hurt himself?'

'I don't think so. I was sewing up a haemorrhaging stump in a farm kitchen at the time.'

He almost felt her shudder of revulsion. 'There's no need to be so coarse, Thomas.'

'There's no delicate way to put it.'

Susannah folded her arms and walked back and forth across the hall, blocking him from entering the house. Her skirts swished when she changed direction. He wanted to go inside and rest, put his feet up, then have something to eat. He felt shaky from the exertion of the amputation.

'The poor boy!' Susannah said. 'To see an arm hacked off like a butcher cutting meat. No wonder he fainted.' Again she shuddered.

'John managed fine,' Thomas said.

'John isn't refined and sensitive like Edward.' She stopped pacing and turned to face him. 'I wish you hadn't allowed Edward to become your apprentice.'

'He wanted it. Especially after you arranged for John to be.'

'You should have said no, you knew my wishes for him to use his real talents and be a lawyer.'

'It's his first amputation. He'll get used to it.' Thomas started to remove his boot. His feet were hot and cramped and he longed to uncurl his toes.

'He's gone towards the brook,' Susannah said. 'Don't you think you should go and talk to him?'

Thomas stood on one leg with his boot half on and half off.

'You don't have to treat him as your own father treated you,' she said.

He could see she was determined to make him go after Edward and he was too tired to argue. He pulled his boot back on his aching foot.

The path was flanked by thorny, arching stems of brambles which snatched at his coat. Where it opened out he emerged into a clearing. The brook ran slowly, bare tree roots exposed on its banks, and the sun hung low behind a cluster of trees. No sign of Edward.

Susannah's last remark had stung. Their father had trained Thomas and William well. They'd both attended Guy's and become apothecary surgeons, but at times he'd been harsh and Thomas had confided this to Susannah. On his deathbed he'd ranted, saying William should take over the practice, he was more suited, making Thomas feel inferior.

Thomas heard a creak and looked up into a tree, its bare branches silhouetted against the slanting light. Edward sat on a branch, his boots dangling.

'Come down, Edward, I want to speak to you.'

'Why don't you come up here?'

'I'm too old and sensible to climb trees.'

Edward didn't move. Thomas sat on a fallen trunk nearby and picked up a dried leaf. He stripped it down to its skeleton. After a few minutes Edward jumped from the branch, landing heavily, and sat next to him. Thomas threw the leaf aside.

'It's not unusual to faint at major operations,' Thomas said. 'At Guy's students were always leaving the operating theatre because they felt unwell. I felt faint the first time I watched William Lucas cutting for bladder stones. We stood on the standings packed like herrings in a barrel. The patient was tied to the table, his knees pulled into his chest and his hands bound to his ankles. The screams when they cut into his scrotum were terrible.'

'I didn't faint. I felt dizzy from my fast ride to fetch your saw.' Edward tossed his hair off his forehead. 'Otherwise I could easily have held the arm.'

'You don't need to lie to me, Edward.'

'At my uncle's I saw many operations.'

'It's nothing to be ashamed of.' Thomas's hand reached towards Edward's shoulder.

'But you're ashamed of me, aren't you?' Edward shrugged off Thomas's hand.

In the brook the water circled in eddies and became trapped in hollowed-out areas near the banks.

'As I said, it's very common. Eventually the students got used to it.'

'You didn't answer my question.'

'That's because it doesn't merit answering.' He wanted to tell him, no, I'm not ashamed of you, but he found he couldn't speak. How could he tell him not to lie but do so himself? They sat there for some time, a chill in the air settling over them, until wisps of mist rose from the river.

'I'm bored by Edmonton.' Edward ground his heel in the dirt. 'Southgate is more exciting. Can I go to William's again?'

'I can help you get over this, become as you were before.'

'There's nothing to get over. William will teach me new things. I'll make more progress there. You have John to help here.'

On the opposite bank the mud was smooth. An animal must have slid down into the water. On the near side desiccated, tangled brambles trailed in the brook. Rocks protruded in shallow places, the water trying to run over them but having to divert around. The light was fading.

'I'll meet Joseph Green again and maybe Henry Cline or even Astley Cooper. Think how it will help me become a dresser when I start at Guy's.'

So he still wanted to be a surgeon and had confidence he could be. That was encouraging. Thomas heard Susannah's words in his head. *You don't have to treat him as your father treated you.*

'If that's what you wish and William agrees, you may go for a while,' Thomas said. 'I can spare you for a month.'

They walked back in the near dark, tripping on tree roots hidden in the shadows, walking in single file to avoid the brambles. When they arrived at Wilston Thomas retired to bed, exhausted. He knew he would hear Robbie's screams in his nightmares.

Thomas was famished. In the kitchen he found a plate of cold partridge, ripped the meat from the bones and ate it. Mr Norton of Ponders End had fallen from his horse and broken his leg. John and Thomas had set and splinted the fractured femur, but it had been hard physical work, coming only a few days after the amputation. He was again impressed by John. They'd ridden back late at night side by side in the wind and rain, then John had headed to his lodgings and Thomas to Wilston.

Thomas added more wood and puffed the fire with the bellows. The whoosh of air fed the flames and they leapt high. Now he was warm and content in the stone-flagged kitchen, with its pots and pans and bowls and herbs. Martha's kingdom as the surgery was his. He ate more partridge and drank some ale, then sat in a chair, sleepy and happy to rest. After a while he heard the front door opening and female voices in the hall.

Eliza entered, throwing aside her wool cloak. She wore a green evening dress which suited her, and her dark hair was pinned up. She reminded him of Susannah as a young woman.

'Mama has worn me out,' Eliza said. 'I need coffee.' She put the kettle over the fire.

'Thomas!' Susannah stood in the kitchen doorway, wearing a fine blue dress, and Thomas rose to his feet. 'We've had such a good evening. William Godolphin Cobb danced with Eliza three times.' She stepped into the room, flapping her fan. 'I think he may be in love with her.'

'Don't be silly, Mama.' Eliza added coffee to the pot. 'He hardly knows me.'

'But he listened so attentively and looked so handsome in his naval uniform. The Godolphin Cobbs are descended from Sir Wolstan Dixie Bart!'

Eliza bent her head as she set out the coffee cups and spoons. She moved gracefully around the table. 'That isn't the most important thing about a husband, Mama. I'd like him to be well educated and read books and discuss them with me.'

'So what's your opinion of this Godolphin Cobb, Eliza?' Thomas asked. Thomas had met the father years ago and found him rather arrogant.

'He's quite old.' She raised her eyes to Thomas and bit her lip.

'He's only thirty!' Susannah said. 'An excellent match. My first husband was much older.'

Eliza concentrated on making the coffee. The liquid bubbled in the pot and the smell diffused throughout the room.

'You don't need to rush into marriage, Eliza,' Thomas said. He watched her profile, her delicate features. She looked too innocent to marry. Since the episode with John, Eliza and he had grown apart; she didn't confide in him anymore. He doubted she would still refuse to marry any man who lived more than a mile from Wilston as she'd said in the garden last summer.

'I was already widowed at her age,' Susannah said.

Thomas didn't point out Susannah had been married to a rich, older man to support her family who had fallen on hard times.

Eliza poured the coffee and set out cream and sugar. They all sat down at the table.

'Have you had a good day, Father?' Eliza asked.

'John and I set a fractured femur. I really think John should apply for a year at Guy's to become a surgeon.'

Susannah, who was adding a heaped second spoonful of sugar to her coffee, spilt the sugar on the table.

'Are you sure that would be in his interest, Thomas?' She brushed the grains of sugar into her hand and added them to her cup.

'He has the attributes of a good surgeon.'

'Is this the same boy you said hadn't the character to be an apothecary half a year ago? The boy who insulted you and called you a quack?'

'Things have changed since then; he's matured and learnt to control his temper. His natural talent for surgery shines through.'

'Has he changed, or have you changed?' Susannah gave him a piercing look.

'John shouldn't be a surgeon!' Eliza said. 'It would be a tragedy. He loves words too much, his Shakespeare and poetry.'

'Unfortunately they don't pay the bills,' Susannah said.

'John's very talented, Eliza,' Thomas said. 'It would be a waste for him not to be a surgeon.'

'I hope you won't neglect Edward, Thomas.' Susannah fanned her face which was red from the heat of the fire.

Thomas ticked off a mental list: fevers – intermittent, continued and eruptive; smallpox, measles, scarlet fever and typhus; typhoid and dysentery; gout, lumbago and rheumatism; dyspepsia, colic and jaundice; tumours; rashes; bladder stones and strangury; convulsions, palsy and paralysis; quinsy and chincough; asthma; apoplexy; insanity; rickets and fractures; scrofula, consumption, phthisis and pleurisy; and not to be forgotten lice, ticks and worms. John had now seen or had knowledge of many of these. He was skilled at practical procedures and mixing medicines. Apart from the odd day John's melancholy had lifted and Thomas breathed a sigh of relief. It was time to talk to him again. He just needed to pick the right moment.

Robbie lay in bed upstairs in his small cottage, staring at the wall. Thomas asked his wife if she'd given the laudanum earlier as instructed. She nodded and disappeared downstairs with the baby on her hip. Thomas could see she'd been crying and was frightened to see her husband's stump.

'Today Mr Keats will dress your wound, Robbie,' Thomas said.

John looked alarmed, but Thomas opened his bag and handed him fresh lint and bandages. John had watched Thomas dress the stump for the past three days; today it was his turn.

John bathed Robbie's bandages, which were yellow from leaking fluid, in warm water. Robbie shuddered and bit his lip. John paused a little then continued, glancing at Thomas for reassurance. He unwrapped the soiled bandages and started to remove the old lint. This was the part which could be most painful if the lint had stuck and wasn't moistened enough. Speed lessened pain but too much could tear the delicate healing tissue.

'I used to do this at Guy's,' Thomas said, trying to distract Robbie. 'On my first day as a dresser I collected my tin box filled with tow fibres and strips of lint cloth. I carried the box on the ward rounds with Mr Lucas. It was a status symbol. When he'd gone I had to dress the patients' wounds.'

He didn't tell them how he'd had to grit his teeth to dress the foul-smelling, suppurating sores at first, but had hardened himself and it became easier. He'd got to know a lot of the men during the dressings, heard about their families and lives. Their good and bad luck.

'You've seen other people like me?' Robbie asked, the first sign of interest since the operation.

'Yes. Many who'd had accidents or been injured in war.'

'What happened to them?' Robbie asked.

'They went home. Back to their lives.'

'How can I live my life without my arm?' Robbie said. 'I can't even wash or dress myself.'

'You can still do many things.' Thomas struggled to think what. A scythe needed two hands, as did an axe, a pitchfork. 'You'll discover what's best.' He felt embarrassed at his blundering. The man had lost an arm. 'You have a lovely wife and baby.'

'How am I going to support them?'

John had exposed the stump, which Robbie avoided looking at. It was healing well and there was no smell or pus, no sores. Robbie was lucky. Thomas handed John the *Unguentum Apostolorum* and he applied it, then a fresh lint pad and cotton strips to bandage.

'You'll soon be up on your feet,' Thomas said.

'At least you didn't cut my legs off.'

The room fell quiet as a crypt. Thomas held his breath. He wished that after nearly thirty years he knew what to say. Astley Cooper would know.

John snorted, a great explosive snort, and laughed, his body shaking with it. Robbie joined in, until tears came to his eyes.

'Stop!' Thomas shouted, but they both kept laughing. He saw they couldn't stop; they were out of control. Thomas shook John by the shoulder and he calmed down a little but then started again. It was half an hour before both men were calm enough to leave. He told Robbie to get some rest and they would see him tomorrow. He had no idea whether the fit of laughing would help or hinder Robbie's recovery.

Grey clouds billowed across the sky and a light rain fell. Sheltering under the calash, Thomas drove himself and John back in the carriage. He was wondering how Robbie would cope with his one arm, when John shouted to him to stop. As Thomas pulled Cinnamon up hard, worried maybe they were about to hit something, John leapt down.

'Look!' John pointed across the bare fields where the sun had emerged from behind the clouds. He wore no hat and raindrops settled on his hair and cheeks.

A rainbow, its colours intense, arched over the landscape.

'Isn't it beautiful?' John said.

'It's pretty enough. But it's only light split by a prism as Newton told us.'

'I hope Robbie can see it; it will make him feel better.'

'How can a rainbow make a man who's lost his arm feel better?'

'Because beauty does that.'

'But it's transient. Even if he appreciates it, which I doubt, it will only last a few minutes.'

'No. Beauty stays with you forever in memory and imagination.'

'I still think it has no point, serves no purpose.'

'You're wrong.'

'Get back in the carriage. You'll catch your death in the rain if you get chilled.'

John looked with longing at the rainbow then climbed back up beside Thomas but craned his neck around the side of the calash until the sun went behind a cloud again and Thomas guessed the rainbow had dissolved.

Back at the dispensary it was quiet and they both mixed medicines.

'What happened to the patients at Guy's?' John asked. 'The amputees.'

'Some of them coped well, others less so. I think it was harder to lose a leg than an arm. A few were out of bed in days; some cried because they still felt pain in the phantom limb. One walked out the gates of the hospital on his crutch and straight under a carriage. Another returned with his family to thank me and bring me a bottle of rum.'

'Will Robbie cope?'

'Let's hope so. He's young and has a sense of humour.'

John bowed his head over the mortar. The scent of lavender rose from his bowl.

'You dressed the wound well, John,' Thomas said. 'You

165

could become a surgeon, as I suggested after you helped me with the amputation.'

'But I'm training to become an apothecary.'

'You need to do six months at Guy's anyway. If you do twelve you can take the surgical courses and exams as well.'

John raised his eyes. 'Do you really think I could?'

'You have a natural talent for surgery. You work hard and your Latin is good. I'll help you prepare for your admission.'

'I'm not sure.'

'You'll be better able to support your brothers and sisters. I'm sure your grandmother would have thought it a good plan.'

'Will Mr Abbey approve?'

'As a surgeon you'll be able to earn more money so the extra expense will be an investment. I can talk him round.'

'I'm not sure I'm capable.'

'Astley Cooper says a surgeon needs the eye of an eagle, the hands of a lady and the heart of a lion. I think you might have those qualities.'

'I don't think I do.'

'That's the melancholy speaking, John. It steals self-belief. With time you'll embrace the idea. Surgery will give you a purpose in life. And think of the good you could do. Much more than being just an apothecary.'

'That's true.'

'I'll talk to Mr Abbey. I'm sure he'll agree. Then in October you can sign up for twelve months at Guy's.'

'You will?'

'That's settled then. You'll be a surgeon.' Thomas was pleased he'd convinced him.

'Yes. I think I will.'

Chapter Eleven

Thomas hardly recognised the man standing at the door with his short hair, long sideburns, close-fitting, pale trousers rather than breeches and a new dark coat. The month at William's had passed and Thomas had insisted Edward come home.

'Edward!' Susannah embraced him. 'Don't you look handsome and dapper?'

'He looks like a puffed-up dandy,' Eliza said. 'What have you done to your cravat?'

Over dinner Edward was excitable, answering Susannah's questions, telling stories about Southgate and talking rapidly. He drank several glasses of wine and his cheeks became flushed. Susannah hung on his every word and pride beamed from her face. Harriet wanted to sit next to him and he teased Mary Ann gently. Eliza watched, mostly silent, but made the odd acrid comment to him.

'Do you think Napoleon will invade, Father?' Edward asked. 'I've heard he's heading to Paris.'

'Don't talk about it, Edward, please,' Susannah said.

For many years people had been frightened, even in Edmonton, of Napoleon. There had been jubilation in the village the previous year when he'd surrendered in Paris. But that sense of safety and security had ended with his recent escape from Elba.

'If he invades, I'll go straight to the coast to fight!' Edward said. 'Or if the battle is on the continent, I'll volunteer and travel to join the Duke of Wellington.'

'How can you torture me like this, Edward?' Susannah said.

'You can't be a soldier,' Thomas said.

'Why not?'

'Because you're destined to be a surgeon.'

'I could be a soldier first, or a surgeon on the battlefield. But I'd rather fire a gun or stab with a bayonet than wield a scalpel.'

'The only time you may fight Boney is if he turns up on our doorstep. You need to study your Latin more to make sure you'll do well at Guy's.'

Edward slumped in his chair and fiddled with his cravat, which was tied in an outlandish series of knots ending in a bow. 'Can't you let me do what I want just once, Father?'

'I let you go to William's. John and I have been exceedingly busy these past few weeks.'

'Please, Edward,' Susannah said. 'I couldn't bear to lose my only son.' Her voice wavered with panic, on the edge of tears.

Edward ran his hand through his short hair. 'He probably won't invade anyway. Don't fret, Mother.'

Susannah sat Harriet on her lap and held her close. 'At least my girls will never have to fight.'

After the ladies retired Thomas poured two glasses of port from the finely cut decanter that had belonged to his father. They moved their chairs in front of the fire and Edward adjusted the sleeves of his new coat.

Thomas reached out and touched the fabric. Worsted. Smoother than his own coat. It was no secret to Thomas that Susannah often gave Edward small sums of money, but these new clothes were expensive. Finely tailored. The cost would probably support Robbie Brown and his family for a year. An apothecary surgeon's clothes were always getting stained and dirty. It had been wasteful of Edward to buy new when his old breeches and coat still fit him, but Thomas didn't want to argue with Edward on his first night home.

Edward drained his port and placed the glass on the mantlepiece. Above the fireplace hung portraits of Thomas's grandfather, Robert Killingly, and father, John Hammond. Robert sat at his desk in a red coat and grey wig, looking thoughtful, his hand resting on his chin. Thomas had never met him but heard he was a kind man, a good apothecary to the village and workhouse. John wore a black coat and a white wig and stared at the viewer. A skull rested at his elbow. When he died a gentleman's magazine reported he was a man of strict integrity and a friend to the poor.

Thomas was the third generation of this family dynasty and Edward would be the fourth. He felt proud Edward would continue the family tradition and realised he didn't feel ashamed of him anymore about fainting at the amputation.

When Thomas went upstairs to bed Susannah said, 'Be kind to Edward, I'm worried he may run away to be a soldier.'

'Of course I'll be kind to him. He's my son.'

Thomas hummed as he and John readied the surgery for the day's work. They had their routine, John dusting the jars and sweeping while Thomas mixed pill paste. Thomas was looking forward to Edward's help and seeing what he'd learned at William's. It would be much easier with three of them.

Edward arrived in his new clothes, his hair and sideburns brushed. Thomas tried to reconcile this new, neat Edward with the boy he remembered with long hair flopping in his face and curling over his collar.

'Perhaps you should wear your old coat and breeches?' Thomas said. 'You don't want to get blood on those.'

'If you want a good clientele you must dress for them. Patients judge you by your clothes.'

'I hope my patients judge me to be thrifty and practical then.'

'My old ones are too worn. I can give them to John, like you did before.'

John stopped dusting. 'I don't need your charity,' he said. Mr Abbey had authorised the expense of a new coat after his grandmother died, but it was still inferior to Edward's, badly fitting and rough cloth.

The patients were pleased to see Edward and many asked to see young Mr Hammond, remembering teeth he'd pulled or pills he'd prescribed for them. The morning passed quickly although it was crowded and busy. Edward was quick and energetic in all he did and the best at pulling teeth of all of them. John was slower but was conscientious and thorough, checking with Thomas if he was unsure.

Near the end of the morning Thomas heard arguing coming from the dispensary and went to investigate. He paused at the open door. John and Edward faced each other across the bench.

'You've no right interfering with my patient!' John said to Edward.

'She's Father's patient and I do have a right when I know more than you.' Edward was pouring a reddish-brown liquid into a smaller bottle. John was bashing something green in the pestle and mortar. The clang of iron on iron rang out.

'Mrs Dalton would be best treated with feverfew.' John laid down the pestle and leant on his hands. His colour was high.

'Laudanum will be better.'

'It's too strong. It will make her drowsy and careless.'

'It will cure her headaches and help her insomnia.'

'There was no need to talk like that in front of her and make me look ignorant.'

'I was only trying to help. My Uncle William recommends it.'

'Your father recommends feverfew and he's an experienced surgeon.'

'But out of date.'

Thomas entered the dispensary. 'Quiet, boys,' he said. 'The patients will hear you. Out of date, am I, Edward?'

'Uncle William says feverfew doesn't work for headaches. Laudanum is the new thing. He hears about it from all the best surgeons at Guy's.'

'But John's right, it has side effects.'

'The patient is calmer and happier.'

'I disagree.'

'Do you dispute with Henry Cline and Joseph Green?'

'I read medical journals.'

'That's not the same as being at the hospital.'

Edward sealed the laudanum bottle and wrote the label. Laudanum for a headache? Surely not. But perhaps his son was right and Thomas was old-fashioned and behind the times.

'When I'm at Guy's the surgeons will tell me all the latest treatments,' Edward said. 'I'll learn from great men, like Astley Cooper.'

'When I'm at Guy's the surgeons will tell me all the best treatments too,' John said.

'They won't be interested. You're to be an apothecary.'

'No. I'm to be a surgeon.'

'Don't make me laugh.'

'It's true.'

'I don't believe it,' Edward said. 'You've no family tradition, no connections. Your father groomed horses.'

'He was an innkeeper! Your father suggested it and convinced me. After the amputation.'

'That can't be. Father wouldn't ask you.'

'Well he did.' John looked at Thomas. 'Didn't you, Mr Hammond?'

'That's correct.'

'No.' Edward's face lost its usual self-assurance and jauntiness. He looked forlorn, shorn of his locks and dressed in fashionable clothes too grown up for him.

'John, I'll deal with Mrs Dalton,' Thomas said. 'Why don't you go and dress Robbie's stump by yourself today? Take my bag and go now.'

John hesitated then picked up the bag and left.

'I was always the one going to be the surgeon,' Edward said.

'And you will be still. It's not a competition.'

'Yes, it is. There's only a limited number of dresserships.'

'Which you'll work hard to try and get.'

Edward sat on the stool and touched a drip working its way down the side of the laudanum bottle. His fingertip was stained reddish brown. He licked his finger and pulled a face.

'Don't you believe in me anymore?'

'Of course I do, you have great talent and skill. Look at how the patients asked for you this morning.'

'You're still ashamed about the amputation, aren't you?'

'No, I'm not. It's the honest truth.'

'John's fooled you with his sycophantic ways and his sad

little orphan boy act, but he's really a cuckoo in the nest, pushing me out.'

'Edward, he's a boy like you. He needs a profession to support himself and his family.'

'Why a surgeon? He could have done that as an apothecary.'

'He has talent too.'

'So you're championing him over me?'

'I'm helping both of you. You have the advantage of William and his connections.'

'At least I can rely on his support.'

'Go and give the medicine to Mrs Dalton. The laudanum won't poison her. Let's see whether those clever surgeons at Guy's were right.'

Edward picked up the laudanum and left the room. There were drips of dried blood on his new pale trousers.

Edward's subdued mood continued, although he was charming to the patients and his popularity grew. Susannah sided with Edward and harangued Thomas about his support for John becoming a surgeon. Edward and John fought like two cats whenever Thomas left them alone together.

One morning Thomas had asked Edward to mix a medicine from the *Pharmacopoeia* while John rolled pills. Thomas went to the herb garden to cut fresh sage. On his return he heard their now-familiar raised voices.

'I'll be dresser to Astley Cooper,' Edward said. 'I've met him at my uncle's. I think he took a shine to me.'

'No, I'll be dresser to Astley Cooper,' John said. 'Once he learns how good my Latin is. And I've been studying anatomy and reading some of his treatises.'

'My skills will impress him more.'

'I very much doubt it.'

'Less talk about how wonderful you both are and work more, please,' Thomas said.

Edward took down a jar and poured liquid from the spout into a beaker.

'What are you doing, Edward?' Thomas asked. 'That's far too much oxymel of squills.'

'It says a beakerful.'

'No. It says *cochlearium*, that's a spoonful.'

'Is it?' Edward poured most of the liquid back into the jar through the spout, spilling some.

'Was that carelessness or poor Latin?'

Edward didn't answer and kept his eyes down.

'Since I don't wish to believe it was carelessness, I see we need to improve your Latin. John, perhaps you could help Edward with his Latin tomorrow afternoon?'

'Of course, Mr Hammond. I'll bring *The Aeneid*.'

'The *Pharmacopoeia* would do, but if you prefer—'

'I don't need help,' Edward said. 'My Latin is adequate.'

'I think you do,' Thomas said. 'Now finish that mixture.'

The next afternoon both boys sat in the dispensary, their heads bent over John's book. Thomas noticed how Edward's dark short hair contrasted with John's reddish-gold long curls. But both boys possessed light and dark inside. John pointed at the text with his finger.

'That's nearly right,' John said. 'Try again.'

'Oh, forget it, what's the use? I've no interest in the ancient Greeks.'

'*Caelestius* is celestial.'

'That's never going to come up in a recipe.'

'Let's keep going. It's a great story of war.'

'The only war I'm interested in is with Napoleon.' Edward's elbow jabbed the book and it fell to the floor, a sheet of paper fluttering from it.

'What's this?' Edward picked up the paper. He read aloud. '*Ode to Apollo. In thy western halls of gold. When thou sittest in thy state.*'

'Stop!' John yelled. 'Give me that.'

'It's in your writing, John. *Bards, that erst sublimely told heroic deeds, and sung of fate.*'

John reached for the paper but Edward turned his back so John couldn't reach it.

'*With fervour seize thy adamantine lyres, Whose cords are solid rays, and twinkle radiant fires.*'

'That's mine!'

Edward held it too high for him. 'You wrote a poem. It's terrible.'

'Give it back!' John jumped to try to get the paper.

'Edward!' Thomas shouted.

'What's adamantine mean? And twinkle? Really, John, twinkle? Couldn't you think of a better word?'

John jumped higher, grabbed at the paper and it tore in two, each boy holding half.

'I can write poems too. There was an apprentice John Keats, who liked a selection of meats, and sucked on an old cow's teats.'

'Look what you've done.' John stared at the torn sheet.

'Are you going to hit me again like you did over the leeches? I should have hit back that day.'

'I thought you did.'

'Not only do you think you can be a surgeon, you think you're a poet too. That's laughable. Pathetic.'

175

'I can write poetry if I choose.'

'But not good poetry. Who do you think you are? Lord Byron? You're a ragamuffin, a waif and stray.'

'I am not!'

'You're so conceited! You've ideas above your station. You're an upstart and impostor.'

'Edward,' Thomas said. 'That's enough.'

Edward threw down his half of the paper and left. John tried to piece the paper together. His face took on the expression it had when he suffered from melancholy. Thomas felt his sadness oozing into the air.

'I apologise for my son,' Thomas said. 'Try to ignore him. His head's been turned at William's and I think he's jealous of you.'

'He's right,' John said. 'Who do I think I am? I'm no Shakespeare, Milton or Spenser. And I never will be.'

'You don't need to become a poet,' Thomas said.

John placed the torn sheets between the pages of his book and closed it tight.

'But you will be a surgeon and a good one at that.' Thomas wondered if he was giving John false hope. Would John's Latin and learning and skill be enough with no supporters apart from Thomas? Edward had Joseph Green and Henry Cline on his side. Perhaps Thomas should approach his one important connection from his past. If he agreed to help John that would make all the difference.

His breath caught in his throat at the idea. No. Thomas couldn't face the shame he would feel, the memories it would bring up, which he'd spent nearly thirty years trying to bury so deep they would never see the light of day again. Never to be resurrected.

'Mr Hammond, come quick. Mrs Collins is bleeding to death!' One of the lads from the workhouse ran into the dispensary where Thomas was mixing a milk thistle medicine for a liver complaint.

'My son's there. Why don't you get him?' he asked.

'No, he's gone. It was him that cut her and there's blood everywhere.'

Thomas grabbed his coat and ran after the boy back to the workhouse. Mrs Collins, an elderly woman, lay on her bed, white and sweating, the veins in her hands collapsed into gutters. The bandages applied after bleeding were soaked in blood, which dripped onto the blankets and floor. Thomas raised her legs to help her circulation, applied new bandages tightly to stem the flow and stayed to check it had ceased. Mrs Collins's colour revived and she thanked him. When he asked Mr Pike where Edward was, Mr Pike didn't know.

That evening Thomas sat in his study, waiting for Edward to appear. The clock ticked past ten on the mantlepiece and he was about to go to bed when Edward walked in swaying.

'Mother said you wanted to see me?' His speech was slurred.

'Edward, I had to rush to the workhouse to see Mrs Collins. She was still bleeding.'

'I'm sure the bleeding had stopped when I left. She must have exerted herself.' Edward perched on the corner of the desk.

'An elderly bedbound woman can hardly exert herself.'

'Maybe she turned over or tried to get up?'

'You should know by now one of the first rules of bloodletting is to check the blood has stopped before leaving the patient. Surely your uncle has taught you that in all your time there?'

'At my uncle's we don't attend to old women at the

workhouse. He prefers to treat the ladies of Southgate. They call for him when they feel faint or dizzy and he mixes medicines for them, but even his presence, the touch of his hand calms them down.'

'That's because there's nothing wrong with them except a lack of purposeful activity. I know that sort of woman who swoons and needs the surgeon. I give them short shrift.'

'William says he helps them and they pay well.'

'Do you still want to be a surgeon?'

'Of course. William says it's good to train as an apothecary and a surgeon to make a good income.'

'But do you want to be a real surgeon? To try for a hospital post?' Thomas held his breath.

'Yes. I met Astley Cooper at William's, he came with Joseph Henry Green one day. Mr Cooper seemed well disposed towards me, and my uncle recommended me to him. Perhaps I'll be his dresser.'

His arrogance astounded Thomas. Didn't he realise one had to be exceptionally good or very well connected to be a dresser to a hospital surgeon? There were only twelve appointed each year out of seven hundred medical students. Thomas had been lucky to be chosen by William Lucas Senior in his time.

'You do realise I need to sign a testimonial that you've done five years as my apprentice for you to attend Guy's?'

'That won't be a problem, will it? My five years are nearly finished.'

A problem? Thomas had taught him the basics; Edward was competent in many things and yet…

Thomas stood and gripped Edward by the shoulder.

'Where have you been all afternoon?'

'In the dispensary mixing.'

'You were at the Golden Lion, weren't you? I can smell the alcohol on your breath.'

'I only had a few drinks.'

'Not only are you uncaring, you're also a liar.' Thomas stepped backwards towards the window, to get away from him. 'You must take life more seriously. If you're to apply to Guy's next summer to become a surgeon you must work harder.'

'Work, work, work! That's all you ever care about. Never enjoying life or having fun, or just being.'

'My work puts bread on the table and clothes on your back. If it weren't for my work you'd be a pauper in rags. I won't always be here to support you; you must be able to earn a living.'

'You'll be around for many years yet, Father,' Edward said. 'Don't drive me so hard, let me have some life. I don't want to be like that miserable gnome John Keats.'

'That miserable gnome worked all afternoon.'

'I wish I was back at William's.'

'I'm not letting you go back there. That's where you've learned these bad attitudes.'

'At least there I was appreciated.'

Edward left the room and slammed the door. The draught of air was like a slap in the face. Thomas felt like chasing after Edward, grabbing him by the lapels, shouting at him, telling him a few truths. That he was lazy and conceited and had no integrity. That he was spoilt and cossetted by his mother and William. His fingers flexed and squeezed into fists. He felt like hitting him, but that made him feel ashamed. He didn't want to be like his father and lash out in anger. He must control himself. He unclenched his fingers, sat down and placed his head in his hands.

Thomas couldn't sleep. If he could fuse the two boys together he would have the perfect apprentice and future surgeon. Edward was decisive, enthusiastic and energetic. The patients warmed to him. John shone at mixing, his Latin was outstanding and his knowledge was good. He could be hesitant, but he was careful.

Thomas turned over and over, tangling his nightshirt around his legs. What would Astley Cooper make of Edward, and Thomas's teaching of him? It wasn't only Edward's poor Latin that troubled him. Or his attitude to John. The more he saw of Edward's medical practice the more he doubted him. He used laudanum far more than Thomas thought wise, he didn't measure ingredients accurately, he was slapdash in his bloodletting and his bandages unravelled. Thomas had tried to talk to Edward about these things, but his son wouldn't listen.

Soon he would have to sign the certificate to say each boy had satisfactorily completed five years as his apprentice, to gain admission to Guy's. William had expressed no concerns. In fact he had sung his praises. Was William's practice all it should be? Edward's ideas about laudanum must be coming from someone.

But today Edward had reduced a difficult, displaced Colles fracture brilliantly. And he'd staunched a haemorrhage when Mr Green cut his leg on a rusty plough. Surely he had a bright future as a surgeon.

One Sunday in April after morning service Thomas greeted the vicar and spoke to a few patients who approached him then wandered in the graveyard among the headstones, the raised ledgers and tombs. A sweet scent floated from the gnarled, twisted crab apple tree full of pink blossom. Swallows dipped down from the sky, a blur of wings with occasional flashes of their white breasts. He was puzzled how he could see this beauty in the midst of the burial plots. Beauty and death, existing side by side.

His father's gravestone stood in one corner. Green lichen encroached on the lettering, but the inscription was still legible.

John Hammond Apothecary Surgeon of this parish
Died 15th April 1790 aged 57 years

Twenty-five years ago today since he died. He hadn't been that old, only eight years older than Thomas was now. His father had been strict but fair. Thomas remembered the time when he was quite young and his father had sent him to collect leeches, but it was such a fine day he stayed by the brook trying to catch minnows. The minnows were almost transparent in the clear water, holding themselves against the current, but darted away as soon as they saw the shadow of his hand. His father had been so stern when he returned late he'd felt ashamed and that had been the end of lingering outdoors on his errands.

Then when Thomas was his father's apprentice there was the time he'd found Thomas writing a label incorrectly, two spoons instead of one. It was only a syrup of hyssop to ease a cough, it wouldn't have harmed the patient, but he'd impressed on him the seriousness of his mistake.

His father had fretted on his deathbed, wanting William to take over the practice at Wilston. Perhaps if Thomas had become a surgeon things might have been different. Thomas was glad he never knew of his shameful secret.

What would his father make of Edward? Thomas had reviewed a case Edward had attended the day before and found the rash of spotted fever. Edward denied it had been present when he visited, but it was so florid Thomas wondered if he'd even looked at the patient's skin.

'Thomas?' Susannah stood by his elbow. She wore a bonnet trimmed with flowers which suited her. 'Are you coming home?'

'I was thinking about my father. He was a good man.'

'I'm not sure he approved of me, apart from my money.' The long ribbons tied under her chin gave her a girlish look. 'You look so serious. Is something wrong?'

Perhaps if he discussed his concerns with her it would help. Her advice to take John back after the row with Abbey had been sound.

'I'm concerned about Edward's competence.'

'But I've heard him tell how he's pulled teeth and bled and cured diseases. William talks highly of him and the patients like him.'

'There's more to being an apothecary surgeon than popularity. He needs to build his character.'

'Do you demand he's miserable and suppresses his natural vivacity?'

'He lacks… conscientiousness and dependability.'

'How can you assess those qualities?'

'It's lots of little things. He doesn't listen to me, takes shortcuts, does his own thing, thinks he knows best.'

'William may have taught him to do things differently from you, that's all.' She turned around as if to leave.

He'd let him spend too much time at William's. Edward had picked up bad habits and attitudes. Blossom blew from the crab apple tree and landed on the dark mound of soil on a nearby fresh grave. The grave of a young boy with smallpox Thomas had been unable to save.

'I'm starting to doubt whether I can vouch for his five years' training with myself.'

She turned to face him so quickly the long ribbons of her bonnet swung out from under her chin.

'Will you vouch for John?' Her voice was sharp as the crab apples from the blossom would be.

'Yes.'

'Your charity has gone too far. You think more of him than your own son.' She clutched her prayer book tight in her white gloved hands.

'If Edward wasn't my son I wouldn't even consider signing the certificate.'

'And if you don't sign?'

'Edward will have to do another year as my apprentice.'

'I think you're being cruel to hold him back when you send John, and all Edward's friends and relatives expect him to go.'

'I must protect patients from harm.'

Susannah looked at him for so long he had to avert his gaze. He should have realised she would always put family before patients, but he couldn't.

'Are you sure you're not doing it to punish Edward for spending so much time with your brother and praising him?'

'He isn't ready for Guy's.'

'Have you no feelings? He'll learn what he needs at Guy's. Think carefully. A good father would sign.'

She marched towards the gate which led to Church Street, past the rows of headstones, some straight, some leaning, some new, some ancient. He turned back to his father's headstone, but he felt no connection with the man and received no comfort.

Chapter Twelve

Thomas was called to see Mary Curtis's little girl, Rachel, his miracle, who was nearly five years old. He'd treated her for minor illnesses and maintained a fondness for the child after her difficult birth. Mary met him at the door, holding her six-month-old baby, her three-year-old boy tugging on her skirts.

'Rachel's so weak she can't get out of bed,' Mary said. 'She says her hands and feet hurt her like insects crawling under her skin.'

Rachel lay in the only bed in the cottage, tossing and turning in her sleep. Her cheeks, nose and lips were red. Her hair was thin.

'Has she had a fever or sore throat?' Thomas asked.

'No, but now she won't eat because she says her teeth wobble.'

Rachel woke and cried out in pain. Mary sat her up and rubbed her hands and feet. A rash was visible on her neck and saliva drooled from her mouth. Mary wiped it away with her own dress.

Thomas took the child's hand and examined it. The nails were coming away from their beds and the skin peeling on her fingertips. He asked her to open her mouth and gently touched a tooth. It fell out under his finger, as did another. He closed his hand around them and offered them to Mary, but she shook her head so he slipped them into his pocket. He told Rachel to close her mouth and patted her on the cheek.

'Have you given her any medicines you bought from anyone?' he asked. 'The horse doctor or midwife or druggist?'

'I always call for yourself, Mr Hammond,' she said. 'Your apprentice left a medicine a few weeks ago, and I've been giving it to Rachel every day.'

'Can I see it?'

She rose to fetch the bottle from a shelf and he asked, 'Which apprentice?'

'Your son, Edward. He was very good with Rachel. He said we should give it three times a day until she was better.'

The large bottle was brown glass, crusted around the stopper. It was nearly empty. Thomas read the ingredients: peppermint, jalap, coriander seeds, cream of tartar. He struggled to read the last one, struggled to decipher Edward's messy handwriting. Mercury. And the directions: to take one spoonful every three days.

His hand shook and he nearly dropped the bottle. Rachel began crying again and despite Mary's efforts wouldn't stop. The noise caused a physical pain in his head. He took a deep breath to calm himself.

'This medicine doesn't seem to be working. Let me take it back with me and I'll send out something to help with the pain. She must also have beef tea to build her up.'

'She will recover, won't she?' Mary stroked Rachel's hair and a clump fell out. She stared at it in disbelief.

'She's very ill, but there is hope,' Thomas said. 'There is always hope.'

During the rest of the visits Thomas's stomach knotted with worry about Rachel. He hurried back to the surgery to find Edward sat on a stool yawning, unshaved with dark circles

185

beneath his eyes. His new coat, the one he'd arrived home wearing in February, had a rip in the sleeve and his cravat was all askew. The *Pharmacopoeia* and an empty pestle and mortar rested on the bench in front of him.

'What can I mix for a headache and nausea?' He rubbed his temple and groaned. Thomas knew he meant for himself, not a patient. He suspected he hadn't come home from The Golden Lion 'til the early hours.

'A large dose of mercury? The same medicine you prescribed for Rachel Curtis a few weeks ago.'

'Who?' Edward fiddled with one of his cuffs, which was dirty and had the sleeve button missing. Thomas hoped he hadn't lost it as it was silver and a gift from Susannah.

'The little girl in the cottage at the end of the main street. Why did you even prescribe it?'

'Constipation. That's one of Uncle William's favourite remedies.' His face brightened as he talked of Thomas's brother.

'She's been taking it three times a day instead of every third day as it says on the label.' Thomas put his hand in his pocket, withdrew Rachel's two small teeth and held them in his open palm in front of Edward. Their enamel shone pure white, unlike the yellow of adult teeth. The insides were black hollows. 'Her teeth are falling out.'

'Milk teeth do fall out in children.'

'I've never seen all the baby teeth come loose at once due to natural causes. She'll need a liquid diet, which is inconvenient and expensive. Her nails are coming away from their beds and she's in great pain. All symptoms of mercury poisoning from an overdose.'

'It's not my fault the mother gave too much. Can't she read?'

'Mary Curtis grew up in the workhouse then became a servant, but she's not stupid. If you'd told her the dose several times she would have remembered.'

'How was I meant to know that?'

'There's no use prescribing a medicine the patient doesn't know how to take.' Thomas placed the milk teeth on the bench.

Edward appeared to be studying the *Pharmacopoeia* and turned its pages, which crackled. Thomas took down the jar of milk thistle seeds, *Silybum marianum*, which he needed to mix the medicine for Rachel to try and counteract the mercury. He placed the jar so hard on the bench he feared it might break. An angel looked at him from the glazed surface with questioning eyes, his large feathered wings spread above the label then curved inwards to almost meet underneath. Thomas removed the vellum lid to discover the jar was nearly empty. He would need to travel to the druggist in Southwark for more, but he could make a small quantity of medicine now. Milk thistle was expensive, but he wouldn't charge Mary for it. He would also send Martha with liquid foods and hope Mary would accept them.

Thomas weighed the small shiny black seeds and ground them in the mortar with the iron pestle. They were difficult to grind to the fine powder he needed and his fingers cramped from the effort, but he persisted. Edward continued to study the *Pharmacopoeia*.

'She may not survive,' Thomas said. 'I saved that little girl the day she was born. The midwife wanted me to use the destructive instruments, but I refused.'

'I didn't intend to harm her.'

'No apothecary surgeon intends to hurt patients, but your lack of care has injured her, using dangerous ingredients and not checking the mother knew the dosage.'

Edward hung his head and scraped the pestle on the side of the bowl, which made an annoying noise. His shoulders were hunched, his spine bent. He looked pathetic. How could this boy be his son?

'Stop making that terrible noise!' Thomas added alcohol to the milk thistle powder and left it to soak. The alcohol vapour stung his nose but cleared his head. 'I think we need to discuss your future.'

Edward raised his eyes. 'I'll start at Guy's in October and train to be a surgeon as we planned.'

'I think you would benefit from more teaching and experience before you go to Guy's.'

They faced each other across the bench, the scarred bench where they'd measured and weighed ingredients and mixed medicines together, where Thomas had taught him, corrected him and tried to instil integrity and proficiency in him.

'I'll have done five years with you soon.'

'You've spent too much time at William's.'

'He has more patients than you and runs three carriages. The local gentry call for him when they're ill.'

'He hasn't taught you well.' Was it disloyal to be critical of his brother? But the safety of patients must come first.

'By your methods and standards, you mean?' Edward's voice was barbed with sarcasm, but Thomas took his words at face value.

'Exactly. Edward, I think it best if you stay and do another year as my apprentice.'

Edward pushed back his stool and rose to his feet, taller than Thomas across the bench. 'Father, I can't bear to spend another year running errands and doing lowly tasks.'

'You must, Edward.'

'And if I wish to go to Guy's anyway, against your wishes?' His eyes bored into Thomas. His jaw was set. Thomas was reminded of the time as a child when Edward insisted on staying in a tree even though it was getting dark. Susannah and Thomas called and called, and Thomas threatened but he would not come down and in the end they left him there.

'You can't because I won't vouch for your five years.'

Edward's face darkened; he picked up the pestle and dropped it into the empty mortar. The clang echoed in the surgery and Thomas tried to swallow but his mouth was dry.

'But you'll vouch for John?' Edward tugged on his lapels, his fists clenched.

'Yes, I'll vouch for John.'

Edward paced up and down in front of the apothecary jars. He turned on his heel several times. 'Then I'll ask my uncle to vouch for me. He can use his influence with Astley Cooper and Joseph Green.'

'He may agree, although strictly he shouldn't. However, there is one more obstacle.'

'What's that?' Edward stopped pacing.

'Money. I won't pay for you to attend Guy's unless you do one more year as my apprentice. I very much doubt my brother will offer to pay your fees.'

Edward breathed deeply and started pacing again. 'This isn't fair!' he shouted. 'You're always criticising me, thinking John is better. Just because he's sycophantic to you. You can't stand my independence, that I disagree with you. Well, I'll show you what I think of you.'

Edward inserted his hand behind the end jar on one of the shelves holding Thomas's father's apothecary jars, the blue and white stoneware painted with Latin names, flowers, birds and

189

cherubs. He ran his hand along behind them and pushed the jars over the edge of the shelf. Thomas reached out for them with outstretched arms but couldn't catch them. Angels and cherubs fell to earth. The crash was tremendous, like a volley of muskets firing. The jars broke into thousands of pieces. Shards of all shapes and sizes lay on the floor, some razor-straight, others jagged. The contents of the jars oozed out and pools fused together, liquids swallowed dry seeds and powders. The smell of aniseed and linseed and sage, cardamom and clove and cinnamon, mixed with sickly rosewater, overwhelmed Thomas.

Thomas caught sight of Edward's distraught face. Edward stood motionless, his shoes islands in a sea of fractured china and contaminated medicines. Thomas saw that Edward realised he'd done something terrible, but Thomas could find no forgiveness in his soul.

'Get out of my sight!' Thomas shouted. 'And don't come back.'

Edward ran out of the surgery, leaving a trail of sticky footprints. On the floor before Thomas, in the debris, fragments of china showed peacocks with their tails cut off, flowers broken from their stems, angels and cherubs with no wings, and Apollo with a crack across his face.

Thomas didn't know how long he stared at the broken apothecary jars, but he came to his senses and realised he must finish the medicine for Rachel. He bottled it and also prepared a small bottle of laudanum. His hand shook so much he could barely write the label. His writing was spidery and blotched.

'Mr Hammond?' John walked into the dispensary, returning from a visit to bleed a patient at the workhouse. 'What's happened?'

'There's been an accident.'

'How could this be an accident?'

Thomas concentrated on writing the labels for the bottles. If he could write perfectly maybe everything would go back to normal.

'Your precious jars… all those ingredients…'

He must help Rachel, save her.

'Shall I clear it up?'

'I want you to deliver this medicine straight away and explain to the mother how to take it.' Thomas handed John the two bottles and gave the address. 'Go quickly.'

After John left Thomas took a bucket and dumped the remnants of broken Delftware in together, wearing gloves to protect his hands. There was no point trying to salvage the jars. Some broken things can't be mended. He was filled with yellow bile, the parched dry heat of summer, the flames of a burning fire. It built in him until he could stand it no longer and thought he might combust.

In the garden he threw the pieces in a corner. They flew through the air and landed in a pile. He made several journeys, then mopped the floor, pushing hard, finally sinking to his knees to scrub the last of the stubborn stains. Some of the liquids had penetrated the wood and the marks wouldn't come away however hard he scoured. Dark, overlapping patches remained. The empty shelf on the dresser kept catching his eye. What had possessed Edward to do such a thing? Thomas would need to buy new jars and ingredients, but he would never be able to replace the jars. They weren't manufactured anymore.

Could Edward be mended? Susannah had spoilt and pampered him. William hadn't been firm with him. Edward had a weak character, prone to influence. Thomas should have been stricter with him. Others were fooled by his outward enthusiasm and high spirits. Sometimes Thomas thought only he saw his real character, what was underneath. His father would have seen it if he were still alive. He'd have beaten Thomas severely if he'd broken even one of his jars on purpose.

Thomas was grateful to be called out on a visit and concentrate on treating the patient. Then there was a difficult childbirth miles away and he returned late in the evening. On the ride home, the reins loose in his hands, his horse's hooves clopping on the road under him, his body swaying in the saddle from fatigue, he felt calmer and told himself Edward needed his help and guidance. If only he could convince him to do another year he could save him. Edward could still be a surgeon. He thought of going to Edward's room to talk to him, but he worried his anger might resurface and undo all his good intentions. He would talk to him tomorrow.

That decision to wait 'til the morning returned to haunt Thomas over the coming months. He was woken by Susannah telling him Edward's bed hadn't been slept in and she couldn't find him anywhere in the house. He told her he hadn't seen him since yesterday afternoon.

'Did something happen between you two?' She hadn't brushed her hair or put her daytime cap on and looked oddly young and vulnerable. 'He was in a bad mood at dinner but refused to tell me why.' She twisted her long hair in her fingers.

Thomas sat up in bed. 'I told him he would have to spend another year as my apprentice.'

'How could you? After we discussed it.' She sank onto the bed next to him and pulled at the counterpane with nervous fingers.

'He nearly killed a little girl with mercury.'

'You're exaggerating.' Her expression hardened and she folded her hands in her lap.

'He smashed my apothecary jars to shards. They're ruined and all their contents.'

'You must have pushed him to it, by being angry with him.' She drew her shawl tight around her shoulders.

'I wasn't angry. I was calm and logical. I told him the truth.'

'You're angry now, I can tell, underneath that calm exterior.' She stared at him, seeming to see right into his heart. But he wasn't going to admit she might be right. What Edward had done was beyond the pale.

'Perhaps he's making medicines in the surgery,' Thomas said. 'I'll go and check.'

He dressed quickly, passed a few waiting patients on his way to the surgery, and entered the dispensary, greeted by the unpleasant lingering smell of yesterday's spilt medicines. Edward wasn't there. He was about to leave to tell Susannah when he saw a scrap of paper on the bench, with Rachel's two milk teeth on top of it. The note was dotted with ink stains and the signature underlined. He tried to decipher Edward's messy handwriting. His eyes saw the words, but their meaning didn't register. He read the note again.

Gone to fight Napoleon, Edward.

It was quiet in the surgery apart from some chatter from the patients outside and a phrase of birdsong. Yesterday Edward had sat across the bench from him. Now there was this inexplicable note. He walked slowly over to Wilston, telling the patients John Keats would soon arrive to see them.

Susannah's eyes scanned the note and her lips mouthed the words silently. Then she repeated them aloud.

'He can't mean it,' Thomas said. 'He's only trying to frighten us.'

'Thomas, you must ride after him, you may still catch him,' she said. Her face was pale and her body shook. She grabbed his hand and held it so tightly it hurt.

Edward's horse was missing from the stable. Thomas saddled Cinnamon and headed along the road to London, asking after Edward on the way. A few people had seen him last night, riding south, and Thomas was hopeful he would find him asleep under a tree, his horse grazing nearby, or eating at an inn, but then the trail went cold. The further away from Edmonton he travelled, the harder it was to ascertain if people had seen Edward or another boy. If only he had a distinctive horse, but bay geldings were commonplace. Thomas kept telling himself his son was a silly boy, he must be hiding because he was embarrassed to come home. He might even be home now. The yellow bile was still within him and waves of anger spread over him about the events of yesterday and today. Edward was inconveniencing him greatly and taking him away from his patients. John would have to cope with all the work. Thomas had told him he needed to be away for a short time and instructed him to call for William if he needed help.

Thomas skirted the City. If Edward's note were genuine, he would head for the coast. On the road towards Kent he questioned a group of soldiers camped by the side of the road, but they hadn't seen a boy matching Edward's description. They told him they were being sent to the continent. He explored some side roads, in the blind hope Edward might have headed down one. He rode further towards Dover and saw cannons and wagons being dragged over potholes in the road. A tightness settled on his chest. For the first time he thought maybe Edward really had run away to fight Napoleon. He remembered him waving wooden swords in playfights when he was young, his recent comments and enthusiasm about being a soldier. Then he told himself of course not, Edward wouldn't do anything so rash. But despite this the tightness on his chest turned into a feeling of dread, and as he became more worried his anger towards Edward sank with the sunset. The sun was an orange ball, aflame, the sky streaked with pink and purple. He could see the beauty of it, but beauty had never felt so hollow.

The inns were full so Thomas tried to sleep beneath a hedge. The ground was hard and unyielding and he lay awake for a long time. His words spun around his head like a whirlpool in Salmon's Brook: *Get out of my sight. And don't come back.* Over and over, round and round, he couldn't banish them. He wished he could take them back, eat them, swallow them, even if they poisoned him. Edward was a headstrong, foolish lad who'd been spoilt by his mother and indulged by his uncle, but Thomas was the one who'd driven him away. He would forgive Edward everything if only he came home safely.

Thomas woke to a steady drizzle and grey light. He was stiff from sleeping on the ground and picked grass from his hair and clothes. More soldiers marched past on the road; carts and wagons rolled by. He wasn't going to find Edward like this. It was hopeless. He headed for home.

Susannah ran out of the front door of Wilston to meet him, her face falling when she saw he was alone. She burst into sobs.

'There's no sighting of him after a few miles,' Thomas said. 'I tried my best but there are so many ways he could have gone.'

'Can't you go further?' She held tight to his arm as if someone might try to drag her away.

'I went down the Dover road. I asked many soldiers, but none had seen him.'

'You can go back tomorrow. Go all the way to Dover.'

'Susannah, it's no use. He's disappeared. And I can't leave the patients too long.'

Susannah lifted her hand and slapped his cheek. The sharp noise rang across the front garden. His head jerked to the side and he was so surprised he nearly fell over. His skin stung as if he'd fallen into a patch of nettles.

'Thomas, for once, put your family before your patients. For years I've endured you putting them first and held my tongue, but this is too much.'

'They need me. John can't cope alone.'

'Edward needs you. I need you to look for him.' She swayed on her feet.

Thomas led her into the drawing room, sat her down in a chair and knelt beside her.

'Looking for him would be a fool's errand, like looking for a grasshopper in the orchard.'

'I blame you for this. If you'd vouched for him and not favoured John, my son would still be here.'

This felt too much for Thomas. If she hadn't spoilt him things might have been different. He knew he shouldn't hurt her more, but he couldn't resist, saying, 'You're the one who manipulated me into taking John, remember?'

She let out a keening wail, the sound he heard from the poor mothers when their babies died. 'Do you think I haven't thought of that?'

He tried to put his arms around her, but she pushed him

away with force. He left her in the drawing room. He should check John was coping with the patients but first he needed a few moments alone. His cheek tingled with the shame of being hit by his wife.

In his study he sat with his head in his hands. His cheek burned where his palm rested against it. He breathed in and out deeply. Thoughts of Edward swirled in his mind: where he was, if he was safe. The books on the bottom shelf were in his view. He remembered the night he'd read some of *The Tempest* when Eliza was so ill. The bones of coral. He still sometimes saw them in his dreams. He pulled the book from the shelf and turned the pages, starting at the beginning. He read aloud hesitantly, stumbling over unfamiliar words. A rhythm emerged and he continued. A storm was raging and the men were in danger of drowning. Of course, a tempest was a storm. Like the storm in his own household. He wondered if the men would drown. Then an old man and his daughter. The daughter asking him to stop the storm. Like Thomas and Eliza. He still had Eliza, and the girls, whatever happened to Edward. And he still had to look after John and help him become a surgeon. Storms could be weathered.

He felt calmer; only a faint sensation of heat persisted in his cheek. He closed the book, returned it to the shelf and headed to the surgery.

Chapter Thirteen

The empty shelf in the dispensary brought on feelings of loss. Loss of his father's precious jars and loss of Edward. Thomas tried to push them away. A boy in a black coat stood with his back to him, mixing, his head bent over the bowl. What was Edward doing here? He'd run away. The boy raised his head and turned around, reddish-gold hair catching the light. It wasn't his son.

'Everything fine?' Thomas asked.

'Can you see James Cory?' John asked. 'He fell off his pony yesterday. His elbow was painful and swollen, but the radial pulse was absent.'

Fear seized Thomas. A supracondylar fracture of the humerus. He imagined the boy's arm developing gangrene and turning black.

'I called for your brother as you told me, but he was on another visit.'

Thomas should have stayed with his patients. A poor young boy would lose his arm because he was on a fool's errand after his wayward son.

'So I tried to reduce it and splint it myself.'

'You did what? How did you hold him down?'

'His father helped. I was anxious at first, but I knew speed was vital. I read Mr Cooper's treatise again before I attempted it.'

'Did the pulse come back?'

'Yes. I told his father to call me if the arm went cold or white.'

'Excellent. Well done, John. Let's go and visit him now to review it.' Thomas picked up his bag and headed out the door.

'Is Edward ill?' John asked. 'I haven't seen him for three days.'

Thomas thought of lying, of saying Edward had gone to William's, but he didn't see the point. The truth would come out eventually.

'He says he's gone to fight Napoleon,' Thomas said.

'Napoleon?' John's mouth was agape.

'He's a silly boy. He doesn't know what he's doing. We had an argument.' Thomas looked at the empty shelf of apothecary jars.

'Was it he who broke the jars?'

'Let's go and see young James Cory.' Thomas was full of admiration for John. He'd been brave and strong at the amputation, but this showed initiative and skill as well. He could make a great surgeon, but Thomas knew he would need help to do that, would need someone with influence and power on his side. Thomas really should ask his connection to help John, but every time he thought of it panic engulfed him. John would have to forge his own path.

Thomas scoured *The Times* for news of Wellington and the allied armies amassing on the Continent. Each day brought more speculation war was approaching. He felt flattened by a grey cloud of dread hanging above him. At night Susannah slept on a bed in the younger girls' room. She rarely spoke to Thomas but accused him with her eyes. Those deep brown eyes he loved, the same as Edward's eyes, reproached him and made his heart ache. He told her they didn't know Edward had gone to join Wellington. He could be anywhere.

A few days after his abortive search, Thomas passed Edward's room and felt a strange sensation someone was in there, as if Edward might be sleeping and he only needed to push open the door to find him. He heard a noise inside, held his breath and looked in. Susannah knelt by Edward's bed, holding one of his shirts and burying her face in it.

'What are you doing?' Thomas asked.

'It still smells of him,' she said. 'I'll never let it be washed.'

'Susannah,' he crossed towards her and held the arm of the shirt, 'this isn't rational.'

'Rational? You expect me to be rational when my son has run away and is likely to be killed any day now?'

'I don't think it's helpful.'

'Well, I find it a mite comforting, and it's all the comfort I have. Don't deny me that.'

Thomas tried to take the shirt from her, but she pulled in the opposite direction and he feared it would rip.

'Leave me, Thomas, leave me alone.' She lay on the bed and sobbed. He stood there, helpless, not knowing what to do, her pain cutting into him. He didn't know how to comfort her. It hurt too much to see her sobbing and he left.

The next day, coming in late from a visit, Thomas knocked on Susannah's sitting room door and opened it. Susannah didn't look up from brushing Mary Ann's hair. Harriet played with a doll at their feet.

'Your dinner is in the kitchen,' Susannah said.

'Will you come down later?'

'No, I'm tired. I'll go to bed soon.'

Sitting eating a plate of cold lamb, Thomas felt very alone.

He missed Susannah's company, her chatter, even the village gossip. Thomas heard footsteps coming towards the kitchen, but it wasn't Susannah. Eliza came in and warmed her hands over the fire. He suggested they could sit in the drawing room, but she said she'd rather stay where they were.

They sat in silence. The flames lit her face, and she frowned, but he couldn't guess what she was thinking.

'I've been invited to the Godolphin Cobbs' tomorrow,' she said. 'But I don't know if I should go.'

'Is your mother accompanying you?'

She shook her head. 'She says she needs to stay here, in case Edward returns, but Mr Godolphin Cobb's sisters can chaperone me.'

'Why don't you go then? It will be a break for you.'

'Where do you think Edward is?' Eliza asked.

'I really don't know. Maybe on the continent, maybe anywhere. I wish he would contact us.'

'It's funny but I miss him. Even though he was so conceited and annoying.'

'Me too.'

'I sometimes think Mama would rather I were missing.'

'I'm sure that's not true.'

'She's very cross with you.'

'She blames me for driving him away. I was cross because he nearly killed a little girl, Rachel Curtis. He didn't even seem to care. Perhaps I was too harsh on him.'

'I don't think it was your fault, Father.' She placed her soft hand on his and he felt tears well in his eyes.

Thomas threw himself into work to distract himself. When he was involved with patients he could often forget about Edward,

201

until something reminded him: a difficult tooth extraction Edward would have enjoyed, an amusing patient, a broken bone he'd have liked to set. Then he had to push away the thought of him. Patients asked where Edward was, but he told them he was visiting friends.

It was busy with just the two of them again, but he and John worked well together. John bled and cupped and blistered. He dressed ulcers, prescribed medicines and lanced abscesses, but he also listened to people, his whole attention on them. He lacked Edward's supreme confidence, but perhaps that wasn't a bad thing. He was kind.

As they worked side by side from early in the morning 'til late in the evening, Thomas was more and more impressed by John. His fatherless apprentice deserved the chance of a bright future. Thomas had been deluding himself thinking John could just walk into Guy's and become a great surgeon. It would take more than that. John had no connections apart from Thomas, no family in the profession. Thomas doubted William would agree to introduce him to Joseph Green and Henry Cline. Thomas knew a way he could help, but that meant Thomas would have to do something he'd thought impossible. To confront his fear.

The Guy's Hospital anatomy theatre was packed. Thomas had made enquiries and planned to arrive at the end of the lecture, but it must be running late. Not that the students cared. The only sound from the two hundred or more of them was their pens scratching. Perhaps he should turn around and go straight back to Edmonton. No. He'd come here for a purpose. He crept up the steps to the top row of seats and squeezed onto the end. All the way on the journey here he'd felt nausea, which now intensified to the verge of retching.

The elliptical room was illuminated by light pouring through the skylight. Below him Astley Cooper paced the floor. It was the first time Thomas had seen him in twenty-eight years. Astley's face was slightly plumper and more red-cheeked, but still handsome. His hair had receded from his forehead, making him look more learned. Astley spun a revolving table, picked up a femur from a small selection of bones and began discussing hip fractures. For all his fame and success his voice hadn't lost its Norfolk twang. He placed his leg, clad in tight black breeches and white silk stockings, on the table to demonstrate hip movements. He'd always been vain about his legs, a strange trait for a man with such a brilliant mind.

At the end of the lecture students gathered round Astley to ask questions. Thomas remained at his bird's-eye view. Eventually they left and Thomas descended the stairs as Astley tidied up the bones on the table.

'Astley?' Thomas said. He'd forgotten how tall Astley was. The sight of him, the nearness of his physical presence, was like the bodysnatchers forcing the iron bar under the coffin lid, prying it open, to expose Thomas's shame.

Astley looked up from examining a femur, but for a few seconds Thomas feared his former friend and colleague didn't recognise him. Had Thomas changed so much since they'd last met? Perhaps Thomas had aged more or perhaps he was just less memorable.

'Thomas?' Astley asked. 'Is it you? Welcome.' Astley grasped Thomas's hand and shook it firmly with both of his. Thomas felt the strength of hands that could saw open skulls and tear limbs apart but were also so delicate they could stitch a severed artery back together. He felt calmer.

'I was in the Borough to see a druggist. I hoped I might find you.'

'How's provincial practice?'

'Not so exciting as hospital, I'm sure.'

'Why have you been hiding? You should come out to Abernethy's place in Enfield. He's forever debating with Lawrence about Mr Hunter's theory of life. Do you remember the discussions we had about that?'

Of course he remembered. Their enthusiasm, their hopes for a better world, their beliefs they could make great discoveries, cure disease and alleviate suffering.

'My apprentice will be applying to Guy's in October,' Thomas said. 'Would you take him under your wing?'

'I've already met your son at your brother's. A fine lad.'

'Not Edward. My other apprentice, John Keats.'

'Why should I help him?' Astley had always been direct and said what he thought.

'He has the potential to become a great surgeon, but his father was an innkeeper. He'll need a patron. You know how necessary that is to advance. Your uncle was a surgeon at Guy's, my father an apothecary. John has nobody.'

'I'm not sure. I don't know him.'

'He's a hard worker and already shows skill in surgery. He's assisted at an amputation and held firm. He's set bones and performed difficult deliveries. Why, the other day when I was away, he reduced a supracondylar fracture according to your treatise.'

Astley ran his finger along the shaft of the femur on the table, pausing at the sites where the tendons attached, the bumps and ridges. He cupped the spherical head in his hand. Where had the bone come from? A corpse stolen by bodysnatchers or an amputation at the hip, one of the most prolonged and painful operations ever performed by Astley.

'I can't help you, Thomas.'

'But—'

'Do you know how many fathers ask me to help their sons? Wanting me to give them special attention. I can't do it. It's impossible.'

That was it, the definitive answer. He'd been a fool to even think Astley would help, just because they shared a past. Astley was the great surgeon in silk with regal bearing, Thomas the mere apothecary in his worn coat, drab and slouching.

Someone entered the lecture theatre. 'Have you got those bones, Astley? I need them for a teaching session.'

Thomas knew that high, nasal voice. His skin crawled as if infested with lice. He forced himself to turn around and saw a tall, ungainly man with stooping shoulders and a shuffling walk. Someone he'd hoped never to meet again.

'Billy,' Astley said, 'you remember Thomas Hammond, don't you?'

'What?' Billy Lucas Junior put his hand to his ear. He always had been deaf as a post.

Astley repeated his words and Billy looked at Thomas intensely. Thomas wanted to disappear, to gallop home and be back in the surgery at Edmonton, anywhere but under this man's gaze.

'Yes, of course.' Billy slowly offered his hand and Thomas reluctantly took it. Billy's palm was like onion skin. Thomas let go as soon as he could without actively tearing his hand away.

'What are you doing here?' Billy asked. Perhaps he thought he'd banished Thomas forever from Guy's, that he had no right to come back.

'I came to see Astley.'

'His apprentice is starting in the autumn,' Astley said.

'I need that bone.' Astley gave him the femur and Billy excused himself.

'Please give my regards to your father,' Thomas shouted after him, but he wasn't sure he'd heard. His palms were sticky with sweat.

Astley rearranged the bones on the table: half of a pelvis, a tibia and fibula.

'How was he awarded a surgeon's post?' Thomas asked. 'He was always so delicate he was never in the dissecting room with us.'

'The post was left vacant by his father, that's why,' Astley said. 'Unfortunately he didn't inherit any of his father's skill or flair. He's the worst surgeon in the hospital, rash in the extreme, cutting amongst important parts as if they were only skin. I spend a lot of my time sorting out his mistakes. He cut the flap for an amputation wrong so the bone was left uncovered and I had to amputate the leg higher up.'

The scar on Thomas's hand itched. He tried not to scratch it but couldn't help himself. The skin around it flared up red and angry.

'Remember this?' Thomas showed his hand to Astley. When they were medical students Billy's hand had slipped during an operation and cut Thomas with a scalpel. Pure carelessness. Thomas had spent a week worrying he might die if the wound became infected, agonising days inspecting his hand for a red line creeping up his arm signalling death.

The scar throbbed and Thomas felt lightheaded. 'Can we sit down?' he asked.

Thomas and Astley sat on the front bench, the bench

students fought over to be close to the lecturer. They'd been here side by side as students listening to Henry Cline, Thomas copying Astley's notes.

Astley sat in a relaxed posture. His face was serene, almost jovial, as if he might crack a pun any second. It didn't bear the agonies of all the suffering he'd inflicted on his patients over the years. Their pain wasn't carved into his features, wasn't preserved in deep furrows and lines on his face.

'Do you ever think of the boy from that night?' Thomas asked. The question felt risky but necessary.

'Briefly, when you appeared today.'

'I do, often.'

'I have other things to think about. Operations and research and how to help patients.'

How many limbs had Astley sawn off, how many skulls had he trephined, how many bladders had he cut and how many babies had he destroyed piecemeal? Thomas couldn't imagine. He saw a pile of limbs high as a house.

'How can you operate every week, knowing you cause such pain and distress, witnessing it?'

'During surgery a surgeon must be deaf to the pains of his patient and forget any present anguish in the pursuit of his lasting goal, otherwise he couldn't do it.'

'So you're indifferent to it?'

'Perhaps I was as a younger man. I'm lucky I feel little physical pain myself and find I can tolerate that of patients. A natural talent.'

'And now you're older?'

'I have sympathy for my patients. Real feeling for the suffering of others prompts a wish to relieve those sufferings as naturally as the needle points to the pole.'

'But what if the feelings flood and nearly drown you?'

'That's rarely happened to me. I cried when operating on a fourteen-month-old girl who reminded me of my daughter who died and I was greatly disturbed by a woman who cut her throat and stomach. Not by her wounds but by her despair and hopelessness. Most of the time I can control my emotions.'

'How do you control them?'

'Practice, I suppose. Strength of will. I've always said a surgeon needs an eagle's eye, a lady's hand and a lion's heart.'

Thomas remembered that night, the boy's screams, his distress at the pain Thomas inflicted to try to help him. He could never have the strength of will to withstand that, but he did have the strength of will to try to help John.

Astley stood up and crossed back to the table with the bones. Thomas followed him.

'You would like Keats,' Thomas said. 'As well as surgical skill he shows sympathy to patients.'

'The question is, do I trust your assessment?'

'You know my capabilities. If things had gone differently I could have been a surgeon too.' Thomas paused and assessed Astley's face. What was his massive brain thinking? Did their closeness nearly thirty years ago mean anything to him now? Thomas saw nothing hopeful in his countenance and spoke in desperation. 'I know it was my fault, but I think you owe it to me, Astley.'

Cooper snorted and rubbed his nose. 'Ha, ha!' But he looked discomfited. He twirled the table with the bones. It span round and Thomas feared the bones might fly across the theatre, but they blurred into a white circle.

'I've never told anyone you assisted me,' Thomas said. 'At least you kept your career.'

'I regret what happened to you. I would have tried to help but I became ill with fever soon after then went to Edinburgh.'

'I've never asked you for anything before,' Thomas said.

Astley stopped the table spinning, picked up the tibia and tapped his palm. The skylight was obscured by cloud and the room dulled.

'I'll keep an eye out for Keats and help him if I can.'

'Thank you. Perhaps you would consider him becoming your dresser?'

'Wouldn't you rather your son became my dresser? I heard Edward wants to be a surgeon too.'

Thomas hadn't prepared himself for that question. He felt struck dumb. How could he answer it without sounding disloyal to Edward? Or admitting his son had run away to fight Napoleon? He struggled for an answer until he found something he could say to Astley.

'Edward already knows Joseph Green and through him Henry Cline. He doesn't need my help.'

'I see,' Astley said, but Thomas wasn't convinced he did.

'Keats won't disappoint you.'

Astley thumped Thomas on the back. 'You must come out to Gadebridge House for dinner one day soon. We have so many years to catch up on.'

'Thank you, that's very kind,' Thomas said, but he suspected he would never receive an official invitation. He wasn't important enough in Astley's world. Even if Astley did invite him, Thomas would feel inferior, a mere apothecary surgeon amongst Astley's high-powered connections. Thomas hadn't written treatises or pioneered new operations. He treated patients with common illnesses: headaches, fevers, coughs.

They said goodbye and parted. Thomas hoped he'd done

enough to secure John's future. He didn't see how he could have done more.

On the way back to fetch his horse Thomas saw a bookshop, but this wasn't Cox's medical library where he bought his medical books, and he hesitated outside, staring in at the high, packed shelves. He pushed the door and entered into the dim interior, the smell of smoke and leather. The bookseller appeared beside him, balding and dressed in a dark coat. Respectable. Thomas felt like running away but stood his ground.

'Is Sir looking for anything in particular?'

'I want a poetry book.' Thomas wondered if Astley ever read poetry or literature. He wished he'd asked.

'That shelf.' The assistant pointed.

The books stood next to each other in their leather covers, brown or blue or even green or burgundy. So many of them. Some with gold-tooled lettering. He didn't recognise most of the names. How to choose?

'I want a present for a young man who enjoys poetry,' Thomas said. 'As appreciation for his hard work.'

'Has he read Byron? He's very popular.'

'I don't think so.' Thomas had never seen Byron on John's bookshelf or seen him reading it.

'Perhaps *Childe Harold's Pilgrimage* Cantos One and Two?'

Thomas nodded and handed over coins. He left clutching the volume in his hand. He hoped John would like it.

The carriage careened up to the gate of Wilston and Susannah leapt out before it stopped. Her stout figure ran up the garden path and hammered on the door. Thomas, returning from a visit in the village, was startled to see her so uncharacteristically active.

'Susannah!' He hurried to her. 'What's happened?'

'Oh, Thomas. I have news.' Her face was red, her eyes wet and her lower lip trembled. She leant on his arm, panting.

Thomas waited, convinced it would be bad news. Edward had been killed in a fall from his horse, a fight, a shooting accident, a bayonet slip. Martha opened the door and Susannah stepped inside, pulling Thomas with her.

'He's found!' Susannah said.

'Master Edward?' Martha helped Susannah remove her cloak.

'Where?' Thomas asked.

'I must sit down. I feel all giddy.' Susannah went to the drawing room and lay on the chaise longue. Her chest rose and fell rapidly.

'Is he well?' Thomas asked. 'Tell us.'

'Let me catch my breath. Yes. He's at William's. William sent a note so I took the carriage straight away to Southgate. I tried to find you, Thomas, but no one knew where you were.'

'Oh, Mistress. I'm so relieved.' Martha wiped her eyes with her apron. 'I did miss the young master.'

Thomas found his legs wouldn't hold him and sank to the end of the chaise longue by Susannah's feet. Edward wasn't two hundred miles away on the continent but two miles up the road. He was alive. The wall restraining Thomas's pent-up emotions tumbled down. He didn't know whether to laugh or cry. He felt like doing both at once.

'Martha, could you fetch me a drink?' Susannah said. 'I think I need a glass of brandy. Have one yourself too.'

Thomas declined a drink and waited while the women drank theirs. Then Martha went back to the kitchen and Susannah sat upright.

'But what happened?' Thomas asked. 'I thought he went to fight Napoleon.'

'We must tell the girls!' Susannah said.

'In a bit,' Thomas replied. 'Tell me what happened.'

'Well, Edward did head for the coast and Dover. If you'd continued you might have found him and saved me a lot of worry.' She poured herself another brandy. 'But he couldn't find a way to cross the Channel and had to sleep rough and it was cold and wet and he changed his mind about fighting and came back to Southgate.'

'But why did he go to William's instead of here? Perhaps he called and we were out, but Martha would have been in. It's very strange. I don't understand.' He stood up and paced in front of the fireplace, in front of the cockatoo fire screen.

'Calm down, Thomas.'

'There's something wrong, isn't there?'

'Thomas, you must go to William's.'

'Why didn't you bring him back with you?'

She put down the empty glass and clasped her hands. 'He refuses to come home because of your argument. You said unforgivable things.'

Get out of my sight. And don't come back.

'So did he. And what about my apothecary jars?' What about angels and cherubs falling to earth, smashed shards of pottery littered on the floor, medicines oozing around them, Apollo with a crack across his face?

'Go now in the carriage and apologise and he'll come back. I'm sure.'

'Apologise for what? He's the one who nearly killed poor Rachel. No. He must come and apologise to me for his behaviour.'

'Thomas, you must go and ask him to come home.'

'Why is William sheltering him? He should make him come home to us.'

'He won't because he supports Edward. He understands him.'

'Understands him? That's laughable. I suppose he understands why he almost killed a child with mercury.'

'I beg you, Thomas.'

'I won't.'

She stared at him and he wondered if she would slap him again. He felt the ghost of the sting on his cheek.

'I despair of you, Thomas. Will you never learn? I'm going to tell the girls the good news.'

Thomas thought John liked his gift of the volume of Byron. At first John had looked surprised, but maybe that was just because Thomas was giving him a book. Thomas explained it was for all his hard work. John had read the title and a frown appeared on his forehead but was quickly erased. He'd turned the pages and thanked Thomas, but Thomas never saw him reading it in the dispensary as he did with many of his other poetry books.

After his visit to Astley, part of Thomas felt lighter. When he looked at John he saw what a good surgeon he would make and was pleased he'd asked Astley to help him. He'd confronted his fear of seeing Astley again and remembering the boy's suffering from that night long ago. He often thought about their talk. Two patients soon presented the challenge of putting Astley's advice into practice.

Mrs Straw's youngest had pneumonia. The baby struggled

to breathe, his tiny ribs pulling in and out, and his lips were tinged blue. Mrs Straw cradled him in her arms. When he first saw the baby Thomas felt the familiar hopelessness. The baby could well die and the mother would be distraught, but he thought of Astley's words. He would think of it as an operation. He assessed the child and decided on the best medicines, dispassionately. Now you can show sympathy, but don't let it overwhelm you. Control yourself. You are more help to the baby and mother that way. He told the mother the baby was very ill, but he would mix some medicines. The mother cried and he patted her arm, telling her he would do his best. Outside the house he found he was shaking, but he hurried back to the surgery to mix the medicines.

To his relief the baby survived. He couldn't have kept this up if it had died.

Mr Lee fought for breath. He'd suffered with his lungs for many years, but the situation had deteriorated. He coughed and coughed, trying to expectorate phlegm. He was very thin and weak. Thomas felt his coughs were wracking his own body. He felt overwhelmed. What would Astley do? Do all that was necessary medically. He assessed Mr Lee and decided a cough linctus might help and a small dose of laudanum. Show sympathy. He talked to Mr Lee kindly. But control it. He found he could manage it.

Practice, strength of will, a lion's heart. If he did this enough he would become better at it; he would learn to control his feelings.

Chapter Fourteen

October 1815

October 1st was a crisp autumn morning. The trees displayed leaves of yellow, orange, russet and copper along the main road to London. John rode a hired horse, which was too big for him, but he handled it well, while Thomas rode Cinnamon. Thomas remembered making this same journey thirty years ago with his father. He'd been so excited. That day he knew his father was proud of him.

'I don't see why autumn is seen as the season of decay,' John said.

'Because things die,' Thomas said. 'Those trees will be stripped bare after the next gale.' That was a pity; he would like them to last longer.

'But there's so much abundance. Everything is full and ripe. Apples and fruit and nuts.'

'I suppose you have a point,' Thomas said. He wondered why John was thinking about autumn instead of the great adventure ahead of him.

'Shall we go faster?' Thomas asked. 'To get to Guy's quickly?'

'Yes! I can't wait to arrive and start.' John spurred his horse onwards, Thomas following.

The City of London rose before them, smoke-free at this early hour, with no hint of the poverty and suffering held within it. Other people appeared, heading towards London on foot, in carts, on horseback or in carriages.

When they reached Bunhill Fields John halted his horse. Through the railings lines of headstones, stone slabs, chest tombs and obelisks stretched as far as the eye could see. The graves and monuments of dissenters and nonconformists. John looked at the ground in front of the gates and a dark expression clouded his face.

'Is something wrong?' Thomas asked.

'Somewhere here is the place my father fell from his horse,' John said. 'He hit his head and was found bleeding. I wonder exactly where it was?'

'John, don't distress yourself.'

'He'd visited me and George at school. I was eight years old. Perhaps if he hadn't visited us, he wouldn't be dead.'

'We can't change the past,' Thomas said. 'I'm sure your father would be immensely proud of you today. As would your mother and grandmother.'

'The world is full of troubles. Suffering is the only certain thing. There's so much pain.'

'Come, John. This isn't a day to think like this. It's a new beginning, a fresh start. You will be learning how to relieve suffering, as you asked me that day you first came to the surgery.'

They stabled the horses at Moorgate, near the Swan and Hoop where John had lived as a child, next to Bedlam with its statues of melancholy and raving madness, then crossed the City on foot. It was Sunday and bells rang out chiming and singing good tidings.

After crossing London Bridge, they entered the Borough, that dirty, crowded, heaving slum. It hadn't changed since

Thomas had taken lodgings there as a medical student. A crowd of people crushed them and Thomas put his hand in his pocket to protect his money. Slops came flying out of windows, requiring quick dodging, and a stink arose from open ditches full of sewage. Urchins covered in crusty scabs, their hair alive with lice, their legs rickety, watched them with large, hungry eyes. Thomas knew better than to give one a farthing; they would all demand the same and hordes more would appear. A group of men gathered round dogs fighting and John watched, fascinated, until Thomas pulled him away.

A man in tattered clothes and a battered top hat sat next to the gate of Guy's. Thomas would have walked past him if he hadn't spoken. 'Something for a veteran of Waterloo, Sir?' he asked and held out his hand. The man's face was brown from dirt, his hair long and matted, but he was young. He sat on a trolley; his breeches were tied in knots where his knees should be. Thomas fumbled in his pocket and handed him several coins, a mix of florins, shillings and sixpences. That could have been Edward if he'd gone to Waterloo. What must it be like for a young man to lose both legs? To have stumps?

'Come on, Mr Hammond,' John said, and they walked through the gate into the courtyard of Guy's.

'There's the statue of Thomas Guy, the founder,' Thomas said as they walked past. 'He built the hospital for incurables, which other hospitals wouldn't take. Hope for the hopeless.' Thomas Guy had left a great legacy. He'd still be remembered in two hundred years.

Behind the statue was the grand facade of Portland stone. Above a row of arches, columns soared upwards from the first to third floor. A grand pediment surmounted the columns. Between the columns were bas reliefs of a child with a leech, a child with a tourniquet and a child with a lancet. Thomas remembered the excitement, standing here thirty years ago, with his father, the feeling he was going to be admitted to the mysteries of surgery like his brother William and prove himself.

'It's like a Greek temple,' John said, his eyes bright.

They entered under the middle arch into two inner quadrangles divided by a colonnade. Two men carrying a patient on a stretcher bumped into them and John leapt out of the way. Patients wandered seemingly aimlessly along the cloisters at the edge: some heavily bandaged, women carrying tiny babies, amputees dipping and swinging on crutches. One with his nose destroyed by a syphilitic gumma, leaving a hole in his face, walked straight up to John and startled him. Thomas saw the look of horror on John's face. He remembered the feeling of being the minority of well among the sick, the worry they would drag him down to join them.

'Remember, this is the place of the sick,' Thomas said. 'But you're not one of them.'

The smell of smoke drifted from the open fires on the wards, not quite hiding the taint of festering wounds. 'Those are the wards, above the cloisters,' Thomas said. 'That's where you'll follow the surgeons on ward rounds. The wards are the most modern in London with flushing toilets.'

'I can't wait to follow Astley Cooper,' John said. His eyes were wide, glistening, taking it all in.

Pairs of young boys and older men hurried towards the Guy's counting house. A queue had formed outside the door which was not yet open. Thomas and John were jostled and John nearly hit back when pushed, but Thomas counselled restraint. From the conversations around them he gathered many of the boys were with their fathers, who were apothecary surgeons. An ache arose in him. He'd always imagined bringing Edward to register at Guy's, as his father had brought him. He must push that feeling aside. John had worked hard and deserved to be here. John was his apprentice; he'd trained him for five years. Wasn't that what mattered, not blood ties?

At last the door opened and they tumbled in like water through a sluice. John registered as a surgical pupil for twelve months and handed over his fee of twenty-five pounds and four shillings. A large expense, but well worth it, as Thomas had convinced Mr Abbey.

Next they queued on the stairs leading to the lecturers' room, which was by the anatomy theatre, on the same floor as the dissecting room. Thomas detected a whiff of decay from the dead house. They were squashed in the lobby outside the lecturers' room, but John elbowed his way through and Thomas followed. Astley Cooper stood there with his book.

'Astley,' Thomas said, 'this is John Keats.' Would Cooper see the potential Thomas knew was there? What if he didn't think much of him?

Cooper surveyed John from head to foot. Perhaps he thought him too short? Too common?

'Your master has persuaded me you have talent,' Astley said. 'I hope you live up to his promises.'

'I'll try my best, Sir,' John said.

'And you're happy with the lodgings at St Thomas Street? Sharing with a dresser and surgeon's apprentice will be helpful to you.'

'It was most kind of you to arrange it, Sir,' John said.

John paid Astley ten guineas for his lecture series on anatomy and the same for dissections, and Astley wrote his name in his book. Thirty years ago Astley had been a pupil like

Thomas; now he would give the lectures. John then signed up with the other teachers for lectures in the theory and practice of medicine, chemistry and materia medica.

John would need to buy medical instruments from the gunmaker, textbooks at Cox's medical library and notebooks bound in soft, thin leather. Thomas would have liked to stay and help him, but he needed to return to Edmonton.

They walked out of the hospital. In the courtyard with the statue, Thomas saw the chapel on his left. It had only been a few years old when Thomas started, the stone shiny and new, but it now looked faded and worn. Thomas had crept there after that terrible night, sitting in one of the pews, his head bowed, praying, but it hadn't given him solace. He hoped John's career would fare better than his.

The veteran of Waterloo was still begging at the gates and Thomas walked a few paces further along the street.

'I should get back to my patients,' Thomas said.

John thanked him and said he would return to Edmonton to visit soon. Watching his short figure walking down the street, Thomas thought about what lay ahead for John. Getting up early for lectures, going round the wards with the surgeons, watching operations in the theatre and dissection. Thomas wanted to run after him, give him advice, keep him safe, but he restrained himself. It was a difficult path, but he didn't doubt John could follow it. John's future was in his own hands now. Thomas's job was done.

Thomas walked back through the Borough reluctantly. He'd enjoyed feeling part of a new beginning and been happy for John. John was starting again, as Thomas wished he could. He was proud to have attended Guy's, he had affection and nostalgia for it, but also felt shame about what had happened there. As he crossed over London Bridge his legs felt heavy and he felt fatigued.

Thomas collected his horse and rode towards home. Thirty years ago his father must have ridden home this way, full of pride and hope. What had happened to that? Thomas hadn't lived up to his father's expectations and his pride had turned to disappointment then indifference.

As he rode further towards home a melancholy descended on him. A cold mist arose from the ditches at the side of the road. He'd imagined this day in his mind for many years, the pride, the excitement. Coming to Guy's, signing up at the counting house, but it had always been Edward he was bringing. His son would continue the family name of Hammond in the medical world. His son would achieve what Thomas hadn't and become a surgeon.

John was a good lad and talented, but he wasn't his flesh and blood. It wasn't the same.

The bright leaves no longer shone. Piles of rotting leaves lay by the roadside, matted together, an earthy smell rising from them. John was mistaken. Autumn was the season of decay, not fruitfulness. He should have brought Edward today.

Susannah was right. He must swallow his pride and ask Edward to come home.

Everywhere he looked Thomas saw expensive items Susannah would love. The chandelier with crystals refracting light, the shining silver vases, the thin porcelain, the pictures and the velvet curtains. William lifted a cut-glass decanter and poured him a glass of brandy. Thomas tasted it and tasted its worth. He'd never kept brandy that good at Wilston.

'So nice of you to visit,' William said, settling into his chair in front of the blazing fire. 'I haven't seen you since when?'

'Before Waterloo.' Before Edward ran away.

'You must have been busy with only one apprentice to help.'

Thomas drained the brandy, shuddering at its kick, and placed the glass on an inlaid table next to him. He pulled his cuffs down. 'I've come to take Edward home.'

'But will he want to go?' William stroked his sideburns with one hand. These and his thick hair gave him a leonine appearance. Did William possess Cooper's heart of a lion?

'You've been very kind keeping him, but he's my son and I want him back with me.'

'I don't know why you made all the fuss. He's a perfectly capable apprentice and could be a good surgeon.'

'He nearly killed one of my patients. A little girl.'

'You're making a mountain out of a molehill.'

Thomas felt six years old again, arguing with William, knowing he'd lose because he was younger and smaller and weaker. Some of the anger at that powerlessness stirred in him.

'He prescribed mercury as a cure for constipation and the mother accidentally gave too much.'

'That's a perfectly acceptable remedy. I use it often.' William didn't even look perturbed.

'He learnt it from you.' Thomas's anger surged. 'You may use it, but Astley Cooper advises against mercury, except for venereal disease.'

A flicker passed across William's face, a preparation for combat. He leant forwards in his chair, squashing his belly in its straining, embroidered waistcoat. 'How do you know what Cooper thinks when you haven't seen him in nearly thirty years?'

'I read his treatises.'

'I don't understand you, Thomas. You trained with him

yet avoid him like the plague. What happened between you? I heard rumours of something unsavoury. Was it a woman?'

'I saw him the other day when I took John to Guy's.'

'You've registered John at Guy's, but what about Edward? Will you sign his certificate?'

'That's my business.'

'Surely you want him to qualify as a surgeon? To continue the family name?'

The family name of Hammond. The Hammonds of Edmonton. What would have happened if William had taken over the practice and Wilston as their father wanted? Would there be anyone to treat the people at the workhouse? Would the drawing room look like this, drowning in wealth? Thomas still didn't know why their father had wanted William. Because he thought he was the better medical man, or because he'd heard rumours from Guy's about Thomas's secret?

'I suppose you want Edward back to help you now you're on your own,' William said, pulling Thomas out of his thoughts.

'Has he been helping you?'

'A little, round the surgery. I'm grateful. I have James too, of course.'

Even in this William had bettered him, having a son who'd attended Guy's, been dresser to Astley Cooper and passed the exam of the Royal College of Surgeons. Where had Thomas gone wrong?

'He's my son and I want him to come home. Will you call him for me?'

William drained his brandy and left the room.

Thomas wished he could have another glass of brandy, or swig straight from the decanter. Five months was a long time not to see one's only son. *Get out of my sight. And don't come back*. Edward had obeyed him for once, taken him at his word. He remembered the look on Edward's face, after he'd smashed the apothecary jars, the realisation he'd done something terrible. If only Thomas had found it in his heart to forgive him then.

Edward took three paces into the room and stopped. Thomas stood and stared at him. The relief. His son was here, alive. As if somehow Thomas hadn't truly believed it and it was only a rumour he was staying at William's. His face had filled out, too many of William's rich dinners, no doubt. His hair was shorn short and sideburns long, not the wild curls of his boyhood. Thomas wanted to embrace him. He stepped forward but Edward avoided him and sat down. Thomas was shaken at the rejection.

'William said you wanted to see me,' Edward said. Cold as ice on the brook in winter despite the heat from the fire.

'I'm so pleased to see you, Edward.' Thomas sat back down. 'I want you to come home.'

'Why?'

'So I can prepare you for Guy's next year.'

'I've done the five years I need.'

'You've missed the entry this year, but you may as well come back with me. Your mother misses you.'

'I suppose that poisonous gnome Keats has started.'

'This is nothing to do with him.'

'If that's what you think, you have no idea.' Edward took a handkerchief from his pocket and twisted it round his finger so tightly Thomas worried he might cut off the blood supply.

'Let's make a fresh start as father and son. I have a new apprentice, a fourteen-year-old. He'll do most of the chores and you can teach him.'

'I should be at Guy's attending lectures and ward rounds.'

'I can see now the mercury was an accident, a misunderstanding about the dose. I don't approve of mercury, but you weren't to know that.' He must try and be charitable, understanding.

'William uses it.'

'I overreacted about Rachel. I was much too harsh on you.' His tongue thickened at the lie. Could Edward hear the insincere tone in his voice?

Edward untied the handkerchief and folded it back in his pocket. This was it. He was preparing to come home. He stood.

'No, Father, I'm not coming home.'

'I insist. You can't stay here.'

'Uncle William says I can stay as long as I want. I'm very welcome.'

'Your mother misses you. And your sisters.'

'Mama visits here often. She can bring the girls.'

'But your mother said if I apologised you'd come home.'

'That was months ago. You've left it too late.'

'Please...' The heat from the fire was intense. Thomas's brow sweated with it.

'I'm not even sure I want to be a surgeon anymore.'

'You don't mean that. I've been preparing you to be a surgeon for years.'

Edward walked from the room. Thomas wanted to grab the tails of his coat, to claw him back, but he couldn't move. Too late. Too late. All around him reflections hurt his eyes, from the chandelier, the silver, the fire. He wanted to pick up the cut-glass brandy decanter, throw it across the room and smash it.

Many plants in the herb garden had withered or died with the end of summer and onset of autumn. Some had gone to sleep,

225

hiding underground as roots, tubers, bulbs or seeds. Thomas picked green, notched leaves of vervain, *Verbena officinalis*, from a large bush. The weak sunshine gave no warmth, and a light breeze contained a nip of the coming winter. A figure came towards him and he saw it was Eliza, dressed up in her long pelisse. She removed her bonnet and swung it in in a wide arc by its ribbons. Her hair was pinned up, but small curls had escaped, framing her face, and her cheeks were pink from the wind.

'What are you gathering?' she asked.

'Vervain.'

'Strengthens the nervous system, treats migraines and headaches of the bilious kind.'

'You remember!'

'You taught me well.' She removed her gloves, picked a leaf of vervain, twirled it in her long, slim fingers and let it fall to the ground.

'Did you enjoy your visit?' Thomas continued to pick the leaves into a bowl.

'William Godolphin Cobb has asked me to marry him,' she said.

Thomas stopped midway in picking a leaf, so his fingers held the hairy surface, but he didn't pull it from the stalk. Even though he knew Godolphin Cobb had been courting her, he hadn't expected this to come so soon. He tugged the leaf; the stem bent and the leaf tore away.

'Will you accept his proposal?'

'Do you think I should, Father?'

What did he think? He thought he couldn't bear not to see her face and talk to her every day. She was only twenty, plenty of time to get married. She would most likely conceive and childbirth would endanger her life. He wanted to keep her here at Wilston forever, the Eliza who'd run in the orchard with her sisters and asked him to teach her about plants.

'He's from a good family, well mannered, a gentleman,' Thomas said. And yet he detected something superficial and dull in him. He'd retired from the Navy yet had no burning desire to do anything else.

'He doesn't read books or discuss poetry, but he's kind and I think he truly cares for me,' she said.

'Do you want to marry him?' He tried to remain calm, but the thought of Eliza leaving made him feel panicky. He put down the bowl of vervain leaves, worried he might spill them.

'I think so.' She drew the edges of her pelisse together, overlapping them over her dress, and shivered. Her bonnet hung slack from her arm. She put it back over her dark hair, struggling to tie the ribbons in a neat bow, and turned her back to him.

'What does your mother say?' Thomas asked. Advice on affairs of the heart was Susannah's department more than his.

'I know what her answer will be. I wanted your opinion.'

Eliza ran her hand over the seedheads of honesty, next to the vervain bush. Silvery, translucent, papery ovals held the seeds inside. The ovals were attached to the plant by thin brittle stalks and Thomas worried they would all fall or blow away in the wind. They didn't have a medicinal use, but he'd planted them because Eliza loved them.

'I think you should do what you wish.'

She turned to face him again. 'If you agree I would like to marry him.'

'If you're sure that's what you want you have my blessing.' He put his arm around her shoulders and drew her close.

Perhaps it wouldn't be so bad. They might live nearby and he could see her most days.

'There's one more thing I need to tell you,' she said. 'We will live in Brentford.'

Brentford. It must be twenty miles to Brentford. The honesty rattled in the wind. He saw some seed pods were torn and ripped, others split in half and empty of the seeds which had been so carefully protected inside.

The remaining leaves withered on the trees and fell to the ground. Gales blew in from the west and the wind constantly whined, setting Thomas on edge. Work was unceasingly busy, Thomas's new apprentice Samuel slept in the surgery in John's old room, but he was a mouse-like boy, quiet and easily startled. Thomas missed John's experience and steadiness.

But the amazing thing was that Thomas found it easier to cope with the pain and suffering he saw. Instead of the terror of seeing patients in agony and being overwhelmed by their pain, he found he could control his emotions. It was difficult but the more he practised the easier it became. The feelings of hopelessness lessened, and the need to block his feelings out completely. And he could still be sympathetic. That trip to Astley had shifted something in him.

At the end of October Thomas travelled to Southwark to acquire some medicine from a druggist, and after he'd procured this he decided he would visit John. He should be free after afternoon dissection.

On the way to John's lodgings he came across a crowd shouting and jeering. At the centre of their circle a bear was chained to a tall stake by a metal collar. It rose on its hind legs while a pair of English bulldogs snapped at it. One of the dogs plucked the bear by the throat. The bear clawed at him in vain. Its coat was bare in places and the skin bleeding. A man in a purple outfit and floppy hat took money for wagers on the match. Thomas turned away. In his youth he enjoyed watching such sport, but now he felt it was unfair on the bear, the odds stacked against him.

It was already getting dark when he arrived at 28 St Thomas Street. A young man let him in and directed him to John's room. The house smelt strongly of tallow and on the ground floor were great vats where the chandler dipped wicks to make his candles. It wouldn't matter if the stench of dissection came home with John, for this smell of dead cows and sheep was as bad.

'Mr Hammond! What are you doing in the Borough?' John turned from his desk, where several tallow candles burned, rose to meet him and shook his hand.

'Some business. I'd forgotten how brutal this area is. I've just passed a bear being baited in the street.'

'Did the bear swipe at the dogs like this?' John gave an impression of the bear. 'Then the dog growls and crouches down.' He acted the part. 'And the ruffian character in the purple hat was there? I love watching the spectacle.'

'I thought it cruel, but at your age I also enjoyed watching.'

On John's desk lay a notebook, its open pages covered in John's small, neat hand with doodles of flowers in the margins. *Physiology* was written at the top. 'How are your studies?'

'Mr Cooper's lectures are most entertaining and informative.'

'He always was the showman.'

'And he's considerate to the patients when he goes round the wards. His manner is like physic.'

The London Dissector lay on the desk. 'Ah! They're still using this.' Thomas flicked through, looking at the drawings. The images brought back memories of his time studying at Guy's. 'How's dissection?'

John was quiet and Thomas noticed the smell of the dissecting room on him above the smell of tallow from the house, and the stains on his sleeves. He'd probably been there half an hour ago. Thomas remembered the maggots, the smell and the livid colours of decaying flesh.

'I have a strong stomach,' John said. 'At least the corpses don't feel anything. The operating theatre is a trial. If only we had something other than laudanum and alcohol for pain.'

'The Holy Grail of medicine.'

'Sometimes I can't stand the cries and must leave.'

'That's a common reaction. You must concentrate on the good the surgeon is doing, that the suffering will be worth it. When you learn that your skin becomes thicker.'

'I hope it doesn't take long.'

John trimmed the candles, and when Thomas expressed concern he was being profligate burning so many he confided they pinched them from the chandler downstairs, who charged them enough in rent. The room was sparse with just a bed, desk and chair. On a shelf were the books John had brought to the surgery years ago and new ones. It was getting cold as the fire wasn't lit. The room faced onto the street and coaches trundling by shook the floor like a shiver. But it was close to Guy's, convenient for lectures and the wards and dissection.

'There's good news,' John said. 'Mr Cooper told me I'm to be appointed to the next vacant dressership.'

'John, that's wonderful! I knew you'd impress Astley Cooper.'

'It might be with Mr Forster or Mr Lucas.'

'I'm sure it will be with Astley Cooper.' Thomas patted him on the shoulder. 'You're on your way to becoming a surgeon, John. I feel it in my bones.' Astley was helping John as he'd asked. Thomas felt proud he must agree with his assessment of him.

'The money is a worry. I hope Mr Abbey will release the funds...'

'I'll see to it he does. It's an investment in your future.'

John picked up his quill and walked in front of his desk, separating the barbs of the feather so it looked messy. 'I wonder if I'll cope, helping at operations and dressing the stumps.'

'Your fellow dressers will support you. The patients will be grateful. We should go for a drink to celebrate!'

John tidied some papers on his desk. 'I've a lecture on surgery soon, with Mr Cooper, and study to do later.'

'You mustn't miss your lecture. We can celebrate another time.'

'Yes.' John looked up and waited.

Thomas felt perhaps John wanted him to leave, but he didn't want to go back to Wilston, where his new fourteen-year-old apprentice who knew nothing would be waiting for him. He was thrilled to be so close to Guy's and surgery and Astley Cooper through John, and longed to prolong the experience.

He picked up a book from the desk, expecting perhaps one of Astley Cooper's treatises.

'What's this?' he asked. '*Poems by William Wordsworth*,' he read aloud, '*including Lyrical Ballads*.'

'Wordsworth is excellent. There's been no such poet since the days of Spenser and Milton.' John's face shone with the passion Thomas had seen the first day he came to his surgery.

Except then the passion was for medicine. 'He's even written a poem about a leech gatherer.'

Thomas noticed other poetry books on the desk, and scribbles which might be poems.

O Solitude! if I must with thee dwell,
Let it not be among the jumbled heap
Of murky buildings; Climb with me the steep

John saw he was reading and snatched away the paper.

The sight of the poem angered Thomas. He placed the Wordsworth heavily down on the desk.

'It's only a few lines I wrote because… I felt a bit lonely,' John said. 'And I miss the countryside.'

'Take care poetry doesn't distract you from your true calling, John.'

'I'm fully committed to my studies,' John said. 'I'm busy but I can still read and write poetry. They won't interfere with each other.'

Thomas wanted to believe that was true. A man put his head around the door and asked if John wished to play billiards or whist and have a drink. John replied he would after his lecture.

'I should probably head back to Edmonton,' Thomas said, half hoping John might ask him to stay and join them. He remembered fondly drinks and discussions at the inn with his fellow students.

'Yes, it's dark already. Take care on the road.' John's face flickered in the candlelight. Outside the window a crowd shouted and Thomas wondered if the bear was being taunted again. 'How's Edward, Sir?'

232

Thomas found his breath caught in his throat. The smell of tallow was suffocating.

'Fine, very fine,' he said. 'I hope he'll be joining you at Guy's next year.'

'That's good news,' John said.

'Yes, it is.' Thomas's eyes became moist and he nearly cried. It must be the effect of the tallow.

Thomas passed the bookshop where he'd bought the Byron for John. John loved poetry books as much as Thomas loved medical books. Thomas was curious why. He found himself pushing open the door, entering the crowded space with bookshelves looming above him. The assistant came forward and Thomas asked if he had a poem by Wordsworth about a leech gatherer.

'Ah, *Resolution and Independence*,' the man said. He found the book of poems for Thomas and Thomas found himself stood outside the shop clutching the volume. Then he headed for the confectioners' shop.

Susannah sat bent over her sewing in the drawing room in the yellow armchair. Ever since Eliza's engagement she'd been busy sewing her trousseau.

Thomas handed Susannah a box wrapped in colourful ribbons. 'A present for you,' he said. 'I bought it in town today.'

'Put it on the table.' Susannah continued stitching.

'Aren't you going to open it?'

'I'm too busy.'

Thomas pulled the ribbons undone, opened the box and unwrapped the layers of tissue paper, revealing macarons and jellies and marzipan fruits. He held it so she could see them.

'Don't you want one?'

'No, thank you. I've lost my appetite for sweets since Edward left.'

Thomas closed the box and placed it on the table next to her. 'You might like one later.'

She continued to sew, concentrating on the tiny stitches, pleating the fabric. It looked like a sort of nightdress for Eliza on her wedding night. Thomas felt nausea at the thought. He sank onto the chaise longue and stroked the worn yellow velvet. The silence was thick as lard.

'We can think about reupholstering the chair and chaise longue if that will please you,' he said.

She ignored him and continued sewing.

'Don't punish me, Susannah. I can't bear this silence, this indifference. Please talk to me again.'

'I will when Edward comes home.'

'I told you I begged him to come home but he refused.'

'You should have asked earlier.' She bit the cotton with her teeth and started a new seam.

'Have you seen him lately?'

'I went today.'

'What does he do? Is he helping William?'

'A little, but he says he's not sure he wants to be a surgeon, or even an apothecary.'

'I'm sorry, Susannah. For what's happened. I wish I could go back and change it. I never thought it would come to this.'

'So am I. Take those sweetmeats away. You can give them to the girls.'

Something soft and fluid in Thomas which had been willing to forgive Edward and try again hardened in him. Edward should have come home by now. He was just being spiteful.

Late that night Thomas opened the Wordsworth in his study and read the poem about the leech gatherer, *Resolution and Independence*. It was a long poem and he read it several times. The words were easier to understand than he'd expected. He found himself on the lonely moor, with the hare. He saw the old man, with his long grey staff, his body bent double, gathering leeches. The man should have been miserable, being old and poor, but he was cheerful and kind with a firm mind. Thomas liked the poem. He was starting to see a little of what John saw in poetry, but it was no substitute for medicine.

Chapter Fifteen

March 1816

John was an infrequent correspondent, but Thomas lived for his letters. With Edward entrenched at William's, Eliza married and living in Brentwood, and Susannah hardly talking to him, they were an escape to another world. He relived his own days in the dissection room, attending lectures and ward rounds, watching operations, discussing cases and theories with fellow students. Thomas would keep the most recent letter folded in the top pocket of his coat and reread it several times during the day. He held the latest envelope, addressed in John's neat hand, and savoured the anticipation. This might tell him John had started his duties as a dresser.

Thomas remembered his own days as dresser to William Lucas, a fine man and skilled surgeon. Thomas had been on call for a week at a time, living in the hospital and tending to emergencies. He saw many accidents and obstructed hernias. It was both exciting and terrifying, but Astley, who was apprenticed to Henry Cline, was often around and advised him.

Operation day was Friday and he assisted. At first he found it difficult, being so close to the patients and their screams, watching the blood dripping from the operating table onto the sawdust on the floor, but he concentrated on the surgery, trying to learn. His skin became thicker and his ears plugged.

He performed endless bloodletting, tooth-pulling and dressings, applied lotions and plasters and linseed meal, but he enjoyed it. On the wards he had to grit his teeth to dress the foul-smelling festering sores at first, but he hardened himself and it became easier.

He also had dissection and lectures to attend. He was young and enthusiastic, learning from great men and gaining valuable experience. He saw his future amongst them. It was the best time of his life. Until that fateful night nearly thirty years ago.

Thomas took his letter opener, slit the envelope and unfolded the paper. John's reply was short. He'd been appointed dresser to William "Billy" Lucas Junior. Although he was disappointed not to be working for Astley Cooper he would try and make the best of it.

Thomas stood in the hall with the letter in his hand. He read it again. Dresser to Billy Lucas Junior. Billy was nothing like his father, Thomas's esteemed master William Lucas. Astley had admitted Billy was a terrible surgeon. John would learn nothing and Billy might even take against him because of Thomas and their past history.

Why hadn't Astley appointed John as his dresser? Couldn't he see John's potential? Thomas wanted to saddle his horse and gallop to Guy's to see him but couldn't spare the time. He went to his study, seized paper and quill, and wrote to Astley. His quill pressed deep, scoring the paper, and ink spots flew across it.

Astley's reply didn't arrive. Thomas reconsidered if he should visit. His anger made him shaky and caused him stomach pains. He was irritable with patients and Sam, his apprentice. Then Astley's reply arrived saying he was sorry but he could do no more. The first vacant post was for Billy and he had to stick to the rules.

Thomas ripped the letter into pieces which fell to the floor. Astley had said he would help John. Didn't Astley remember he'd agreed he owed Thomas something? Had he forgotten that night? The boy being admitted semi-conscious, the blood, the sound of rain pouring down on the roof of the theatre, the theatre lit by oil lamps. Had he forgotten his part in the tragedy?

In the evenings Thomas often found himself reading the book of Wordsworth poems. He found the tragic stories of poor people interesting, reminding him of some of the villagers of Edmonton he'd known over the years. He recognised much of the countryside described, although the lakes and mountains were more spectacular than the area around Edmonton. But most of all he liked them because he felt a link to John. Maybe John was also reading these poems, at the same time. Perhaps they were helping him cope with working for Billy Lucas Junior.

Sam rolled misshapen pills, even worse than Edward used to make. Thomas was mixing the paste, thankful this was the last batch then they could stop for the day. Thomas's coat was still wet from being caught in April showers on his visits. One minute the sun had been out, the next cold rain had soaked him. The noise of a commotion reached him. Something must be happening outside in Church Street.

'Mr Hammond, come quickly!' Ned Clark, a labourer, appeared at the door of the surgery. 'There's been a terrible accident.'

Thomas's stomach felt as if he'd plunged from a height. Terrible accidents occasionally turned out to be false alarms but more often involved crushed limbs, speared bodies or protruding bones. He told Sam to fetch his bag and they followed Ned. Outside, a little way along Church Street, a group had gathered. Further away someone held a frightened horse, which pawed the air and snorted. Bright sunrays, emerging from behind dark clouds, lit the scene.

The crowd parted for Thomas. A boy of about Edward and John's age lay on his back in the road. He had fair hair, surrounded by a pool of blood like a strange halo. His eyes were open in surprise. Thomas recognised Mark Hill, who used to climb trees with Edward in the orchard years ago. Thomas crouched in the dirt next to him.

'His horse kicked him in the head,' Ned said.

'Mark, it's Mr Hammond.'

'It hurts,' Mark said, and groaned.

'Help me move him,' Thomas said to the crowd, and two burly men came forward. The three of them rolled Mark like a log onto his side. There was a deep cut in the back of his scalp. Thomas tried to tell himself it didn't mean the injury was serious, it didn't mean the skull and brain underneath were damaged, but his bilious stomach feared it.

'I'm just going to feel your wound.' Thomas felt gently around Mark's skull, in ever-decreasing circles, closer and closer to the source of the bleeding. Near the gash Mark's hair was matted with blood. Thomas, feeling for the scalp where he thought it should be, met nothingness. He lowered his fingers and probed a deep hollow in the skull. Mark cried out.

'Everything will be fine, Mark,' Thomas said. 'Try and stay calm.' A depressed skull fracture with a laceration over it. The bone needed elevating and removing to avoid brain compression and injury. The same injury as the boy at Guy's had that night so long ago.

Vomit appeared next to Thomas's boots and for a moment he thought it was he who'd been sick, but it was Mark. Pieces of a meat pie swam in a pool smelling of beer. Vomiting could be a sign of complications, but on the other hand Mark's pupils weren't dilated and he was conscious. Thomas knew he should carry him into the surgery, trephine a hole in the skull next to the wound, insert a thin probe, raise the depressed fragments from underneath and remove them. The alternative was a long, bumpy journey to Guy's or another London hospital during which Mark might develop pressure on the brain and deteriorate. Mark would be in great pain as laudanum was too risky to give; it would make him drowsy and hard to assess.

'What's happened? Oh, my poor boy.' A woman fell to her knees, oblivious of the vomit, and clasped Mark's hand. Thomas recognised Mark's mother, a small woman with a pinched face beneath her frayed bonnet. She raised her eyes to Thomas. 'Help him, Mr Hammond.'

'He needs an operation,' Thomas said.

'Is it that serious? Will you do it, Mr Hammond? I trust you.'

Mrs Hill looked at him. He remembered her first stillborn baby, then Mark's difficult birth and Mark nearly dying of croup. Her husband had survived typhus, under Thomas's care, only to drown in the brook. She had supported herself and Mark by taking in sewing, until Mark was old enough to earn a wage.

Could Thomas perform the operation in the surgery with Sam assisting? He heard his apprentice's noisy breathing behind him. Sam was fourteen years old and inexperienced. He'd never seen any major surgery. That other time Thomas had been in the operating theatre at Guy's with Astley holding down the patient. He remembered the boy's screams, the way he'd fought Astley, his frightened eyes, his garbled speech, then silence. Thomas felt physically weak at the thought of doing the operation.

'We must transport him to Guy's Hospital,' Thomas said. 'To Mr Astley Cooper, the best surgeon in the country.'

The sun slid behind a cloud and the world went grey. Thomas asked a woman to go to Wilston and ask Martha for a blanket to keep Mark warm. He sent Ned to borrow the publican's carriage, as it was larger than Thomas's and enclosed, and would be better than an open cart. He told Sam to fetch a plank of wood from the carpenter, to use across the seats. A local man volunteered to harness the horses and drive the carriage. Meanwhile Thomas bandaged Mark's head wound. Martha ran out with a blanket and they covered him. Coldness settled on the land and crept into Thomas's body.

When the carriage was ready and Mark lying on the plank inside, his mother wanted to accompany him, but Thomas told her there was no room. Martha put her arm around her and led her back to Wilston, where she would clean her dress and comfort her.

The carriage rattled and bumped on the London road, and Thomas shouted to the driver to slow down a little. Mark cried out with each jolt. Thomas talked to keep him awake. Every so often Thomas asked him to squeeze his hand and the boy responded. The feel of Mark's hand in his reminded Thomas of holding Edward's hand as a boy, when they would walk down to the brook to catch minnows. He felt a longing to see Edward, to know he was safe.

Thomas told Mark he would be fine. He was taking him to the best surgeon in the country. And Thomas told himself it was true, Astley would do a better job than Thomas, give Mark the best chance. If Mark survived the journey.

Mark opened his eyes. 'Mama?' he said with the voice of a small child.

'She's at Wilston.' Thomas thought of Mrs Hill, sitting in the kitchen with Martha, waiting for her only surviving child to come home safely.

Mark muttered something unintelligible. Perhaps this was the first sign of deteriorating consciousness. The sky darkened and sharp drops of rain struck the carriage top and windows, reminding Thomas of the rain on the operating theatre roof. If they had stayed in Edmonton the operation would be finished by now. He was a coward. Shame ate away at him. He wanted to rid himself of it but couldn't. It was bound to him, mixed in like an ingredient in a medicine. The shame of all those years ago and the shame of today. He wanted to turn the carriage round and race back to Wilston and do the operation there, but he knew it was too late and also that he wouldn't be able to carry it through.

Night had fallen. The carriage made its way onward in the dark, its lamps lighting a few yards of the road in front. They passed London Wall and carried on into the city. Blood leaked from Mark's wound and stained the bandage. It was too dark to assess his pupils. He talked but most of the words made no sense. His grip when Thomas asked him to squeeze his hand was weakening.

'Hold on, Mark,' Thomas said. 'We're nearly there, nearly at Guy's.'

The smells of sewage and stews cooking crept into the carriage. Dark figures ran alongside, disappearing when their driver cracked his whip at them. There were strangled cries which sounded like people being murdered but were probably fighting cats. Figures lurked in alleyways. Prostitutes or thieves. The journey seemed endless.

'Mark, can you hear me?' Thomas asked.

No reply.

'Squeeze my hand.'

No response. He pinched Mark's earlobe hard and the boy flinched. Some hope yet. He thought of what awaited Mark at Guy's. The circular hole drilled into the skull next to the fracture. Although Mark wasn't fully alert he would feel the pain intensely. As the other boy had and screamed. His eyes, filled with horror, would stare at the surgeon. As the other boy had stared at Thomas. Then the raising of the bone fragments would cause anguish. Thomas told himself he mustn't think about this. Control. Strength of will. A lion's heart.

They drew up in front of the gates of Guy's, and the gatekeeper held up a light. Mark was silent but still breathed and had a pulse. Thomas lifted his patient's eyelids. One pupil reacted to the light, but the other was large, dilated and didn't constrict. Pressure on the brain. Time was critical now. Thomas sent for two porters to bring a stretcher. It was cold waiting in the carriage and he tucked the blanket around Mark.

Thomas followed the stretcher as the porters carried Mark through the courtyard, past the statue of Thomas Guy and through the entrance John had compared to a Greek temple. He wondered if John was the dresser on call. Perhaps John could help save Mark and atone for Thomas's failure in the past. No. What was he thinking? If John was on call, that would mean Billy Lucas Junior would be the surgeon covering, and Billy would kill Mark. He knew it.

At the door to the ward Thomas felt as if he might collapse. Staying upright was an immense effort. A young man appeared and introduced himself as the dresser on call. Thomas explained the situation.

'You will call Astley Cooper?' Thomas said. 'Promise me? He's an old friend of mine.'

'Of course. Do you want to wait for him?'

Thomas knew he could come in and wait for Astley and watch the operation, but he couldn't face it. It was too similar to the other time. He'd brought Mark this far, but he could go no further.

Thomas was shaking with cold and his teeth chattered as he headed back across the dark courtyard, lit by a few lamps, to the carriage and back to Edmonton. How was he going to talk to Mark's mother and bear her distress? He must show sympathy and kindness. He must control himself as Astley had told him. Practice. Strength of will. The heart of a lion. But lions weren't cowards, were they? He wished he still had the blanket to wrap himself in and keep warm.

Spring continued damp and grey, as melancholy as Thomas's mood. Susannah was still hardly speaking to him. He missed Eliza and rarely saw her. Edward remained at William's and John was still dresser to Billy Lucas Junior.

Thomas stood outside the cottage, bracing himself to enter. A dog rose surrounded the doorway, but it was a poor specimen with a few tattered flowers. Inside Mark Hill lay propped up on pillows in a bed downstairs, where he'd lain for the past six weeks since he'd been discharged from Guy's. The hair around his head wound had been shaved and was now like stubble. Mrs Hill greeted Thomas. Her face was more pinched than he'd ever seen it and her fingers red where she'd pricked herself sewing. Now Mark couldn't work she had to earn a living again.

'I'm worried about his chest,' Mrs Hill said. 'He's coughing.'

'I see. Mark? How are you today?' Thomas crossed to the bed. Mark's head lolled, his tongue protruded and he dribbled. He coughed, which sounded moist. He was a little warm and his pulse raced. He tried to speak, forcing sounds out with great effort, but Thomas couldn't make out the words.

Thomas had promised Mark everything would be fine: Astley Cooper would save him. Astley had operated but Mark hadn't recovered. His brain was damaged. The greatest surgeon in Britain hadn't been able to save him, or maybe the long journey had been the reason. Astley had been sympathetic and apologetic to Mark and his mother, but then he had sent them back home to Edmonton. He didn't have to be reminded of his failure every day the way Thomas did. Mrs Hill called often because Mark had fits, which frightened her. Thomas's medicines had reduced their frequency but only a little. She was in danger of being evicted because she had no income from Mark, yet she never once blamed Thomas but thanked him for taking Mark to Guy's and making sure Mr Cooper operated on her son.

Mark made guttural sounds and pulled Thomas closer. The effort involved was painful to watch, the muscles in his throat and jaw bulging, and the sinews tightening. Thomas listened carefully, looking into Mark's eyes. Mark squeezed his hand, reminding Thomas of their carriage ride together. The pain was acute. For a moment Mark's eyes cleared and Thomas saw the desperation of a young man trapped in a damaged body. A young man who would never walk again or speak normally.

'You're talking about the hospital?' Thomas guessed.

Mark shook his head. He tried again. More animal sounds, more effort.

Mrs Hill came round to the other side. 'Don't upset yourself, Mark,' she said.

'Let him speak,' Thomas said. 'He's trying to tell me something.' Thomas leant closer and strained with all his attention, closing his eyes to help him concentrate. The words were indistinct, but a mumbled message came through.

Thomas jerked back. Mark was telling him he couldn't bear to live. Or was he imagining it? Mark roared and beat his fists against Thomas. Thomas held his wrists to restrain him.

Mrs Hill tucked the bedclothes. 'Now, Mark. Don't upset Mr Hammond. He's been so helpful to us.'

'Could you fetch his medicines for me?' Thomas asked, and Mrs Hill went to the kitchen.

Thomas held Mark's wrists. What would he want if this boy were Edward or John? Perhaps it would be kindest to give Mark a dose of something poisonous, to end his suffering. Or a massive dose of laudanum. Thomas was aware that laudanum often hastened the death of many patients, but they were dying anyway. It was different to actively end a life. His whole being was repulsed by the thought. It would be a sin in the eyes of God, murder. Only God could end Mark's suffering, in his own time when he chose.

'I can't do it, Mark,' Thomas whispered. He let go of Mark's wrists.

Again for a few seconds Thomas saw clarity in Mark's eyes and expected a furious assault with his fists, but Mark collapsed back on the pillows, his head lolling and mouth dribbling.

Thomas's eyes moistened and tears flowed down his face. They started slowly but increased until they were an unstoppable torrent like Salmon's Brook after the thaw. He made no effort to wipe them away. They dripped onto his cravat, his waistcoat, his hands. Hot, salty tears.

'Mr Hammond, what's wrong?' Mrs Hill appeared from the kitchen, holding Mark's medicines on a tray. 'Are you ill?'

The tears continued to flow. His throat was so clogged he couldn't speak. The old helplessness returned. He couldn't control his feelings about suffering; they overwhelmed him. He couldn't cope with being compassionate and caring, couldn't do it every day whatever the circumstances. It was too difficult. He was a failure as a man and a doctor. He had no strength of will, no courage.

Thomas saw the fear in Mrs Hill's eyes at his loss of control. The poor woman was terrified. He must go back to his old ways and block everything out, harden himself. He struggled to gain control over himself, over his speech. He must conquer his weakness.

'It's nothing,' Thomas said. 'Something in my eyes.' He wiped his face with his handkerchief and blew his nose. 'Now let me check those medicines.'

When he arrived home Thomas knocked on the door of Susannah's sitting room, but she was busy with the girls. He asked to speak to her, but she told him to wait. He went to his study, picked up his book of Wordsworth poems and threw it at the wall. What had he been thinking of, reading poetry? Poetry was no use, no help, no comfort.

Chapter Sixteen

Summer didn't arrive. Instead the weather turned backwards. Jack Frost paid extended visits and nipped tender plants; skies were overcast, winds cold and incessant rains fell, causing Salmon's Brook and Pymmes Brooks to flood. Fields were barren and farmers worried about their crops. Thomas had to ride rather than take the carriage as the smaller lanes were impassable from mud. Some days the hens would roost at noon and people had to light candles as if it were midnight.

In July a letter from John brightened Thomas's world. John had passed the examination to become a Licentiate of the Society of Apothecaries. If he wasn't continuing his training to become a surgeon he could have started work as an apothecary. Thomas wrote to congratulate him and insisted he come to dinner at Wilston to celebrate.

'You've done what?' Susannah sat at the desk in her sitting room preparing the accounts.

'I want to see him.' Thomas stood just inside the doorway, unsure if he was welcome in the room. 'His success is partly my success.'

'So you've invited John, but you haven't invited your own son to dinner?'

'Edward wouldn't come, you know that.' Thomas hadn't seen Edward since the time he'd refused to come home when Thomas asked him nine months ago, although Susannah visited him often.

'When did you last ask him?' Susannah asked.

'It's not John's fault Edward ran away.'

'No, it's yours.'

This had become a frequent accusation, whenever they discussed Edward. Thomas wished she could see his point of view, just a little bit. It wasn't completely his fault. Edward had nearly killed Rachel Curtis through carelessness. Thomas wondered if it was worth persisting. He could retract his invite; it would make his life easier. But he wanted to see John and tell him he was proud of him, discuss Guy's and his duties as a dresser.

'You can ask Edward to dinner anytime you like, Susannah. But John is coming next week whatever you say.'

She tightened her lips but didn't argue.

John arrived dressed in a loose coat and baggy trousers. Instead of the high collar and cravat everyone else Thomas knew wore, he had his collar turned down and a thin black ribbon around his bare neck. The effect was disconcerting, as if he was exposing himself in public. His hair was longer than Thomas remembered.

'Welcome, John.' Thomas shook his hand. John looked older than when he'd last seen him at Guy's nine months ago. Thomas supposed he'd done and seen a lot since then.

Susannah greeted him without warmth, while Mary Ann and Harriet hid behind her. Thomas introduced Sam. John seemed to be looking for someone else. Thomas had told him of Eliza's marriage in his letters, although he mostly wrote about the surgery and patients, but Thomas hadn't mentioned Edward.

'Edward's at his uncle's, helping in the surgery,' Thomas said. 'He's learning a lot. Let's go into dinner.'

John tucked into his meal heartily and drank a glass of claret. Sam seemed in awe of John and was quieter than usual.

Mary Ann lowered her eyes shyly whenever John looked her way, then raised them when he wasn't looking. At thirteen she was growing up and Thomas sighed. Why couldn't his girls stay young forever?

'So you're now a Licentiate of the Society of Apothecaries,' Thomas said. 'How was the exam?'

'I must admit I was shaking a little when I walked through the grand entrance of the Worshipful Company of Apothecaries,' John said. 'Their coat of arms shows Apollo, in gold, straddling the wyvern. Either side of him are gilded unicorns, above him a blue rhinoceros and underneath the motto *Opiferque Per Orbem Dicor*.'

'I know a little bit of Latin,' Mary Ann said. '*Orbem* is world?'

'That's right. Throughout the world I am called the bringer of help,' John replied. 'It's from Ovid. *Metamorphoses*.'

Mary Ann blushed.

'The Great Hall was very imposing with all its portraits, but translating the *Pharmacopoeia* and physicians' prescriptions from Latin was easy,' John continued. 'Mackereth, who shares my lodgings, failed and protests it's a test of classical more than medical knowledge.'

Sam stared at John, dumbstruck, his jaw hanging down. Presumably he could never see himself passing the same exam in five years' time. Mary Ann's Latin was better than Sam's.

Thomas poured John more claret and John complimented the lamb. Thomas told him it was from the butcher, Mr Trew, in exchange for services rendered.

'Do you remember the time you cut too deep and he screamed and claimed you were trying to kill him?' Thomas asked.

'Thomas, no discussion of work at the dinner table, please,' Susannah said.

Silence enveloped the table like a heavy cloth. The discomfort was palpable and Harriet jabbed Mary Ann and giggled.

'What do you plan to do for the summer, John?' Susannah asked, and Thomas was pleased she was at least making an effort.

'Visit Margate with my brother Tom. I hope the sea air will improve his health.'

'Is he ill?' Thomas remembered the thin boy from his grandmother's funeral.

'Not seriously, but I worry about him… he's pale and listless.'

Thomas read his thoughts. The shadow of consumption hung over the family and John feared Tom was ill with it.

'Let us hope the sea air will bring colour to his cheeks and strengthen him,' Thomas said.

Susannah talked at length about Margate, which she had visited with her first husband. Thomas had never had the time nor money to take her there. From their portraits Thomas's father and grandfather looked down on them.

After the meal John and Thomas retired to his study, where John inhaled snuff from a small decorative box, a new habit, and they both sipped brandy.

'Do you remember James Cory?' Thomas asked. 'The young boy with the fracture you reduced when I was away? I saw him the other day. The arm is a little twisted but perfectly functional. I suppose you've seen many more serious fractures now.' In his mind's eye Thomas saw John walking the wards with Astley Cooper, describing cases to him, carrying his tin box for the dressings. Except he was dresser to Billy Lucas Junior.

'Yes, I have, many requiring amputations,' John replied, and Thomas winced at the thought of Billy performing an amputation. He'd seen him in action, the zeal in his eyes turning to panic and ever more desperate hacking with the saw.

'I could lend you my books, for the examination of the Royal College of Surgeons next year,' Thomas said. 'But perhaps they're out of date? Astley Cooper has devised new procedures and although I try I can't keep abreast of them all.'

John stared out of the open window where grey clouds merged, blocking out rays of sun falling in shafts and dimming the study. 'I sometimes wonder if I would make a better poet than a surgeon,' he said.

John continued to look at the clouds and Thomas wondered if he'd heard correctly. Perhaps John was jesting, but there was no smile on his lips. A coldness settled on Thomas, as if the grey clouds were touching him with damp fingers.

'Your talent lies with surgery.'

'I had a sonnet, *O Solitude! If I must with thee dwell*, published in *The Examiner* in May. Leigh Hunt has also published Byron and Shelley.'

'Your name is next to Lord Byron?'

'My poem but not my name. I sent it anonymously.'

'Then no one knows you wrote it.'

'I do.' John's voice expressed a confidence Thomas hadn't heard before.

'You can write poems for amusement when you have time,' Thomas said. 'But you can do so much more that's worthwhile as a surgeon.'

John turned to Thomas. The room was even darker and

the lamp threw a circle of light across John's face. 'Can't poetry help people?'

'I don't believe so.'

'Milton says *apt words have power to swage the tumours of a troubled mind, and are as balm to festered wounds.*'

'That's nonsense, John. Poetry can't save lives.'

'But it can offer comfort and consolation, which are also important and always needed.'

John looked towards the volumes of Shakespeare on the low shelf, some of which he'd read to Eliza all those years ago. He knelt on the floor, took one out and opened it. The stiff brown leather of the spine creaked.

'*A Midsummer Night's Dream* helped Eliza recover.'

'That was just relieving boredom during her convalescence. Don't let poetry take you away from your true calling, John.'

John flicked through the pages of the book. A slight breeze entered through the window and lifted a few strands of his hair.

'I'm not sure I can survive working for Mr Lucas 'til next March,' John said. 'The past four months have been difficult.'

'I've heard he's not the most skilful surgeon.'

'He's speedy, which is important, but reckless, even Mr Cooper says so. He makes us all shudder from the apprehension of his opening arteries or some other error.'

'His father Billy Lucas Senior was as swift as a bird in flight and kind with it when I was his dresser.'

'Patients suffer, intense suffering, even with a good surgeon. Sometimes the treatments seem worse than the original illness.'

'The word patient, from the Latin, means one who suffers. Perhaps we can't completely relieve it but only try our best.'

'But what's the purpose of suffering?' John still knelt on the floor, looking up at Thomas.

'A vicar would tell you it's a punishment for the fall and a soul will be rewarded in heaven.'

A bolt of lightning lit up the murky sky, followed by a clap of thunder. Heavy rain began to fall, drumming on the roof, drenching the garden.

John hung his head and although his kneeling posture and bowed head, his hands holding the book, suggested prayer, Thomas knew at that moment John didn't believe. And Thomas wondered if he, Thomas Hammond, believed. Thomas attended church and said his prayers, but in his heart he often doubted. He'd discovered long ago it was safest not to question.

'Come, sit up.' Thomas offered his hand to John, who took it and pulled himself up. John sat back in the chair and placed the book on the desk. The desk where they'd signed the indentures six years ago. On that day a storm had also raged. Thomas saw he was still holding John's hand and let it go.

Lightning sparked again and thunder rumbled beneath the sound of the rain. 'How did you find being a dresser?' John asked.

'Not easy at first, but I hardened myself to it.' That was true. The rain fell in sheets outside the window and the smell of wet earth crept into the room.

John hesitated and inhaled another pinch of snuff. 'When I see Mr Lucas cut through a leg, I feel it in my own. A searing pain.'

'Feeling their pain doesn't help them but only immobilises us. Astley Cooper told me it requires strength of will to control one's emotions but still be sympathetic. A lion's heart.' Thomas thought of Mark Hill and felt a fraud. Tears had run down his face, unstoppable, overwhelming him. How could he tell John how to cope with suffering when he couldn't cope himself? 'But if that sounds too difficult you must put on a coat of armour like those knights you played at with Mrs Foster's son.'

'Won't the armour cut me off from myself? Make me cold and unapproachable?'

'Perhaps, but it makes it possible to work and survive. That's the most important thing.' Thomas truly believed that, but he had no idea if John did.

John looked down at his hands, and Thomas detected a slight agitation in the rubbing of one thumb against his forefinger.

'When Mr Lucas discovered I was your apprentice,' John said, 'he told me you'd done something terrible when you were a dresser at Guy's.'

Thomas held his breath. What had Billy told John? Shame engulfed him. For a moment he couldn't reply, then did so with a great effort. 'I made a mistake which harmed a patient. I deeply regret it and am sorry.' Thomas wondered if John would lose any respect he had for him now. Billy was still trying to destroy him. He waited for more questions on the matter, but none came.

'A few times the melancholy has come upon me again. The blue devils.' John raised his hands and fiddled with the ribbon around his neck. It reminded Thomas of a noose.

'You must work hard, do something meaningful. Help patients.'

John lifted his head and his eyes fixed on Thomas's face. 'I asked you to teach me how to relieve the pain caused by suffering.'

'I've tried my best.'

'You've taught me how to fix broken bones, extract teeth, cut abscesses and give medicines, but it isn't enough. Your herbs and leeches and potions, Mr Cooper's scalpels and saws, can only do so much.'

Outside the rain was still falling, the sky remained dark and cool air blew into the room.

Thomas didn't know how to respond: he'd taught John everything he knew. He felt he'd failed. He remembered the day Mrs Foster coughed blood. When John had asked him how he coped with suffering and he hadn't known the answer.

'Yes, they can only do so much, but it's better than nothing. Keep going, John.'

Thomas drank the rest of his brandy down in one and his body shivered.

The rain which fell when John visited Thomas continued all summer. If one could call it summer. Thomas became soaked running between Wilston and the surgery. The carriage wheels stuck in the churned-up mud so he rode Cinnamon. His overcoat was heavy with rain, water dripped from the brim of his hat, trickled inside his boots and ran from his hands along the reins. The seat of his breeches and his stockings were damp. He hung his clothes to dry in the kitchen at night by the embers of the fire, but they never fully dried. He felt sorry for Cinnamon, rubbed him down well and gave him extra oats and blankets.

On his rounds, in the incessant rain, Thomas thought of John at Guy's, on the wards, in the operating theatre, struggling to cope with the suffering he saw. The rest of their evening had been short and John had left to travel back to Guy's. If only Thomas could have helped more, said the right thing. A gnawing pain came to his stomach, often.

Chapter Seventeen

October 1816

As the rain-soaked, dead leaves of autumn rotted in ditches beside the road, Thomas's stomach pains worsened. He found eating aggravated them and started to dread mealtimes. It must be an ulcer; he'd had one years ago which had got better with Trisnitrate of Bismuth. He followed a light diet and treated himself with the same remedy, but it was taking a long time to work.

A rare visit from Eliza lit up the dark autumn days. She hurried in from her carriage, throwing back the hood of her cloak, her cheeks glowing.

'Father!' She embraced him and he held her tight.

'You must be cold, come and sit by the fire.' Thomas led her to the parlour.

She removed her gloves and held her hands out to warm them. Her hair was pinned up and she looked like a lady. She was mistress of her own household now, he reminded himself.

'How are you?' he asked. 'It's so nice to see you.'

'Very well, thank you, but I have pains in my joints and wanted you to advise me on some medicine.'

Thomas swelled with pride. His daughter trusted him more than her local apothecary surgeon, quite rightly, of course. He asked her some questions, palpated the joints in her hands for warmth and swelling, and said he would prepare a medicine.

When he returned from the dispensary with the saffron crocus syrup, he found her talking to Susannah, their heads nearly touching as they sat before the fire.

'I was telling Eliza about your stomach pains,' Susannah said. 'You hardly touched your meal last night.'

'It's nothing, just an ulcer. I'm taking some medicine,' Thomas replied.

'You work too hard, it's making you ill,' Susannah said.

'My patients need me and Sam needs my supervision.'

'You must slow down,' Susannah persisted.

'I've told you I can't.' Thomas felt irritation rising in him. The pain was affecting his disposition.

'You won't be any use to anyone if you don't look after yourself.' Susannah's voice was strident, further fraying his temper.

'You expect me to just stop and lie in bed eating sweetmeats?' Thomas's voice came out louder than he'd intended and he saw alarm on Eliza's face. He took a few deep breaths.

'You must consult someone,' Susannah said.

'I know what it is and I've mixed some medicines for myself.'

'To be perfectly frank, they don't seem to be working.'

'A physician should be able to heal himself.' He tried to ignore the pain flaring in his stomach.

'Why are you so stubborn? Ask William. Surely a family of surgeons can help each other?'

'But if patients find out I'm ill they may stop consulting me.'

'That's ridiculous. William will be discreet.'

'Perhaps I don't want him to know I'm unwell?'

'Why not? He's your brother.'

He couldn't explain it to her. He could hardly explain his reluctance to himself. Because he didn't trust William's medical skills, his fondness for mercury? Because if he visited William he might see Edward, whom he hadn't seen for over a year?

'Father,' Eliza said, reaching out to him, 'you do look unwell. Your face is thinner and drawn. Please consider consulting William.' The concern in her voice and the soft touch of her hand on his arm made him feel he couldn't refuse.

Thomas stood outside William's house in the cold staring at the closed curtains in the upstairs windows. Perhaps Edward lay in bed there as it was early morning. For a few seconds Thomas longed to see his son, to have him home for Christmas in a few weeks' time, erasing the feeling of a missing limb in the family. But the memory of their last meeting came sharp into his mind, the light glittering on William's glass and silver, the intense heat of the fire, Edward dismissing Thomas's apology and offer to come home, saying he wasn't sure he wanted to be a surgeon. Susannah visited regularly and brought news, but there had been no suggestion of him registering at Guy's this October to complete his training. The boy was wasting his life away.

In William's treatment room a roaring fire burnt in the grate, the thick velvet curtains kept out the cold and the whorls on the walnut table gleamed.

'What symptoms do you have, Thomas?' William asked. Thomas was again reminded how closely William resembled their father physically, although his manner was very different.

'Nothing much.'

'You haven't sought my opinion for years.'

'Susannah insisted. I have some stomach pains.'

'Have you lost weight?' William assessed Thomas with a shrewd look. 'Your face looks thinner.'

'A little. I'm sure it's an ulcer. Brought on by overwork and rushing meals. Since the harvest failed there's so much illness in Edmonton.'

'What are you taking for it?'

'A light diet and bismuth. For a few weeks.'

'An ulcer should be improving by now. It could be something more sinister.'

Thomas knew what he was alluding to. The ghost of their father appeared between them. His stomach pains and wasting away, his last months in agony, only eased a little by large doses of laudanum. Thomas had seen him every day, treated him, lived in the house, taken on his practice, while William had mostly stayed safe in Southgate. Thomas never understood how William had been able to deny their father his desire that William would take over the practice at Wilston.

'I'm sure it's not what Father had. A few more weeks of the bismuth and I'll be fine.'

'Why don't you consult Astley Cooper? Or Abernethy? To be sure.'

'There's really no need. Can you bleed me now?'

William rolled up Thomas's shirtsleeve and tightened a tourniquet around his upper arm. He removed a shiny lancet from a mother-of-pearl case and cut Thomas's engorged vein. Thomas was surprised how sharp the pain was, but it felt a relief, a release. Thomas's blood flowed into a white china bowl decorated with gilt.

William held Thomas's elbow with one hand. Thomas found his touch comforting, the strong, warm fingers of a trained apothecary surgeon. He glanced at the bowl of blood. He felt as if poisons had been released. He was being cared for, looked after. William was highly trained, but he was also his older brother. All would be well. A feeling of warmth and calm spread over him.

'Do you remember when you made me be your patient and bled me and it wouldn't stop and blood went everywhere?' Thomas asked. William must have been about fifteen and Thomas nine. His brother had persuaded him they should play doctor and patient.

William laughed. 'Father told me I should practice.'

'I was terrified I'd bleed to death.'

'Father was furious with me.'

'He was? For the mess?'

'No, I think in case I'd hurt you.' This was news to Thomas and he wondered if there were other things about his father he didn't know.

At last William loosened the tourniquet, pressing with lint over the wound. Thomas's arm tingled. William gestured to him to press and sat on the chair opposite him.

'Let me mix something for you,' William said.

Thomas pressed harder on the lint. 'I really don't think it's necessary.'

'Don't be so stubborn.' William stood up and went towards the door. 'Come to the dispensary. Rhubarb with calomel might help.'

'No mercury.' Thomas remembered the feel of Rachel Curtis's teeth in his hand, the row with Edward, his apothecary jars smashed on the floor.

'It's only calomel.'

'It's still mercury.'

William must have seen his determined expression. 'If you insist.'

Thomas followed William's broad back, the maroon coat straining across his shoulders, into the corridor. William walked slowly as if his knees troubled him and Thomas worried his brother was getting old. The noise of a pestle pounding in a mortar was audible in the narrow space, and Thomas wondered if Edward might be in the dispensary. His calm mood fell away from him, replaced by nervousness. William pushed the door and a boy looked up.

'Hello, Uncle Thomas.' James stood at the bench, his hair long and wild. 'How are you?'

'Fine, thank you.' Thomas tried to keep his disappointment from his voice.

'James, can you mix a tonic of gentian and cascarilla?' William said.

James began taking down the jars he needed, all patterned glass or white china decorated with gilt. He weighed ingredients and mixed them.

'Have you heard Astley Cooper is talking of operating on abdominal aortic aneurysms now?' James asked. 'He thinks he'll soon be able to ligate the vessel and the patient survive.'

'Nothing would surprise me where Astley Cooper is concerned,' Thomas said.

It was pleasant to be in the room with his brother and nephew, reminding him of those early years with his father and William. Perhaps he should come here more often and join in their discussions. Or even attend the evenings at Abernethy's that William had mentioned some time ago where they discussed Mr Hunter's theory of life. Thomas had nothing to fear from seeing Astley Cooper now if he also came.

The door opened, a figure rushed in bringing with him cold and damp, and slammed a pot of pills on the table.

'Mrs Grant wants gold pills like Mrs Cole, even though I've told her these are just as effective. Now I'll have to make them again!'

Blood pounded in Thomas's ears and the wound in his arm throbbed. Edward wasn't asleep upstairs as he'd imagined. Edward lifted his eyes and stared at Thomas. It was all wrong. It was Edward, but it wasn't Edward. Thomas searched for signs of the small boy who'd climbed trees and teased his sisters, the boy who'd smashed his apothecary jars and run away to fight Napoleon, but found a stranger.

'Father?' Edward's eyes glanced at the lint Thomas pressed on his arm. 'Are you sick?'

Thomas tried to swallow but his mouth was dry. He hadn't prepared for this. He should have asked William to keep Edward away. He must remain calm.

'Just a little tired from overwork,' Thomas said.

Edward watched him intently. Thomas couldn't think how to bridge a gap of ill feeling which had lasted more than a year. He reached out his hand then let it drop. He couldn't face another rejection from Edward.

'We hear your protégé is acting strangely,' William said.

'Sam?' Thomas asked.

'No. John Keats. Joseph Green tells me he hardly attends dissection and is always off with his artistic and literary friends.'

'That can't be.'

'Turning into Byron and writing poetry.' James stopped mixing and lifted his head. 'Someone even told me he was in *The Examiner* this week!'

'See, Father?' Edward said. 'He always was rather strange.'

Thomas placed his palms flat on the bench to steady himself.

'I'm not surprised.' William laughed. 'I warned you he was trouble. The word is he'll fail his exams and never be a surgeon.'

Thomas's legs felt weak and he struggled to stay upright. The pound of the mortar was like a hammer on his skull. He saw William's laughing face, his wobbling jowls, his overlong sideburns, his wild bushy eyebrows, his fat belly.

'I think I'll sit down next door,' Thomas said.

Thomas walked back to the parlour, blackness encroaching upon his vision, and sank into an armchair, placing his head on his knees. Someone entered the room and shut the door.

'Keats would have made a perfectly good apothecary,' William said. 'Why did you have to fill his head with ideas of greatness?'

Thomas sat up straight. 'Because he could be a great surgeon. He showed passion and talent and skill. Shouldn't a master help his apprentice aim for the best?'

'Thomas, you delude yourself,' William said. 'About Edward too. All Edward really wanted was to work somewhere like here, but you kept pressuring him into being a hospital surgeon.'

This was too much. Thomas was still reeling from the news about John, plus felt faint from the bloodletting and heat of the fire, but he wouldn't stand for this from William.

'You're the one who ruined Edward.' Thomas rose to his feet and pointed his finger at his brother. 'Filling his head with ideas of money and mercury, corrupting him.'

'Why did he spend so much time here?' William remained unruffled. 'Because we enjoy our work and our life and treated him well, respected him. Look at James. He was happy to go to Guy's and be dresser to Astley Cooper then work with me.'

'You held him back,' Thomas said.

'Just because you never made it as a surgeon, doesn't mean you have to push these boys.'

Thomas felt drained, as if his brother had taken quarts more blood from him. William said he looked pale and urged him to sit down, but Thomas resisted and kept standing.

'I never made it because I had to take over Father's practice. If you'd done your duty, I could have become a surgeon.'

'I don't know exactly what happened back then, but I heard the rumours. You did something scandalous and that's why you didn't become a surgeon. Taking over Father's practice saved you.'

That wasn't how it happened. It wasn't true. 'You're talking hogwash,' Thomas said, and turned to leave.

'Don't forget the tonic.' William went to the dispensary and returned with the medicine, which he handed to Thomas. Thomas wanted to push it back into William's hand, but he felt too weak. He took it with him, grabbing his coat on the way out.

A chill breeze blew under the hood of the carriage, but Thomas was glad he'd brought it as he didn't think he could have ridden home. William's accusations that Thomas had forced Edward into aiming to be a surgeon were ridiculous. Edward himself had wanted it. If William hadn't poisoned his mind, Edward might now be training to be one. As John was. John was due to take the exam of the Royal College of Surgeons in March; he was nearly a qualified surgeon with a great future ahead of him. The things William and James had said about John were just vicious rumours. They'd never liked John and had only heard Edward's side of their disagreements. There couldn't be any truth in them.

Back at Wilston Thomas called for Sam to stable Cinnamon and went to the dispensary. He took off his coat and saw the wound where William had bled him had opened and left a large red patch on his shirt. He found some lint and pressed hard then tied a bandage around his arm. He tried to mix some medicines but couldn't concentrate and kept reading the same thing over and over. He paced up and down. It was malicious gossip. And yet… John had written a poem here, at this very bench. He'd read Shakespeare to Eliza when she was ill. There had been a volume of Wordsworth's poems on his desk in his lodgings near Guy's. What did James mean by John's artistic and literary friends? He was being corrupted by people he'd met after he left Thomas. John's comments in the summer about suffering should have warned him. Why hadn't Thomas seen the danger and stopped it?

No, it was nothing. A few instances of playing at poetry. That didn't add up to anything. Except James had heard it from Joseph Henry Green, who saw John often and taught him anatomy.

Thomas could write to John, but would he tell him the truth? And he might not reply straight away. Thomas couldn't wait.

In the bumpy stagecoach from Edmonton to London Thomas read the latest *Examiner* dated December 1st 1816. He'd decided to buy it, despite his objections to its politics, because James had said John was in it. The front page was about Bonaparte in St Helena. Pages two and three were a list of bankrupts. On page four there was an article about a reform meeting in Spa Fields, then a theatre review and he reached the Literary Notices on page nine.

Young Poets. He read about the new school of poetry. *Its only object being to restore the same love of Nature, and "thinking" instead of mere "talking".* Hunt wrote about Percy Bysshe Shelley, then John Henry Reynolds. *The last of these young aspirants whom we have met with, and who promises to help the new school revive Nature and to "put a spirit of youth in everything", is, we believe, the youngest of them all and just of age. His name is JOHN KEATS. He has not yet published anything except in a newspaper; but a set of his manuscripts was handed to us the other day, and fairly surprised us with the truth of their ambition, and ardent grappling with Nature.*

Then followed a poem by John: *On First Looking Into Chapman's Homer.*

> *Much have I travelled in the realms of gold,*
> *And many godly states and kingdoms seen;*
> *Round many western islands have I been*
> *Which bards in fealty to Apollo hold.*
> *Oft of one wide expanse had I been told*
> *That deep-browed Homer rules as his demesne;*
> *Yet did I never breathe its pure serene*
> *Till I heard Chapman speak out loud and bold:*
> *Then felt I like some watcher of the skies*
> *When a new planet swims into his ken;*
> *Or like stout Cortez when with eagle eyes*
> *He stared at the Pacific – and all his men*
> *Looked at each other with a wild surmise –*
> *Silent, upon a peak in Darien.*

Thomas thought the poem was good, as good as Wordsworth's, maybe even better, but it troubled him. John mentioned

Apollo, but not as the god of medicine. Thomas had never read Homer. The ancient Greeks had no relevance apart from Hippocrates and Galen, who had passed down invaluable knowledge of medicine. Homer only told stories.

Hunt was being irresponsible, encouraging John, maybe making him think he could be a poet, and that might take him away from being a surgeon. Thomas couldn't let that happen.

The Thames churned with grey heaving water as Thomas crossed London Bridge on foot, the tall masts of ships docked at the Pool of London wharves swaying in the wind. He still felt a little weak from the bloodletting the day before. Rather than go to John's lodgings he decided to search Guy's for him. At the gates sat the same beggar, the veteran of Waterloo he'd met the day he brought John to the Counting House. The beggar didn't recognise Thomas, but why should he? He asked for money and Thomas threw him a shilling.

Thomas walked through the arch and under the colonnade which led to the wards. The wind blew cold on him through the open sides. He entered the first ward he came to, which looked the same as it had when he was a dresser with beds lined up along each side and across the far end. Some light entered from the large arched windows, but on such a grey day tallow candles were also lit. It was cold despite the open fires, the smoke unable to disguise the smell of festering flesh. Many of the women lying in the beds moaned and cried. There were no surgeons present.

'Can I help you, Sir?' a nurse asked.

'I'm looking for Mr Keats,' Thomas said. 'Mr Lucas's dresser.'

'He'll be in the operating theatre.'

Of course. Friday was operating day.

Thomas headed towards the theatre and was nearly there when he wondered if this was a sensible idea. There would be surgeons and dressers operating, apprentices and many students watching. His steps slowed and he felt reluctant to enter the theatre he'd not seen for thirty years, the scene of his disgrace, but it was late afternoon so they must be nearly finished. As if it was a sign Billy Lucas Junior – his face spattered with blood – shuffled past Thomas on the way out of the theatre. Thomas shrank into himself and held his breath, but Billy didn't recognise him. The sight of Billy spurred Thomas on; he might be the reason John had lost heart. Throngs of students emerged and Thomas pressed against the wall to let them pass. He waited until their numbers had thinned then climbed the stairs to the theatre.

The door brought him in at the back, steeply shelving rows dropping away before him. He clutched the handrail, the same rail he'd held tight as a student when he felt faint. He almost heard the cries of "head, heads" his fellow students had made – trying to make the surgeons and dressers bunched up around the table below move so the students could see – and almost felt the crush of bodies around him again.

When he'd been promoted to dresser, he'd stepped into the centre below, with its operating table and circle of chairs for the surgeons to rest on, and others watched him. He'd listened to the cries of the crowd, like a mob in ancient times.

But on that fateful night the theatre had been deserted apart from Astley, Thomas and the boy. Dark and lit by oil lamps. He half expected to hear the cries of the boy, trapped in the vault of the roof after all this time, coming to haunt him, to exact revenge.

269

Today a few students lingered on the wooden rows. Light shining through the glass skylight illuminated the dressers congregated by the operating table. Thomas knew as the most junior dresser John would be expected to clear up. When John was the only person left Thomas descended the stairs. John was picking up blood-soaked sawdust from around the wooden operating table and putting it in a sack.

'John,' Thomas said, 'I need to talk to you.'

John looked up and alarm showed on his face. 'Is something wrong? Tom or George?'

'No. As far as I know they're well.'

'Then what?' John wore a blood-stained apron. Thomas remembered the feel of the weight of the apron heavy with blood, the pull of the strings on the back of the neck, increasing as the afternoon wore on.

'I'm concerned about you,' Thomas said. 'I've heard rumours you're not attending dissection.'

John continued to fill the sack with the reddest sawdust. Thomas saw bone fragments in it. John's hands and arms were bloody, his rolled-up shirtsleeves rust-brown from dried blood.

'Today we cut for the stone,' John said. 'The patient was tied, his knees pulled up to his neck, his hands trussed to his ankles, drunk on whisky. Mr Lucas cut and the patient screamed. Mr Lucas couldn't find the stone and the patient screamed louder. Mr Lucas probed and searched with forceps, cursing the poor man, until Mr Cooper arrived and extracted the stone.'

'You must look to Mr Cooper for your model. He's a good surgeon and helps patients.'

'I don't possess Mr Cooper's skill or certainty. Performing surgery the arteries and veins are so close, the nerves entangled.

270

One must be quick but could sever an artery or nerve or pierce an organ and kill a man in a stroke. When I cut I feel such fear I've done wrong I'm almost destroyed.'

'That will improve with practice. The more you do, the surer you'll become.'

John shook his head. 'I've decided to abandon surgery.'

The words echoed in the empty theatre, rising to the back rows and up to the skylight. People abandoned babies, or ships, not surgery. Thomas must have misheard.

'What did you say?'

John stopped picking up sawdust and dropped the sack.

'I'm giving up surgery.'

Thomas felt as though William had cut him open and all his blood was draining out. His now-familiar stomach pain gripped him.

'You can't.' Panic spread through Thomas. 'You have such talent.'

John hung his head and didn't speak.

'Astley Cooper picked you out for a dresser. He saw the potential in you.'

'You can't persuade me to change my mind, Mr Hammond.'

Blood dripped from the table onto the floor. A slow drip onto the sawdust which softened the noise of it. John took a cloth and wiped the table, exposing its worn oak rings underneath. John couldn't give up. Thomas had trained him for five years, guided him, prepared him for Guy's, brought him up to the counting house when he started. As if he was his own son.

'You can still be an apothecary surgeon like myself, or even an apothecary.'

John continued to wipe the wooden operating table but couldn't remove the blood stains. Some were probably decades old, maybe from Thomas's own time here. John put down the cloth and faced him.

'No. I will give up completely.'

Thomas leant against the operating table for support. The wood of the table was smooth under his palm. He must be logical, not give in to sentiment. He tried to think of arguments to convince John to continue. He saw in his mind's eye Alice Jennings the day Susannah arranged for John to be Thomas's apprentice. Mrs Jennings had been so grateful, so honoured.

'You promised your grandmother on her deathbed,' Thomas said.

'I promised to complete my studies with you, which I've done. I think she'd understand my decision. As would my mother.'

John hadn't talked about his mother for years. Her ghost hovered between them, the woman John had loved most in the world, the woman Thomas hadn't been able to save. Thomas saw he must fight back.

'What about all the money spent on your training? It must be fifteen hundred pounds. What will Mr Abbey say?'

'I'm of age now so he can't stop me.'

'Think of your family: George, Tom and Fanny. How will you support yourself and them?' Thomas dreaded the answer, which he already knew but needed to hear from John.

'By writing poetry.' John looked up towards the skylight and his face shone with the passion Thomas had once seen in his surgery, when he first took John on, except then it had been for medicine.

'But there's no future in it. No income.'

'Haydon has sent one of my sonnets to Wordsworth.'

'That means nothing. It won't put food on the table.'

'I met Leigh Hunt less than two months ago, but already he's written and published an article in *The Examiner* on three young poets – Shelley, Reynolds and Keats. He's included my sonnet on Chapman's Homer and enthuses about a new school of poetry.'

'You're giving up a promising, well-paid career in medicine for these scraps of flattery?'

'Before I met him and his friends, who are the most wonderful, interesting people, I never saw how I could make a living from poetry. With their belief in me, I trust it must be possible.'

'You'll sink into debt and starve.'

'Hunt's essay predicts great things to come. I must seize the opportunity.'

'You're surrendering your chance of being remembered for your skills at surgery, your chance of immortality. Leigh Hunt is an immoral reprobate. Don't listen to him.'

John's mouth was a straight line and Thomas saw the contracted muscles at the angle of his jaw. John's breathing quickened. 'If you can't say anything other than insults, please leave.'

His words hurt Thomas. John valued the advice of his new friends more than his old master. Thomas was his mentor; he'd known him far longer, known his family and background, seen him grow up and develop. Thomas reached out and touched John's shoulder for a moment.

'You mustn't waste your gifts. You could do so much good in the world through medicine.'

'I am ambitious of doing the world some good,' John said. 'By using my gift for writing poetry.'

'How can poetry compare to medicine?'

'When I see a thing of beauty or lose myself in a poem I feel healed, restored, renewed. My burden is eased.'

'If you're searching for redemption, treat the body and you'll find meaning in life by helping patients.'

'It isn't enough for me to heal the body. I can't ignore the world of the senses and the imagination.'

'A beautiful sunrise or pretty flowers can't cure illness and disease.'

'But to me they're at least as important as leeches and lancets and medicines.'

Thomas's head span with all these strange ideas. Medicine was about treating the body. Thomas believed that, Astley Cooper believed that, all his books told him that.

Standing in this spot next to the operating table in the failing light, the sawdust under his boots, the smell of blood, all reminded him of the biggest failure in his life. The pain cut deep, opening old, scarred wounds. No poem could possibly ease it.

'It's my fault, isn't it?' Thomas said. 'I've not taught you well enough, not been a good role model.'

'If I were different you would be the best master. I see how dedicated you are, how hard you work for your patients, how they admire you. You're a good doctor.'

'How little you know me. I did a terrible thing once right here in this theatre. Because of my ambition to be a surgeon. From pride and self-interest.'

'I understand. I would do anything to be a poet.'

'Even risk someone's life?'

'Is it the thing Mr Lucas hinted at?'

'It's too distressing to tell you.'

'I've trained to be a surgeon. I know what it feels like to cut, to cause intense pain, to fail. The risks, the dread of making a mistake, the responsibility of holding a life in your hands. I want to know.'

John's expression, his desire to know, swayed Thomas. It would be a relief to tell someone after all this time and he felt he owed it to John somehow, after all their years together as master and apprentice. Perhaps this strange boy with his love of poetry would see something in his story, see how ambition could lead one astray, would understand. He might even be inspired to still do medicine so he could act differently to Thomas.

'I was ambitious, competitive with Astley Cooper, whom everyone praised. I wanted to reach the top and impress my father. A young lad about my age, twenty-one, came in late at night with a head injury, confused and agitated, vomiting. I was the duty dresser and should have called Mr Lucas. But I decided to take him to theatre to impress Mr Lucas and asked Astley to come with me to restrain him.'

In the otherwise empty operating theatre with clouds scudding across the skylight, altering the light, Thomas found he couldn't keep looking at John's shining eyes, his rapt expression, his innocence. Thomas turned and addressed the empty rows, where past generations of students had stood and observed immense suffering. His voice carried. He spoke without stopping, not checking John's face for his reactions, concentrating on telling his story, getting to the end.

The theatre had been dark that night and they'd lit lamps and candles. At first it went well. Astley held the boy and Thomas inspected the wound and positioned the trephine. He turned the trephine and the boy seemed to tolerate it so he continued. But after a few turns the boy opened his eyes, thrashed his limbs and screamed. Thomas had never heard such screams before or since. Like a vixen in heat curdling the blood.

Thomas begged Astley for help, but Astley had to hold the boy from behind, by his chest and arms, and told Thomas he must continue drilling into his skull. Thomas forced himself to turn the blade over and over, deeper and deeper. With every turn the boy shrieked more and his eyes begged him to stop.

Thomas felt such pity for the boy at the pain he was inflicting that his body seized up. His limbs refused to move as if he'd taken hemlock. Blood poured from the wound all over his hands, down his arms like a butcher.

The boy started crying for his mother. Thomas was incapacitated by his own anguish. He couldn't do what he needed, to turn the trephine more and raise a flap of bone. Astley shouted at him, but he was deaf. He stood there while the boy bled to death.

Astley went to find a porter to dispose of the body. Billy Lucas Junior had come in and recognised the boy as the son of the hospital treasurer. Billy told his father. Thomas was lucky to keep his place, but that was the end of his surgical career. No one wanted a surgeon who put himself and glory before a patient.

'Mr Hammond?'

Thomas didn't want to be standing by the table, where a real surgeon would stand. He didn't deserve it. He sat down sideways on the first tier of benches, behind the waist-high wooden partition. It was empty and lonely.

'Now I see how you try to cope with suffering,' John said. 'By working harder and harder. But you can never bring that boy back.'

'Look.' Thomas pointed to the motto in large letters on the back wall of the theatre, above the surgeons' frockcoats stiff with blood. *Miseratione non Mercede.* 'For compassion, not gain. That should have been my creed.'

'And you wanted Edward and me to be surgeons to atone for your mistake.'

Thomas shook his head. 'That's not true.'

'Isn't it?'

'I wanted you to be surgeons because I know you're both talented and have skill and could do good. Because it was right for you.'

'But it's not right for me.'

'I still don't understand,' Thomas said, 'how you can give up when you know you could do so much good as a surgeon.' Pain gripped Thomas's stomach and he doubled over. He wanted to cry out but held back.

'Are you ill?' John wiped his bloody hand on his breeches, reached across and touched Thomas's coat sleeve. 'Shall I fetch someone? Mr Cooper?'

'There's no need.' Thomas tried to be strong, to conquer the pain. 'I want to go home.'

'I had hoped for your blessing,' John said.

Thomas shook his head and tried not to sob.

Thomas took a cab across the city because he felt too ill to walk. John couldn't be giving up surgery. After all the training and work. It must be a mistake. If Thomas returned to Guy's he could convince him to continue. Or ask Astley to talk to him. There must be some way. He leant forward to ask the driver to turn around, but his stomach pains started again. He couldn't go back now.

For John to come so close: nearly a surgeon, nearly a member of the Royal College of Surgeons, nearly able to apply for a hospital post. The prize just within reach and John had been talked out of it, his head turned by those radicals like Leigh Hunt.

Thomas's pains reached a crescendo then fell back only to build again. Perhaps it wasn't an ulcer; maybe it was something more sinister as William had suggested. His body shook with fear at the thought.

The streets north of the river were busy with crowds of people, many dressed in rags, and the coachman shouted to them to get out of the way, but they didn't seem to care. The coachman brandished his whip to try to scare people out of his path, but it hit one man on the arm and drew blood. The large man came over to the carriage and shouted. Thomas was behind glass but heard the man's words accusing him of being rich and well fed, a parasite, while he and his family starved. The coachman urged the horses onwards and they left the man behind, but Thomas felt shaken by the encounter.

Rain pelted the roof of the stage the rest of the journey home, drumming an insistent rhythm like someone hammering nails. The stage jarred and Thomas's thoughts rattled round his head. All he'd wanted was to train a good surgeon. Someone skilled, who would do good in the world and make a difference. Edward wasn't going to be an apothecary or surgeon, and John was to be a poet. All his hopes were gone.

When the stage reached the inn in Edmonton it was still pouring with rain. He had to walk the last part and arrived home with water dripping from the brim of his hat, the tails of his coat and his sleeves. His boots had leaked. He shivered uncontrollably, his teeth chattering.

Susannah opened the door. 'Thomas! You'll catch your death.' She didn't ask questions but helped him undress, dried him, gave him brandy and put him to bed, where he fell into a deep sleep.

Thomas woke to warm sheets, soft pillows, the noise of a crackling fire and a cool hand stroking his forehead. Susannah sat on a chair next to the bed. Behind her sunlight came through the half-drawn curtains. He felt safe and content. Until he remembered John was giving up. He tried to sit up, but Susannah gently pushed him down.

'What time is it?' he asked. It must be late morning from the height of the sun.

'Shh. Rest, Thomas,' Susannah said.

'But the patients will be waiting.' Thomas sat up. 'It's too much for Sam to deal with.'

'I sent them away.'

'You can't do that.'

'Why not? You need to rest.'

'But they need me.'

'You'll be no use to them dead. There are other apothecaries and surgeons they can see if they can't wait.' Her voice had a hint of iron and he knew it was useless to argue.

Thomas sank back onto the pillows. Susannah looked tired this morning and he wondered if she'd sat with him all night. She smoothed the blankets which covered him.

'Did you consult William as I asked?' she said.

'Two days ago. He bled me but wasn't overly concerned.'

'I found this in the surgery.' She held out the bottle of gentian and cascarilla tonic, with Thomas's name written in William's hand. She poured the tonic into a spoon and held it out for him. He forced himself to swallow it.

She rose from the chair and walked around the room,

279

folding his clothes from yesterday, pulling trapped hair from his brush, arranging his sleeve buttons in their tray.

'Where did you go yesterday?' she asked.

'The Borough.' He struggled to say the words.

'Why?'

Thomas closed his eyes. He couldn't tell her. It was too painful and would only prove her right. She'd hear soon enough about John from someone else. He saw his life's work, to pass on his knowledge, to Edward, to John, was wasted. John no longer looked up to him. Thomas knew from experience the only way to help was through action. How could words compare with diagnosis, leeches, bloodletting, medicines and surgery? John was lost to him. There was no hope.

'You frightened me,' Susannah said, 'arriving home late, drenched and shivering.'

'I'm sorry.'

'You must take more care of yourself. What would the girls and I do without you?' She squeezed his hand tight, let go and kissed his cheek.

Chapter Eighteen

Thomas hauled himself out of bed on Monday morning and dressed slowly, not bothering to shave. The room was chill, a cold draught with a whisper of ice on its breath whistling under the window frame.

The surgery was dark, the fire not lit. Thomas climbed the stairs to the room above where John had once slept. Sam lay with one arm flung outside the blankets.

'Sam?' Thomas said. Couldn't the boy even rise in time for work? 'Time to get up.'

Sam moaned in his sleep.

'Sam!' Thomas shook him by the shoulder; Sam yelped and sat up.

'What?'

'You're late. Get ready now.'

'Sorry, Mr Hammond.'

Thomas went back down to light the fire. The wood was damp and hard to light, smoking instead of burning. The acrid smell filled his nostrils and his eyes watered. He remembered the fire sparking the day John returned to work for him after their argument about Mrs Foster. Everything he'd taught John since that day was now wasted.

Sam swept the floor while Thomas made pills. He ground the ingredients with the pestle, round and round, crushing them against the mortar, then added glycerine. The mixture became stiff and unyielding, and he forced the pestle through it. He gathered it in his hands and rolled a tube of paste. How many hundreds, thousands, millions of pills had he made in his life? What good had they done?

'Any patients I should know about?' Thomas asked Sam.

'Mrs Hammond sent them all away.'

When Thomas opened the doors a flood of humanity surged in, all rags and smells and scabs and colds and infirmity. There was Mr Trew with another sore throat, Mrs Wilson with her headaches, Ned Fisher's leg ulcer had opened up again, Sam Tricker's dyspepsia hadn't settled, Rachel Curtis's eczema made her skin dry, itchy and scaly. They were all hoping he'd cure them, but he hadn't over all his years here, so why did they still come?

Morning surgery went on late into the afternoon. Thomas set Sam to bleeding and mixing medicines while he dealt with the more complicated cases. Sam spilt a bowl of blood on the floor and couldn't read a Latin recipe. Thomas remembered John's head bent over the *Pharmacopoeia* and felt his loss. Several patients asked if Thomas had been ill and he said briefly but he was better now. He saw the fear in their eyes. If the doctor couldn't treat himself, how could he hope to help them?

The visits were long, driving the carriage through snow and hail. Darkness descended at noon, he had to light the lamps to see the way and his rounds dragged on into the evening. Mr Brown was in severe pain which even laudanum didn't relieve. Mrs Dunn was dying of dropsy, struggling to breathe. Baby Rudd was wasting away and wouldn't last long. But instead of his usual helplessness he felt detached from them, as if they didn't matter, and his sense of futility deepened. All his leeches and lancets, potions and medicines, were no more than quackery.

Thomas lay unable to sleep that night. The place in the bed next to him was empty, marked only by the dip in the mattress, the sheets cold; Susannah still slept in the younger girls' room since Edward had run away.

Thomas struggled through the next few days. All he'd learnt, all he'd practised, all he'd taught Edward and John felt useless. His stomach pains became more frequent and he felt angry. Why were they afflicting him and not William? He wondered how many more endless years he had ahead of him, pretending to ease suffering and cure illness.

In the bedroom he shrugged off his coat and unwound his cravat. The yards of cloth reminded him of the bandages he'd used to dress the stumps at Guy's. He'd tried to be gentle, but the patients had grimaced or cried out in pain. He pulled his shirt from his breeches. Without the fabric stuffed in them they were loose where he'd lost weight. He sank down onto the bed, rested his stockinged feet on the floor and found he had no desire to do anything, even undress further and go to bed.

Susannah came into the room in her nightdress but not her night cap. Her long dark hair tumbled over her shoulders. Every evening she brushed her hair at her dressing table which was mahogany with brass handles and a mirror on top, brought from Ludgate Hill, given to her by her first husband. She'd made a bad bargain with Thomas. She probably wished he'd died instead. She drew her ebony brush through her long hair, strands of which rose and floated in the air. How Thomas longed to touch it, to feel the crackle beneath his fingers.

She caught his eye in the mirror and put down her brush. 'What's wrong? You're not yourself since you went to the Borough.'

He remained silent. She rose and came towards him, her white nightdress pale and simple with a deep V at the neck. The candlelight threw shadows on her face, revealing glimpses of her beauty.

'Tell me.' She sat next to him on the bed and laid her hand on his. Her small fingers which could write and do accounts and sew, were warm and soft. Her silver wedding ring caught the light.

'I went to the Borough to see John,' Thomas said. 'He's giving up medicine.'

He felt her stiffen at his side, the slight spasm of her hand.

'How can he? After all your work with him?'

Because John valued words more than actions, fancy phrases more than pounding and grinding and mixing medicines. Thomas waited for Susannah to tell him off, to blame him for favouring John over Edward.

'I'm sorry, Thomas, I know how much it meant to you.' She rubbed his hand with her thumb.

'Neither John nor Edward will be a surgeon. My life feels wasted.'

The linen bed curtains hung around them, faded and fraying. He could draw them and hide inside the bed like a funeral vault.

'That's not true. Think of everyone you've helped over the years.'

'I'm a fraud. I never really cured them. John saw that.'

'But your compassion and counsel must have helped them.'

'Even if that's true, there's always suffering I can't relieve.'

'God knows you work hard.'

'But it's never enough. I can never make amends.'

'For what?'

His stomach cramped with pain. He needed to tell her the secret he'd kept from her, the secret he'd wanted to confide many times. It was eating away inside him, rotting, gangrenous. She might reject him, but he had to take that risk. Perhaps if he told her the pains would disappear.

'I did a terrible thing years ago, at Guy's.'

She didn't speak but looked at him with puzzled brown eyes.

He told her the story, as he'd told John but with fewer upsetting medical details. Her hand squeezed his so tightly his bones hurt. When he told her about the boy's screaming she asked if Thomas had stopped and he felt her shrinking back from him. He said no and continued to talk. The look of fear on Susannah's face pierced him. He'd never seen her frightened of him before. Proud, tough, no-nonsense Susannah. This was all wrong. She would never speak to him again, maybe leave him and take the girls. But he had to finish the tale; he couldn't leave it there.

At the end Thomas couldn't bear to look at Susannah. He waited for her judgment; certain she would condemn him as he condemned himself. He deserved it. He took her silence for disgust.

'I had nightmares and kept seeing the boy's face. I felt such shame. It felt like a small part of me had died with him that day. I thought about giving up medicine.'

'Why didn't you?'

'Partly because I didn't want to disappoint my father, partly because I didn't know what else I'd do. I also felt an obligation to the boy, to continue surgery.'

'That sounds more like a punishment for yourself.'

'No punishment could atone for it.'

She still held his hand and he focussed on that. She hadn't thrown it aside. Her breath travelled in and out next to him. He smelt her lemon cologne. A few strands of her hair brushed his face.

'Thomas, it's a terrible thing to have done, but you were young.'

'That's no excuse.'

'It was a long time ago. You need to forgive yourself.'

'I can't.' He leant on her shoulder and wept. He was sobbing for the suffering of the boy at Guy's, the suffering of all his patients: for Frances Keats, Isabella, Mrs Foster, Mark Hill. But he was also sobbing for himself, his own lost soul which couldn't bear to witness their pain.

'You must.' She held him tight for a long time. 'Only once you've healed yourself will you be able to better heal others.'

The envelope was addressed in a neat hand Thomas recognised and he tore it open. He hoped John wanted to tell him he'd changed his mind. There was one sheet of paper written very small, in John's hand.

Dear Mr Hammond, this is a poem I wrote when I suffered melancholy after my grandmother's death and you helped me recover.

To Hope

When by my solitary hearth I sit,
And hateful thoughts enwrap my soul in gloom;
When no fair dreams before my "mind's eye" flit,
And the bare heath of life presents no bloom;

Sweet Hope, ethereal balm upon me shed,
And wave thy silver pinions o'er my head.

Whene'er I wander, at the fall of night,
Where woven boughs shut out the moon's bright ray,
Should sad Despondency my musings fright,
And frown, to drive fair Cheerfulness away,
Peep with the moon-beams through the leafy roof,
And keep that fiend Despondence far aloof.

Should Disappointment, parent of Despair,
Strive for her son to seize my careless heart;
When, like a cloud, he sits upon the air,
Preparing on his spell-bound prey to dart:
Chase him away, sweet Hope, with visage bright,
And fright him as the morning frightens night!

Whene'er the fate of those I hold most dear
Tells to my fearful breast a tale of sorrow,
O bright-eyed Hope, my morbid fancy cheer;
Let me awhile thy sweetest comforts borrow:
Thy heaven-born radiance around me shed,
And wave thy silver pinions o'er my head!

Should e'er unhappy love my bosom pain,
From cruel parents, or relentless fair;
O let me think it is not quite in vain
To sigh out sonnets to the midnight air!
Sweet Hope, ethereal balm upon me shed,
And wave thy silver pinions o'er my head!

In the long vista of the years to roll,
Let me not see our country's honour fade:
O let me see our land retain her soul,
Her pride, her freedom; and not freedom's shade.
From thy bright eyes unusual brightness shed –
Beneath thy pinions canopy my head!

Let me not see the patriot's high bequest,
Great Liberty! how great in plain attire!
With the base purple of a court oppressed,
Bowing her head, and ready to expire:
But let me see thee stoop from heaven on wings
That fill the skies with silver glitterings!

And as, in sparkling majesty, a star
Gilds the bright summit of some gloomy cloud;
Brightening the half veiled face of heaven afar:
So, when dark thoughts my boding spirit shroud,
Sweet Hope, celestial influence round me shed,
Waving thy silver pinions o'er my head.

Thomas read the poem several times. What was John trying to tell him? Should he hope John would go back to surgery? Was he thanking him for caring for him when he was melancholy? He folded the paper and slid it into his top-coat pocket.

The church was lit with rows of candles and smelt of pine boughs. Thomas knelt on the lumpy hassock, which hurt his knees, and listened to the vicar. Susannah knelt beside him and he peeped at her; her eyes were shut, her face full of grace, the lines relaxed. He'd sobbed for much of that night, four nights ago, but she'd held him and he fell asleep in her arms, to find her still there when he awoke. If she could forgive him, perhaps he could start to forgive himself.

The prayers this Sunday were about peace, goodwill, the joy of angels, the birth of the Christ child.

'A child is born, a son is given,' the vicar said. Thomas had been given the gift of two sons: Edward and John. Neither of them would carry forth his knowledge, his work. If Edward and John weren't surgeons or even apothecaries, Thomas had no legacy. He left nothing and therefore he'd achieved nothing. A son is given, but however hard we try to guide him and shape him he may not turn out as we wish. Had he been a bad father? Could he have done things differently? Would it have altered the outcome? He didn't know.

'God of light and hope.' The vicar's words sounded loud in his ears. God of hope, but Thomas didn't gain much hope from him. Lines from John's poem *To Hope* came into his head. It still rested in his top-coat pocket, but he had read it so many times the paper where it was folded had deep creases, the ink worn away. He knew the first few verses by heart. Sweet Hope. He whispered the poem to himself whilst the vicar continued with the prayers.

John was calling on hope for help. When he felt solitary or had hateful thoughts, or no dreams for the future or felt melancholy. When he felt despondent, disappointed or despairing. Hope was like the moon, breaking through the clouds and chasing away bad things. John was asking Thomas to have hope for him, to believe in him.

At the end of the poem Thomas knew he had a choice. Accept John as a poet or lose him completely and live the rest of his life full of bitterness. He'd already lost Edward and couldn't bear to lose John as well. As the prayers ended, the congregation rose to their feet and notes from the organ swelled towards the roof. Thomas decided he would write to John and give him his blessing.

Dark clouds which had threatened rain all morning spat fat drops. Thomas stood outside the Fosters' cottage, clutching his bag tightly and bracing himself to knock. It was over two years since Mrs Foster had died and he'd visited infrequently for minor ailments, but each time he found it difficult, wondering if Charles Foster blamed Thomas for failing to save his wife.

The maid, who he remembered was called Molly, opened the door with the youngest child peeping from behind her skirts. 'Master Fred has a cold.' Molly led Thomas through the house. 'He was so bored in bed we brought him downstairs.' Fred lay on the same chaise longue, covered by a blanket, where Thomas had treated and bled Mrs Foster. The boy looked dejected, a different child from the boy who'd leapt out and waved his wooden sword at John. Charles Foster sat next to his son on a chair, clasping his hands together.

'Ah, Hammond!' Foster rose to his feet and shook Thomas's hand. 'Thank you for coming.'

Fred's face was flushed and a light sweat lay on his brow. He looked thinner than Thomas remembered, although he was now ten years old.

'How's the patient?' Thomas said.

'Fred's not picking up as we hoped,' Foster said. 'I'm sure it's just a cold but wanted to call you as a precaution.'

'Of course.' Thomas was aware Fred was listening to the conversation.

'How long have you been unwell, Fred?' he asked.

'Two weeks or so,' Mr Foster said. 'He's had a cough for a while, a bit of fever.'

'Are you coughing anything up?' Thomas asked Fred.

'Some yellow muck. I don't like being ill.'

'No, of course not. We'll get you better.'

Fred stared at Thomas, his face reminding Thomas of his mother. The reddish-gold hair, the wide mouth, the large eyes. 'Like you got Mama better?' Fred asked, refusing to drop his gaze. Thomas felt pinned by it, a specimen pegged down.

'Fred!' his father said.

Thomas felt his detachment crack and a chasm open up to his old helplessness. Fred could have consumption, like his mother, and be on the road to a slow, painful death. How could he even tell the boy that? Or the boy's father.

Thomas felt Fred's pulse, the skin on the back of his hand, observed his breathing. It was too early to tell if it was definitely consumption, but he couldn't rule it out.

'I'll send some medicines to help the cough,' Thomas said. 'It may well be a simple chest complaint.'

But if it wasn't? Thomas thought of himself mixing more medicines, unable to slow the decline, applying leeches, bleeding Fred's thin arms, watching Fred waste away, his cheeks go pale, listening to his noisy breathing, watching blood pour from his lungs, watching him die as his mother had. Knowing he couldn't help, couldn't ease his suffering.

He couldn't bear it. He couldn't do it anymore. He would give up, ask Fred to see another apothecary.

'Where's Mr Keats?' Fred asked. 'He was always great fun, sword-fighting with me. Can you send him with the medicine?'

'Mr Keats has left me to study in London. He was training

at Guy's Hospital to be a surgeon, but now he's going to become a poet.'

'A poet?'

'Yes. Strange as it seems.'

'I don't like poetry.' Fred slumped back on the pillows.

Thomas remembered John in this room, lifting Mrs Foster, sitting her up, handing her his handkerchief when she coughed the blood. Asking to read to her, helping Eliza choose books, playing with Fred. Quoting the poem on her deathbed. How had John coped with her suffering when it was so like his own mother's? He hadn't been cold like Thomas's father or controlled like Astley Cooper, but he hadn't broken down either. He'd been himself, kind, caring, enthusiastic about poetry and books. At those times and when John questioned Thomas's treatments, read to Eliza, quoted poetry at the confused old woman, laughed with Robbie, he'd shown Thomas something. His humanity. His compassion.

Perhaps Thomas could learn from him, learn to fill this gaping void of pain, to fill it with caring and hope. He saw that all along John had shown him things. His love of the beauty of nature. His love of words. The poem he'd sent about hope. He saw now what he must do to save himself, the only way forward. The master must learn from the apprentice. And he must start right now.

'I'll send the medicines, Fred, but perhaps you would like your father to read to you? An adventure book about pirates?' Thomas felt wooden and awkward. He'd be talking about dragons next.

'Oh. yes. But soldiers. I like stories about battles.'

Mr Foster looked slightly alarmed but agreed he could try that.

'And I think my son has some tin soldiers at home,' Thomas said. 'He's far too old for them. I'll bring them for you if you'd like.'

'Can I paint them like Wellington and the French and replay Waterloo?'

'Of course. If you wish.' It wasn't going to cure Fred's possible consumption, but the boy had a smile on his face. That was something.

On the way out Mr Foster stood in the hall.

'Thank you for cheering him up.' He paused. 'You don't think... Could it be...?'

Thomas wanted to rush and say of course not, it's not consumption, as he usually would, but something stopped him.

'I hope he'll recover, but I can't promise you.'

Mr Foster nodded his head. 'Thank you for being honest. I miss her, you know. I miss her so much.'

Thomas reached out and placed his hand on his shoulder. He looked deep into the man's eyes. He saw the pain and hurt. He felt it in his own heart but didn't break his gaze.

'I know you do, Charles,' Thomas said.

Outside the house he paused for breath. The rain had stopped but the air was damp and cold. A single orange rose he hadn't noticed on his way in bloomed by the front door. A spiral of infinite petals, bunched at the centre. Beads of moisture clung to them, perfect rainbow spheres. The delicately veined petals, yellow-tinted at their edges, unfurled soft and smooth. It would be gone soon, with the next storm, but it gave him joy in that moment.

Chapter Nineteen

Illness flourished in the cold weather and it was easier for Thomas to carry on in his old ways of a leech for every ill, a medicine for every complaint. He found himself wanting to instigate John's ideas but was unable to see how and despaired he could change. Then a glimmer of hope appeared.

Colonel Pitt had suffered a paralysis of the left side of his body a few months before, but he could still speak. Right-sided paralysis was almost always associated with loss of speech.

'How are you today?' Thomas asked.

'How do you think I am?' Colonel Pitt replied. He sat in a chair with a blanket over his knees. His left arm hung uselessly by his side and his mouth drooped at the left corner. On the table next to him sat several of Thomas's medicines in bottles.

'Any improvement with the last medicine I prescribed?' Thomas asked.

'None at all.'

'I can try a different remedy.' Thomas racked his brains for something which might help.

'You and I both know, Hammond, that it won't help. You may as well give me snake oil.'

'I believe in the medicines I prescribe, Colonel.' Years ago when John had called him a quack he'd been angry, but now the colonel implied it he only felt frustration he couldn't help him.

The colonel's head sagged forward and he gave a long sigh.

He was completely changed from the man who used to boast about his exploits in the American wars and ride in the local hunt.

'I'm not going to recover, am I?'

Thomas sat in the chair opposite him. 'You may regain some strength in your limbs with time. I've observed that with similar patients.'

'Balderdash! I always thought you were the kind of man to tell me the truth.'

'You won't walk or ride again.'

The colonel closed his eyes and the room fell quiet. Thomas wondered if he'd been too direct. Perhaps he'd taken away his hope. Tears emerged from beneath the old man's lids and ran down his cheeks. Thomas stood up to leave. Grown men don't like to be seen crying, even by their surgeons.

Thomas had reached the door of the room when the colonel called out, 'I knew that. I don't know why I call for you. Throwing my money away.'

'I won't charge you for today.'

'Don't be ridiculous. What else can I spend my money on now? Come back and talk to me, earn your keep. How's that soldier son of yours who ran away to fight with the Duke of Wellington?'

'Edward is...' How to describe Edward?

'Send him round to talk to me. That would cheer me up.'

'He's not at home anymore. Perhaps there's something else I could do for you?'

'I want to hear hymns. I haven't been able to go to church.'

'Shall I call the vicar?'

'That sanctimonious man? No. I want you to sing for me.'

In all his years of practice Thomas had never had such a request. It was preposterous.

295

'I can't sing for you.'

'Why not? You sing in church, don't you?'

'But I'm an apothecary surgeon.'

'So? There's a hymn book on the shelf over there.'

The old stubborn goat. Thomas bet he wasn't even taking his medicines. And he'd been drinking, Thomas smelt it on his breath.

The colonel sat as straight as he could in the chair. 'Sing for me,' he said. It was an order. Thomas saw how he must have been in command of his men, fierce and proud.

Thomas took the hymn book from the bookcase. 'Any requests?'

'You choose. Something rousing. Sorry there's no accompaniment.'

Thomas flipped through the hymn book, stopped at a page, cleared his throat and sang. '*Guide me, Oh thou great Jehovah, pilgrim through this barren land.*' His voice was thin and weak. He kept going, feeling totally ridiculous singing a hymn to a crotchety, incapacitated old man in his drawing room. What if someone walking by heard?

The colonel mouthed the words and waved his good hand in time. Thomas sang louder and his voice filled the room. He remembered as a boy singing out in church. These days he hardly sang along. '*Bread of Heaven,*' he sang loudly.

'*Open now the crystal fountain whence the healing stream doth flow.*' The colonel's bass voice joined Thomas's tenor. The colonel was enjoying himself so much Thomas thought he might overdo it and meet his maker sooner than expected. At the end the old man settled back and smiled.

'Thank you,' he said. 'Come back next week and do it again.'

'I don't think—'

'That's an order, not a request, Hammond!'

Thomas found himself laughing out loud and knew he would come back next week to sing for him again.

The pain bent Thomas double and he struggled not to cry out. Deep breaths, he must take deep breaths, prolonging the exhalations. Breath hurtled from his lips. He dismounted, straightened up a little and rested his forehead against Cinnamon's flank. The smell of the horse's coat and sweat distracted a little from the pain. After some time, he had no idea how long, but it felt endless, the pains eased and he walked to the dispensary. The pains were becoming more frequent, stronger, lasting longer and not responding to his medicines. They made him melancholy.

It had been nearly dark since midday and the lamps shone in the dispensary windows. He dragged his bag along the passage, feeling weak and tired, cold air blowing around his knees. Sam was talking to himself, which was unusual. Except there were two voices, one much deeper. He wondered who Sam had let into the surgery, against his strict instructions, no doubt a patient seeking Thomas.

'Take the paste and roll it into a tube.'

Thomas knew that voice. He hurried the rest of the way and flung the door open. Edward stood next to Sam at the bench, in front of the shelf where he'd smashed the apothecary jars the last time Thomas had seen him in the surgery. When Thomas had told him to get out of his sight and not come back.

Thomas stared and stood silent.

'Your apprentice makes even worse pills than I used to,' Edward said, 'so I thought I'd give him a few tips.'

'Yes, good idea,' Thomas said. He put down his bag and sat on a stool opposite them. His stomach pain sat like a stone in his middle. He wanted to reach out and touch Edward, to see if he was real. Perhaps he was seeing a vision because of the pain.

Edward's long, thin fingers held the paddle of the pill machine and rolled perfect spheres. It couldn't be him; Edward never made perfect pills. Edward looked up and Thomas bent his head, looking at his hands, afraid to look his son in the eye in case he scared him away.

'I didn't expect to see you…' Thomas said.

'Mama asked me to visit for a few days over Christmas.'

That didn't explain what Edward was doing in the dispensary. Perhaps Susannah had told Edward that Thomas was unwell.

'Your pills have improved, immensely,' Thomas said.

'All the practice I've had at William's.' Their eyes met. Edward's gaze was strong and direct.

'How are William and the family?'

'Well.'

Edward told Sam to put the pills in a bottle and what to write on the label. Sam looked cheerful for a change.

'That's much neater than my writing,' Edward said. Thomas remembered how Edward always used to try and make John write the labels.

'I need to mix a medicine for Mr Yates.' Thomas reached for the *Pharmacopoeia* and turned the stained pages, keeping his eyes focussed on them. He took down the jars he needed, some of them new stoneware, placed them on the bench and weighed out the first ingredients. He was aware of Edward close to him.

'Can I help?' Edward asked.

Thomas saw the shards of his beloved apothecary jars on the floor, smelt the scent of the spilled ingredients, saw the cracked face of Apollo. He remembered holding Rachel Curtis's teeth in his hand, the feel of their jagged edges.

'Don't you trust me?' Edward's voice contained a hint of anger, resentment, a challenge. 'William does.'

Thomas felt confused. This was the boy who'd smashed his jars, but he looked grown up, a man, with his full face and serious expression.

Thomas handed him the pestle, laying it in his outstretched palm. Edward weighed it in his hands, placed it in the mortar and started mixing slowly. Thomas held his breath, listening to the faint sounds.

Edward's hands soon took up a rhythm and the herbs were ground down to a powder.

'We used to make this often,' Edward said. 'With John.'

'Could you add the cascarilla for me? You need three drahms. Do you remember how to weigh the ingredients?'

Edward picked up the drahm weight and rubbed it with his fingers. The small brass square had lost its sheen; a dark patina covered it. 'Of course I remember,' he said. He found the cascarilla jar, picked up the scales and placed the weight in one pan. It tilted down and he balanced it with the herbs. 'You taught me.'

Sam watched them mixing.

'Edward,' Sam looked up from his writing, 'is it true you fought at Waterloo?'

The air in the room was like fragile glass until Edward's snort of laughter cracked it.

'Who told you that?'

'I only want to know what it was like. Everyone in the village says you went.'

'No, I didn't,' Edward said.

'Sam, why don't you deliver those pills?' Thomas said.

Sam gave a last puzzled look towards Edward and left carrying the pills.

Edward bent his head over the mortar, blending the cascarilla. Thomas set up the small stove to decoct the mixture. Once it was simmering away he sat down and watched Edward. Thomas wanted so much to ask what had happened when Edward ran away to fight, he decided he must speak.

'Why didn't you go to fight?' Thomas asked.

Edward picked at the skin around his thumbnail. The bubbles rose and popped in the mixture; the flame flickered.

'I intended to, but no one seemed to want me and I couldn't get a passage across the Channel. I was cold and hungry, so I decided to come back.'

'Why didn't you come back here?' Thomas asked.

'Because I knew you'd think I was a coward.' Edward's voice cracked.

Thomas reached for his son's hand, covering it with his own. Edward's body was stiff, motionless, his face full of despair.

'We all lose our resolve sometimes,' Thomas said.

'But you would have carried it through, if you'd decided to.'

'When I was at Guy's operating there were cases where I couldn't continue and Mr Lucas had to take over.'

'You, Father?' Edward looked at him and Thomas saw surprise on his face and felt something had changed. He felt the warmth of Edward's hand, the connection between them.

'I don't think you're a coward,' Thomas said. 'I'm just glad you came back alive.'

Faces sparkled in the candlelight, the smell of evergreen and spices filled the air, and the table was laden with goose, potatoes and vegetables. Thomas felt blessed, surrounded by his family: Susannah, his wonderful wife; Edward, his son who had extended his visit and was helping mix medicines, even bleeding and pulling teeth; his daughters, Mary Ann and Harriet, with their pink cheeks and glowing smiles. And Martha, who joined them for the meal. Eliza wasn't here and he missed her, but he knew she was safe with her husband and his family.

He hoped John was with his brothers today. No letter had arrived from John and Thomas worried if John had received his. Maybe John couldn't forgive him for the things he'd said that day in the operating theatre at Guy's. Thomas's stomach squeezed with pain. He must try and ignore it and enjoy this time with his family.

Thomas rode up to the farmhouse at Shaw's farm, past the field where the tree had fallen and crushed Robbie Brown's arm nearly two years ago. That was the first time he'd had doubts whether Edward was fit to be a surgeon and the first time he'd seen John's true potential.

The farmhouse kitchen was warm, filled with the smell of bread baking. Mrs Shaw wiped flour from her hands and invited Thomas to sit down. They sat at the kitchen table where Thomas had amputated Robbie's arm.

'I've felt a lump,' Mrs Shaw said, placing her hand against her left breast. 'You remember my mother had one?'

'Yes.' He'd performed a mastectomy on her mother but sadly she'd died from spread of her tumour. 'Could I examine you?'

'Can you do it here where it's warmer?' she asked.

The lump was the size of a hen's egg, hard, craggy and fixed. As soon as he felt it he knew her prognosis was dark. As he felt glands in her axilla and neck a creeping dread invaded him. He'd have to tell her.

'Will I need an operation?' she asked.

She smoothed her apron with her hands and sat waiting for his reply, her face pinched with worry. The kitchen was hot, too hot, and the smell of freshly baked bread which had been pleasant before now overwhelmed him and made him want to gag. She was Susannah's age, a wife and mother.

'I could perform a mastectomy,' Thomas said. 'Or send you to Guy's Hospital to see Mr Astley Cooper.'

'Remove my breast, like my mother?'

'Yes. But I don't think it would stop the disease.'

'Why not?'

He could lie to her, gloss it over, try to decrease her worry. But was that the right thing to do? Didn't she have a right to know her fate?

'You have hard lumps in your armpits and neck. I fear the tumour has spread.'

Her face struggled with this news, but she made an effort to be brave.

'You're telling me you can't cure me?'

'That is correct.'

'Do I have long?'

'Maybe a few months, perhaps longer.'

'There's no hope?' she asked.

'There is always hope, but I am being realistic. I can try and keep you pain-free and comfortable.'

'That's not enough. I'm needed to help with the farm and the children. What will they do without me?'

He felt her distress, her wish for things to be different. The old hopelessness stirred in him, but he knew he had to conquer it to help her.

'What do you wish for with the life you have left?'

'I wish to stay as well as I can for my family. Will you help me?'

'Of course, to the best of my ability.' He knew it wouldn't be easy, but he would try with everything he possessed.

The thud, thud, thud of metal on wood reverberated in the night air of the graveyard. Astley Cooper was hammering on the lid of a half-excavated coffin with an iron bar. He wrenched the lid off, revealing a shroud which he unwound, yards of cloth spooling over itself, but it was empty. He grabbed Thomas and began to wrap the shroud around him. Thomas struggled, but the cloth pinned his arms against his sides. Then Astley and several others lifted him and jammed him into the coffin. Astley grinned, the flesh of his face dissolving to leave only the bare bones of his skull. He replaced the lid, blocking out the moonlight, and hammered it shut.

Thomas awoke sweating, his heart pounding, his limbs tangled in his sheets. The noise of the coffin lid being hammered shut continued. Someone was knocking at the front door.

He fumbled through the bed curtains, lit a candle and grabbed his robe. The clock in the hall struck two. Downstairs a boy at the door told him he was needed for a sick child. Thomas told the boy he would come and sent him away. He dressed and headed to the stables, collecting his bags from the hall on the way.

Outside the sky was black, pricked by stars. He tilted his head back and stared at their beauty. The universe stretched all around him, who knew how far? Perhaps it was infinite. Usually he enjoyed being out by himself at night, the feeling he was one of few people awake, doing important work, but tonight he felt alone. Although he expected his apprentices to work hard, he didn't make them saddle his horse at night. Since his stomach pains had become worse he found rising from his warm bed to dress and get the horse ready increasingly hard. He shivered in the cold air and looked up at the window above the surgery, the room where Sam now slept, and missed John.

The stable door creaked as he opened it and he knew Cinnamon heard him. The horse blew gently into the air. Thomas lit a lamp and saddled him, placing his bags in the saddlebags, then put on the bridle, and led him out.

The child had asthma and Thomas administered ipecacuanha to induce vomiting. She improved and he said he would send a syrup of lemon and cinnamon later. It was still dark when he left the cottage, the cold piercing. He felt too tired to ride hard and let the horse go at his own pace. Back at the stables he opened the door to see a light, which was strange because he was sure he'd extinguished the lamp.

The lamp threw shadows on the walls, the stalls, the straw. The shadows flickered and looked like phantoms. In one corner of the stable, someone was curled up on a bed of straw under one of the horse blankets. Dark hair emerged from the edge of the blanket.

'What are you doing here, Edward?' Thomas shook him to wake him. Every day, especially as twelfth night approached, Thomas had expected Edward to declare he was returning to William's, but he hadn't, and Thomas was glad.

Edward was disorientated but after a few seconds leapt to

his feet, went to the horse and unbuckled the straps of the saddle.

'Go to bed, Father. Get some rest.' He removed the saddle, lifting its heavy weight, and started on the bridle.

'How long have you been waiting here?'

'I heard you leave and came down after that.'

'But why?'

'You look tired and I want to help, if I can.' Edward began grooming the horse, brushing his flanks with sure strokes.

Thomas patted Cinnamon's muzzle and rested his cheek against the horse's neck, felt his warmth on his skin. His eyes welled up. He didn't understand why. Edward was only unsaddling his horse.

'Thank you,' Thomas said, his voice husky with unshed tears.

'Father,' Edward said, 'I can see you're in pain and you're so thin.'

'It's just an ulcer from too much work.'

'Mama told me you weren't well. That's why she asked me to come home and help a little. But it's much worse than I imagined. Perhaps you should consult William.'

'There's no need, I'm fine.'

'Are you sure?'

'Of course I'm sure.' Thomas patted Edward on the back. He was touched by his son's concern.

Edward looked uncertain but continued to groom the horse.

Thomas walked back to the house. The sky was lightening ever so slightly in the east, the black turning to indigo. He no longer felt so alone.

Thomas stared at the small body lying on the quilt on the bed, her skin red from the angry rash of measles, her dark hair matted, leeches attached over her ribcage. He laid two fingertips on her chest: no movement. Felt the pulse at her neck: nothing. Lifted her small eyelids: dilated pupils. An engorged leech detached itself and tumbled onto the bed. Thomas had done all he could to save her, but none of the medicines, the dill or chives or wormwood, nor the bleeding had worked.

Mrs Dean knelt motionless by the bed and held her daughter's hand. Surely she must see any small signs of life were gone from her daughter. But he wasn't sure. He dreaded the words he had to say. Speaking them would make it real.

'She's gone, I'm afraid,' he said.

Mrs Dean raised her eyes to him. Thomas expected protests or the wailing and keening so common when a mother lost a child, but all she said was, 'Take them off her. Take the bloodsuckers off her.'

Thomas removed the leeches, swollen and sated with blood. Red trickled from the wounds their jaws had left. Mrs Dean reached out her thin arms, covered in coarse grey wool, for her daughter, scooped her up and held her. Thomas led her to a chair and sat her down. She clutched the naked child tight to her chest.

'Is your husband nearby?' he asked.

She shook her head. Thomas sat down opposite her. He felt angry he hadn't been able to save the child, but he saw that it wasn't his fault. He felt helpless in the face of this woman's silent grief. It would be easier to bear if she screamed and shouted, ranted and raved. Images of the boy at Guy's flashed before him, the same feeling. He was inadequate, he couldn't help.

In the past in this situation he would have left, thinking it wasn't up to him to try to console her; he'd done his job. He might have offered to send a message to a relative, friend or the vicar, or prescribe a sedative. Yet something meant he couldn't leave. The woman's tight grip of the child seemed to grip him too.

How must it feel to lose a child? He remembered when Eliza was ill, how anxious and desperate he felt, so he knew a little. But this wasn't his child, and Eliza had survived.

'I'm very sorry that I couldn't do more,' he said.

'She's my only one,' Mrs Dean said. 'I tried for years to have a baby, you know that. And when she came it seemed a miracle.'

'There may be more children for you,' Thomas said.

'No. Because I couldn't bear the pain of losing another one.'

He didn't know what to say. He could argue, but he didn't think that would help her. He felt a pain as if he'd lost a child. He remembered the pain when Edward ran away. He'd thought he couldn't bear that any longer, but he did.

'I see,' he said. And he did see how it must be for her. 'Let me wrap her in a blanket. We don't want her to get cold.' Was he going mad? The child was dead, of course she would get cold. He reached for the girl. Mrs Dean loosened her grip to let him take the child, and he wrapped her in a blanket and gave her back. Mrs Dean rocked her baby gently. Thomas sat quietly with her, his hands resting on his knees, the fading light softening the edges of the furniture, the objects, the mother and child. He saw he could bear it, if she could. He could overcome his helplessness by sharing her grief. Only a small part, it wasn't his child after all, but he would be a witness and she wouldn't be alone. He rose to light a candle and the flame threw a circle of light in the near darkness.

When her husband arrived home and they'd talked, Thomas left. Outside the sky was a sulphurous yellow streaked with pink. Clouds were backlit by the sun behind, their edges gilded. The quality of the light was so pure, he gasped.

How could he see beauty when the child had died and the mother was grieving? How could it exist when there was such sadness in the world? But it did. And what harm would it do to be moved by beauty and accept it?

The letter rested on a silver salver on the hall table. Thomas recognised the hand from a distance and picked it up, thinking to rip it open, but then hesitated. The letter shook in his trembling fingers. Perhaps John would reject his approaches, his suggestion they meet. This might be the end.

He unfolded the sheet of paper and read the dense script, cross written at right angles. John thanked Thomas for his letter and apologised for the delay in replying. He was spending much of his time at weekends at the Vale of Health with Leigh Hunt, and if Thomas wished he could visit him there. Thomas felt a stab of envy but tried to banish it. Hunt could help John in his new career.

Thomas folded the letter and placed it in his top-coat pocket, next to John's poem. He swore a warmth spread from the sheets of paper across the front of his chest.

John had replied; John had accepted Thomas's blessing. Thomas hadn't lost him.

Work was busy with only Edward and Sam to help. Illness was always severe in the middle of January, the darkest and coldest time of the year. Ague, bronchial complaints, fevers, croup, wheezing, angina, rheumatism, whooping cough, Boulogne sore throat. After the light and joy of Christmas, spring felt a long way away and Thomas's pains continued.

One afternoon he went to the herb garden to dig angelica root. In the summer the plant grew tall, as tall as Thomas, but had to be cut down before it set seed. The flowers were large globes composed of tiny pale green flower clusters. Martha candied the stems and added them to sweetmeats. The root when boiled into a tea was good for bronchial complaints and indigestion. Perhaps it would help his ulcer. Susannah kept begging him to consult William again, but he'd refused.

Dark clouds gathered in the sky, threatening more rain. The herb garden was nearly bare at this time of year. Dried stems rattled in the chill wind and plants rotted on the compost pile. Thomas knelt on a sack and dug, trying to remember the exact location of the tall stems.

The soil was damp and dark. He forced the blade of his trowel deep into the earth, over and over, until he hit something hard, then dug all around to loosen it. He removed the earth, exposed the thick grey root, worked his fingers beneath it and pulled with his bare hands but he couldn't free it. Fibres trapped it in the soil. He tugged and tugged, but it wouldn't come away. He felt exhausted and sat back on his heels to rest. Moisture had permeated through the sack into his breeches, chilling him.

Rain began to fall. He lifted the sodden, black earth and cut off a piece of the angelica root with a knife. The cut root smelt of gin. He wiped his hands on his breeches to brush off the dirt and they left great smears, but his hands remained dirty.

Thomas's stomach cramped with pains and he retched. The contents came up and flowed across his soil-engrained hands.

A red stream. It couldn't be. His eyes must be deceiving him. Maybe he'd eaten or drunk something red. He knew he hadn't.

How could he have been so stupid? Any fool would have realised. He held his life blood in his hands, a perfect ruby colour against the black soil. Angelica root wasn't going to save him. That blood was his death warrant.

Chapter Twenty

A few inches of snow fell overnight and the world looked fresh and new, sunlight bouncing off the brilliant white. Everything was covered, softened. Thomas was reminded of John's poem *The swan his neck of arched snow*. How could the world look so beautiful when he was dying?

In church weak light shone through the stained glass onto the congregation, bathing them in pastel colours. The church was half empty, due, Thomas supposed, to a combination of the cold outside and illness.

'Let us pray,' the vicar said.

Thomas knelt and tried to concentrate on the vicar's words, but his mind wandered. Did he, Thomas Hammond, believe that he would ascend to heaven if he had lived a good life? Did he believe in the resurrection of the body? When he thought of the body in the coffin he'd dug up with Astley, the bodies in the dissecting room, he found this vision of eternal life fantastical. Yet now he faced towards the darkness. He clenched his hands tighter in prayer.

How does a man or a woman live the rest of their life when they know they will die soon? Many denied it. Some put a gun in their mouth and pulled the trigger. Even those who believed in heaven were reluctant to leave the sight of blossom, the sound of birdsong, the touch of warm sun, the taste of blackberries, the smell of violets. Unwilling to leave the warmth of family and friends.

What does an apothecary surgeon do when his body fails and he knows he can't fix it? He might have weeks or months, like his father who'd suffered with a similar tumour in his stomach. His father had raged against it, but that hadn't helped.

He must work; that was his life. He must work for as long as he could, help patients. And care for his family, show his love for them.

The snow melted in the sunshine of the next few days but refroze every night, so the path was slippery and treacherous. Cinnamon walked slowly, picking his way over the glassy, icy patches.

Mrs Shaw took her time to answer the door, a small girl clinging to her skirts. Thomas saw Mrs Shaw was pale and breathless. They sat around the kitchen table, the child on her knee.

'How are you?' Thomas asked.

'The pain isn't too bad on the laudanum and I'm not too sleepy.'

'That's good. You're taking the tonics?'

'Yes, I feel they're helping a bit.'

'I could bleed you…'

She hugged the child closer. 'No bloodsuckers. The thought makes my skin crawl.'

'That's fine. How's Sally?' The child tilted her head at the sound of her name.

'She's sleeping better since you treated her cough. She clings to me, but I don't mind somehow.'

Thomas understood the comfort Mrs Shaw must gain from the child being close to her, before their final parting.

A spasm crossed Mrs Shaw's face, and Thomas almost felt

the pain as his own. He wondered if he could confide in her, tell her he was also dying. No, that would be a burden on her. He would support her as her doctor and friend. He asked about the rest of her family, how they were coping with her illness.

Thomas held a book by Abernethy in his lap, *An Enquiry into the Probability and Rationality of Mr Hunter's Theory of Life*, but he couldn't concentrate on it, couldn't bring up his youthful enthusiasm for the subject. Even though now the question of whether he had a soul should be of utmost importance to him.

'Thomas,' Susannah was working at her embroidery, forming tiny stitches in pink thread, 'William's sending James to assist you.'

'Why on earth?'

'Because I asked him. You need help you so you can rest more and recover from your ulcer.'

'James sees rich ladies with the vapours. He wouldn't have a clue how to treat the washerwoman's leg ulcer or the farmhand's backache.' Susannah was meddling, as she had when she told Alice Jennings that John could be his apprentice without consulting Thomas.

'He was good enough to be dresser to your idol Astley Cooper.'

'That was years ago. Anyway, we can't take him away from William.'

'William agreed. James starts tomorrow.' Susannah looked up from her sewing straight into his eyes. 'I'm only trying to help you.'

Thomas was sure Susannah asking John to be his apprentice all those years ago had been self-centred, but that couldn't be the case now. And for all the problems with John, Thomas wasn't sure he'd go back and change the situation even if he could.

'I'm sorry,' Thomas said. 'James's help will be useful. Thank you.'

'I'm glad you appreciate my efforts. William also asked how you were and said you should consult him again.'

'There's no point.' She didn't know about the row William and Thomas had the last time they met, but that wasn't the main reason he hadn't consulted his brother again, or Astley Cooper or anyone else.

'You're ill, Thomas, anyone can see it. You've made yourself ill caring for patients, they're the ones to blame. Calling you at all hours, dragging you out of bed, making you ride around in all weathers.'

'But I wanted to do it. It's my life.'

Susannah held the needle poised above her hoop, the thin pink thread connecting it to the white fabric where Thomas saw she'd embroidered roses, full blooms. There was a silence in the room. She tucked the needle into the fabric and carefully laid the hoop next to her chair. Folds of white spilled from it. She stood up and warmed her hands in front of the fire with her back to him, her dark dress contrasting with her white cap. Strands of grey hair escaped at the nape of her neck. Behind her, on the mantlepiece, Greek mythical figures on her blue jasper Wedgwood vases were forever trapped in time.

She then turned towards him, her eyes wide.

'Aren't I your life?' She looked so young and vulnerable, not the tough woman he thought her.

'Of course, but—'

'Work always came first, didn't it? Above me and Edward and the girls.'

314

'That's not true. You've always been important to me. And the children have too.'

'Do you remember when we first met? I thought you were devoted to me. I thought being a surgeon's wife would be worthwhile, helping you to help others, but I soon saw I wasn't really needed and felt neglected.'

'I *was* devoted to you. I adored you. I couldn't believe it when you agreed to marry me.'

'So what happened?'

'I don't know. My work was always so busy, so demanding.'

'All those times you were late for dinner, all those times I wanted to talk to you but you rushed off or read your books, all those times the children needed you.'

'You're more important than my work, Susannah.'

'You've failed to show me that.'

'I'm sorry.' How could he not have shown his love for her? He thought she knew it was there, felt it every day. 'You know the boy I told you about, at Guy's. I think I was always trying to make amends, to atone for that, by working harder and harder. But of course I never could.'

'All I wanted was to feel needed.'

'In my heart I've always needed you.' He must tell her about his illness, but he knew it would hurt her. He wished he could be the colourful cockatoo on the fire screen and fly away to distant lands. 'I'll need you more than ever in the next few weeks.'

'What are you saying, Thomas? You're frightening me.'

'The ulcer is a tumour.'

She took a sharp intake of breath and held her hands crossed over her heart. Her face aged before him, the skin dragged down.

'Can something be done? You must consult Astley Cooper or Abernethy.'

'They can't save me, it's too advanced. I don't have long left, Susannah. Maybe a few weeks or months.'

'It can't be true.'

'I need your help. I can't go through this alone.'

To his shame his body shook and he started sobbing. For the loss of his youth, their love, his work, his life. He buried his head in his hands.

Thomas heard the rustle of her skirts, the step of her slippers, felt the air move about her. The rustling came closer. He smelt her scent of citrus cologne; she knelt by him and put her arms around him. They were soft and gentle, but he felt their strength too.

'You won't be alone,' she said.

On the last Saturday in January, after seeing the sickest patients, Thomas asked Sam to harness the horse and ready the carriage, and they drove towards Hampstead. It was a cold but sunny day and they placed blankets across their knees. Sam was in high spirits, sensing a jaunt away from his usual grounds. Thomas's stomach pains had been severe in the night but then settled.

They arrived at the Vale of Health, a group of white-painted cottages in a dip surrounded by patches of undrained marsh. With all that stagnant water its name was ironic. Thomas became nervous, wondering if he'd be welcome, but he wasn't going to turn back now.

The man who answered the door obviously wasn't a servant. He was about thirty, tall and his black hair fell thickly from a central parting. He smiled at Thomas.

'Mr Hunt?' Thomas asked, and the man nodded. 'I'm Thomas Hammond.'

'How can I help, Mr Hammond?' Rowdy children ran around behind him.

'I'm an apothecary surgeon. I'd like to speak to John Keats.'

'Is he ill, poor boy? He didn't tell me he'd called for you.'

'He was my apprentice.'

'Ah! The apothecary! You've come a long way. Come in and bring your boy.' He signalled towards Sam.

Was this really the man who'd been to prison for insulting the Prince Regent? Who was going to bring about a revolution? He looked far too harmless and cheerful. Hunt waited while Sam tied up the horses, then directed him to the kitchen and invited Thomas inside. The house was crowded with piles of books everywhere, mementoes and trinkets. Hunt led Thomas to a door, knocked and opened it. John sat at a desk in a tiny parlour, writing. He looked up.

'John, you have a visitor,' Leigh Hunt said, and left them.

'Mr Hammond.' John stood up.

'You don't mind me calling? I wanted to see you.'

'Not at all. I hope you've recovered from your illness.' He put down his quill. The desk was covered in pages of writing. No doubt a poem he was working on.

The room was crowded. As well as the desk there was a piano and busts were displayed which dwarfed Thomas's of Hippocrates. The walls were crowded with engravings of castles, fauns, satyrs, nymphs and vine leaves.

'Is this where you write?' Thomas asked.

'Yes. I've finished two long poems. Libertas often lets me sleep on the sofa.'

Seeing John in that room, looking so at ease, Thomas

317

felt a great change had been wrought in him since his time at Wilston mixing medicines. The honest, hardworking surgeon had been transformed into a pasty intellectual. Part of Thomas felt John should be holding a scalpel, not a pen. He wished he could go back in time. He had to remind himself of his vow to accept John's choice of career.

'Could we talk outside, get some air?' Thomas said. 'It's stuffy in here.'

Sam was playing with the children and eating cake. John and Thomas put on their coats and set off from the Vale of Health across Hampstead Heath with its grassland and scrubby bushes. Thomas struggled to keep up with John, who slowed his pace. Clouds scudded across the sky, obscuring the sun. They climbed a small hillock and looked at the view. Below lay a pond, in the mid distance trees and far distance countryside.

'Are you still doing surgery?' Thomas asked.

'Yes, but I'm not taking the exam of the Royal College of Surgeons. I'll finish my dressership then stop.'

'What does Mr Abbey say to that?'

'When I told him that I intend to rely on my abilities as a poet, he told me I was either mad or a fool to talk in so absurd a manner. He also called me a silly boy and prophesied a speedy termination to my inconsiderate enterprise.'

'He has strong opinions,' Thomas said.

'He wanted me to set up in practice as an apothecary somewhere near Edmonton.' John stuffed his hands in his pockets and stared into the distance.

Thomas had a soaring hope that John could come to Wilston and take over his practice. He was still unsure what would happen to it after he was gone, but with John there his teaching would endure. Thomas would live in John.

'Come and work with me,' Thomas said. 'It will be like it used to be, between us.'

The wind blew across Thomas's face. He watched John's profile, the upper lip protruding above the lower, the weak jaw which belied his strength of character. John turned and his eyes stared directly into Thomas's. 'I'm sorry, Mr Hammond, but I can't go back.'

Thomas wanted to persuade, cajole, argue, anything to make John change his mind, but he saw this wasn't what John wanted and held his tongue. Tears pricked Thomas's eyes and he stared at the far distance: the dark trees, the sandy track winding away, the shades of purple and blue in the sky.

'Perhaps Edward will work with you?' John said.

'Perhaps. He helps a little at the moment.' The clouds moved across the sky, casting shadows. 'John, you asked about my health earlier. I'm not telling you this to make you come and work for me but because I want you to know.'

'What is it?' Thomas heard alarm in John's voice.

'I have a stomach tumour and only a few weeks or months left.'

John's face turned pale and his pupils widened. 'That can't be. You can't die.'

'We will all die, John. We're not immortal like your Greek gods and goddesses.'

'But so soon. There's no hope?'

Thomas shook his head. 'To Hope,' he said. 'What were you trying to say when you sent that poem?'

John thought for some time. 'I wanted to give you something because you trained me to be a surgeon and I let you down. But I also wanted you to understand how I love poetry and can't live without it. To see how I see the world.'

'Do you remember the day in my surgery, when you looked at my father's delftware jars? I told you Apollo was the god of medicine and you said he was also the god of poetry.'

'I do.'

'I'm starting to see now. Something can be more than one thing. It doesn't mean it isn't the other.' A boy could be a son and a surgeon, or a son and a poet.

'I know poetry can't heal a fever or stop a pain, but I feel it can do some good in the world.'

'Your poem affected me. It made me wish to keep my connection with you.'

'I'm sorry,' John said, 'that I disappointed you.'

'Don't be. You've helped me see the world in a new light, its beauty and its poetry. And through your compassion you've helped me find a new way of dealing with suffering.'

They stood together under the winter sky.

'It's beautiful, isn't it?' John said. The sun emerged from behind a cloud and sunlight poured down on them. 'It's like a medicine.'

'Yes, it is.'

Thomas saw that John was content, doing what he wanted. Thomas felt a bond with John, as if he really were his son.

'If you need anything let me know,' Thomas said. 'I wish you well.'

'Thank you.'

'Promise you'll come and see me.'

'I promise.'

James was proving surprisingly helpful. He rode over three days a week and helped Thomas with surgery and the visits. Edward and Sam mixed most of the medicines and made the pills. Despite his illness sometimes Thomas found himself feeling happy. It reminded him of times when he was young working with his father and William.

One evening James had headed back to Southgate and Sam was delivering medicine when Thomas was called out on a visit. The snow and ice had thawed; Edward offered to drive the carriage and Thomas accepted gratefully. He was tired. They visited an old woman who was dying of dropsy and sat for some time with her. With enough laudanum to calm her, she died peacefully.

On the way home Edward held the reins and looked straight ahead into the darkening gloom. The carriage rattled in ruts and over bumps, jolting Thomas's thin frame. He held his stomach as pain gnawed at him.

'It's not an ulcer, is it?' Edward asked. 'Your illness.'

Thomas turned to his son, observing his profile, his aquiline nose and dark hair, in the fading light. A painful surge of love clutched his heart. He wanted to protect Edward from the news.

'No. It's more serious.'

'How serious? Tell me the truth, please.'

How to prolong Edward's ignorance a little longer, to spare him? Impossible.

'It's a tumour.'

Edward swallowed and didn't take his eyes from the road. 'I knew it must be something like that. The pain, the weight loss, your tiredness. You must see Astley Cooper or Mr Abernethy. Uncle William will ask them.'

Thomas placed his hand on the sleeve of Edward's coat. 'It's no use. They can't save me.'

Edward stared straight ahead and Thomas saw he was crying, but he kept driving the horse, taking them home.

Dinner was a mournful affair. Thomas made a vain effort to swallow the soup Martha had cooked especially for him, Susannah had dark circles under her eyes and Edward looked melancholy. Even Mary Ann and Harriet were subdued. Afterwards Thomas and Susannah sat in the drawing room close together by the fire. Susannah tucked a strand of her grey-streaked hair, which had escaped, back under her cap.

'We need to talk,' Thomas said. 'About what will happen to you, Edward, the girls and the surgery after I'm gone.'

'I don't wish to think about it.'

'You must, Susannah. Perhaps James can stay and help you. He seems to like the work and get on with the patients, but he may want to return to William.'

'Let's talk about this another time.'

'If he goes you must hire an apothecary surgeon to keep the practice going. One who can continue to train Sam. Edward can help him with mixing. That should still leave enough income for you and the girls, I hope. I'm sorry I can't provide for you better.'

Susannah's eyes brimmed over and she wiped them with a handkerchief with an embroidered bunch of violets in one corner.

'What's wrong?' Thomas asked.

'Oh, you know what's wrong. You hardly eat anything and you're wasting away.'

'I'm trying my best.'

'I know you are. It's just...' She stopped, mute with emotion, but he saw the despair in her face. She sobbed into her hands and he put his arm around her shoulder. Her body shook beneath him.

'Shh. Shh. It's all right.'

'No, it's not. Don't leave me, Thomas.'

A knock at the door and Martha entered. 'Sorry to disturb you, but the midwife's asking for you, Mr Hammond.'

Thomas stood up.

'Who's it for?' he asked Martha.

'Mrs Walsh, a long labour.'

'Can you send Edward?' Susannah said, her voice cracking.

Thomas felt himself torn. Mrs Walsh might need forceps.

'Let me fetch him,' Martha said.

Edward came into the room and stood in front of Thomas. 'Can I help?'

'Can you perform a forceps delivery if it's needed?'

'I'm willing to try,' Edward said.

Thomas looked from Susannah to Edward. A pressure built inside him. Edward might not cope. It might go wrong.

'I've seen several at William's.'

Thomas remembered the first time he'd performed a forceps delivery by himself, without his father there. Thomas had been terrified but the baby had survived.

Susannah's small hands held tight to her handkerchief, squeezing it so tightly he thought her tears would drip from it.

'I'd like you to attend Mrs Walsh. You can call me if there are problems.'

'I will.' Edward turned and Thomas wanted to reach out to him, to call him back, but he stopped himself.

Susannah leant into him. How many more times would he feel her warmth? Even heaven, if he was admitted, would be a cold place without her.

He remembered the first time he'd met her at William's party, her beauty and her laugh, her interest in his work. The early years at Wilston, the passion, the nights she waited up for him to return from night visits. Then the fear clutching his heart as she gave birth to Eliza. Repeated with Edward, Mary Ann and Harriet. He saw her at her desk doing the accounts, her quill scratching, the dark ink flowing across the page. He felt her hand resting on his head, in the orchard, the sun shining through dappled leaves. The hours after dinner, by the fire, chatting or quiet, doing embroidery or stitching the shirts he wore every day, mending them and patching them. The softness of her fingers later felt in the shirts.

'I wish I could have given you the grand life in London you wanted,' Thomas said. 'You deserved better.'

'I've had a good life here, Thomas. My only regret is you're leaving it so soon.'

'I put my work first, before you.'

'What do you think attracted me to you? Oh, your looks and manner, of course, but I thought your profession was a noble cause.'

'But an apothecary in a small village?'

'When I was married to William Styles—'

'Don't. I don't want to hear it.'

'He was rich and I had a fine house and furniture, china and dresses. He was much older than me but a good-looking man and treated me well. I persuaded myself I loved him, but I see now I never did. He was a businessman, but he had no greater purpose in life. All he did was turn sugar into gold. When I met you I knew you were different, but I became frustrated your work took so much of you and I felt neglected. I thought success and money were important. And success for Edward, good marriages for the girls, but all along I secretly admired your devotion, your dedication, your commitment to your patients. You're a good man, Thomas, and have lived a good life.'

Thomas held her hand and it was as if they were twenty-three again. 'I want to ask you something,' he said. 'I want to see your hair.'

She took off her cap and unpinned her hair, which fell across her shoulders in thick waves. He reached out and touched it, remembering the first time he'd done so. She reached up and stroked his cheek.

Chapter Twenty-One

'Father, what's wrong? You look so ill.' Eliza entered the room in her fine clothes, her cheeks pink from the cold air.

Thomas asked her to sit down and told her about his illness. She cried and cried, wiping her eyes with her handkerchief until the skin around them was red raw. He put his arm around her shoulders. When she was empty of tears Thomas suggested they put on their coats and go out.

The air was fresh and they walked round the herb garden several times. It was nearly bare but a few herbs still grew. Thomas crushed rosemary between his fingers, inhaling the scent.

'Did you hear about John Keats?' Thomas asked.

'What about him? Is he a famous surgeon now?'

'He's given up medicine for poetry.'

Eliza knelt and picked a sprig of parsley, which she twirled in her fingers. She stood and turned towards Thomas.

'You must be disappointed. You always had such hopes of him, Father.'

'I did mind, but I've made my peace with him now and wish him well.'

'I'm glad for him. I remember we talked of love-in-idleness, how it grew here in your garden. He made me see the beauty of the world with words.'

Her gaze was far away, in the distance, in the past. Had Thomas been wrong to forbid her from associating with John?

Thomas didn't know and it was too late to change. Eliza shook her head and came back to the garden, now bathed in thin winter sunshine.

'I haven't told you my news,' she said. 'I'm expecting a baby.'

'A baby?' The word sounded like a foreign tongue to Thomas.

'Yes, Father. It's not unexpected, surely?'

'That's wonderful. I'm so pleased for you.' Thomas grabbed her hands. 'When is it due?'

'July, I think.'

Five months. He wouldn't live to see his grandchild, to hear its cry and feel its tiny fingers wrapped around one of his. He wouldn't live to see if Eliza survived or if she perished like so many young women he'd attended. Eliza, his beautiful, kind, loving daughter. The girl who'd chased her sisters through the orchard and laughed with them, who'd learnt the names of herbs in his garden. The young married woman who held herself with grace and smiled.

'But tell me do you have a good apothecary surgeon nearby?' Thomas asked. 'You must engage the best midwife you can.'

'Don't worry. I will.'

Thomas knew even that might not be enough, but he couldn't live in fear. He thought of all the babies he'd delivered safely, all the mothers who had survived. He must hold on to that and hope all would go well in her confinement and delivery.

'If it's a boy I'll call him Thomas,' she said.

One day in early February, when the sky outside was swirling with snowflakes, Thomas sat at the dispensary bench studying the *Pharmacopoeia*. Next to him Edward stood bent over the mortar, his face in shadow. The fire burned behind them. A weariness settled on Thomas which he tried to fight.

'You've been very helpful in these busy times, Edward,' Thomas said.

Edward continued to mix. 'If I hadn't run off, I could have been an apothecary by now, and much more helpful to you.' The bitterness in his words was like milk thistle.

Thomas rubbed the paper of the *Pharmacopoeia* between thumb and forefinger. The page was stained by past concoctions. 'Maybe I was wrong the way I treated you…'

Edward twisted the pestle in the mortar. The tendons in his wrist stood out like cords.

'If you wish I'll sign the certificate for Guy's, so you can apply this year.' Thomas felt a spasm of pain in his stomach.

Edward kept mixing, his eyes fixed on the crushed herbs. 'I'm not sure that's what I want. I thought I'd go back and help William, but now I'm starting to doubt his methods.'

'You are?'

'What good does covering pills in gold leaf do apart from make the apothecary richer? Some of your patients are much sicker than his, but he wouldn't treat them because they're poor.'

Thomas held his breath. Edward's words warmed his heart. He wanted to urge him to go to Guy's, then take over the practice, but he held his tongue.

'You must do whatever is best for you.'

Thomas reached out his hand and touched Edward's arm through his sleeve. It was the coat he'd bought on one of his visits to William's. The expensive worsted was worn now, shiny in patches. Edward didn't draw back and Thomas left his hand there.

They sat by the glow of the lamps and the fire as darkness fell outside. Thomas decided the medicines could wait 'til tomorrow.

'You must look after your mother when I'm gone.' Thomas put his arm across Edward's shoulders and they walked across to Wilson together, Thomas leaning on his son.

Now he could no longer work Thomas sat in his study with Hippocrates and his books, including *The Tempest* and Wordsworth, a blanket across his knees and another over his shoulders. James or Edward or Sam might come and ask his advice, but it was for show, to make him feel useful. He slept badly but every morning dressed and came downstairs. The effort was immense; it took him an hour to do what used to take minutes. Susannah fussed but he sent her away because he didn't want her to see him weakened and struggling. He would call Edward to help him down the stairs and leant his weight on him. Edward's body was strong and Thomas felt the life in it as his ebbed away.

It was only a fortnight since he'd seen John. It was too early to expect him to visit. He knew that, but he listened for a knock at the front door, the lion's head knocker announcing his arrival.

'Mr Hammond,' Martha stood at the study door holding a cabbage, a basket of eggs and a scarf, 'what should I do with these?'

'Where are they from?'

'Your patients leave them at the kitchen door. Someone's been talking, it's not me, honest, but they know you're sick.'

'We can eat the eggs and cabbage. Keep the scarf for yourself.'

'And they keep coming to the kitchen door at all hours and asking to visit you, but I send them away.'

'Let them in, Martha. It will occupy me and help pass the time.'

'Are you sure, Mr Hammond? There's all sorts.'

'Yes, I'm sure.'

And so, when they presented themselves, Martha showed the patients into the study. Every day there were more. Old Mr Yates stood, cap in hand, thanking Thomas for the time he'd fixed his broken arm twenty-five years ago. Thomas noticed the arm still wouldn't fully straighten. Mr Trew the butcher, looking a mite tearful, thanked him for all the bleeding he'd given him for his sore throats. George Smith's daughter thanked him for treating her father's dropsy and making him comfortable before he died. Robbie Brown came with his one arm and told Thomas he was glad he'd saved him, that he still had a life worth living.

Mary Curtis and her daughter Rachel stood at the door to the study. Mary encouraged Rachel forwards and the child handed Thomas a bunch of snowdrops.

'Thank you, Rachel, they're beautiful,' Thomas said. The white petals hung on stems of vivid green. A sign of new life, the first flowers of spring.

Rachel smiled. There was a gap in her teeth where she'd lost some from the mercury poisoning, but her adult teeth were now coming through.

'Mr Hammond,' Mary said, 'I can't believe you're sick. Who will I call when I need help? You saved Rachel twice, on the day of her birth, and then again two years ago. How can I ever thank you?'

Thomas's throat closed up and he couldn't speak for a while. He felt he should be the one thanking Mary, for letting him look after her little girl. Especially after what had happened with Edward and the mercury.

In the streams of patients there was no sign of Mr Foster or Fred. Thomas wondered how the boy was. The last time he'd been able to visit Fred his fever was lower but still present. Thomas knew he wouldn't live to see whether Fred would grow up, but he hoped he would. Thomas fell asleep and Mrs Foster, Frances Keats and the boy at Guy's drifted through his dreams, reaching their hands towards him, calling out to him but their voices were silent.

He woke to see Mrs Hill standing in the doorway. He thought maybe he was still dreaming, but she spoke and he heard her words.

'May I come in?' she asked.

'Of course,' Thomas said. 'Take a seat.'

She advanced hesitantly and perched on the edge of the free chair, twisting a handkerchief in her hands.

'I wanted to thank you for looking after Mark,' she said.

'I'm sorry about what happened,' Thomas said. He imagined Mark drooling and groaning, asking him to end his life. He thought of how this woman had nursed her son and still did so, with love.

'I know you tried your best,' she said. 'And I appreciate how you've kept coming, not given up on Mark.'

'But I've not been able to do anything for him.'

'You've been there. You've been a witness to his suffering, and mine, and that has made it possible for me to continue. Knowing you cared.'

Thomas felt his eyes well with tears. This time he let them roll down his cheeks, let her see he was crying for her son, and her pain and himself.

After she'd gone he watched the flames leaping and falling in the hearth. Their warmth touched his face. The number of visitors and amount of gratitude was overwhelming: all these people, old and young, those he'd cured and those he thought he'd failed to help, some whom he remembered well and some hardly at all. Being an apothecary surgeon here, in this village, had given him the chance to get to know his patients, to see their children grow and have their own children, to be part of their lives, see their successes and failures, share their sorrows and their joys. It had been a privilege. Being an apothecary surgeon had been a greater, far more meaningful life than being a grand surgeon.

But there was one person who hadn't come. Every time there was a knock at his door Thomas wondered if it was him, only to be disappointed.

Chapter Twenty-Two

February 1817

Snow falls, covering the fields and the orchard. Thomas stays in bed and Martha doesn't bring the patients to see him but accepts their gifts and passes on their messages. His body is so wasted he resembles one of Astley Cooper's skeletons in the anatomy museum. His pain is nearly constant and he takes laudanum, but it befuddles him at times. Edward brings him medicines he's mixed and Thomas drinks them for his sake. They leave the taste of liquorice and peppermint on his tongue.

Susannah stands by the bed, her face white and drawn, her eyes red, and asks if he's well enough to receive a visitor. Thomas say yes if it's for a short time and before he can ask who it is she says she will send them up. Thomas hears the tread of a man's boots on the stairs to his bedchamber, the door creaks as it swings open, and John steps into the room.

'Mr Hammond,' John's voice reaches Thomas's ears as if travelling through water, 'may I sit by your bed and talk with you?'

John sits on the chair next to the bed. The chair where Susannah normally sits to be with him, read to him or hold his hand. John wears a flowing neckerchief, his poet's clothes. He holds a sheaf of paper in his hands. His surgeon's hands which are even now stained with ink.

'I'm sorry it's taken me so long to come. I've been busy

with my dresser duties. I only have a few more weeks 'til I stop working for Billy Lucas Junior.'

'You're still determined to give up medicine for poetry? No regrets?'

John looks away towards the window, where ice crystals freeze on the outer pane. Rays of late afternoon sun struggle to shine into the room which is shrouded in dimness.

'I will be a poet.' The sunrays shine on his face.

'You have such talent for surgery. I understand your doubts but I know you could do it if you wished.'

'Mr Cooper says no one should become a surgeon unless he has the temperament for it. A surgeon needs the eye of an eagle, the hands of a lady and the heart of a lion. I don't possess the heart of a lion.'

'I believe you do, John.'

'I have the heart of a poet. But you, Mr Hammond, you have the heart of a lion.'

Thomas closes his eyes because he knows he's about to cry. He wishes he did have the heart of a lion, for then he would be brave and not afraid of dying. Pain starts in his stomach, builds in intensity and racks his body.

John touches his shoulder. 'Shall I call for Mrs Hammond?'

Thomas opens his eyes and shakes his head. 'Pass me the laudanum.'

John hands Thomas the bottle from the table by the bed. It's light in Thomas's hand, nearly empty, but he tips it up and drains it. He's got used to its bitterness and prefers it to the sweets Susannah brings which make him gag. He sees the poppies it comes from, in his garden, their large papery petals crinkled in the wind.

'I'm publishing a book of my poems in March,' John says.

334

'I wish you success.' Thomas fights against the pain.

'I've brought copies of some of them for you.' John offers a thick tight wad of paper and words.

'Thank you. Perhaps you would read a few to me? I remember when you read to Eliza, all those years ago.'

'Of course.'

John's voice is low and soft, and at first all Thomas hears is the rhythm, which begins to soothe him. He wants to drift into sleep but his pain holds him in the room. He distinguishes single words, then phrases which he doesn't understand. He sees he doesn't need to understand them; he can let them wash over him and flow around him. Thomas is collecting leeches, floating in water, swimming in Salmon's Brook.

His attention comes and goes. He catches fragments of John's poems and images form in his head.

Let me thy vigils keep 'Mongst boughs pavilioned, where the deer's swift leap, Startles the wild bee from the foxglove bell. Foxglove, *digitalis purpurea*, used to treat dropsy. Pink tubular bells hanging from tall spikes, spotted inside with dark purple daubs, inviting the bee to enter. Fairies' gloves, witches' thimbles, witches' hats. Flora slipped one on her thumb and touched Juno's stomach to help her conceive the god Mars. It makes the heart beat stronger.

Thomas's pain relaxes its fierce grip and his body rests. He knows it will come again but just for now it's gone. He feels safe.

That I should never hear Apollo's song, Though feathery clouds were floating all along The purple west, and two bright streaks between, the golden lyre itself were dimly seen. Both John and Thomas heard Apollo's song, but different versions of it. Thomas chose medicine and John chose poetry, but they're connected somehow. Through Thomas and John. And Edward? Had he heard the song? Thomas saw Apollo, his face painted on his father's apothecary jars, smashed to smithereens. But Thomas thinks now Edward hears the song whisper, in his thoughtful selection of herbs and careful mixing of medicines. What he does with it is up to him.

Thomas comes back to the room and his pillows and snow falling outside the window and John's gentle voice. *He mourns that day so soon has glided by: E'en like the passage of an angel's tear That falls through the clear ether silently.* Thomas mourns. Where has his time gone? Those days splashing in the brook as a child, riding along country lanes, courting Susannah, his children growing up. So many nights visiting patients under the stars. The moon hung large over the fields of green wheat the night John discussed poetry in Thomas's carriage.

John asks if he should stop but Thomas wants him to continue. *Sleep and Poetry.* Thomas is so tired, he longs for sleep, but not the final sleep. He wishes to wake renewed. *Life is but a day; a fragile dew drop on its perilous way From a tree's summit.* Dew drops the mornings he returned to Wilston with the dawn. The sky streaked with indigo. *A laughing school-boy, without grief or care, Riding the springy branches of an elm.* Edward as a young boy climbing trees and refusing to come down. How playful he'd been before all his troubles.

Thomas hears a sound in the room and opens his eyes to see Susannah and Edward sitting by the bed, listening to John. Thomas will miss them, but he knows they will care for each other. He wishes Eliza was here too. The poem is long and Thomas is pulled away into the past. Susannah is a young woman smiling at him. He's kissing her.

And I rose up refreshed, and glad, and gay, Resolving to begin that very day These lines; and howsoever they be done, I leave them as a father does his son. Thomas is leaving his sons, Edward and John on this earth without him. He'll be gone but live in them. They're his legacy, like John's poems will be his.

It's quiet in the room. Susannah muffles her sobs. Edward hangs his head. John holds his words, his thoughts, his gift, in his hands. Thomas asks John to read *To Hope*, and John finds the right pages. Thomas mouths the words with him. *Should disappointment, parent of despair, Strive for her son to seize my careless heart.* He won't despair. He felt despair the day he took John to register at Guy's, because he should have taken Edward, but now Edward is returned to him. He felt despair the day John told him he was giving up medicine, but now Thomas knows John is following his own path.

Lines of poetry float in the air and he tries to catch them, to hold on to them, but they swirl away from him and rise skywards to heaven. *Sweet Hope, ethereal balm upon me shed, And wave thy silver pinions o'er my head.*

Afterword

John Keats died tragically in 1821, at age twenty-five, of consumption (tuberculosis), the same illness that had killed his mother and his brother, Tom. He published three books of poetry but never found success in his lifetime. He was derided for being lower class (unlike Byron and Shelley) with no right to aspire to be a poet. His poetry was criticised as vulgar, self-indulgent and overwrought. He struggled to earn enough to live. It was only when the Pre-Raphaelites rediscovered his poems in 1848 that he became recognised and today is thought one of our greatest poets.

Not much is known about Keats's years as an apprentice from 1810–15. There is little historical record of Keats from this time as his first surviving letter is from August 1816. I used Andrew Motion's biography as my main source, and although my story is fiction, I have tried to be true to the few facts that are known. Nicholas Roe argues Keats split from Hammond in 1812, but I have kept to the other dates for my novel. There is more known about his surgical training years at Guy's from 1815–17. Again, I have tried to stick to the known facts. Keats started writing poetry during his apprenticeship, although none of his best-known poems are from that time. In my story I've only referenced and quoted the poems he wrote then.

Even less is known about Thomas Hammond, apart from bare facts about his birth and death, parents, marriage, children, and medical training. His grandfather and father were both apothecaries. He trained at Guy's and would have been a contemporary of Astley Cooper. The main liberty I have taken is omitting his two eldest sones from my story. One worked for the East India Company and the other was apprenticed to a surgeon at The London Hospital in 1810.

Hammond was trained as a surgeon and an apothecary, hence the title apothecary surgeon. He would also have learnt obstetrics in his time at Guy's. Irvine Loudon writes that in 1783, eighty per cent of medical men in provincial England were apothecary surgeons. Physicians were much fewer and only treated the rich. These apothecary surgeons evolved into general practitioners. (The earliest use of the term "general practitioner" was in 1809.) Thomas Hammond was one of the first GPs in England.

Wilston, the house at 7 Church Street, Edmonton, where Hammond lived and had his surgery in the garden, was demolished in 1931. A blue plaque on 3 Keats Parade, above a shop which used to be a chemist but is now an estate agent, marks the site in what is now Edmonton Green, London.

The Royal College of Physicians Museum, London, has a magnificent collection of Delftware apothecary jars (the Victor Hoffbrand collection) and other medical artefacts. The Royal Pharmaceutical Society Museum, London, also has a wonderful collection. The operating theatre in the Old Operating Theatre Museum and Herb Garret, in Southwark, is very similar to the ones Hammond and Keats would have attended.

Keats House in Hampstead has a display of items related to Keats's medical training and tells the story of his life after Guy's. At Guy's Hospital there is a statue of Keats in the grounds where you can sit next to the great poet.

See my website mellanyambrose.com for more information on Keats, Hammond and medicine in the Georgian era.

Acknowledgements

I'd like to thank the following for all their support and encouragement.

My parents Jock and Angela. My sister Keren. My sons Adam and Jamie. My friends Susan Rich, Maggie Coffey, Louise Hopkins, Tan Wood and Julie Thomas. My writing group Sandra Mcdonald, Eileen Aird, Su-lin Dow, Emma Rea and Janine Scoggins. My book club Naomi Hillel, Berry Birdsall and Denise Sheen. Kylie Fitzpatrick for mentoring. And last but by no means least my husband Danny.

Books I found especially useful for my research are:

Motion, Andrew. *Keats*. Faber and Faber Ltd, 1998.

Roe, Nicholas. *John Keats*. Yale University Press, 2013.

Keats, John. *The Letters of John Keats*. Edited by Maurice Buxton Foreman. Geoffrey Cumberlege, Oxford University Press, 1947.

Keats, John. *John Keats: The Complete Poems*. Edited by John Barnard, Third Edition. Penguin Books, 2006.

Burnby, Juanita. *The Hammonds of Edmonton*. Edmonton Hundred Historical Society, 1973.

Loudon, Irvine. *Medical Care and the General Practitioner, 1750–1850*. Oxford University Press, 1987.

Crosse, V. Mary. *A Surgeon in the Early Nineteenth Century: The Life and Times of John Green Crosse, 1790–1850*. E. and S. Livingstone, 1968.

Burch, Druin. *Digging up the Dead*. Vintage Books, 2008.

Humphries, Alan, Oakeley, Henry and Hoffbrand, Victor. *English Delftware Apothecary Jars and Their Contents: The Victor Hoffbrand Collection*. Oakeley Books, 2017.

South, John Flint. *Memorials*. Introduction by Robert Gittings. Centaur Press Ltd, 1970.

Bynum, Helen. *Spitting Blood*. Oxford University Press, 2015.

Sources of quotations:

Keats, John. *John Keats: The Complete Poems*. Edited by John Barnard, Third Edition. Penguin Books, 2006.

Spenser, Edmund. *The Faerie Queen. The Poetical Works of Edmund Spenser*. Edited by J. C. Smith and E. De Selincourt. Oxford University Press, 1942.

Cowper, William. "Light Shining out of Darkness". *Poems: William Cowper*. Edited by Hugh I'Anson Fausset. J. M. Dent and Sons Ltd, 1931, pp 188–9.

Milton, John. *Samson Agonistes. The Poetical Works of John Milton*. Oxford University Press, 1941.

Shakespeare, William. *The Comedies of Shakespeare*. Geoffrey Cumberlege, Oxford University Press, 1946.

Shakespeare, William. *The Tragedies of Shakespeare*. Geoffrey Cumberlege, Oxford University Press, 1948.

The Examiner. 1st December 1816, British Newspaper Archive, www.britishnewspaperarchive.co.uk.

Williams, William (1745), translated by Williams, Peter (1771). "Guide me, Oh Thou Great Jehovah". Published in 1747 Hymnals. Hymnary.org. Accessed 13 Oct. 2022.

About the Author

Mellany Ambrose worked as a hospital doctor and general practitioner in the NHS for nearly thirty years. Her interest in Keats's medical career arose when she discovered he'd trained as an apprentice close to where she was working as a GP. She spent many happy hours researching in the British and Wellcome Libraries and visiting sites related to Keats's life and Georgian-era medicine.

About the Author

 Matador